ACCORDING TO Thy Word

ACCORDING TO *Thy Word*

by Karen Kelly Boyce

According to Thy Word

Published by iUniverse, Inc., Lincoln, NE

Published by Cloonfad Press, Cassville, NJ

Book design by Andrew Gioulis

Published by: KFR Communications, LLC
148 Hawkin Rd
New Egypt, NJ 08533

ISBN-10: 0-6920-0920-5
ISBN-13: 978-0-692-00920-8

Printed in the United States of America

www.kfrcommunications.com

Dedicated to

My earthly mother Kate who taught me how to talk
My heavenly mother Mary who taught me what to say

My earthly father Ed who taught me the faith
My heavenly Father who gave me the gift of faith

My earthly love Michael who by "hanging on" gave me his life
My heavenly love Jesus who by letting go gave me eternal life

The Principal's Office

I have dealt with great things that I do not understand; things too wonderful for me, which I cannot know. (Job 42:3)

Ten year-old Mary Catherine O'Rourke walked down the hall with her fists clenched at her side, and her face flushed red. A path should be worn in the linoleum leading from my classroom to the principal's office, she thought, as she scuffed her worn, penny loafers along the familiar path. Mary Catherine was especially upset this time because she could not remember doing anything to warrant this summons. *How was she supposed to plan a defense that would pacify Sister Clements if she didn't even know what she did?* She reviewed the week since her last trip to the office. It was a quiet one. Mary Catherine couldn't remember any fights or insults, none Sister Clements could have found out about, anyway. This was the worst way to be called into the office. It happened a few times before, and usually involved someone's parents.

Mary Catherine liked to be in control. She hated working in the dark. The more she thought about it, the angrier she became. Sister Clements always said Mary Catherine's temper would be her downfall. *Easy for her,* Mary Catherine thought. *She didn't understand what it was like for Mary Catherine, nobody did!* It wasn't that Mary Catherine didn't like Sister Clements, everybody did. It was just Sister Clements didn't understand. That formula might work just fine in the nun's world, where everybody knew 'turning the other cheek' was the rule. But, it didn't work in Mary Catherine's world.

Once, after a really long meeting with Sister Clements and her mother, Mary Catherine truly tested the system. The day after the meeting, when Ann Marie Higgins called her a name, she just mumbled and turned away. With her short auburn hair and the numerous freckles scattered over her nose and cheeks, Mary Catherine looked like mischief. Her petite form gave most the impression of weakness, but Mary Catherine was solid muscle. Her blue eyes sparkled with confidence in her own physical strength. Ann Marie, large and blonde, overestimated herself.

Ann Marie's flat face was alight with amusement as she pushed Mary Catherine. Mary Catherine tried to ignore the shove. With her blonde hair tossed behind her, and feeling brazen, Ann Marie poked Mary Catherine hard in the back. Still, Mary Catherine, using all the strength within, tried to walk away. She kept repeating those Bible passages about controlling her temper, as Sister advised her to do. Then Ann Marie decided to call her a dork, and hit Mary Catherine over the back of her head with her books. All Mary Catherine remembered was the look of shock and expectation on everybody's face in the hall. Her next memory was of sitting in the principal's office, while Mrs. Higgins went on and on about Ann Marie's bloody nose.

Mary Catherine had to give it to Sister, she was a real pro. Somehow, she managed to calm Mrs. Higgins down, and convince her Ann Marie started it. Sister ended it all by giving both young people a two-day detention. To Mary Catherine, the way Sister Clements fixed everything showed off the nun's way with people. The way she got the truth into the open was a real victory on Sister's part. Nevertheless, when Mary Catherine told Sister this after Mrs. Higgins left, the nun increased Mary Catherine's detention to three days. Well, there was no way of figuring out nuns, Mary Catherine decided. If you complimented them, you got punished the same as if you insulted them.

Despite her foot dragging, Mary Catherine finally reached the office only to be told by the secretary to sit in the chair just outside the office. The outer office had two large desks and numerous files that sat behind a long counter. The two middle-aged women who worked behind the metal desks always seemed to be busy with piles of papers, but still had time to help any adult who came to the counter for help. They seemed less inclined to stop working and gossiping when a child stood waiting.

Windows in the hallway gave full view to the outer office. A large wooden door behind the counter in the outer office led to the Principal's office. This dark door always seemed to be closed unless some trouble developed. Outside the office, in the hallway below the office window was a row of small wooden chairs. Mary Catherine was directed to wait in one of these chairs in the hallway.

This was the worst possible situation. Usually, when Mary Catherine waited in the hall, it meant Sister was getting an earful about her from some irate person. It also meant Sister would have her mind made up concerning Mary Catherine's guilt. Not knowing why she was here put Mary Catherine at a real disadvantage. Mary Catherine's ignorance made it easier for Sister to trap her with just a few short questions. Not only did she have to sit out here and ponder the upcoming punishment, but soon all the classes would be letting out and the other kids would see her.

Sister Clements just didn't understand what it was like for Mary Catherine. All the kids knew she and her brothers were charity cases. Being poor was bad. Living in the trailer park was worse. Everyone knew the parish let her brothers and her go to Catholic school because of the long friendship between Sister Clements and Mary Catherine's mother. Everyone knew her family was too poor to afford the tuition. Well, they may have just suspected it until John Reilly's mother, a financial secretary, made it common knowledge.

Sure, the kids harassed her over it, but having wimpy kid brothers was worse. Her brothers couldn't even fight for themselves. Whenever Mary Catherine didn't respond to the other kids' harassment about being poor, they would just pick on Danny or Johnny. It then became a matter of defending the family name, though Sister Clements didn't always see it that way. It was bad enough to have wimpy, charity case brothers, but it was still worse to have a charity case for a father.

Imagine, on top of everything else, Mary Catherine's father drank too much. He drank so much that he couldn't seem to keep any job. Why, her mother even got him the job as the school janitor. And to top it off, thought Mary Catherine, he only showed up for work about three days a week. The nuns were kind enough to cough and look away on the days his breath betrayed his drinking. The majority of the teachers and staff at the school ignored the fact he spent most of his time asleep in the janitor's closet. The nuns, for the love of Mary Catherine's mother, overlooked these things but the other kids didn't, and therein lie the trouble.

Everybody loved Mary Catherine's mother, but no one more than Mary Catherine. She never understood how someone as educated, beautiful, and gentle as her mother got herself into such a situation. It must have been kindness, Mary Catherine concluded. She thought her mother was the kindest woman ever born. She never had a harsh word for anyone, even those who were less than kind to her. She was calm and joyful, even in the most adverse circumstances. *She is too kind*, Mary Catherine thought, *too kind to all the people who give her grief.*

Oh sure, Mary Catherine loved her father, despite his many problems. He was a small, thin man with a handsome face and thick auburn hair. His smile was infectious. When he was sober, he was a merry and loving man. On Sundays after Mass, her father Patrick used to bring the family to the dollar zoo. He would jump and scratch in front of the monkey's cage. The monkeys would get mad and screech at his poor imitation. Then they would jump and scratch in anger exactly like him. Her father's antics and jokes always made Mary Catherine and her brothers laugh. Patrick could always bring a smile to her mother's face. Mary Catherine's stomach ached with the laughter. Johnny and Danny jumped around with Patrick and the monkeys would jump even more.

The younger boys were towheaded like Mary Catherine's mother. Their freckled features matched the father. The sight of the monkey's screeching anger brought laughter even to the people passing by. The laughter doubled Mary Catherine over.

Nevertheless, her father's sadness would return, and with it the endless empty bottles. Patrick O'Rourke was never mean, even when drunk. Her mother said his drinking made it impossible for Dad to care for the family. Her father couldn't even keep a decent job. Mary Catherine's mother added he wasn't always this way. Once, they supposedly had money, and her father owned his own business. Mom said that when she was a baby, they lived in a fine house, and were very happy. Mary Catherine didn't remember this. Mom also said her father drank because he was too trusting. His business partner had stolen everything and destroyed the business her father built. In trying to save the business, her father used all of their savings, and then spent all of her mother's money. As the money dwindled, his drinking increased.

When all was lost to Patrick O'Rourke, except the comfort he found at the bottom of a bottle, they ended up in the trailer park, living in poverty. Mary Catherine had no doubt her mother loved her dad. She saw the love in the gentle comfort her mother always displayed to her father. It would calm him during his worse depressions, and her father would be good for a few weeks. However, it never lasted, and for this Mary Catherine resented him. Still, her mother just sighed and said that soon he would get better. Mary Catherine prayed, just as Sister and her mother asked, but God never seemed to answer her prayers. Perhaps, she was too bad for God to listen to her.

The ringing school bell roused Mary Catherine from her musing. Oh no, Mary Catherine thought as the other children flooded the hall, everybody will see me now. And who was at the head of the approaching pack but Ann Marie Higgins. Mary Catherine quickly assumed a defiant pose and gave Ann Marie the raspberry. How was Mary Catherine supposed to know Sister Clements was standing right behind her?

A light touch on her shoulder startled Mary Catherine and alerted her to Sister's presence.

"Mary Catherine, come with me into my office." Sister Clement's voice was soft. Both her voice and her face gave no indication she was going to address the behavior she just witnessed.

This must be bad, really bad, thought Mary Catherine, as she followed Sister into the oak paneled office which always smelled of lemon oil. Sitting in the leather tufted chair in front of Sister's large desk, Mary Catherine decided since Sister was acting so funny, it would be best if she remained silent. She would allow Sister Clements to lead the way. Sister Clements was tall, thin, and dark skinned. She was so different from Mary Catherine's mother, who was small, blonde, and petite. Still the two women had been best friends since a childhood shared in this very school.

Usually Sister got right to the point, but this time she stared out the window at the beautiful gardens below and seemed to forget Mary Catherine was there. Mary Catherine sat for a few minutes and was about to say something when Sister began speaking quietly as if in a whisper, "Mary Catherine, how was your mother this morning?"

Mary Catherine hesitated, what a strange question she thought.

"All right, I guess." Mary Catherine waited but there was no response. Perhaps Sister wanted her to say more. "Oh, she was very tired. Her hands and her ankles looked very swollen and puffy, but you know, the baby is due any day, so naturally she feels bad."

"Yes," answered Sister in a strangely quiet voice, "she was always fragile." Pausing she continued, "Was she on her way to the doctor?"

"Oh no!" Mary Catherine replied, "She said she was just going to lie down for a while."

Sister never behaved like this before.

In a whisper so low it made Mary Catherine strain to hear, she asked, "Mary Catherine, when was the last time your mother visited a doctor?" Mary Catherine didn't understand what Sister was getting at.

"She had an appointment a while back, but then Johnny needed new shoes, so she canceled it. She made another one, but I had the flu, and there was only enough money for one visit."

Sister had her back to Mary Catherine, as she stood rigidly looking out the window. As if afraid of the answer, the tall nun asked, "So, when was the last time she went to the doctor, Mary Catherine?"

Mary Catherine answered without thinking, "When she first found out she was pregnant, about seven months ago." Sister Clement's shoulders seemed to collapse, as if under a heavy weight.

Suddenly, Mary Catherine understood. She knew what Sister was getting at, and the tears began to flow down her cheeks in heavy streams.

"I know how good she is, I know I should be more like her!" Mary Catherine sobbed between sentences, "I try to be like her, but she's so good, how can anybody be that good!"

Another loud sob escaped her. "I'm just so bad. I don't know who I take after. Please don't tell her, Sister, whatever I've done, punish me for it, but don't tell her. She has enough to worry about!" Mary Catherine looked up to see Sister staring at her in surprise.

"Is that what you think you're here for, Mary Catherine, because you've done something wrong? Come here and sit by me." Mary Catherine climbed onto Sister's lap as her sobs continued.

"You'd be surprised to know, but I understand exactly how you feel." Mary Catherine looked up in amazement, as Sister placed her arm around her, and continued, "You know some people seem to be just born good, and others, like you and me, why, we have to constantly work at it."

"Oh no, Sister," sobbed Mary Catherine "You're so good."

Sister stroked her hair as she continued, "I wasn't always so good. In fact, I still have a bad temper. Your mother was always good.

Despite all my prayers about it, just like you, I still have to work at controlling my temper. I'm very angry right now, and I don't know what to do about it."

"Are you angry at me, Sister?" Mary Catherine asked.

Filled with emotion the nun answered, "No, I'm angry at fate or life, or whatever it is we mere humans have no control of. But I have to remember, your mother wouldn't be angry, would she?"

Mary Catherine answered Sister with a tighter hug, "She's never angry. In fact, I've never seen my mom angry, whenever anything bad happens she just says to trust in God. She always says that it's not for us to understand God's will, just to follow it."

Mary Catherine looked up as she finished, and was shocked to see tears flowing down Sister's cheeks, her mind seemed far away.

"Yes, that's exactly what your mother would say, and she always tells the truth. I want you to remember that, Mary Catherine! Your mother is truly a saint, closer to the understanding of God than us weaker mortals." Sister started to cry harder now, and Mary Catherine tightened her grip on her.

"What is it, Sister? Why are you so sad?"

Sister sighed and started, "Mary Catherine, it's your mother. After you left this morning, she became very ill and collapsed. She's in the hospital. And now you'll be very brave for her and your brothers won't you, Mary Catherine?"

"I don't think I can, Sister." Mary Catherine whispered, as fear and grief gripped her.

"I know it will be hard, but think how your mother would want you to behave, how she would behave," Sister answered, as she stroked the frightened child's hair. "That should make it a little easier, Mary Catherine."

Somehow Mary Catherine doubted anything could make this easier. She felt like she was in a dream. No, it was a nightmare, and she just wanted to wake up.

"I want to see her, Sister. I want my mother," Mary Catherine cried.

With a take charge attitude, Sister Clements answered, "Then come, Mary Catherine, comb your hair and wash your face. We'll pick up your brothers from their classes before we go."

"You're going, Sister?"

"Why, of course, she's my best friend, I love her." Sister's voice betrayed a slight tremor, as she gave Mary Catherine a minute to prepare and calm herself. Mary Catherine was scared. The walk to her brother's classrooms seemed to take so long. She had to wait as the nun talked to her brother's teachers. Mary Catherine wanted to scream. It was taking too long, she wanted to see her mother. Finally, with Johnny and Danny holding her hands they walked out to the convent on the side of the red brick school.

"It won't take us long to get to the hospital," Sister stated, as she directed the three children to the large, blue station wagon. Silently, all the O'Rourke children piled into the back of what the school children called the "Nun-mobile" whenever they saw the sisters riding around town in the dented car.

Sister Clements, in a soft voice, instructed, "Mary Catherine, please, take out your rosary beads and pray as we ride to the hospital."

Mary Catherine cringed as she pictured the rosary beads she was supposed to always carry, sitting on the table at home. She tried to change the subject. "Is my father at the hospital, I mean, could they find him?"

"Yes, Mary Catherine, he's already there. Here, take these beads and keep them. Pray really hard, Mary Catherine, God especially listens to the prayers of children." The frightened girl wanted to ask what exactly was wrong with her mother, but she was afraid, afraid of the truth. Mary Catherine prayed hard, harder then she ever had in her life. Sister directed her way through the heavy downtown traffic of the blue-collar suburban town. Mary Catherine prayed, but despite her efforts, her heart was too full of fear to allow her to concentrate.

Mary Catherine thought the ride to the hospital was a long one, but the time spent in the waiting area was longer. At least the boys seemed quiet. There was none of the usual poking and wrestling. None of the usual, 'You started it' or 'Stop looking at me!' Both boys sat quietly as if in shock. Mary Catherine would have been glad to have the distraction of a noisy diversion.

They sat quietly in the plastic molded chairs outside the room with the sign: Intensive Care. Mary Catherine watched the people, nurses, and orderlies walk around. She couldn't believe how they walked by, engrossed in conversations about their lunches, or that night's date. Didn't they know what was happening? Didn't they know the most important person in the world was sick just beyond the door? She might need them, but they just continued on their way, as if they didn't care. Mary Catherine wanted to scream and spit on them as they laughed and teased each other. Her mother was sick, and they acted as if nothing had happened.

Sister Clements went into the room where Mary Catherine's mother was lying unconscious. Mary Catherine assumed her father was there also. She wanted to run in and see her mother, but Sister told her to sit still. Waiting was the hardest job Mary Catherine ever did. She looked up to see Father O'Brien coming down the hall, and was glad to finally see a familiar face. Father O'Brien was always good to the O'Rourke children. He always had a pocket full of chocolate, and a string of corny jokes ready whenever he saw them. This time, however, his face was grim. He gave Mary Catherine a hug as he greeted them.

"Can I see my mother?" she asked him with a lump in her throat.

"I'll find out," he smiled gently, as he petted both of the boys' heads. "I'm going in to see her now and I'll ask. But you must be calm. The doctors and nurses need time to try to make your mother well. Children would be in their way. I'll find out if you can visit her for a while, but you must be patient."

Mary Catherine was doubtful, patience wasn't her long suit, but she supposed she didn't have any choice. Father O'Brien was worried. He knew these small children had much to face. He had been called to perform Last Rites.

After what seemed like an eternity, Sister Clements appeared at the door. They were to follow her quietly, and they would be able to visit their mother for a few minutes.

"You must be quiet, however, your mother is very sick. You must be brave, and not cry and upset her."

Mary Catherine didn't like the look on Sister Clement's face. It looked as if she had been crying herself. Still, she tiptoed behind Sister, anxious to see her mother. Nothing could have prepared her for the sight she would see. Curtains hid the other patients from the sight of the children, as they headed for the drapes which hid their mother.

When the curtains parted and the children were guided into the bedside, Mary Catherine's courage failed her. Fear invaded every fiber of her body, as her mind refused to accept that the person in the bed was her mother. Her mom's eyes were closed, and didn't open when the children entered. Plastic tubes seemed to be stuck in every part of her body. Machines hummed all around the bed. Other machines with green lights beeped overhead. Devices beeped and hummed with each heartbeat and breath, but her mother didn't seem to hear any of it. She didn't move or even open her eyes. Even though Mary Catherine was frightened, she reached out to touch the mother she loved so much.

"Mom," Mary Catherine whispered, but there was no response.

She felt the tears fall, as she gently touched her mother's hand. The boys were louder in their reaction, and started to sob.

"That's enough," Sister sighed, as she and Father O'Brien led the boys out of the room. So concerned were they over the boys that nobody seemed to notice that Mary Catherine was left behind.

Despite her fear, Mary Catherine was determined not to leave and wait in the hallway outside. She silently retreated to the chair in the corner. The curtain hid her as she tried to be as unobtrusive as she could. The machines, surrounding her mother's bed, ticked moments that felt like an eternity to Mary Catherine, but it was only ten minutes before her father arrived. Her father, when he entered with the doctor, never noticed her. His eyes appeared glued to the angelically peaceful face of his wife. Despite the machines and illness, her face had the porcelain look of another world. The doctor appeared not to notice.

In a deeply concerned voice the doctor said, "You have to make a decision, Pat. I know you love her, but you can't have them both. The EEG's are conclusive. She has a flat line, brain death. You can save the baby though. If we perform the surgery soon, there's a good chance the baby will live. She probably won't make it through the surgery, but the baby will. Think about what she would want, Pat. Don't let your grief make you lose both of them."

Mary Catherine couldn't believe her ears! What was this doctor saying? Her hands gripped the arms of her chair, as she strained to hear her father's answer. She could not believe what she heard.

"Save the baby!" he blurted out. The doctor smiled, as he patted her father's back.

"You're doing the right thing." The doctor went to arrange for the surgery, leaving her father to shed silent tears as he looked at his wife.

Mary Catherine was paralyzed. She didn't know what the letters EEG stood for. She didn't understand what flat line, or brain death meant. She only knew that her father made a choice. He had a choice between the life of the baby and her mother. And he had chosen the baby! Mary Catherine was too stunned to move. Perhaps, she could stop the doctor. Maybe she could talk the doctor into saving her mother instead. She was frozen with fear. *How could she live without her mother?* She knew they wouldn't listen. They never listened to children. They would go ahead and do whatever they wanted, no matter what she said!

Mary Catherine's stomach churned. She never considered her mother might die. It was unthinkable. Mary Catherine could never live without her. She watched in stony silence, as her father, still weeping, left the room. She went over to her mother, and stroked her hand.

With determination, Mary Catherine whispered, "I won't let them, Mom. I'll save you. I love you!"

Mary Catherine could no longer hold back the tears as the sobs rose and shook her tiny body. Covering her face with both hands, she sobbed. The groans came from deep within her, from her very soul. It wasn't long before the nurses heard her, and escorted the weeping child to the hallway.

Mary Catherine sat, gently sobbing, as her father talked to the doctor in the hallway. Everyone was talking and no one noticed her.

Mary Catherine watched as the doctor grasped the shoulders of her father, and her father continued to cry. "You're doing the right thing, Patrick. It's what she would want, and the baby will have a good chance."

Mary Catherine wanted to shout. How did this doctor know what her mother wanted? He didn't even know her mother. Why was her father listening to him? No one loved life more than her mother. She had always been amazed by the joy her mother found in everything from a simple sunrise to a furry kitten. Mary Catherine knew her mother loved life. Anger rose in her as she realized it was her father who hated life. Everything made him sad, that's why he drank so much. Mary Catherine was no longer sad or stunned. She was angry! *Why were they letting her father, who didn't understand her mother's love of life, decide who would live or die?* Sister Clements appeared to be absorbed in her own thoughts, as she stared out the window. Still, Mary Catherine had to interrupt her. It would save her mother's life!

Mary Catherine gave Sister's black sleeve a gentle tug. Sister continued to stare out the window. The next, much harder tug, appeared to shock her out of her deep, silent thoughts. She momentarily stared at Mary Catherine, as if she didn't know who she was. Mary Catherine was temporarily disarmed by Sister's eyes.

She had looked into the nun's eyes on numerous occasions, but they had never looked like this. They looked so old. There was a deep sadness in them, and yet there was something else too. Something Mary Catherine couldn't put into words.

Mary Catherine had to bite her lip to bring herself back to the reality of the situation. As she did, her eyes began to well up with tears.

"What is it, Mary Catherine?" Sister spoke softly as she bent down to Mary Catherine's level.

"You've got to stop them!" Mary Catherine stammered, as the urgency of the circumstance hit her. "They're going to kill my mother!" And now the tears began to flow silently down her cheeks, as the taste of blood filled her mouth. "You've got to stop them! They want to save a baby, a baby no one even knows! And they want to kill my mother to do it!"

"Mary Catherine, what have you done to yourself?" Sister pulled out a white handkerchief and wiped the blood that was trickling down from Mary Catherine's lip. It stung as Sister Clements rubbed Mary Catherine's bitten lip.

As Sister knelt to help her, Mary Catherine, worn from fear and desperation, wrapped her arms around the nun's neck and laid her head on her shoulder.

"Please, help," she sobbed, as Sister stroked her head.

"Mary Catherine, you don't understand," she murmured softly. "Your mother would want us to save her baby, and even if we didn't, we couldn't save your mother now. If we don't save the baby, both of them will die."

Mary Catherine pulled away in surprise. Sister was the same as every other adult here. She wasn't going to help. She was going to let them kill her mother, all for a baby nobody knew!

Mary Catherine shook with anger. No one was going to help her. They would kill her mother and nobody would stop them. The gravity of the thought felt like a heavy weight. The weight pulled the emotions, so intense a moment ago, down into her very core. The tears stopped flowing as she stood in stunned silence.

Sister Clements mistakenly interpreted this as acceptance and walked Mary Catherine back to the chairs. With her senses dulled from the shock of her best friend's impending death, Sister didn't notice the lack of response to the comforting hug she gave Mary Catherine.

Mary Catherine felt empty. Sitting, as if detached, she watched as the nurses wheeled her mother to the operating room. A scream rose from her soul, but died in her throat. She sat empty, feeling useless as they killed her mother. Never had she felt so all alone. It was as if she were invisible. Events whirled around her, and she felt unable to control any of them. No one listens. Even if she screamed Mary Catherine knew no one would listen. She wanted to die. If her mother was going to die, then Mary Catherine wanted to die and be with her.

The hour they all waited seemed like an eternity. Mary Catherine prayed someone would do something to help. No one did. The doctor returned. Dressed in green scrubs, the doctor approached her father and said, "Patrick, you've got a fine new son. He's a little small, but very strong."

Mary Catherine watched as her father's smile faltered, he didn't seem concerned with the news.

"And my wife?" Patrick's face stayed emotionless, as the wrinkles on the elderly doctor's face deepened, etched with sorrow.

Reaching out to put his arm around the shoulder of the concerned husband, the doctor shook his head and announced, "I'm sorry. We couldn't save her."

For a moment the hall remained silent. It was as if God Himself, stopped time.

Suddenly everyone was up, even the boys. They were hugging, sobbing, and gathering around Patrick. No one noticed that Mary Catherine hadn't moved. No one seemed to care.

After a few minutes, Sister Clements approached her and said, "Mary Catherine, come. We'll go down to see your new brother."

Mary Catherine followed everyone as they headed down the hall to the nursery. The group was very quiet, hardly the usual group going to see a new life. But this life started in unusual circumstances. Life, like a phoenix arising from the ashes of death, brought out the supernatural curiosity and awe in people. Grief, so well known to the souls present, suddenly took on the air of eternal destiny. This made the mood one of serious contemplation. Looking at the sleeping newborn through the nursery window, each person present contemplated the mercy of God, each according to his own understanding.

God never entered Mary Catherine's thoughts. She looked with horror at the tiny infant everyone else seemed so interested in. This baby had taken her mom away from her. She couldn't believe how everyone reacted with affection and love when the nurse held the baby up.

Mary Catherine looked with amazement at her father, who, with gentle tears rolling down his cheeks exclaimed, "Ah, he looks so much like her."

Mary Catherine wanted to hit him. When she looked back at the baby, she saw what her father saw. The soft angelic face, the wispy blonde hair, and the gentle features instantly brought back her mother's face. This baby looked just like her. Mary Catherine and her brothers each had some of her features, but this baby had all of them. It made her sick. She wanted to smash the window and the infant who cooed beyond the glass. She didn't want this baby. Mary Catherine wanted her mother. Why couldn't she just have her mother back? Everyone just stood there. They just stood there smiling at this stupid baby. It was as if they already forgot about her mother.

Mary Catherine wanted to scream. The fact that this newborn looked just like her dead mother didn't help. It didn't make her feel better, it made her feel worse. Mary Catherine knew every time she looked at the baby, she would think of her mother. She watched a faint smile emerge on Sister Clement's face.

Sister murmured lowly, "The Lord giveth, and the Lord taketh away."

Mary Catherine couldn't believe how quickly everyone seemed to forget her mother was gone! How could they be happy to see this baby? How could they be concerned about how the baby was and how much he weighed? It disgusted her. As far as Mary Catherine was concerned, the Lord took away the best, her whole life and soul, her mother. In her place, He left this useless thing. She couldn't accept it. She would never accept it! She looked at her father as he cooed at the baby. She hated him. He had killed her mother! She looked at the baby with disdain. She hated them both, and vowed she always would.

Starved for Love

Blessed are they that have not seen, and have believed. (John 20:29)

Elly looked around the small room with a detached feeling of exhaustion. The gleaming white walls and shining chrome fixtures were all so sterile and germ-free. The glass canisters on the counter displayed sprays of tongue depressors and long, wooden cotton applicators. Shining instruments of various shapes, and unknown use, lay neatly lined up in a row. What germs were they afraid of, she wondered? An amusing thought that the only germ-laden object in the room was herself ran fleetingly through her mind. The amusement vaporized as quickly as it occurred. The dark cloud of thoughtlessness soon emptied her mind.

She sat detached until the paper gown the nurse had asked her to don itched her arm. Looking down to scratch where the stiff medical gown irritated her, she was shocked at how thin the arm was. The white, paper gown and paper-lined examining table were uncomfortable. Why was she here? If only Susan, her roommate, had left her alone.

Susan harassed her, until she came just to end the constant nagging. Susan had been nagging her for a month to come to the clinic and have an examination. Well, soon it would be over, and they would leave her alone.

A wave of nausea and blurred vision passed over her. Perhaps it was the low blood pressure the nurse commented on, as she quietly used the pediatric cuff on Elly's thin arm. A few deep breaths and the feeling quickly passed. There was no food in her stomach to irritate it. Sinking back into indifference, Elly did not hear the doctor as he approached the door of the examining room. He took the chart from the holder on the door and read Elly's history. She had been examined a few months ago by the former clinic physician. The previous clinic doctor had done a through examination and history on Eleanor Wilkin.

Dr. Gabe Lopez talked to Elly's roommate Susan just this morning, when she made the appointment for Elly. He knew the story of Elly's recent grief and depression. Still, he was shocked to read the chart and realize Elly had lost twenty pounds. It was a lot of weight to lose in the short time since her last annual physical, at the beginning of the college year.

All students at Northeastern College were required to have a complete physical each September – only four months ago. Eleanor Wilkin's chart showed that at 5'8", and 125 pounds, the examining physician had recommended that she put on some weight. Now the young sophomore was only 105 pounds–grossly underweight. Still the olive-skinned doctor was not prepared for what he saw when he opened the examining room door.

Like a starved and fragile bird, he thought, as the blonde-haired patient lifted her purple-shaded eyes to him. Blue eyes devoid of any life examined him with detached curiosity. He quickly smiled, a lesson he learned early on, to alleviate any fear on the patient's part. He shouldn't have bothered. This patient didn't seem to care.

"Hi, I'm Dr. Gabe Lopez, glad to meet you, Eleanor Wilkin."

A faint smile, the remnant of a polite upbringing, whispered across her face. The eyes reflected no feeling. He proceeded with the examination, looking down her throat, and in her ears. It was really a waste of time. Dr. Lopez already knew what was wrong. Pinching the skin on her arm proved the poor turgidity indicative of dehydration. This girl, only 20 years old, was completely emaciated. She looked like a refugee from a concentration camp. He was, even after five years as a practicing physician, amazed at what power the mind and the spirit of a person had over the body.

The handsome physician addressed the young girl with authority and stated, "You're very ill, Eleanor. I'm afraid you're going to have to be admitted to the hospital."

She raised her head, as if about to speak, but lowered it and just sighed. The young doctor would have preferred an argument. It would have shown some evidence of undefeated spirit. There was none. There seemed to be no fight left in the girl.

Dr. Lopez instructed her to dress and announced to the blonde patient, "It's the end of my shift. I'll drive you over myself. It's on my way."

Elly didn't question the matter. She just wanted to go home to her room at the college dormitory. She wanted to crawl into bed and fall into a mindless sleep. She felt so drained, so tired. But, she was too tired to argue. Nothing seemed to matter anyway.

Leaving the room, Dr. Lopez instructed the attending nurse to help the patient dress. In her condition, he wasn't sure the girl wouldn't collapse. He'd never seen someone so dehydrated, so emaciated, so weak, and still functioning. He lied to her. The hospital wasn't on his way home. He worked voluntarily at the college clinic two days a week. He usually went straight from the clinic to his busy private office and a waiting room of patients. He thought of calling an ambulance for the girl. That would take care of his obligation to her. The hospital would assign an attending physician to treat her. But somehow, he just couldn't do that.

Dr. Lopez called his office and explained to his exasperated receptionist that he would be late. There was just something special about this girl. He wanted to be sure she received immediate and correct treatment. Neither Elly nor her roommate realized she was in danger of death. In her condition, the lack of fluids and proper nutrition caused an electrolyte imbalance. This imbalance could trigger a heart problem at any moment. He had already noted the quickened and irregular pulse. The very lack of heart this girl displayed was affecting her physical heart.

He settled her gently in his car and he started driving toward the hospital. The windshield wipers whirled gently as a misty rain fell. Entering the entrance ramp of the crowded parkway, he turned the defroster on. The car was cold and damp from sitting in the parking lot of the clinic. Looking across the bucket seat of his classic Mustang, he grew concerned about the weakened state of his young patient. She seemed listless, and displayed no interest in the early winter scenery just outside the car window.

The dark-haired doctor asked, "When was the last time you had a full meal?"

Softly, she answered him, in a dull and monotone voice, "I don't know. I've tried to eat in the last few days. I figured it was better to force myself to eat. I'm tired of listening to Susan nag me. But nothing will stay down now, eating just nauseates me. Even the smell of food nauseates me."

This short speech exhausted her. The physician decided to let her rest. Her eyes were half-closed, as she laid her head back against the red leather seat.

Elly had suffered a loss. Susan, her roommate had explained it to the physician, during her call. Elly's fiancé died in a motorcycle accident, three months ago. She received a simple fractured leg while her boyfriend, Michael, died of a head trauma. Still, her reaction to his death was about to cause her own. Dr. Lopez knew there had to be more to the overwhelming grief that triggered this young girl's depression.

The emergency room staff awaited his arrival. He had called them from the clinic as his nurse helped the patient dress. He wanted immediate attention for this fragile girl. He wasn't disappointed. The staff was waiting with a stretcher for the weakened patient. Dr. Lopez lifted her gently from his car to the awaiting stretcher. Following her into the emergency room, he quickly oversaw the initial stat treatments. An intravenous of D5W/2NS with 40 MEQ of KCL to treat the potassium loss was started. Blood tests and urine tests that would tell the tale of the electrolyte needs were taken. A stat EKG and cardiac consult were ordered.

Dr. Lopez ordered a high protein diet and force feeding if necessary. He hoped these meals would quickly fill all the body's nutritional needs. The physician had her admitted to I-West, where, in the past, he noted the outstanding kindness of the nurses on this floor. Last, but not least, he ordered a psychiatric consult. He needed to get at the root of this depression, triggered by the death of her boyfriend. He knew if he didn't, he might win the battle for her life, but lose the war.

Driving back to his office, Dr. Lopez felt a little empty. Going over all his steps, he realized there was no medical recourse he hadn't addressed. But, there was something that bothered him. He had trouble putting his finger on it. There was something about this strange, quiet girl that touched him. It was as if he knew her. It wasn't a physical attraction, although she was probably very attractive when healthy. No, there was something more, something protective. He sensed that his tie to this patient seemed almost spiritual.

"Whoa," he shook his head. "You've been putting in too many hours." He resolved to take a long overdue vacation, and visit home as soon as possible. Not until you make sure she is well, his mind whispered to him. He spent the afternoon attending to the numerous patients who waited at his office. Dr. Lopez took the time to make some phone calls, however. He resolved to take a long vacation in two months. The physician had been working nonstop for the past two years. His practice had grown, as his reputation spread. Dr. Lopez was tired. The daily drudgery was taking its toll. Besides, he hadn't spent any quality time with his family and the young doctor missed them. Dr. Lopez had only been able to make a few weekend visits. One of the calls he made was to a friend and colleague. That colleague could oversee his patients. Dr. Lopez needed some real time with his family.

He made visiting the hospital first on his list each day, and Elly was the first patient he visited. Dr. Lopez was astonished and gratified by the vast improvement each day brought. The high protein diet seemed to do wonders. Some days, the nurses had to force feed the detached girl. Her mind seemed so far away. Her body, so emaciated, rejected much of the food. She often became nauseous. Dr. Lopez ordered Tigan IM for the recurring nausea. She started to fill out and gain weight. Soon she was eating on her own, with little coaxing.

The cardiologist confirmed Dr Lopez's suspicion. The irregular pulse was caused by the temporary loss of potassium, due to the dehydration. There would not be any permanent damage. Within a few weeks, Elly actually gained five pounds.

Dr. Lopez should have been thrilled with her progress. Entering her room, he couldn't see any trace of the physical deterioration she displayed in his office. Her color was rosy, and only faint dark lines beneath her eyes revealed any hint of her recently perilous state of health. Elly's shining blonde hair, just shampooed by the nurse, reflected the healthy increase of protein. The lab tests were all within normal range. As she sat in a chair, with the morning sun flooding around her, Dr. Lopez was struck once again with how beautiful she truly was.

So what was wrong? The blue eyes remained empty. As her physical state greatly improved, her mental state worsened. She was more withdrawn each day, despite her regular dose of antidepressant medication.

Dr. Lopez was followed into the patient's room by the charge nurse of I-West. Gray-haired but energetic, Kathy ran her floor like a well-tuned machine. Most of the nurses on the floor were young and competent, but given to silliness and laughter. In the stress-filled environment, where they were overworked and understaffed, laughter worked well to relieve the overwhelming pressure and fatigue which was all part of the nursing profession.

However, the reaction the young nurses displayed when Dr.

Lopez came to the floor was totally out of proportion. Still, Kathy mused, if she were about 30 years younger, she might feel the same herself. "Dr. Gabe Lopez, Gabriel is a perfect name for such an angel," the older nurse thought as she followed the young physician down the hall and into Elly Wilkin's room.

Gabe Lopez was astonishingly handsome. His dark, muscular persona was further accented by his humble and kind ways. He never yelled, as some physicians tended to do, for snappy attention. He never demanded nursing assistance until one of the nurses was free to help him. He never tried to make the nurses feel like slaves to all of his needs. He was patient while teaching, and never made the nurses feel incompetent if a procedure was new. Kathy wondered whether it was his good looks or great personality that attracted all of the nurses.

Whatever it was, all the young nurses became flighty and nervous around him. Therefore, Kathy tried to be free to help him whenever he needed help. With a puzzled look on his face the doctor questioned the patient, but there was no response.

"She hasn't talked in two days," Kathy whispered, as the patient sat staring out the window.

"I'd like to see all of her work ups. Has Dr. Deluca been in to see her like this?" Dr. Lopez asked as he left the room and headed toward the nurse's station.

"Yes, his consultation report is on the back of her chart." Reaching into the desk bin and sorting through the daily lab reports, Kathy handed him the computer readouts.

"I haven't even seen them myself," Kathy answered.

Dr. Lopez seemed deep in thought, as he read the consultation. Dr. Deluca, the consulting psychiatrist, found little improvement in the patient. He feared the patient was slipping slowly into a catatonic depression. Dr. Deluca recommended shock treatments if the patient continued to deteriorate. Dr. Lopez was stunned. He had no idea her condition was so serious. Her physical improvement was so great he just assumed her mental improvement would follow. Looking over the lab reports, he was pleased to see the improvement in her electrolyte balance but he felt completely frustrated, even angry. He did all he could to heal this patient. She was so young and beautiful. What in the world could send her into such a deep depression?

Shock treatment was the treatment of last resort. What was the missing key in this mystery? Kathy watched the conflicting emotions play across Dr. Lopez's face as he read the reports. She had never seen the light-hearted internist so intense.

Suddenly, as the puzzled physician scanned the lab reports, his face changed. First surprise registered, and then grim determination.

"Shock, I'll give her a shock," he mumbled, as he slammed the reports back on the desk. As he headed back toward the patient's room, Kathy grabbed the reports, and started to read. What could have produced such a reaction from the mild Dr. Lopez?

With an air of determination, Dr Lopez entered Eleanor's room, walking quickly over to her chair. "Hello, Eleanor," the resolute physician announced loudly. Still, there was no reaction. Gabe gently reached out and lifted her chin, raising her face to his direction.

"I know you can hear me, Eleanor." Her face remained deadpan and devoid of all life. Dr. Lopez was determined to reach this young woman.

Staring into Elly's face, Dr. Lopez stated, "Hear me, and hear me well. You can no longer indulge yourself. You, Eleanor, can no longer sit there and just think of yourself."

She showed no reaction.

"Eleanor, you're pregnant," Her eyelids flickered, but her face remained emotionless.

"Do you understand, Eleanor?" Dr. Lopez raised his voice, "You can't just think of yourself any longer. There is a new life growing in you."

She showed no emotion.

Totally frustrated, Dr. Lopez started to leave the room. As he reached the door, he discerned some movement. He looked back and saw the single tear. A single tear slipped down her cheek.

Her hand covered her abdomen, as she whispered to an unknown listener, "Michael."

Gabe quickly spanned the room. Gently grabbing her by both shoulders, he talked, "Eleanor, is it Michael's child?" She appeared confused as a torrent of tears streamed down her face.

"But, that can't be. It can't be Michael's baby. Michael is dead, completely dead! How can his child be alive?" She still talked to an unknown entity, with no acknowledgment of the doctor's presence. He softly shook her, until she looked at him. Looking up into the soft brown eyes of the man who brought her this unbelievable news, her sobbing became uncontrollable.

Dr. Lopez whispered softly, "It's a gift, Eleanor, a gift of life from God."

Elly gulped for air.

"Don't call me Eleanor. Michael is the only one whoever called me Eleanor." She lifted her hands up to her face, and began to sob a cry of the soul.

"What shall I call you then?" Gabe whispered as he took this broken child in his arms. He allowed her to lean her head on his shoulder as she continued weeping.

"Elly, everybody calls me Elly."

He held her closer and allowed her to grieve uninterrupted.

As she cried, the broken girl told her story. Short of breath from crying, Elly gasped for air between each sentence, "I killed Michael. I brought him the motorcycle he always wanted, but couldn't afford. It was for his birthday, and he loved it. But he loved it too much. He said it made him feel free. He was so happy with it and loved to ride it. He just got bolder and bolder." Her body shook with grief.

"He wasn't even looking, when the truck came around the curve. His mother was right. She slapped me at the funeral. She said I murdered him, and she was right. If I hadn't bought Michael that motorcycle, he would be alive today." The young girl's grief and guilt overwhelmed her. Her thin frame trembled as the emotions, so long repressed, were released.

"Oh God," thought Gabe. No wonder she couldn't bear the pain.

"I didn't cry, I didn't deserve to cry and I knew it. I was guilty. I only got a fractured leg and he died. I killed him."

"Shh," Gabe murmured. "It was an accident, you didn't kill him."

She didn't appear to comprehend as she continued crying. It didn't matter–he knew she would be all right now. The pain was out in the open. The healing would begin now. No longer festering in the dark, the light would come and slowly heal the wound. Perhaps the baby would help.

Her sobs slowed. She appeared drained. Lifting her tear soaked face gently up with his hand under her chin, he looked into her eyes, now so filled with life and emotion.

"Elly, God has given you a gift. He is bringing you life out of death."

Elly answered her routine answer, the answer she learned as a child, "There is no God, that's just a nice story. It's a crutch for the weak."

Dr. Lopez said nothing. She was much too drained to understand. This was a time for her to rest. Now, he had his diagnosis. She had no faith. A weakened and lost child was before him.

"What will I do now?" she whispered.

Holding both her shoulders in his hand, Dr. Lopez looked into her blue eyes, "You'll go home and have your baby, Elly."

Two weeks after being told of her pregnancy, Elly did go home. The hospital stay, under the care of Dr. Lopez, strengthened the young blonde girl. She felt able to face the pregnancy.

The baby did make a difference. Suddenly, she believed she had something to live for because a piece of Michael remained with her. She would never be alone again.

Loneliness was such a part of Elly's life. Until she met Michael, she spent most of her life alone, longing for the companionship and approval of others. That approval never seemed to come. And then there was Michael, laughing and accepting, with such a joy for life that he infected everyone around him. His instant acceptance, approval, and love for Elly was a totally new experience for her. Michael laughed at her insecurities and loved all her fears away. Without him, Elly felt totally lost again and undeserving of happiness or joy. Worse, was the feeling that she was responsible for his death.

Dr. Lopez had been so good. Each morning after the day he broke through her depression, he visited Elly. He took the time to sit and talk with Elly about the baby and her plans. He addressed her feelings of guilt and encouraged her to talk out her feelings. These daily visits and talks with Dr. Lopez helped her to start dealing with these feelings. The growing love toward this unborn child of Michael's was the true healing balm. And this child, Elly was determined, would be showered with love. Elly wanted to shower this baby with all the love she felt deprived of during her own childhood. Elly was unable to accept Dr. Lopez's idea of a loving God in this plan, but the idea of never being alone again, and having Michael's child gave her hope.

On the day of her discharge, Elly realized just how important the staff of this hospital had become to her. The nurses all seemed to find their way into her room that morning. A hug and well wishes came from all, from the head nurse to the cleaning woman. Even Dr. Lopez spent time on his final examination and discharge instructions. The doctor and his patient had grown close in a short period of time. Sharing her soul with this man as they talked each morning seemed to break all of the usual barriers. They had become friends. An extended hug from Kathy the head nurse ended Elly's goodbyes. She had never experienced such a warm display of love. It filled her with hope.

The shining morning sun that lit the blue winter sky filled Elly with renewed optimism. But as the southbound train clattered its way home, the sky darkened with storm clouds. Leaving her new friends, especially the kind Dr. Lopez, changed Elly's mood. It seemed that as distance grew between Elly and those who had helped her, the hope that was so strong in the morning was also disappearing.

She had never been happy in that home. The house where she grew up stood elevated on the highlands above the Atlantic. Her only family, her mother, waited there. Any hope Elly had in her future seemed to shrink with the distance which separated her from home. Elly's newfound sense-of-self weakened. By the time the train pulled into her home town station, the young girl's optimism had all but disappeared. It seemed that home and hope were not factors which worked together in Elly's soul. And as Elly climbed the winding footpath up the hill leading to the large house above the ocean, the dark cloud of doubt began to descend.

Sitting on a large boulder just outside her childhood home as she had so many times in her young life, she looked down to the sea. The large shabby home sat like a citadel on the cliff above the ocean. It had always been her home. No, it wasn't a home, it was just a house. A house in which, Elly now realized, she just existed, but never felt loved. The cold dampness of the ocean-mist started to chill her.

There was a time in her memory when she felt loved. A vague memory surfaced, so hard to reach, of school, and friends, and a mother who laughed and hugged her. But that had been so long ago, perhaps it was just a pleasant dream conjured by a lonely child.

Elly never knew her father. He died before she was born. It was always Elly and her mother, alone. Pictures of her father were framed all over the house, but her mother seemed reluctant to talk about him. All Elly really knew was the story her mother told her. He died of a heart attack. He had no family.

Her mother told her that she had no family either. Elly's mother told her that her parents had died many years ago. Since Elly's mother was an only child, they had been left with no living relatives.

Her father's death left Elly and her mother alone in the world. As a small child, Elly remembered her mother often saying it was just Elly and she against the world. But that was long ago. She sensed her mother's resentment. Elly had always felt her mother was sorry to be burdened with a child. It wasn't just her insecurity which made Elly feel her mother regretted her birth. Her mother never failed to let Elly know her daughter took away her freedom and weighed her down.

Looking down to the ocean, dreary coldness enveloped her. Elly never understood the joyful attraction people displayed toward the ocean. Each summer, people flocked to the sea, happily wasting their vacation on sand, sunburn, and fighting the crowds. Elly hated the ocean. As its icy fingers grabbed the shore, it seemed to invite all to enter its steel-gray coldness. The waves of the ocean always seemed to echo that all was empty, cold, and useless, just like itself. Many times throughout her life, it called to her to end the pain. Elly shook with dampness, as it seemed to talk to her now.

Never, never, never, will your mother understand or accept this baby, the ocean waves seemed to cry.

Elly had not told her mother of her pregnancy. She wrote of her illness and hospitalization. She wrote of her impending return home. There was no response, and Elly would have been surprised if there had been. Her mother was indifferent. The coldness of her mother was like the coldness of the ocean below, deep and unfathomable. Elly stopped trying to understand it long ago.

The muffled sound of an early morning church bell dully pierced the Sunday morning mist. Looking down at the town below, to the left of the cliff, memories flooded her mind. The town seemed miniature at this distance. As a child, Elly often sat on this very rock, looking below. She made up stories about the town and the distant ant-sized people. Each Sunday morning, the tiny people would file into the little white church.

"Like, mindless, bumbling, idiots," her mother always said. Elly longed to meet those people, and see if they were anything like the people in the stories she imagined. She fantasized about them during the long, lonely days of her childhood.

Even now, through the morning fog, she could see the people walking around the town, entering the little church. What was it about this place that so disheartened her? When she left the hospital after her last talk with Dr. Lopez she was so full of anticipation. Now, all hope seemed to be gone. Looking to the large home of her childhood, Elly wondered when it became so dilapidated. It was once the finest house in the county. Now, so long neglected, it appeared large and shabby. Still, the outside dampness was starting to permeate her bones, and Elly decided she could no longer put off the inevitable.

As expected, Elly found the front door unlocked. Her mother never locked the doors. Her friends needed access without disturbance of any psychic exercise that happened to be going on. Instantly, Elly was assailed with the strong smell of mildew and decay. Dust and neglect saturated the very air of the dark and dank house. The hall was empty. The murmur of voices from the back living room put the lie to the perceived emptiness. In fact, Elly could never remember the house being empty.

Her mother seldom left the house. There was always the crowd of friends, sometimes large, sometimes small, but ever present. Elly's access to her mother and her attention was always hampered her mother's friends. Elly was seen as an intrusion on her mother's valuable time.

When her mother first became involved with her new friends, they paid a lot of attention to Elly. They tested her over and over for gifts in ESP, reincarnation memory, or precognitive gifts. She didn't display any. When she failed to have any special gifts, she was quickly swept aside and ignored. Her mother added that Elly took after her father, as she herself, was so psychically talented.

Elly soon learned to entertain herself, and not disturb the psychic experiences of the gifted. She spent long, solitary hours reading or playing on the cliffs outside, often wondering if her mother knew or even cared where she was. On the few occasions she ventured into the domain of the psychics while they meditated, read Tarot cards, or studied astrology, she was severely rebuked for destroying the mood of the moment. So severe was the punishment for the smallest intrusion that even now Elly was nervous to enter the back room and announce her homecoming.

As she tiptoed quietly toward the back room, across the old marble floor, Elly coughed from the dust which covered the dark heavy furniture. Everything in the hall was old and neglected. Elly was not surprised to hear some one telling her to stop.

Looking to the left, into the murky and poorly lit dining room she saw Agnes, a long time friend of her mother's casually fingering one of the antique frames on the mantle. Elly got the uncomfortable feeling Agnes was assessing the value of the frame. While the house was dusty and neglected, it was full of expensive treasures which seemed to attract Agnes.

Agnes, a middle-aged woman, always seemed to be in the house. She had been a steady visitor since Elly was a child.

In a haughty tone Agnes announced, "Your mother is busy. She is in the middle of a regression."

Elly knew instantly what Agnes was talking about – after all she grew up around the paranormal. Her mother was in the middle of being hypnotized into a past life which would expose either her great psychic abilities in that past life, or some fact relevant to this life.

"She's found a great new guru with great channeling abilities," Agnes announced, clearly ready to take credit for finding the new talent.

Elly understood. She wouldn't want to see Elly until she was free. Elly could not help but to feel crushed, even after all these years, she came last in her mother's life. It still hurt her deeply. Agnes, knowing Elly since she was a child, picked up on Elly's feelings immediately.

Disdainfully, Agnes said, "You mustn't resent your mother's great skills. It's hard for someone like you to understand how important her work truly is."

Agnes' sarcastic remark was just another slap in the face. Agnes was what Elly called one of the regulars. There was a group of people who, as far as Elly could tell, fed off her mother's fantasies on a steady basis. When Elly's father died, Elly's mother inherited a great deal of money. Elly was sure many of the people who clung to her mother also drained her of much of that money. There were those temporary, gifted stars who dazzled and fizzed out as soon as Elly's mother got bored with them. There were also the steady companions like Agnes. In Elly's opinion, they were all sponges soaking her mother dry.

"You can see her during dinner, in an hour," Agnes advised her.

Elly resented being scheduled to see her own mother, but she was glad to have an excuse to get away from Agnes.

"I'll just unpack in my room until dinner." She quickly ran up the stairs to some much needed peace.

Elly was glad to see her childhood room remained the same, although it obviously hadn't been cleaned or dusted since she left for college. Out of sight, out of mind, Elly mused. She quickly unpacked and decided to clean her room. Elly loved this room, which was so often her entire small world as a child. Like herself, the room was often neglected. It was filled with old furniture and sorely in need of paint. Its isolated spot at the very top of the house, and its odd shaped windows and walls overlooking the ocean below gave the room an almost mystical quality. It encouraged the imagination of the lonely, young girl who occupied it.

It didn't take long for Elly to tidy it up. This room was the one part of this house Elly loved and truly felt at home in. The rest of the large, rambling house belonged to her mother and her crowd.

Opening the window wide, she allowed the cold air to clear the stuffy room and roll over her, as she lay cocooned under the comforter on her bed. She dosed off. Coming home drained her. She had much to face. Elly wanted to tell her mother the truth, and face the future. Her mind was fevered with the events of the past and the unknown future. Exhausted, she fell into a deep sleep.

It was dark when Elly awoke. Disoriented at first, she didn't know where she was, or what time it was. It was dark and frigid cold. Of course, I'm home, she thought. Why hadn't anyone awoken her? She rose and shut the window the chilly wind was blowing through, and turned on the light to discover it was already 9:30PM. Running a comb through her tangled hair, she freshened up and started downstairs, determined to confront Agnes and her mother and find out why they forgot her.

Muffled voices and the only faint light in the house determined they were all gathered in the back room. Elly slowly entered the room, unaware of what she might find. She found the usual. A crowd of people looked up as she opened the door. Some of the faces were familiar, and some were new. Gathered in a circle, they seemed to be just talking. Elly was relieved she had not disturbed some important ghostly development. Still, they all seemed surprised to see her.

"Oh, I knew I forgot to tell you something!" Agnes exclaimed. "Elly got home this afternoon!"

A cunning smile adorned Agnes's face, feigning surprise at her error. Elly's mother seemed annoyed at not being told her daughter was home.

Louise announced, "Elly, you missed dinner."

Louise Wilkin had always been a beautiful woman. Unapproachable and dark, her mysterious deep eyes attracted many men. Even after her youth left her, she remained a handsome woman with great style. Elly was shocked to see the changes in her mother's appearance. She was astonished her mother's face had grown so thin and wrinkled.

In a husky, low voice, Elly's mother Louise addressed her, "I'm sure if you look in the kitchen, you can find something to eat."

"I'm not very hungry, but I need to talk to you," Elly replied, dreading what she needed to tell her mother, but wanting to get it over with.

"So talk," her mother replied in a scratchy voice.

"I have to talk to you alone."

Louise stared at her daughter and announced, "There's nothing that's a secret from my friends, and you can say anything you want in front of them."

Elly was annoyed, and looking past Agnes she noticed the strangers sitting in a circle in the drab room. There were two middle-aged women and a strangely intense-looking young man. Elly had no intention of talking in front of them. The discomfort in her face showed.

Elly was firm, "No Mother, I need to talk to you alone!"

Louise Wilkin looked at her daughter with renewed interest and surprise. She had never seen Elly assert herself like this. She was always such a weak and melancholy child, such a disappointment.

With renewed interest, Louise said, "Well, you hear her, everybody out of the room."

Agnes and the others looked stunned, but they obeyed. No one ever contradicted Louise Wilkin and stayed around very long. Elly was startled and pleased by her mother's order. It was probably the first time in years she would be alone with her mother. Elly definitely knew it was the first time her mother chose her daughter over her friends. But fear soon crowded out any thoughts of pleasure at her mother's decision–Elly knew what she had to tell her mother would anger her. Elly dreaded the angry, screaming scene that was sure to follow her news.

Louise lit another cigarette and started coughing uncontrollably as the smoke hit her lungs. The pain was getting worse, despite what the young healer assured her were signs of improvement. Still, he was handsome enough to keep around just for entertainment purposes. Louise long ago gave up any hope for a cure.

She watched her daughter with some interest. Elly looked so much like her father it shocked Louise every time she saw her. Often, she searched both Elly's face and personality for some resemblance to herself. There was none. Perhaps if there was, she would find her daughter interesting. As it was, Elly and her mild ways bored her. Louise Wilkin was a strong personality who took pleasure in dominating other strong personalities. Elly was too easy to dominate. She wasn't challenging enough to interest her mother.

Elly had never been so nervous in her life. She fingered and twirled her hair as she told her mother about Michael and their love affair. She stopped and started as she told her mother about his death. She kept raising her eyes from the floor to search her mother's face for a reaction. She saw none. She told her mother about her illness and hospitalization. Still, her mother remained impassive. The silence was eerie. But now, Elly arrived at the part of the story she most feared telling her mother.

"What I found out at the hospital surprised me, it shocked me." Elly twirled her hair tighter around her finger, and decided to just blurt it out. She better just say it, before fear overwhelmed her. "Mother, I'm pregnant!" Elly raised her eyes to see the angry reaction she expected. She was startled.

There was no reaction on her mother's face, no sign of emotion. Her mother looked bored.

"Why are you telling me all this?" Louise yawned.

"Well, I just thought," stuttered Elly.

"You just thought what?" interrupted Louise in a cold, sarcastic tone. "You thought I would care about your bad luck in having a dead boyfriend, or did you think I cared about you losing your college education? Well, you're wrong, I'm not surprised at your stupidity, I'm only surprised you're telling me all this."

Elly sat in pale silence as her mother continued. "I was going to pull you out of college anyway. I need you here to take care of me. And you wouldn't have time for any boyfriend, either. I have enough on my mind without all this nonsense. Why are you so selfish, Elly? It seems to me that all you care about is yourself. I am too ill to deal with your petty problems. I found out a month ago I have lung cancer."

Louise paused and lit another cigarette – this was the emotion she most enjoyed eliciting in people –s hock! Elly sat transfixed for a moment.

"Oh mother! Oh I'm so sorry," she reached out to hold her mother, but was quickly pushed away.

"Don't touch me!" spit Louise with a look of disgust on her face. "I don't want your pity or your negative vibrations to affect me."

Spurned, Elly sat, her face whitened with emotion. "What does the doctor say is the best treatment?"

Her mother stared at her as if she were staring at a bug under glass. "You know how stupid doctors are. I have the best healers in the country at my fingertips. All I need from you is help around the house and some personal care, not ignorant advice."

Elly sat silently for a few minutes. She knew her mother would never listen to her about getting good medical care. She would listen to her crazy friends and waste precious time and money on phony psychic healers. Still, she would try to convince her later, hoping it was not too late to save her life.

Elly, so naturally kind, answered, "Of course, I'll stay and help you in any way that I can."

Her mother gloated as she replied, "Good, I'm glad you decided not to be selfish."

Elly stared at the mother who was such a mystery to her. In spite of the way her mom treated her, Elly loved her. As a child, Elly couldn't remember anyone but her mother in her life. She had no memory of her father. Only the numerous photographs throughout the house reminded Elly of the father she never knew. Long ago, her mother had told her about Edwin Wilkin. He was an older man, a banker who died just before Elly was born. Louise had always seemed reluctant to talk about him. Elly deeply loved the only parent she knew. They had once been so close.

She was sorry her mom, always so vibrant and energetic, was now sick. She looked thin and pale. Elly had a faded memory of a mother who hugged and loved her. She remembered times when she was young and her mother whisked her up in her arms and shared her small childhood world with interest. That was long ago. Long before her mother's friends became her main interest. Still, perhaps this illness was an opportunity to regain some of that forgotten love.

She repeated, "Of course, I'll help you, mother. But, what about the baby?" Her mother stared at her for what seemed an eternity.

"What baby, Elly?" Her wrinkled lips pursed in contempt, "you'll get rid of it!"

The Fall of Pride

Not so are the wicked, not so! For they like winnowed chaff shall be driven away by the wind. (Psalm 1)

Joseph McKenna waited for his wife Joyce while she ran up the stairs to change her shoes. He had instructed her to do so. Standing at the bottom of the sweeping staircase, the tall, thirty year old was proud–everything seemed to be going his way. His wife and his home was everything a man could want. The center hall colonial with the stately columns was the home he always hoped for. Polished wood floors warmly matched the shining banisters. Oversized windows flooded the newly built home with light. One of the windows captured the setting sun perfectly. Like a framed picture, the scene of the golden sky was breathtaking. Joseph McKenna took the time to build this stately suburban house with all the small details in mind.

His contracting business had flourished over the last five years. Joseph was patient. He waited until he procured enough funds and success to build this home, the home of his dreams. All of his business associates were impressed by the house. He invited all of them to a cocktail party just a few months ago to show off the house and his apparent success.

Joseph understood the need to let everyone know how well he was doing. It wasn't just to enjoy the envy of those around him, although he had no problem with the thought of others being jealous. "Money goes to money," he thought as he waited patiently for his wife Joyce. It was a principle he learned on his way up the ladder of success. Success attracted more success. No one wanted to invest in a problem. Even if things weren't going as well as one wanted, wear the best clothes and have the biggest house. If everyone thought you were doing well, they called when they needed you. It was as simple as that, and yet so few realized it.

Joyce, his beautiful wife, was the biggest sign of his wealth. *Oh sure, I love her*, the dark, thin man thought, as he waited. But, the fact that she was beautiful and from a wealthy family only added to his aura of prosperity. He was so lucky to have met her, just at the right time in his career.

She, like this new home, was everything he dreamed of as he struggled to escape his former life of poverty. And now, as the beautiful model she was, she had accomplished landing the most desired contract in the fashion industry. The lucrative contract for modeling jeans would put Joyce at the very top. Joseph was beside himself with pride. Wait till everybody heard. It would be the talk of the town. The jeans were by the hottest new designer in the industry.

Dressed in black tie, Joseph was on his way to celebrate. Joyce was so innocent. She didn't even understand what this new contract really meant to him. Imagine, wanting to wear those small pumps with a designer gown, simply because her feet were a little sore.

He gently reminded her of all the important people who would be at the party. Looks were everything. She complained her feet hurt from standing and modeling all day, but he soon convinced her that how she looked was more important than how she felt.

One of the most endearing traits Joyce possessed was her total unawareness of her own beauty. It was one of the qualities he loved most about her. She often seemed puzzled, even overwhelmed by the adoration of others. If he allowed her, she would just run around in sweats without any make-up. She was just too naive. It was lucky for her she had him to guide and protect her. He shuddered to think what would become of her without him. She would be eaten alive by the industry wolves.

Unlike Joseph, she grew up leading a sheltered life. Joyce was the 22 year old daughter of a Park Avenue lawyer. She was educated in the finest Catholic schools in New York City. Joyce had never known pain or prejudice. Her childhood was ideal, a happy one. She owned a trusting heart, believing everyone had good intentions.

Joseph, raised in poverty, clawed his way up the business ladder. He understood the greed, and the hidden motives behind the phony smiles of the social climbers. He didn't need the money Joyce made from modeling. He struggled for years, and was wealthy in his own right. So why did he encourage her career? He supposed it was his ego.

Joyce would probably not understand his need for perfection. Joseph rejoiced in her perfect beauty and form. Imperfection was messy and emotional. He had his fill of ugliness in his childhood. Besides, he asked himself, was it so wrong to be proud of having the most beautiful woman on his arm?

She also needed him, as proved by her shoes. He managed her career with an eagle eye. Not that Joyce even cared about her career. She would be content to stay at home having one baby after another. The thought made him cringe. The idea of having her body distorted by pregnancy made him physically ill. Just thinking of such a monstrosity – a puking, crying infant – sent chills down his spine. Of course, Joyce didn't know this. She kept praying for a baby. Joseph did feel guilty. Nevertheless, in her innocence letting her think the baby would come in time was better. Someday she would be able to understand the truth about his vasectomy. She was too young to realize what a burden a baby could be.

They were married for three years, and she continued praying novenas and rosaries for the baby. It was a hopeless prayer. Joseph had made sure the baby of Joyce's dream would never be conceived. Her superstitious ways continued to amaze him. She was a bright and intelligent young woman. However, her faith seemed to override all common sense. It was another reason he felt she needed his protection. He alone knew what was best for her. He was sure that in the end she would see it that way.

Joseph laughed with delight as Joyce appeared at the top landing. With shimmering blonde curls and flashing green eyes, she spun around in the designer gown and stiletto heels for his approval.

"Perfection!" he yelled as he delighted at her little dance.

"Oh, are you sure now?" she kidded him, "I won't embarrass the mighty business mogul?"

"I could never be anything but proud of you," he commented softly as she gracefully descended the stairs and melted into his waiting arms. "Perhaps we should forget the party. I think it might be unsafe to let any other man see you."

Her laughing eyes betrayed her amusement at the thought. "Well, you know that would be fine with me. You're the party animal in this house."

"Ouch!" Joseph replied with a smile as the truth of her statement hit home.

"We could just stay home and celebrate," Joyce cooed as she softly nuzzled his neck.

He gently untangled her, "I would be selfish to keep you all to myself. It wouldn't be right to not to show you off. Besides, this is the night to celebrate your victory. We'll dance the night away."

Joyce just sighed as Joseph went to get the BMW, for she knew the truth. It was not just a party to celebrate her winning the jeans contract. It would turn into a business affair. Joseph would not spend the night dancing with her. He would be dancing around all the so-called important people in hopes of procuring some new clients. It would not be a night she would enjoy. Nevertheless, as with many other nights and other parties, she would do it for Joseph. The glamour of their life meant so much to him, and she loved her husband so. She could never bear the thought of disappointing him.

Joseph was delighted as he pulled the car around to his waiting wife. She was so gentle and kind. Talking her into doing the right thing was always so easy. The reward for her accomplishment and obedient behavior was in his pocket. A large pair of diamond earrings would be her surprise and reward.

"Do you have to keep those rosary beads on the rear view mirror?" he complained as they annoyed him again. He truly admired the smooth leather, shining paint, and comfort of their expensive new car. The beads detracted from the feeling of luxury.

"Yes!" laughed Joyce, as she responded, "It makes me feel much safer, especially when you drive so fast!"

"It's just medieval nonsense." Joseph muttered.

"It is not! The beads represent what I believe. They show God's protection."

"And you know how I feel about that!" he quickly replied. Joseph decided to drop the issue. He knew it wouldn't get him anywhere. They argued about this before, and in this one area, the area of faith in God, Joyce was unshakable. The more Joseph thought about it, the more it annoyed him. Perhaps it bothered him because it was the only area of Joyce's mind he could not control. It was as if there was a whole part of Joyce that didn't belong to him. And if there was one thing anyone who knew Joseph could tell you, he did not like to be out of control. From his business, to his relationship with Joyce, he needed to control even the smallest detail. As his employees well knew, Joseph ruled with a velvet glove but that glove held an iron fist. Those who suffered the weight of that iron fist never forgot it.

Joyce, on the other hand, never needed it. She was so kind and pliable. Joseph always saw himself in the role of a guiding, gentle father. Still, there was something deep inside her–a core strength of which Joseph caught just a glimpse. On the rare occasion he saw it, it frightened him. He felt it had something to do with the strange belief system that seemed so mysterious to him. However, since it never caused a problem, he usually ignored it. Joseph had confidence. He knew if it ever did cause a problem or conflict, he would win. Winning was what Joseph did best.

Joyce was exhausted. The drive from their large, suburban home into the city was a long one. She felt uncomfortable in the green, sequined gown. Joseph felt it brought out the color of her eyes, but she felt so confined and unnatural in it. She would much rather be at home in a comfortable pair of pajamas. She smiled as she thought of how much Joseph hated her beat-up pair of flannels. Joyce loved them. Well, she would manage to get through the night. At least, she didn't have an early call tomorrow, and could sleep in. She would just smile, and be as charming as Joseph needed her to be.

Finally, they arrived at the posh club an associate of Joseph's company rented. It was hard to believe that anyone would pay this much just for a business celebration. An attendant opened the car door directly under the awning, as Joseph took Joyce's arm and escorted her into the garish lobby. Chandeliers lit the ornate room, reflecting off the gold leaf decorated walls. Plush red carpeting matched the velour-covered walls of this old opera house. It was now a club frequented by the cream of society. A long sweeping staircase led to the club below, to which Joseph, always afraid of being late, quickly escorted her.

Joyce stopped him as they reached the head of the stairs.

"I have to use the ladies room," she whispered. She couldn't help but notice the annoyed look on his face. Already, his associates were waving for him to join them. He hoped to make a spectacular entrance with Joyce. She apparently did not realize the importance of this. Still, he held his tongue, allowing her to leave, as he joined his affiliates below.

John Meyer was the first to greet him, waving Joseph to his table. This was far from what Joseph hoped for. John Meyer was the one person Joseph was trying to avoid.

"Did you get a chance to think about the presentation?" John's voice faltered as he continued, "I know a social setting is not the place to talk business, but I know you realize how important this is to me."

John searched Joseph's face with faith and hope in his eyes. It was more than Joseph could bear. He knew what the old man was counting on. John Meyer's once lucrative company was in big trouble, on the very verge of bankruptcy. The large contract he was hoping to win from Joseph's company would save it. Joseph truly felt sorry for him. He appeared so shriveled in his tux. Joseph could clearly see the deepened worry lines that aged the face before him. The old man rubbed his hand across the thinning gray hair as he waited for a response.

Joseph hesitated, looking into the kind, brown eyes he had known for so long. When Joseph first came to the city as a green youth, John Meyer took a chance on him. No one else, many of them present here, were willing to take a chance on a young man without experience. John Meyer not only took him under his wing, but his company's liberal benefit package paid off most of Joseph's student loans. Even when Joseph, after reaping all the benefits of John's company, decided to leave and start his own company, John wished him nothing but luck. He even threw clients Joseph's way.

Still, Joseph felt his anger rising. *Why did people always expect a return of good treatment? Was it Joseph's fault John was in trouble?* It was probably John's generosity to his employees that landed him in this trouble in the first place. Joseph warned him about it years ago, and John ignored his advice. Now he expected Joseph to save him. The old man was too emotional. It was the many soft decisions lead by emotions which got John into trouble in the first place. Now, he expected Joseph to repeat the same mistakes he had made. Sure, John Meyer's bid was low, but it was not the lowest. Joseph was confident John's company would do a quality job. The quality of work was never in doubt. Still, business decisions should never be made based on emotion. Joseph learned long ago never to mix emotion with business and it was a policy which never failed to earn him the largest profit available. He would not, could not, change his ways now. He had already decided to take the lowest bid.

Turning to John, Joseph groped for the best way to tell him his business was as good as lost.

"Well," he tried to avoid John's questioning eyes, "I have looked over all the bids, and I have got to tell you, that… well, yours wasn't the lowest one."

He tried to avoid looking at John as the old man's face registered shock, then disbelief. John grew pale, then ashen. Joseph, who knew the old man had angina, hoped he wasn't going to beg or make some kind of scene in front of all these people. It would be embarrassing for them both.

Joseph was pleased to see the old man quickly regain his composure. John said nothing, nothing that would embarrass either of them. However, the look in his eyes frightened Joseph. It was not the look of anger or hatred Joseph expected. In fact, that kind of response was one Joseph could handle. It would make the whole thing easy. It would make it easier for Joseph to justify his actions. The expression on the old man's face was one of pity, not pity for himself, but pity for Joseph. For some unexplainable reason, the fact John should pity him, while John was the clear loser, made Joseph inexplicably angry.

With his voice a little louder than he realized, Joseph blurted out, "I always told you business was business, not charity! Perhaps if you listened to me long ago, you wouldn't be in trouble right now!"

John Meyer just smiled and softly replied, "I wouldn't change a moment of my life, or any decision I've ever made. God bless you, Joseph."

Joseph was speechless. The old man squared his shoulders, raised his head, and walked with grace and dignity up the stairs. John Meyer headed toward the exit of the club. Joseph was mortified as he realized others witnessed the scene which just occurred. The others noticed because of his loss of composure. He couldn't understand why he, who always maintained a professional demeanor, lost his temper when faced with the very graceful behavior of his old mentor. The whole situation was quite uncomfortable, and as he watched John Meyer disappear he was glad it was all over.

As John disappeared at the top of the stairwell, Joyce appeared. Joseph's anger turned to pride as he noticed how her beauty captivated the attention of the room. In the shimmering green gown, her beauty lit up the very hall she was entering. Slowly, looking around for Joseph, she spotted him and waved. All in the room, the men anyway, turned their heads to drink in the magnificent resplendence at the top of the winding stairwell.

Eat your hearts out, Joseph thought, *this gorgeous creature is going home with me tonight.* Joseph smiled as he watched Joyce start down the stairs.

It happened too quickly to respond, yet it seemed to happen in slow motion. Joseph noticed the heel of Joyce's shoe get caught in the loose hem of her gown. She didn't. There was no time to yell, no time to run. Joseph stood helpless as Joyce started to fall. He watched speechlessly as she tumbled down the long, winding stairway. He stood, shocked, unable to move, as her body landed on the floor of the club. Others ran to help her as she lay unresponsive on the floor. Her leg was bent in an unnatural position, her lip was bleeding. Joseph was frozen with disgust.

He finally snapped out of it when others, wrongly assuming he was in shock, called him over. He didn't want to see Joyce like this. When he heard a woman yell to call an ambulance, he found his escape.

Joseph ran to the phone. He needed to do something. As he ran past Joyce, he could hear her mumbling his name. It wouldn't look good to the others if he just ran away. Calling for help was the perfect excuse. Later, they would commend him for keeping a calm head in an emergency. No one would realize he just wanted to get away.

As he darted past the crumbled heap surrounded by concerned hands, he heard Joyce whimper, "Joseph, Joseph?"

He pretended he didn't hear. The sound of the moaning cries nauseated him. Memories of his mother, old and bedridden, haunted him. The reaching, the grabbing, and the cries of pain, as his mother lay dying on a crumpled, dirty bed rose up from a part of his past he long ago pushed away.

"Joseph, help me!" the old lady weakly cried over and over for help. His mother cried as he, a young boy, turned away in disgust. The long thin arms always dragged him in, into the smell of death and decay, until he felt as if he were going to suffocate.

He pushed the horrible memories away. He would phone for help. He would compose himself, so he could deal with Joyce. He would take charge. They would fix her up. Money was no object. There would be no imperfection!

Joseph was right. By the time he returned from calling the ambulance, Joyce stopped calling for him. She fainted again, but the others assured him it was probably just from the pain. Her pulse was steady.

"Let me get a cold cloth for her head!" he shouted, as he quickly passed the concerned crowd.

He accelerated his steps. He wanted to get away before someone else could volunteer and he was glad to get in the men's room. He slowly washed his face with cold water and was surprised to find his hands were trembling. *How long would it take for the ambulance to get there?* He knew he couldn't face the crumbled, damaged form of his wife, but he couldn't take too long to get a wet cloth. *What would everyone think?* He walked slowly and deliberately back to the main dining room and sighed with relief as he heard the sirens. Trembling, he placed the cloth on Joyce's forehead. He tried not to notice the blood on the designer gown and ignored the grotesque bend of her leg.

Joseph knew everyone expected him to stay close to his wife. What they didn't know was that he just couldn't do it. He knew they would assume his ashen color was out of his deep concern for her. They would assume the beads of perspiration on his forehead came from his worry for her. Let them think what they wanted. He had to get out of here! He was going to be sick! Just as he was about to bolt, the paramedics came down the stairs. It was just the excuse he needed.

"Everybody back!" he shouted, as he himself moved away. "Give the paramedics some room!"

Everything worked out perfectly. He heard people commenting on his control and calm. Now they would take her away. Someone would fix her up, back into the beautiful woman he was married to. The worst part was he would be expected to go with Joyce and the ambulance to the hospital. Joseph hated hospitals. Hospitals were breeding grounds of germs and imperfection and filled with desperately needy people. Joseph couldn't think of a place on earth where he would least like to be. God! He could use a drink.

Joseph's hope to make a quick stop at a bar on his way to the hospital was soon dashed. A couple of business associates, who were genuinely fond of Joyce, quickly volunteered to follow him to the hospital. Looking in the rear view mirror of his BMW, he could see the Cadillac Deville of one of his business acquaintances following right on his bumper. *Great, just great,* the frazzled husband thought. Joseph knew he would now have to rush to the hospital, as if he couldn't wait to get there. He couldn't even have a stiff drink to booster his courage.

It was not as bad as he expected. The waiting area of the emergency room of St. Vincent's Medical Center was almost empty. A small child, lying on her mother's lap, held her hand over her ear and moaned softly. She was apparently the victim of an ear infection, and Joseph could hardly hear her above the bustle of the hospital staff. Joseph was pleased when the nurses advised him after he signed all the appropriate forms to wait until his wife was stabilized. They seemed relieved when he didn't insist on being with her. His companions engaged him in business talk. He even managed to sew up a lucrative deal while waiting for news of how Joyce was doing.

Time seemed to fly while as he discussed business with his associates and Joseph almost forgot the circumstances. Soon enough, he was interrupted by the nurse telling him the doctor wanted to talk to him. Putting down his coffee, he followed her into a small office. A large burly man with salt and pepper hair pointed to a chair in front of his desk and asked Joseph to sit.

The bulky doctor introduced himself. "Hello," he reached across the desk to shake Joseph's hand, "I am Dr. Andrews, the head of the St. Vincent's emergency room. I've done a careful examination of ..." he paused to look at the chart, clearly tired, "your wife, Joyce. I've got to tell you," he continued, "we seem to be lucky as far as your wife's injuries are concerned."

Joseph felt a sigh of relief as the doctor continued. "There is no permanent damage. We were worried about a skull fracture, but the x-rays show just a mild concussion."

Dr. Andrews forced his way up out of his chair, and clipped some x-rays over a light.

"She has a bad fracture of the left fibula, and simple fractures of the third and fifth ribs. We set her leg in a plaster cast and taped the ribs. It's all very painful, but there should be no permanent damage. We feel safe in saying there is no internal damage." The doctor watched Joseph for a response.

"What do you mean you feel safe there isn't any internal damage?" Joseph clenched his teeth.

The exhausted doctor rubbed his eyes and continued in a quiet voice, "Well, there are no signs of any. We would have to x-ray the entire body to be absolutely sure."

"Well then, call me back in when you're finished doing your job." Joseph slowly rose as the doctor stared at him, completely stunned.

"I'm afraid you don't understand. We only x-ray an area if there are clinical signs of damage."

Joseph took a deep breath as he looked down at the doctor. "No, I'm afraid you don't understand! It's not the trash you're used to dealing with lying in there. My wife is one of the top models in this country. You are to x-ray every part of her. She has to be more than okay, she has to be perfect. If it's money you're concerned about, don't! I have to be sure there is absolutely no permanent damage!"

Dr. Andrews rubbed his eyes, he should have known better than to think this was going to be an easy night.

"It has nothing to do with money, sir, complete body x-rays are unnecessary and may even be harmful."

Joseph stared at him. "You're wrong doctor – it has everything to do with money. If you don't check her from top to bottom, you will find out how much it relates to money from my lawyer!"

"Good God!" thought Dr. Andrews. It seemed to the doctor that more people had lawyers than doctors.

"You don't understand. I can't be responsible for whatever damage unnecessary x-rays may themselves do. Sure, you want peace of mind but these x-rays are an unusual precaution."

"I don't give a damn what you think!" Joseph allowed his voice to rise. "I want that precaution taken. Now are you going to order them, or do I have to call in my personal physician?"

The doctor just sighed. It had been a long night. Rubbing his red eyes with the palms of his hands, he answered in an exasperated voice. "It is a dangerous precaution. If you insist on full body x-rays, you will have to sign a release. I will not be held responsible for whatever damage these x-rays may do."

Dr. Andrews lowered his head and bent over his desk. Joseph, a student of body language quickly assessed he had won his point.

Invigorated with a renewed sense of power, Joseph proclaimed, "I'll sign whatever release you require, just get your job done!"

The doctor slowly rose, and walked over to the waiting nurse. Joseph assumed he ordered the x-rays, since she brought a damage release for him to sign.

The nurse had an edge to her voice when she took the signed paper and said, "Dr. Andrews says you can visit your wife for a few minutes, before she goes for the x-rays."

Joseph almost panicked. "No, I'll see her after you're all done with your job." He quickly walked back to the waiting area, leaving the nurse dumbfounded.

Joseph found his associates back in the waiting area, getting antsy and restless. He was glad to dismiss them with the news Joyce would be fine. They seemed genuinely relieved. He was not surprised.

Everyone loved Joyce. She affected people. Once they were assured Joyce was going to be fine, they left Joseph. He was glad to see them leave. He needed to be alone to think.

Just like everything else, he would have to take control of Joyce's medical care. He should have from the beginning. He learned long ago not to trust others. He made a quick call from his cell phone to their personal physician, who assured him he would drive to the city and check on Joyce. Sitting back in the uncomfortable plastic chair, typical of an emergency waiting room, Joseph planned his strategy. Joseph hated hospitals. Hospitals seemed to attract all the oddities of humanity. Still, it wouldn't look right if he left without seeing Joyce. He would suffer in silence until she was ready.

Joseph was anxious to get past all of this trouble. God knows what germs he was being exposed to as the waiting room filled with all manner of people. A nurse wheeled a stretcher past him, hardly filled with the wasted form of an elderly woman. As they passed, the woman's thin arms and hopeless eyes seemed to reach out to him. His stomach turned in disgust. Again the memories were dredged up. Thoughts of an impoverished childhood surfaced. The recollections of a sick and cancer-ridden mother who depended on him as she wasted away overwhelmed Joseph. She died clinging to her son as if she wanted to drag him with her into the unknown. Her prolonged death left him alone with nothing.

What followed his mother's death was long years of work and more work as the teenaged Joseph struggled to survive. He had no other family. Long hours of school and various jobs filled the empty, lonely hours of his youth. Memories of washing the one white shirt he owned in the chipped, ceramic sink each night filled him with pain. It was never enough. No matter how he tried, he could never wash away the stain of poverty. That stain of poverty never let him fit in with his more privileged classmates. Alone, he struggled. Watching and learning to imitate the rich, he raised himself up. With the best marks in his class, he secured a scholarship to the best college. Still, Joseph worked long hours to pay his keep.

He never had enough to fit in with the others whose wealthy parents paid their way. He saw it in the way they looked at his worn clothes, which were always two sizes too small. His budget could never keep up with his growing body. As he worked menial jobs in the cafeteria and college bookstore to pay his way, he could hear the remarks. The derogatory remarks of his wealthier classmates left deep wounds on Joseph's soul. Poverty tarnished him as the belittlement of waiting on those sarcastic classmates degraded him. Joseph was never able to forget the humiliation.

Determined, he endured their derision with one thought in mind. He would make it. He would make it into the closed world of the wealthy. Never would he be poor again. Never would he be an object of pity. Immediately after graduating at the top of his class, he moved to the other side of the country. Away from anyone who knew his past. He worked hard in John Meyer's company, carefully imitating the mannerisms and actions of his wealthy classmates. No one knew his past. He made up a more suitable one, one that better suited his ambitious nature.

Looking down at the sleeve of the expensive, silk, designer shirt he was wearing, he smiled. He made it! Joyce always laughed because he never wore the same shirt twice. She said it was a waste to throw a shirt away after only wearing it once. She soon gave up, as new shirts were delivered each week. Joyce donated his shirts to the poor without understanding his need to always wear brand new attire. Joyce never knew the desperately ambitious teenager who scrubbed a worn shirt in a small empty room each night.

Joseph felt as if the emergency waiting room was closing in on him. He knew he couldn't sit there much longer. He hadn't thought about his past in many years. He had almost come to believe the wonderful childhood story he created for himself. Joseph felt light-headed and sick to his stomach. Looking around at the poverty and pain surrounding him, he felt like screaming. It had been an hour since he had talked to Dr. Andrews and Joseph couldn't wait any longer. It wasn't fair that he be made to suffer like this. It was more than he could bear. He was about to bolt but a touch on his shoulder pulled him from the painful thoughts. Joseph steeled himself, he needed to regain control.

His personal physician, Dr. Simon, stood behind him. Dr. Simon, a light man in a silk suit, looked clearly out of place outside of his posh clinic.

"Joseph, I'm here now. I am going to examine Joyce," the elegant doctor was concerned with how pale Joseph appeared, "Are you all right?"

Joseph pulled himself up on the seat, "Yes, I'm okay, just tired. How long will all this take?"

"Not long, I'll send the nurse out for you soon as I'm done. Why don't you get yourself a cup of coffee? By the time you're revived, I should know something."

Dr. Simon was true to his word. He came out and got Joseph himself. Joseph had not looked forward to this, but now found he was actually relieved to have something to do. Entering the other side of the emergency room, he followed Dr. Simon past the curtained moans of pain, to the corner cubicle where Joyce awaited. Joseph was relieved. She looked beautiful and frail against the cloudy white sheets. No longer bleeding, and with her broken leg cast and underneath the blankets, Joyce looked more like the beautiful woman Joseph was used to. She appeared groggy, but without pain. It was easier than he thought it would be to touch her and show his concern. Dr. Andrews waited at her bedside to explain his findings.

Joseph started talking, determined to take control. "Did you take the x-rays?"

Dr. Andrews exhaled and answered, his eyes filled with contempt. "Yes, against my better judgment."

Joseph reddened. He was not used to having his orders questioned. "I don't give a damn about your judgment, what are the results?"

Dr. Simon answered as Dr. Andrews slammed the chart on the table and walked out, "There are no internal injuries, Joseph. She'll be fine. The fractured leg has been placed in a cast, and should heal without complication in about six weeks. The ribs will heal. She'll be uncomfortable for a while, but we'll give her pain medication. The important thing is that she will be herself in about two months."

Joseph swallowed hard in relief and asked what he felt was the most important question. "Will there be any deformity?" Quickly getting his emotions under control, he added, "I'm thinking about her career of course." Joseph rejoiced hearing Dr. Simon's answer that his wife would be as perfectly beautiful as ever.

Joyce stirred as the murmur of their voices roused her. "Joseph?"

Joseph joyfully held her hand. "It's me, Joyce, I'm right here."

A slight smile brushed her lips, as she struggled to open her eyes.

Joseph tenderly stroked Joyce's hair and whispered to her, "Just sleep. Everything is going to be all right. You're going to be all right."

Joyce sighed in comfort at the sound of his voice, and slipped quietly to sleep.

The same nurse Joseph dealt with before entered the cubicle and stated, "We'll be moving her to a regular room, now, if you will pardon us." She started to unlock the wheels on the Gurney.

Joseph quickly stopped her and announced, "That will not be necessary, she is being transferred to Dr. Simon's clinic."

The nurse appeared startled and replied, "That would be very painful for her."

Joseph flushed with anger at his decisions being questioned once again. "Well, give her more pain medication. I want her out of this place as soon as possible." Standing up to impose his authority, Joseph continued, "Simon, arrange it. I'll be at the clinic first thing in the morning." A surge of energy ran through his body, as his sense of power returned. Briskly, he left the hospital, glad the whole incident was over.

Driving home, he congratulated himself on his handling of a difficult situation. The ride home was long but seemed to relax him. It gave him time to think. He would have to take control of Joyce's care. He would direct everything he decided, making sure they turned her back into the beautiful wife he loved. It had been a horrific night. Spending the night in the emergency room was horrible. He felt so dirty. He actually got chills thinking of the germs that were crawling on his skin. By the time he reached home, he was anxious to peel off his contaminated clothing.

The large suburban home seemed silent and empty without Joyce. He really missed her. He peeled off his clothing as he entered the bathroom. Joseph intended to take a quick shower and get to bed. He had many important appointments and meetings tomorrow. He'd have to get up early to stop by the clinic. Despite the fact he was exhausted, he found himself taking a long, hot shower. He scrubbed his already reddened skin over and over in the hot soapy water. It was as if he couldn't clean the grime of poverty and disease off. He felt so exposed and dirty. Finally, exhausted, he donned his silk pajamas and fell into a mindless sleep.

A Walk with Darkness

But by the envy of the devil, Death entered the World, and they who are in His Possession experience it. (Wisdom 2:24)

Elly tried to resist the pressure of her mother and her mother's friends to have an abortion. She tried to ignore the accusations of selfishness. She even resisted the humiliation of being told her child would be astrologically dull and ordinary. The threats of being cut off financially didn't work, although they worried Elly. Elly tried to cling to the dream of having her own child to love. She tried to hang onto the thought of Michael, who might now live on through her child.

The words of Dr. Lopez were full of hope, but soon faded amidst the constant barrage of negative comments. What finally worked were Louise Wilkin's assertions that Elly would make a poor mother, unworthy of raising any child. Under such an intense attack, Elly's low self-esteem re-established itself.

Unable to sleep more than a few tossing hours a night, she soon weakened. Louise then attacked what she felt was Elly's greatest weakness, her kindness. She made Elly see how selfish it would be to saddle her mother with an unwanted grandchild, when she was so sick and dependant on her care. Louise's friends cornered Elly at every opportunity to reaffirm her mother's need and Elly's selfishness. Elly was given no time to think. Louise secretly laughed at how quickly Elly capitulated.

The whole process of convincing Elly took only two weeks. Elly had no experience in fighting her mother or her mother's friends. The appointment at the abortion clinic was promptly arranged. Elly never really had a chance. Agnes escorted Elly to the clinic in the small town below. Agnes did not go with Elly to be supportive, or to see the operation went safely. It was simply to make sure the deed was done–to be sure Elly didn't back out of her decision at the last moment. Elly realized this when the abortion was over. Agnes did not even wait. Elly was left to take the long walk home alone. It was all so easy, because Elly had no faith. No faith in herself, or God.

Elly felt numb as she walked through the small town. She mindlessly observed the vaguely familiar stores. She felt detached from the people who milled around her. With each step she felt weaker. Finally, reaching the edge of the town, she found herself in front of the small white church she had seen so often from above. The rest of the walk was uphill, and she craved rest. The announcement outside of the church identified it as the Church of The Immaculate Conception. "Enter all who are weary and heavy laden," the sign further indicated. Elly was physically weary and the cold bench outside was anything but inviting. She decided to rest inside for a short time.

Entering the church, she sat in the back pew. She saw no one there. Surely they would not mind if she warmed up and relaxed here. Thinking no one would see her, Elly decided to lay her head down. There was a sense of peace here. Nevertheless, Elly was too numb and cold to notice her surroundings. She simply fell asleep.

Elly slept for hours. She awoke in response to a slight sound of movement. The late afternoon sun filtered softly through the large stain-glassed windows. Warm, color patterned light flowed from the ornamental window falling on Elly.

She looked up and saw a small, dark woman. The woman stood with a polishing rag in her hand, staring at her. Remarkably, Elly wasn't frightened, in fact she had a strange sense of peace.

"How long have I been asleep here?" she asked.

"A few hours, you seemed so tired. I tried not to wake you," the tiny, older woman answered in broken English, with a Spanish accent. "I clean and polish the church each Saturday for Father. I'm Mrs. Lopez."

Elly sat up noticing the glow of worn wood reflected in candlelight. Funny, she had been too tired to notice the beauty of this small church before. The stained glass windows were magnificent and the soft candlelight cast its flickering spell upon the unique statues. The large crucifix in the front of the church was surrounded with flowers which sweetly perfumed the air.

The cleaning woman softly asked, "Are you hungry? I'm sure Father will be glad to help you."

Elly was embarrassed. She hadn't caught the woman's name, but the woman obviously thought Elly was some needy person. Elly sat up and straightened herself out, realizing how thin and disheveled she must have looked.

The cleaning woman continued, "Are you sure? Many people come here when they need help."

Elly straightened her clothes and protested, "No, no I'm sure. I just got tired during a long walk. I'm sorry for bothering you. I don't live far from here."

The cleaning woman's deep brown eyes reflected her doubt. Elly thought, Funny, the eyes seemed so familiar.

"Why, I'm not even Catholic!" Elly continued. But, the words almost stuck in her throat. A vague memory tried to surface in her mind–the woman's eyes–the inside of this church–no, it was a ridiculous thought. She had to get home. "Goodbye, and thank you again," she stated as she quickly escaped the church.

The cold air outside surprised her as she left the warmth of the church behind. The waning sunlight signified it was later then Elly thought. She still had a long walk home. Summoning all her strength, the cold sense of emptiness invaded her. Elly never felt this alone in all her life. The pain began to overwhelm her, but she pushed on. The numbness returned as she traveled home.

Cold, weak, and tired, Elly finally reached home. She could see the light from the back room as she entered the doorway. No, she decided, she wouldn't even give them the satisfaction. They obviously didn't care whether she was alive or dead anyway. She slowly climbed up the stairs to her room. Her legs felt so heavy. Promptly undressing, she collapsed onto her bed. She knew nobody cared. She wouldn't cry. She vowed she would never cry again. She would never let anyone hurt her again. As emptiness filled her, Elly fell asleep.

Lonely day followed lonely day. Yet Elly's time to be alone did not last long. It amazed Elly how quickly after the abortion her mother deteriorated. Within a week, her mother was too feeble to get out of bed. She lost her appetite and grew thinner. Louise insisted on staying in her third floor bedroom, although this made it very difficult for Elly to care for her.

Elly waited on her mother hand and foot. The tired girl ran up and down the stairs, at least once each half-hour, at Louise's slightest whim. "Fluff my pillows!" or "Get me a drink!" were the typical commands. Elly grew exhausted as the days dragged on. Still, like a robot, Elly continued, in numbness, to perform what she considered her duty.

There were times when she hoped for a simple thank you, but it never came. During the first two months, her mother was too busy seeing the many self-proclaimed healers Agnes dragged to the room in hope of a cure. Elly didn't have any idea how much money exchanged hands between her mother and these charlatans. She was sure they had come just for the money. Her mother never improved after any of the so-called healing ceremonies. In desperation, Louise flew in psychic healers from all around the country.

During the third month, as the pain and emaciation grew worse, both the strange healers, and the friends began to disappear. Elly moved to a mat on the floor and spent day and night attending to her mother's needs. Louise grew so weak Elly spent hours just trying to feed her. Louise cursed and belittled her.

The dedicated daughter maintained the numbness, borne of

hopelessness and exhaustion. She tried to convince herself that her mother's hatred was just an outlet for her pain. Deep down, she knew better.

The pain and behavior grew worse, and the friends completely disappeared. Oh, they still used the house, downstairs, for all the psychic meetings, but the pretense of visiting Louise in her room ended.

Elly tried to convince her mother she should not allow them to use the house. Her mother's response was cool. Elly had enough to do in taking care of her mother's needs. Her mother's friends never cleaned up after themselves, constantly ate all the food in the house, and expected Elly to wait on them as if she were a maid. But Elly's mother continued to defend the very friends who deserted her. Worse, she cursed Elly for being unavailable while she was shopping for, or waiting on, those same friends. None of them offered help or money. Elly finally gave up trying to convince her mother of the truth. Now, as the pain grew worse, at least Elly was able to convince her mother to call a real doctor. She was careful not to say anything until he was actually at the house. She didn't want Agnes to persuade her mother not to see him.

Dr. Crosby, an elderly, balding man, answered the call. He was the only doctor in the small town below. Dr. Crosby was often overwhelmed. The burden of his numerous patients kept him busy and rushed. Seeing the condition of the woman he was called to examine slowed him. He took his time during his visit with Louise Wilkin. The experienced physician was shocked at the condition of the patient. He listened carefully with his stethoscope to the labored and shallow breathing. Only a small part of her lungs were even receiving any oxygen. Her legs were swollen and her nails blue, indicating the poor oxygen absorption. His worried face betrayed his concern, despite his attempt to maintain a soothing exterior.

The woman in the bed was near death. He was appalled to find she hadn't seen a doctor.

Finishing his examination, he said, "I want you in the hospital immediately. We need to run some tests and start some treatments."

Louise gave him a look of distain and answered, "I have no intention of going to the hospital. I don't know why my lazy daughter even called you. She'd like to get me in the hospital, just to get rid of me. Well, she can just forget it. I am not going." Exhausted she fell back against the pillows.

He offered to send a nurse over to attend her, but she refused. The woman didn't have any more than a few weeks to live. Dr. Crosby gave up trying to convince her to go to the hospital. She was, in spite of her illness, strong-willed and extremely stubborn. He was more concerned with Elly, who looked thin and drained.

The doctor gave it one more try and advised, "Your daughter looks ill herself. She could probably use the rest. A short hospital visit will be good for both of you. I can stabilize your condition and find the best pain control for you. She can regain her strength for your return home. You don't want her to become ill from exhaustion do you?"

Still the woman refused, harshly whispering in a raspy voice, "That is what my daughter is here for!" In spite of her condition, he found her selfishness totally disgusting. The best he could do was to order some pain injections and hope they would ease the patient's pain and afford the daughter some rest.

He instructed Elly how to use the needles and the dosage from what was in his medical bag. When he was sure she knew how to give the medication, he wrote out the prescriptions. He encouraged Elly to take a walk into town while her mother slept. He thought the fresh air and sunshine might do her some good, but she refused to leave her mother, so he had the supplies delivered. Before he left, he gave Elly his home phone number and encouraged her to call him whenever she needed him. She seemed relieved.

Over the next few weeks, life did get easier for Elly. Her mother usually slept for a few hours after each pain shot. This allowed Elly to sleep on the mat in the room, until she would hear her mother screaming and demanding some service. Tired from the broken sleep, she was lethargic as she carried out each task. Her mother's abusive behavior continued, and even increased as her body deteriorated. Her insults and curses fell on deaf ears. Elly was empty of any emotion.

Two weeks after Dr. Crosby's visit, Elly awoke from a short nap with a strange feeling. She felt as if someone was staring at her, and was surprised to find her mother was. Usually, immediately after awakening, her mother started her screaming and demanding. To have her mother just lying in the oversized bed staring at her gave Elly an eerie sensation.

"I want to see..." An extended coughing fit interrupted her mother's raspy whisper. Dr. Crosby had recommended oxygen, but Louise refused to use it. Elly offered oxygen to Louise when she saw the frothy blood at the corners of her mouth. Louise just returned her concern with a look of abhorrence. Elly stood silently at the bedside, as her mother gasped for air and finally caught her breath.

"Agnes, I want to see Agnes, now." Her voice was a harsh whisper.

Elly was glad, it would give her a chance to get out of this room, and maybe get something to eat. Agnes was the only one who remained in the house during the last few weeks. The others complained her mother's screaming disturbed their psychic aura. Elly was glad when they left but she couldn't fathom why Agnes remained. Agnes visited Elly's mother about five minutes each day and appeared irritated with Louise, although she hid her feelings well. She never offered to help, and generally used the house as if she owned it.

Agnes did not seem to be very happy when Elly told her she was wanted. Sighing, she rose from the easy chair and stomped up the stairs in anger. She hated having her leisure disturbed, but knew she needed to stay in Louise's good graces.

The small break gave the exhausted daughter a chance to eat. As she fixed a small breakfast, she enjoyed the rare silence. Coffee and toast lessened Elly's feeling of weakness. Dr. Crosby had been right, she needed a rest. Elly felt weak and all her muscles ached. If only I could have a few days off, she thought. Too soon, Agnes disturbed her peace with the news that her mother needed her. Elly didn't like the look on Agnes's face–she looked too smug as she put on her coat.

With a smirk on her face, she told Elly she was going out without saying where. She appeared to be in a hurry as she left, but Elly was in no hurry to return to her mother's room. It was only her mother's outcries that quickened her steps.

"Do you want a pain injection?" Elly asked as she entered the room.

"No! I want nothing from the likes of you!" The look of pure hatred on Louise's face did not shock Elly. She saw it often.

"You are such a disappointment to me, so like your father." Elly braced herself for the verbal attack. "I'm sick of you just taking advantage of me! You have no job, no money, and if you think I'm going to support you anymore you're in for a rude awakening!" A short coughing fit gave Elly a chance to strengthen herself for the coming insults.

"There is only one way to deal with a useless person like you! I've sent Agnes for my lawyer. I'm going to change my will! And you, my dear, will be out in the cold! I'm going to leave this house and everything I own to The Psychic Foundation." Louise's face whitened from the long speech, but her eyes glowed with bitterness.

"You'll no longer take advantage of me. I know who my friends are! You'll have to learn to work, you lazy bitch! And every day that you do, I want you to remember me! Remember what a burden you were to me! Remember how much I despised you."

A coughing fit seized Louise, and it didn't stop. Louise trembled.

Elly watched as her mother gasped for air. Louise's skin turned a blue-gray color, as blood trickled from her lips.

Abruptly, a look of terror came over Louise, as she stared at the corner of the room. Elly looked at the corner but saw nothing. Whatever Louise saw petrified her. Elly never saw such fear. Whatever it was that Louise Wilkin thought she saw horrified her.

"No, no!" she screamed as she sat up in the bed with a look of fright on her face. Elly could do nothing to help her, it all happened too quickly. Her mother fell back, with a look of horror on her face, and took her last breath.

Elly stood at the side of her bed. The feelings of emptiness and numbness left her. As any scientist will tell you, an empty space will always, eventually, be filled. As Elly looked at the body of her mother, dead on the bed, her empty space was filled. It was filled with hatred, hatred for the woman who abused her. The feeling of loathing was so strong she no longer felt any pain.

Elly watched quietly, as her mother's coffin was lowered into the ground. Despite her mother's death, she was feeling better after finally getting some sleep. No one came to the burial other than herself. She expected her mother's friends would at least make a show of it. Elly felt no remorse at her mother's death, but she expected her mother's friends would feel something after all the years they spent together. As for Elly, she was just glad it was over. Yet, she wondered how heartless she could be, not to cry at her own mother's funeral.

As Elly watched the coffin being covered with loosened earth, she couldn't think of her mother. All Elly could think about was the baby who didn't have a burial. It was as if her baby never existed. The strange thoughts running through her mind frightened Elly. She felt as if she were losing her mind.

At least she wasn't screaming like a banshee, as Agnes had. If ever a person appeared demented, it was Agnes. She returned quickly, right after Louise's death, with the lawyer to change Louise's will. As soon as she realized she was too late, Agnes went wild. The paramedics had already arrived and were putting Louise's body on the stretcher when Agnes returned. Agnes began howling. All of the people present, even the lawyer, assumed she was screaming in grief. It wasn't until she physically attacked Elly, that they realized she was screeching in frustration.

Elly reached up and gingerly touched the tender and reddened scratches Agnes's attack left on her cheek. The doctor at the hospital disinfected the wounds, after he pronounced her mother dead. Elly hadn't seen Agnes since that night. No one but Elly attended the one-night viewing Elly arranged.

The pensive young blonde sighed as she was drawn to the present and realized it was time to leave. She took one last look at the freshly turned dirt with the one small bouquet of flowers. There was nothing more to do. The funeral director seemed anxious to depart. Elly turned and started to walk away.

For the first time, she noticed the woman standing some feet behind her. The woman, dressed in black, retreated behind some trees as Elly turned. She didn't recognize the woman as one of Louise's friends, and the woman was gone before Elly could be sure. The solitary girl walked to her car, and drove home alone.

Dr. Gabe Lopez enjoyed watching his mother fuss over the breakfast she was preparing for him. Her face was filled with joy as she waited on her firstborn. Gabe turned the page of the newspaper, and pretended not to notice as her joyful humming resounded through the bright, yellow kitchen. He hadn't realized how much he missed his family and home. The smell of his mother's cooking brought back childhood memories of the large family's boisterous and happy times in the kitchen.

Turning the page of the local paper as he sipped the strong hot coffee, Gabe noticed a name on the short obituary list that looked familiar. "Wilkin?" where had he heard that name before? Then it occurred to him.

"Oh God, Ma! Old Lady Wilkin died."

"Yes, just the other day," his mother answered. "She's being buried today."

Gabe reddened as he remembered the last time he had seen the woman who lived on the hill above the town. He and his friends climbed up the hill to throw rocks. They threw rocks at the shabby citadel they believed was haunted. Another memory tried to surface, but was quickly forgotten as his mother served the hot pancakes.

"Hi, Gabe," Maria said, as she and all of the doctor's brothers and sisters entered the kitchen. Maria, the oldest sister of the Lopez family, flashed a sunny smile at her favorite elder brother. Suddenly the kitchen was full of laughter and joy as the four siblings talked and ate breakfast. The noise pushed the memories of Old Lady Wilkin far from Gabe's mind.

Gabe enjoyed the atmosphere created by a large family. Everyone was home during this visit. Gabe was in luck, and would get to visit not only with his mother, but will all of his brothers and sisters. The only one missing was his father. It had been years since his father's death, but Gabe still missed him.

His father died during an explosion at the oil refinery just outside of town. Gabe would never forget that horrible day. Gabe had been in school when the explosion shook the very ground of his high school which was three miles from the site of the explosion. Many of the windows of the surrounding homes had shattered. The sound of the explosion was so overpowering that some of the cold-war children thought the atomic bomb had finally been dropped. Screaming, many of them dropped and hid beneath their desks. Most of the poorer children immediately knew what had happened as the whistles of emergency called through the smoke-filled air. Fear filled the hearts of the children, who realized the whistles sang danger for their fathers.

The refinery was the largest employer in the area. For the most part, the oil refinery had a good safety record. Jose Lopez had died much too young, but he left a glorious legacy behind him. A loving wife and four children remembered his ways fondly. Gabe was the oldest, and the sense of responsibility cut his adolescence short. He worked to help his mother with part-time jobs. He struggled to get the education he needed while sending most of the money he made home to help out. Luckily, his good marks in school had won him a full scholarship to college and then to medical school.

Since his graduation, Gabe was the main source of support for the family. Mrs. Lopez worked at the church but her income was small, especially in such a poor parish.

"Gabe, do you want more pancakes?" asked Mrs. Lopez.

"No, Mama, I'm full," answered Gabe as he touched his stomach.

"I'll take those," Gabe's younger brother Marco answered, as he laughed and held out his plate to receive the extra pancakes.

Marco was getting ready to commute to the University. It was an hour drive. Marco was a full-time student in his senior year. Gabe was proud he could afford to send his younger brother to college. Marco always dreamed of becoming a teacher. Soon, he would graduate, and after getting a job, they would both help Maria, the sister who was next in line. Maria just needed two years at the community college to become the Registered Nurse she longed to be. As she waited, Maria was saving some money herself from her job as nurse's aide at the local nursing home. This was how their father raised them. Family was everything. It was expected they would always love and help each other. The kitchen was full of noise as the siblings teased each other. All of them were glad to be with their oldest brother. The family had missed him. Gabe enjoyed the noisy sounds of love that filled the kitchen.

. The kitchen grew quiet, as each sibling went off to work or school. Mrs. Lopez enjoyed the activity of having all of her children around. Still, she was glad to sit and enjoy a second cup of coffee in the company of her oldest son. She would have to leave in forty-five minutes and so she was determined to make the most of her free time.

"How have things been at work?" she asked. Mrs. Lopez thought her son looked tired and thin.

"Okay, I guess. I was just overdue for a rest and a visit home," he laughed at her penetrating eyes.

"And some good food!" she answered. A sip of coffee led to other subjects.

"You know," Gabe's mother said with a look of puzzlement on her face, "it's strange about Mrs. Wilkin's death. I could have sworn I saw her daughter in the church a few months ago."

Gabe looked mystified. "I forget her having a daughter." A vague memory surfaced in his mind.

"She was a little blonde thing. She hardly ever came to town. I'm not surprised you don't remember her," the small woman answered.

"Wait a minute, was she the one who caused a fuss in church?" Gabe pondered as he tried to retrieve the long forgotten memory.

"Yes, that is the one. I'll never forget the day. It was just a week before the little one was to make her first communion. You came to the church, and saw Mrs. Wilkins at her worst behavior," said Mrs. Lopez, as she shook her head in disgust.

"Yeah, I remember her screaming. What was that all about?" Gabe asked his mother as she poured more syrup on the last of the pancakes.

"Poor little Elly," Mrs. Lopez exclaimed. "She was so shy, and yet her mother always wanted her to be admired. All of the children, arranged by height, were to walk up the aisle in couples. Elly, being the smallest was to walk up with Pedro Gonzalez. Well that loco woman thought it was too beneath her daughter to walk up the aisle with the Hispanic son of a refinery worker. She was yelling at the Padre, screaming her daughter should be allowed to lead the procession by walking up alone. Ah, I'll never forget what happened next. Little Elly, so shy she never said a word, suddenly spoke up.

'Mommy, I don't want to walk alone!' Mrs. Lopez shook her head in disgust, as she continued her story. "Old Lady Wilkins turned from the priest to her little daughter with a look of disdain. I will never forget it. Pulling her hand back, she struck her so hard the poor thing flew through the air and landed crumpled on the floor in front of the altar."

Gabe's face whitened as the memory started to surface in his mind and asked, "Is that when I came in?"

"Yes, I think so," answered Gabe's mother. "Padre grabbed her arm and told her never to hit that poor baby like that again, and that's when she really lost her mind. Oh, the profanities she used in church! That loco woman grabbed little Elly's arm and dragged her from the church. She was screaming that they would ever come to the church again. Oh how that little bambina cried! I yelled at her to stop, but she dragged that girl down the church steps. It was crazy. She screamed and threatened the Padre with the Bishop. I never saw the little girl in the church again. Not unless it was Elly I saw in the church the other day."

Looking up from clearing the dishes, Mrs. Lopez was stunned at the look on her son's face. His face had gone white.

"Oh, My God, what have I done?" the young doctor whispered to himself as his mind raced back to the girl, so thin and pale, in his office. Elly Wilkin, no it couldn't be, Gabe thought. But even as his mind denied it, he knew it was true. The young, beautiful, and pregnant girl he had encouraged to go home was the same Elly Wilkin. And he sent her home to Old Lady Wilkin.

"Oh God, Ma," he repeated, "What have I done?"

Mrs. Lopez rubbed her troubled son's head. She had never seen him like this before. Gabe couldn't explain Elly's private files to his mother. He had to do something. He sent that weak, innocent child into the lion's den. Possibly into hell itself.

Elly shuffled quietly through the large, silent house. She felt so numb after the funeral. She was glad to remove her black, funeral dress and relax in her jeans. The reality of being truly alone was just starting to hit her. She didn't have any idea of what she was going to do, or where she was going to go. She only knew she didn't want to stay in this large, empty house so filled with hateful memories.

Her mother's lawyer had promised to come by today. Elly hadn't really formed any plans until she heard from him. She didn't want to stay in this hateful house, of that she was sure. How much money will there will be? thought Elly. From the condition of the house and the disappearance of her mother's friends, Elly concluded her mother couldn't have left her much. Nevertheless, whatever the amount, it might help her decide what to do with the rest of her life.

The sound of the doorbell roused her from her thoughts. Elly was keeping the door locked since the attack by Agnes. It made her feel a little safer. Jumping up, she assumed it was the lawyer. Opening the door, Elly was stunned to see her mother.

It took her a moment to compose herself. It wasn't really her mother, but the woman in the doorway looked remarkably like Louise. The eyes were softer, the skin without the harsher wrinkles. The face was more fleshed out and brighter, but the real deciding factor was the smile. Elly never remembered her mother with a bright and loving smile like this woman bore.

Shocked, Elly just stood at the door motionless.

"I'm sorry, so sorry. I should have realized you wouldn't remember me, Elly, I was at the funeral but couldn't bring myself to talk to you. You seemed so lost," the woman at the door said.

Elly remained silent and stared at the woman as if she were seeing a ghost. No, she knew it wasn't the mother she just buried. It was more of a bombshell! It was the mother of her elusive, happy memories, the gentle mother of her childhood dreams.

The woman reached up and gently caressed Elly's face. The recent strain of exhaustion and pain hit Elly full force. The room started to spin and Elly fell limply to the floor as she passed out.

A Mother's Love

Then the Lord God said to the serpent: "Because you have done this, you shall be banned from all the animals, On your belly shall you crawl, and dirt you shall eat, all the days of your life. I will put enmity between you and the woman, and between your offspring and hers; He will strike at your head, while you strike at his heel." (Genesis 3:14)

The closing of a person's life puzzled Mary Catherine with all its oddities. First, came the shopping. The nuns kept talking about Mary Catherine and her brothers looking respectable. Johnny still fit in his dark, navy-blue communion suit, but Danny and Mary Catherine didn't have any clothes that were 'respectable'. Sister Geraldine, who was an old sour puss if Mary Catherine ever saw one, was assigned to take them shopping.

Normally, Mary Catherine and Danny were overjoyed to go downtown to the large mall, but not today. The shock of losing their mother dulled all of the children's emotions. Mary Catherine and Danny were not interested in the sights and sounds of the mall. It had been just two days since their mother died. Johnny and Danny allowed their father to comfort them, but Mary Catherine hated him and wouldn't let her father Patrick anywhere near her. In the confusion and sorrow following her mother's death, no one seemed to notice.

Sister Geraldine was annoyed at dealing with the small children, and made no secret of her feelings. The trip was anything but a joyful one. Danny was fitted and adjusted into a gray pinstripe suit quickly enough. His shoes, tie, and shirt were all purchased in the same store.

As usual, even in this, it was Mary Catherine who caused all the trouble. Apparently, it was difficult to find a dress that was proper enough for a ten year old girl. Sister Geraldine persisted through four stores all lined with beautiful dresses with flowers of yellow, pink, or red. Finally, Sister Geraldine found the dark black and gray linen dress that Mary Catherine thought was the ugliest dress she ever saw. The sales woman offered to have it hemmed and taken in. She even offered to have the long sleeves taken up so they didn't hang below Mary Catherine's hands. But, Sister Geraldine dismissed her.

"It will do! There's no time. Besides, she'll grow into it and get even more wear out of it in the future," Sister Geraldine answered the salesgirl sharply.

Paying for her purchase, Sister Geraldine was relieved to whisk the children home, her duty done.

The Sisters brought all the children to the convent. Again, Mary Catherine was stunned by what she saw. The nuns scurried around cleaning, even though the place already looked perfect to Mary Catherine. One polished and dusted, one vacuumed the carpets, and another wiped down the kitchen counters and cabinets until they gleamed. It was as if they were preparing for a party. The doorbell kept ringing and strange people dropped off food items. Hams, turkeys, and casseroles of all kinds, were crammed into an already full refrigerator.

Sister Clements noticed Mary Catherine's confusion and she put her arm around the small girl and said, "You see Mary Catherine, so many people loved your mother. They all want to do something. After the funeral, most of the people will come here. The trailer is just too small. There's plenty of food now to feed everyone. Tonight you and your brothers will stay with us. Tomorrow we'll get you ready and take you to the wake."

Mary Catherine looked up into Sister's soft eyes. "What is a wake?" the tiny girl asked, as tears flowed gently down her cheeks. Mary Catherine looked up at Sister Clements with a flicker of hope on her face, "Is Jesus going to come and wake my mother up?"

Sister held the small girl closer and said, "No, Mary Catherine, your mother is already with God. Her soul is in heaven. The wake is for us, the ones left behind. In a wake, they dress the body of the person in their finest clothes and place them in a silk-lined casket. Beautiful flowers and Mass cards are placed around them. It's for us to see her one last time. It's for us to say our goodbyes. The wake is for us, Mary Catherine. The day after, there will be a funeral Mass, and they will bury your mother's body. All of this helps the living to say goodbye."

"I don't want to say goodbye!" Mary Catherine sobbed, as Sister held her on her knee.

"Well, it's not really goodbye. It's more like 'til we meet again'. Someday we'll be with your mother in heaven. Until then we can pray for her. I believe she is watching over all the people she loves, until we get to heaven with her."

Sister's words calmed the tired child.

Mary Catherine was still confused and asked, "Why are they having a party? Are they glad my mother died?"

Sister Clements held the girl closer and gently answered, "Oh dear! No child, but we are celebrating that she has eternal life in Christ. All her earthly pains and troubles are over. She is in perfect happiness with God. The get-together after the funeral is for the living, so we can talk and remember her. We can comfort each other."

Sister Clements held and rocked the small girl in her arms. Mary Catherine wept softly for 15 minutes. Sister knew that death was too much for a 10 year old to fully comprehend. This child just wanted her mother. The whole situation was emotionally draining. The girl must be exhausted. She held Mary Catherine in her arms until she fell asleep. Sister Clements looked down at the now sleeping child.

How strange the ways of adults must seem to children.

The next afternoon, dressed in the ugly dress Sister Geraldine had purchased, Mary Catherine and her brothers were driven to the small funeral home in town. Mary Catherine kept the fear she was feeling to herself. She didn't want to further upset the boys who were already crying. She didn't want to see her mother in the coffin like Sister Clements had described to her. She didn't want to say goodbye. Mary Catherine took a deep breath, as she tried to keep the tears from starting again. She didn't want to see her mother at all, unless her mother was alive. The last time she saw her mother, it had been horrible.

The memory of her mother in that hospital bed filled Mary Catherine with sorrow. She didn't want to see her mother if her mother couldn't touch her. Mary Catherine touched her mother in the hospital, and she didn't even move. She didn't want to see her like that. When they arrived at the white stucco building with the wrap-around porch, the nuns led them through the double front doors, and into the room where her mother's body was being viewed.

Despite her misgivings, Mary Catherine admitted that seeing her mother amid the flowers and candles brought some small comfort. Her mother looked as if she were asleep. Without machines, tubes, or doctors surrounding her, she smiled peacefully.

Time seemed to pass by in a blur of sorrow, pain, and disbelief. Mary Catherine was grudgingly surprised at her father's good behavior. He didn't have one drink. He greeted, talked to, and comforted everyone, everyone except Mary Catherine. She wouldn't let him near her, and watched him suspiciously from the far side of the room.

She had to go home with him, she knew that. There was no one else. He seemed good for Danny and Johnny. She watched him talking to them and drying their tears, but they didn't understand what he had done. Mary Catherine knew she would pretend to trust him, for the boys' sake. They needed him.

She resolved she would pretend, but not in her heart. In her heart, she would never forgive him. In her heart, she would never love him again. She vowed someday she would make him and that stupid baby pay for killing her mother.

By the time Patrick brought the children home from the funeral, they were exhausted. Thank God, the baby is still in the hospital, he thought. Taking care of a baby who looked just like his dead wife would be more than he could bear. He undressed each sleepy child, carefully dressed them in pajamas, and tucked them into bed. Watching them sleep like angels could almost make him forget the unstoppable energy they displayed during the day. He reached behind the cabinet and pulled out the unopened bottle of Jim Beam.

Patrick O'Rourke sat at the small table and poured himself his first drink since his wife died. Looking at the children, he wondered how he would care for them. Halfway through the bottle, he decided he couldn't take care of four children. At the bottom of the bottle he decided it was all right to leave them alone while he went to buy more whiskey.

Three weeks later, and five states to the west, Patrick O'Rourke continued to pour whiskey onto his open wounds. The wounds ached with guilt for leaving his family, but the family was fading into a distant memory. Whiskey seemed to be the cure. Soon, he would doubt the true existence of the family he would never see again.

When Mary Catherine awoke and saw the empty bottle and glass, she knew what happened. She threw away the bottle and washed the dirty glass. What would her mother do? She would do the same. She would pretend nothing happened and she would take care of the boys until her father came home.

The nuns had sent plenty of good food back home with Dad last night. The refrigerator was stacked with casseroles, breads, and meats. There was 16 dollars in singles and change on top of the dresser. It was enough for now. Mary Catherine laid out the boy's clothes and started eggs boiling before she woke her brothers up. In a few days, her father's binge would be over. Everything would be all right. She just had to be strong like her mother.

Mary Catherine was able to keep the house going for over a week. By Friday, however, she was down to $1.25 and one casserole. Still, there was no sign of her father. Mary Catherine knew she needed to get money somewhere. The boys would need milk money on Monday, and she had to buy food. Mary Catherine worried. She only had the weekend for her father to come home. What will I do if he doesn't come home?, Mary Catherine wondered. There wouldn't be enough money for school on Monday.

Sometimes Mrs. Ryan, the owner of the trailer park, would give Mary Catherine a few dollars for doing odd jobs like picking up the grounds or straightening out the storage garage. She decided to go see her Saturday morning. It was the best she could come up with. Mary Catherine just prayed her father would show up. He always had in the past. She decided not to panic. Her mother was always brave. Why couldn't she be more like her mother?

Maybe, if I just act like her, I'll grow to be like her, thought Mary Catherine. Whatever, Mary Catherine decided, tomorrow morning I'll just go by and ask Mrs. Ryan if she needs any help. Her father was sure to come home soon. With this problem firmly solved in her mind, Mary Catherine quickly joined her brothers in a well-earned slumber. The young girl didn't see the angels that watched over them, but her mother did.

Mary Catherine never got a chance to ask Mrs. Ryan for chores. The call came early in the morning, while she was still in her flannel nightgown. The hospital called to say Baby Thomas could come home. She was supposed to tell her father the baby should be picked up by 11. Mary Catherine said she would tell her father, and hung up the phone in a panic. She knew that baby was nothing but trouble. How was she going to hide this? Even if she could somehow get him home, how was she going to take care of a baby? Mary Catherine's stomach hurt.

What would her mother do? Her mother would say, 'Don't let worries pile up. Take one thing at a time!' Mary Catherine decided she'd worry about taking care of the baby later. First, she wanted to get him home.

She thought it was a great idea when she called Sister Clements. Lying to a nun didn't make Mary Catherine feel good, but sometimes a person had to lie. What else could she do? She told Sister her father was on a day trip visiting his brother. Mary Catherine told the nun her father left just before the hospital called. As casually as she could, Mary Catherine asked Sister if she could pick up the baby and drop him off. She hated to put Sister out of her way, but the hospital would be upset if they left Thomas there for another day. Sister seemed awfully quiet. Sister Clements told her to stay right where she was and she would be glad to help.

Mary Catherine was astounded and overjoyed that the nun seemed to believe her. She lived with this illusion until the two nuns arrived.

As soon as Mary Catherine saw the two nuns at the door without the baby, she knew, as her father always said, the jig was up! She tried to maintain the lie she was living as well as she could. The two nuns, Sister Clements and Sister Geraldine, scanned the trailer and in one glance sized up the situation. They were impressed at the order and cleanliness. Johnny and Danny seemed surprised to see them, but were enjoying a hearty breakfast while watching cartoons. Mary Catherine nervously flitted around the trailer. Her face was reddened, and she was avoiding eye contact.

Sister Clements took pity on her and decided to question the boys. "Hi, Danny, where's your father?"

Danny, with the large innocent eyes of childhood, answered, "Gee Sister, I haven't seen him since the funeral."

Sister Clements turned to Johnny and asked with wonder, "Really and how have you children been getting along?"

"Okay, Mary Catherine is taking care of us." Suddenly Johnny's face puckered and tears began. "But I want my mom and dad!"

Mary Catherine lowered her head and the sobbing began. Soon, the two nuns had their arms full. Three weeping children seemed glad to have adults to share their burden with.

Sister Clements gently reprimanded the tearful young girl, "Mary Catherine you've done a fine job! But you shouldn't have lied. You should have told me your father left."

Mary Catherine protested, "I just want to be like her. She never complained. She just waited for him to come home!"

"Why, you're just as brave and strong as your mother." Sister Clements stood with Mary Catherine directly in front of her, and held her by both shoulders. "But these shoulders are too small, Mary Catherine."

Mary Catherine looked confused, "Too small for what, Sister?"

Sister Clements looked the young girl straight in the eyes. "Too small to carry such a big load. Until you grow, I'm afraid you're going to need some help. And I've got just the friend to help you. Did I ever tell you about my good friend, Sister Immaculata?"

Mary Catherine stopped crying. Sister Geraldine bustled around the small trailer kitchen, washing the breakfast dishes for Danny and Johnny. Maybe the nuns could help us, thought Mary Catherine. Perhaps everything was going to be all right after all.

Sister Clements started to tell Mary Catherine about Sister Immaculata, "She takes care of problems just like yours. Perhaps, she could help you until your father comes back."

Mary Catherine rubbed her running nose on her sleeve.

"Do you think she would, Sister?" Mary Catherine placed her arms around the soft-hearted nun's neck.

The children were brought back to the convent by the nuns. The three of them stayed at the convent for a month while the police looked for their father without success. It seemed hopeless. Sister Clements called her friend, Sister Immaculata, who ran an orphanage. Mary Catherine heard Sister Clements making arrangements with Sister Immaculata on the phone. From what she overheard, they were to leave for this new place next week. They would have to take a train. Mary Catherine didn't want to leave. The thought of leaving was overwhelming. She tried not to think about leaving during the week. She knew that once again she had no control over what would happen.

It was all so scary to Mary Catherine and her brothers. If we have to, let's go just go and get it over with, thought Mary Catherine. The truth was she was afraid to leave. She didn't want to leave her only friends. The nuns had been good to them. Mary Catherine didn't want to leave the convent, or the only town she ever knew. She didn't want to leave her school. Why was all this happening? She wished her mother had never died. She was so angry. Mary Catherine hated her father. He ran away, leaving them all alone. He was the cause of all this pain.

It was so excruciating to be separated from all the people she loved. It was so painful Mary Catherine just wanted it over. If this trip has to happen, just let it happen fast, she prayed. Early on Saturday morning, the three children waited at the train station with the nuns. Mary Catherine thought the train would never arrive. Even though they were only at the train station for thirty minutes, she was so nervous it felt like they were sitting in the station for hours.

Mary Catherine never traveled on a train. She never really traveled at all. Normally, this would be a great adventure, but this trip frightened her. Many interesting people milled about the station. Mary Catherine usually enjoyed watching strange people. She liked to make up stories about strangers. But, it was hard to make up ideas about others when Mary Catherine didn't have any idea what her own future held.

The police tried to find Patrick O'Rourke, but he seemed to disappear. Mary Catherine wasn't anxious to see him at all. But because he could not be found, they were leaving the school, the trailer, and the town they always called home. They would have to go to a place called an orphanage, until a new family could be found for them. Sister Clements explained how Sister Immaculata would find a family to adopt them, if their father couldn't be found.

Mary Catherine didn't understand why they couldn't just stay at home. She could take care of the boys, just like before they ran out of money. It wouldn't take much, the cost of the train alone was probably enough for a few months, Mary Catherine figured. It was hard to understand grown-ups. They always said they were doing the best for you, when they were simply making you unhappy. For some reason, whatever made you happy, turned out to be bad for you. Mary Catherine couldn't understand it. But she knew this much, it all would have turned out better if it wasn't for that stupid baby.

It was the baby's fault they were discovered. It was the baby's fault she couldn't take care of her brothers. She even suspected it was the baby's fault her father ran away. *Who wanted to take care of a baby?* A baby needs so much attention. They were all in a pickle, and she was sure all of it was the stupid baby's fault.

Mary Catherine looked at the bundled, cooing baby wrapped in flannel blankets. Sister Geraldine held him, while Sister Clements played with him. Adults, who normally had decorum, made complete idiots of themselves in the presence of a baby. They made faces and silly noises, just to make the baby laugh. Well, she would never be amused by this baby. She hated it, and she vowed she always would.

Finally, the train pulled into the station and they all climbed aboard and found seats. The porter carried their luggage, which wasn't much. It amazed Mary Catherine that all they owned could fit in just two small suitcases. She held her stomach, as fear of the unknown caused a painful cramp. She felt sick! She wanted her mother! Her mother would make everything better. But her mother was gone. Mary Catherine was determined not to cry, so she took a deep breath.

She knew the boys were watching her. If she didn't show any fear, then they wouldn't be afraid. She looked at them and smiled. They seemed to relax almost immediately. She was determined to watch out for them, as she always did.

Sister Clements cried, however, as she kissed them all goodbye. It seemed hard for her to leave the train. She promised she would call, and she would visit them as soon as possible. Mary Catherine felt a strange tug, as the nun left the platform. In the past, Mary Catherine always tried to avoid the nun. Seeing her usually meant Mary Catherine was in some kind of trouble. Now she wanted her. She wanted to hold her and be near her. But it was too late.

Sister Geraldine would travel with the children and take care of the baby until they got to their new home. The train clattered its way out of the station. It ripped Mary Catherine from everything and everyone.

They traveled for about an hour. The boys were fascinated by the train. Sister Geraldine lavished all her attention on the baby. Mary Catherine quietly watched the changing landscape roll past the train window. They traveled northward, to a very rural part of New Jersey, and Mary Catherine couldn't see anything but hills and trees by the time they reached the last station. This was their stop, the end of their old life, and the beginning of the new.

A nun in a different habit and with a young, kind-looking face greeted them. Mary Catherine ignored her friendly overtures. She knew what happened to people you loved. She would never start loving any one again.

Mary Catherine swore that she had never seen so many trees as in the half hour from the station. They were climbing a small mountain, and the engine of the old car screeched as it strained its way upward. At times Mary Catherine was not even sure the dented up car would make it. But the nun, who introduced herself as Sister Immaculata, changed gears and the engine sputtered back to life again. She laughed as if they were on a big adventure, and enjoyed the challenge of getting them to their destination.

Mary Catherine was eager to see her destination. It was nothing like what she expected. At last, they reached a small town. It had a cute main street with plenty of little shops. It looked like a rich town. All the stores matched, and even had matching green and white awnings. The street lamps were old-fashioned black iron. The trees were all trimmed to the same size. It was all so neat and planned.

Mary Catherine never saw such clean sidewalks and benches. The sidewalks were made out of the same brick as the stores. The park benches sparkled in the sun from fresh, hunter-green paint which coordinated with the shutters on the store windows. Mary Catherine never saw such rich people. No bums slept on the benches. She only saw large beautiful houses with manicured lawns. The car turned off the main street. The only thing in the town that seemed to be out of place was the old beat-up car they were traveling in.

The car struggled into a gravel drive and pulled up to a large iron gate. As Sister Immaculata got out to open the gate, Mary Catherine looked around. The top of the rusty gate had the name, Blessed Trinity Orphanage. Sister Immaculata pushed the old gate open as it creaked in resistance. The drive circled up a hill which Mary Catherine later learned was called Strawberry Hill because of all the wild strawberries which grew there. It led to a large three-story, main building surrounded by smaller and more recently built structures. The hill was filled with walking paths and large, white statues and benches. The entire property was surrounded by an iron fence and overlooked the town they had just passed through.

Mary Catherine held her brothers' hands as she entered the strange brick building.

The young nun directed them through the large entry, and into an office of gleaming, polished wood. Mary Catherine and her brothers sat on a sofa, as the nun handed another much older nun, their paperwork.

"This is the O'Rourke family, three boys and one pretty girl." The young nun looked at Mary Catherine as she introduced them. Sister Geraldine handed the older nun the small baby, and said her goodbyes to the three older children.

"I'm sorry, but I have to leave now if I'm going to make the last train home. Please be good and make us all proud of you," said Sister Geraldine as she picked up the phone to call a taxi.

Sister Immaculata placed her arm around Danny and said, "Children, I know you're scared right now. But we'll make you as happy as possible. Right now you must be hungry, and anxious to see your rooms. Sister, why don't I take them to eat, and then I'll show the children where they'll be staying."

The older nun, who held little Thomas, smiled. Sister Immaculata was taking over what was usually part of her job. She trusted the instincts of the kind-hearted, younger nun. If Sister Immaculata wanted to stay with the O'Rourke children, she must have her reasons.

Danny tugged at Sister Immaculata's sleeve, "Where are you taking Thomas?"

The pretty nun reassured him, "Oh, he's being taken to the nursery. He'll be fed a bottle and changed there. That's where he'll be staying. He's too young to stay in the boys' dormitory."

Mary Catherine's heart quickened with a new fear, and she quickly asked, "What do you mean, boys' dormitory, won't we all be together?"

The nun put her arm around Mary Catherine's shoulder and answered in a calm and gentle voice, "Let's get something to eat, and I'll explain it all to you."

Mary Catherine and her two brothers were shown to a large cafeteria where uniformed women prepared large servings of food. The hungry children filled their trays with hot beef and gravy, mashed potatoes, green beans, and milk. They were given cookies for dessert. Mary Catherine was surprised at how famished she was, as the nun explained the situation here.

The young nun spoke kindly as she explained, "There are many other boys and girls here. The girls stay in this building and the boys stay in the white building next to us. The babies under three stay in the nursery where the sisters are trained as nurses. I'll bring you to meet your roommates after we eat."

Mary Catherine didn't like the whole idea of being separated from her brothers, and asked, "You mean that I won't see Danny and Johnny?"

Sister Immaculata noticed Mary Catherine didn't ask about

Thomas, but she kept it to herself.

Sister Immaculata tried to reassure Mary Catherine, "No, no, Mary Catherine, you'll see your brothers each day. We all go to Mass each morning. And we all have our meals together, even breakfast before school. During recess the children all play together. And you'll be able to visit your brothers each evening after dinner if you want. You'll just have to ask if you want to visit the nursery to see Thomas. It's just you'll be sleeping in the girls' dorm, and they will be together in the boys dorm. It's just easier for us to care for you that way."

Mary Catherine didn't like the thought of being separated from her brothers. *Who would watch out for them? What if somebody picked on them?* Still, Mary Catherine didn't say anything. She figured nothing she thought mattered anyway. Grown-ups never cared what children thought. She just resolved she would find a way to take care of Danny and Johnny anyway. Woe to anyone who even tried to hurt them. She wasn't concerned about Thomas. He didn't matter to her. She actually hoped she would never see him again.

She was sad when another nun took Danny and Johnny to the boys' dormitory. Sister Immaculata led her to the girls' dorm. Mary Catherine focused her thoughts on establishing her own protection.

It took Mary Catherine a few days to realize she could let down her guard. The room she shared with nine other girls was not bad. The girls varied in age from five to 15, and all of them seemed nice. Mary Catherine was ready to fight with whoever was the bully, but it seemed there wasn't one. The girls stuck together, maybe because they were all in the same boat. They never tattled on each other no matter what, even if they all took the punishment. They helped each other with chores and homework.

The older girls watched out for the younger girls. Mary Catherine was treated quite nicely and felt she made some friends within a few days. She especially liked the girl who bunked next to her, Jeannie, who was happy to show Mary Catherine around. She was the one girl closest to her age.

Life soon fell into a routine. Each morning the girls washed and dressed and went to Mass. During breakfast in the cafeteria, Mary Catherine sat with her brothers. After breakfast the O'Rourke children went to separate classes in the school. During recess, Mary Catherine played with her new friends, but kept an eye on her brothers to make sure no one was bothering them. Each night she visited Johnny and Danny and was glad they bunked together. They were growing closer to each other. Mary Catherine never asked about Thomas. She never asked to see him. She never even thought of him. Sister Immaculata, who was also Mary Catherine's Geography teacher and her dorm 'Mother' did notice, and resolved to get to the bottom of the situation.

After a few weeks, when Mary Catherine was starting to feel at home, Sister Immaculata sent for her. Mary Catherine was not too happy about losing her recess time with her friends, but she was concerned something might be wrong with the boys. Sister Immaculata had a small office, up one flight of stairs from the cafeteria. It was close to the girl's dorm room, and the nuns' quarters. Sister Immaculata was nice and Mary Catherine wasn't afraid to talk to her.

Sister Immaculata started, "Mary Catherine, sit down, I called you here to ask how you're adjusting to your new home."

"Just fine, Sister, I miss my home and old school, but it's okay here. I guess I'm all right." Mary Catherine squirmed in her seat. She wanted to go play with her new friends.

Sister Immaculata asked, "And how are your brothers doing, Mary Catherine? Are they happy here?"

Mary Catherine smiled, "Oh yes, Sister, they seem pretty happy. And there's no trouble yet, at least that I know of."

Sister Immaculata smiled at Mary Catherine's assessment of Johnny and Danny's situation. She was concerned with Mary Catherine's lack of attention to her youngest brother. She watched the child's face carefully as she asked a pointed question, "And Thomas, you're satisfied with how he's growing?"

Mary Catherine looked at her shoes. She hadn't even given

Thomas a thought, never mind seen him.

"Oh, I really haven't had a chance to visit the nursery," Mary Catherine said trying to act casual about her lack of concern.

The nun noticed the girl couldn't look her in the eye. Sister stated, "That's really a shame, Thomas has already grown so much! Well, don't worry – you'll soon be seeing plenty of him. As you know all the girls and boys here are given chores to help out. After all, this is your home now and we like you to help out, just like you would at home. We wanted to give you time to get used to us before we assigned you a job. We also wanted to wait, and see what job you might be best at. You don't mind being given a job, do you Mary Catherine?"

Mary Catherine was relieved this was all Sister wanted to see her about. She knew all the children were assigned weekend chores, and she secretly hoped to be given cafeteria duty with her new friend Jeannie.

Mary Catherine was quick to answer, "No, Sister, I don't mind doing my part."

"Good! Sister Nadine needs help in the nursery on the weekend. I've watched you with the younger girls, and with your brothers. You have a way with younger children. I think you'll be a big help to Sister Nadine in the nursery. You'll get to see Thomas too, as an added bonus." The nun was curious to see the girl's reaction.

Mary Catherine was stunned. She didn't know what to say.

The nun didn't want to give the girl any time to create an excuse not to see her baby brother. Standing up, she stated, "Come on, I'll show you the nursery and introduce you to Sister Nadine." Mary Catherine followed the nun out of the back of the building to the small white building behind them which contained a nursery and infirmary. She wasn't thrilled with the idea.

The windows on the double glass doors that led to the nursery were decorated with cardboard chicks and bunnies. Everything was painted in soft pastels. The large room was lined with five cribs and a number of rocking chairs and tables. Mary Catherine couldn't help but know which baby was Thomas because he was the only boy there.

All the other cribs had pink sheets and blankets. Even if she didn't notice, there was no way to escape Sister Immaculata, who led her right over to Thomas' bedside.

Mary Catherine was shocked when she saw Thomas raise his head up. He hadn't been able to do anything but lay like a lump the last time she had seen him. She was stunned to see bright blue eyes–her mother's eyes–stare at her. He looked more like her mother than before. Mary Catherine could hardly keep from crying, she missed her mother so much.

Sister picked up Thomas and told Mary Catherine to sit in the rocking chair. Mary Catherine compressed her lips. Her chin stuck out in stubborn determination. Nobody is going to make me like this stupid baby. This baby ruined my life, thought Mary Catherine as she sat in the rocking chair.

Sister handed the cooing bundle to the small girl on the rocking chair and said, "Mary Catherine, please hold Thomas for a moment while I go find Sister Nadine. I want her to explain your duties to you." Before Mary Catherine could object, Sister placed the wiggling baby in her arms. Mary Catherine held him stiffly and tried not to look at him, as Sister left to search for the other nun. She hated Thomas and wanted nothing to do with him.

Sister Nadine, a soft-spoken, middle-aged nun popped out of the nearby closet where she was stocking the supply shelves. Mary Catherine still held the baby stiffly, refusing to look at him. Sister Nadine, who had discussed Mary Catherine's lack of feeling for her brother with Sister Immaculata just this morning, smiled at the young girl's attempt not to look at her brother. Sister Nadine was sure that the plot she and Sister Immaculata hatched would force Mary Catherine to open up to the baby.

Sister Nadine cheerfully said, "Oh I'm so glad you're going to help me, Mary Catherine. I could really use the help with the babies. I mostly need help rocking and feeding them. Oh Mary Catherine, let me teach you how. Thomas is due for his bottle."

Sister Immaculata watched from the adjoining room as Sister

Nadine handed Mary Catherine a warmed up bottle of formula and showed her how to hold the baby and feed him. Mary Catherine was forced to look at Thomas, despite her resolve not to. She quickly picked up the art of holding and feeding a newborn.

Sister Nadine smiled, "Oh, you're doing great! You're a natural at this! Just keep doing what you're doing while Sister Immaculata helps me put the rest of the supplies away. I really appreciate this."

Mary Catherine was horrified. She didn't want anything to do with this stupid baby. Her face was flushed with anger at the two nuns. She knew they were playing a trick on her and Mary Catherine didn't appreciate it. She didn't want to feed this baby, any other baby–but not this one. They had a lot of nerve forcing this on her. Maybe I should just put the baby down and leave. That would teach them, Mary Catherine's mind was fevered with anger. As the nuns left the room, she looked at the baby who was greedily sucking the bottle. He stopped as her eyes meet his. He waved his little hand in the air and drooled some of the formula out. She bent down to check if he was all right and that's when his little hand reached up and brushed her cheek. It was just like her mother used to do. And then he smiled at Mary Catherine. It was her mother's soft gentle smile.

As the two nuns watched hidden behind the door of the supply closet, the tears flowed down Mary Catherine's cheeks. The baby cooed at her, and that's when Mary Catherine fell in love with her baby brother, Thomas.

Approached by Truth

For He will give his angels charge of you to guard you in all your ways. On their hands They will bear you up, lest you dash your foot against a stone. (Psalm 91:11-12)

Elly awoke on the worn living room sofa. Her thoughts were hazy. Looking into the face of the woman who greeted her at the door, the loving countenance glowed with concerned compassion. The resemblance to her mother still astonished Elly.

"I'm so sorry, Elly. I guess I should have known you were too young to remember our last meeting. I'm your Aunt Sarah, your mother's twin sister."

So conditioned by her mothers stories, Elly's response was immediate. "My mother had no living family!" Instantly, Elly realized the lie of her statement. The woman had to be her mother's twin. It was the only possible explanation. Sitting up, Elly pushed the blonde strands from her face and explained, "My mother told me there was no family."

Aunt Sarah's face flushed red, but she quickly regained her composure and said, "Now I understand. That's why you never let us know Louise was ill. You were too young to remember us. When I read about her death in the paper, I had to come. We are all so sorry for your loss, Elly."

Elly tried to focus on the situation. We? What did her Aunt

mean by saying the word we? Elly pondered.

Elly was quick to ask, "You mean there are more relatives?"

Aunt Sarah stroked her niece's hair and answered, "Yes, not only cousins, but you have an uncle and another aunt."

It was too much for Elly to understand. The doorbell rang and Elly tried to collect herself. Aunt Sarah answered the door. Elly expected to see the lawyer. She shook with amazement when Dr. Gabe Lopez entered the room.

"Dr. Lopez, what are you doing here?" Instantly her hand, as if by subconscious command covered her flat and empty abdomen. Dr. Lopez's eyes followed her hand and the evidence it revealed, but he didn't refer to what he obviously noticed.

Dr. Lopez quickly walked over to the couch where Elly sat and with true contrition in his voice started, "I came as soon as I made the connection. I'm so sorry, Elly – I didn't know who you were when I sent you home."

Confused, Elly shook her head. "I don't know what you mean, Dr. Lopez."

He addressed Elly as if she were the only person in the room, "Elly, call me Gabe. As it is, it turns out we are not strangers." The handsome physician continued, "I grew up in the town below, I knew your mother. I knew you as a child."

Elly couldn't remember any of it, but that meant nothing. Apparently, her memory left a lot to be desired.

"Are you okay?" he asked, as he sat by her side and felt for a pulse.

Elly was a little shaken and answered in a confused manner, "I'm just fine–just, well, I've had a few shocks recently."

The worried doctor was pleased to find her pulse was steady, although she appeared a little too thin.

A loud knock on the door drew everyone's attention. The lawyer, with a no nonsense attitude was a little shocked when Aunt Sarah answered the door. Aunt Sarah explained her relationship to the deceased, as she led the lawyer into the living room. Dr. Lopez and

Elly were on the couch talking when Aunt Sarah and the lawyer entered. The lawyer walked quickly to the chair opposite the couch Elly and Dr. Lopez sat on. Opening his briefcase, he seemed in a rush and said, "Hm-mm, I hate to interrupt your reunion, but I do have another appointment. If you'll excuse us, I must present Louise Wilkin's will."

Elly suddenly didn't want to be alone. She felt so comfortable now that the doctor was here. He had been so kind to her in the hospital. She couldn't believe that the man she trusted so much had appeared, just when she needed him. Elly gently grabbed the physician's hand as he started to leave, "Stay, I would feel better if you just stayed."

Dr. Lopez's eyes glowed warmly as looked at her with tenderness, "Are you sure, Elly?"

Aunt Sarah, always a shrewd observer of human emotions, couldn't help but notice the feelings displayed in this short conversation. So Elly wasn't completely unloved after all.

The reading of the will was a short affair. As if to emphasize her hatred of her family, Louise left both her brother and sisters, and each of her nieces, the sum of one dollar.

Aunt Sarah didn't seem concerned. "I'm not interested in her money Elly, I'm only interested in you."

"Don't worry, Aunt Sarah, I don't think there is much money anyway, just enough to get me started somewhere else, I hope."

The lawyer looked at Elly with sympathy. He had spent years dealing with this gentle girl's mother. Louise Wilkin was a bully. He witnessed Agnes' attack on Elly as the paramedics placed Louise's body in the ambulance. He was pleased the horrid woman never had the chance to change her will.

Rubbing his balding head, the lawyer started, "Well, that's where you're wrong, young lady. Your mother left everything to you, including the house. And by everything, not counting the house, she left you cash and stocks worth over six million dollars."

Elly sat in stunned silence. She didn't know what to think.

As the color drained from her face, Elly exclaimed, "I don't believe it. She had all that money and she lived like this."

"You'll pardon me for saying so," answered the lawyer, "but it sounds like your mother was a bit of a tight-wad. Still, it's all very true, Elly. I'll leave the papers, bank books, and portfolio for you to look over. If you wish to make any changes, I'll also leave you the name of your mother's accountant. Now, I hate to rush off, but I have to be on my way." Looking to the doctor and Aunt Sarah, he continued, "I'm sure that I'm leaving you in very capable hands."

Elly was able to remain cordial, despite the revelations of this astonishing day. She walked the lawyer out and returned to find Dr. Lopez and her Aunt Sarah talking. When the handsome doctor looked up, she was drawn to his deep dark eyes. His bright smile lightened the room. Elly felt safe whenever he was around. She lost all the faith and hope she had when she left the hospital and this man. He filled her with that hope, during his daily visits to her hospital room. Somehow, after she came home, she had lost that sense of trust in the future. Elly was so ashamed of what she had done. He would have to notice she was no longer pregnant. She felt she disappointed him by not having the baby. If he was aware of what she did, he didn't say anything. She was grateful for that.

Aunt Sarah was the first to speak, "Elly, it is wonderful that you will have the money you need to start a new life."

"I just can't believe it. This house is so dilapidated. I thought she had let it fall apart because she didn't have the money to fix it up."

Looking around at the dark and dusty house, Aunt Sarah shook her head, "I guess she just wasn't interested in how the house looked."

Elly started to weep. It had all been too much for her. "I guess not. She only cared about her friends. She didn't even hire a nurse to help care for her. Why should she? She had me. I took care of her. Night and day, without sleep I waited on her hand and foot. All this time she could have hired someone to help me. I guess she just never cared."

Sitting on the chair, Elly continued to weep. Aunt Sarah put her arm around her niece and allowed her to cry it out. The poor girl had been through so much. The young doctor seemed at a loss over what to do. Aunt Sarah decided to draw him out.

"Dr. Lopez, how well did you know my sister?"

The handsome man seemed glad to be included in the conversation and said, "Please, both of you, call me Gabe. I didn't know her well. It is more like I knew of her. I'm afraid as a child I joined in with the other children in town. We had some crazy idea that she was a witch. We very seldom saw the woman so she seemed mysterious to us. And as with most things you don't understand, we grew to be afraid of her. I'm afraid I wasn't very kind to her. The last time I remember seeing her, my friends and I climbed up here and were throwing rocks at the house."

Aunt Sarah smiled as Elly's sobs ended. She noticed the compassion in Gabe's eyes as he looked at her niece. She liked the young man. He was just what her lonely niece needed in her life. She decided to help the struggling romance along. With a smile, Aunt Sarah started, "You remember Elly as a child?"

Gabe reddened, "I'm afraid that I didn't at first. She was my patient recently and I didn't realize who she was. You see, I volunteer at the college clinic where Elly attended. I'm afraid I didn't recognize her when I met her there. Now, I remember her as the small and shy little girl who lived on the hill. I didn't make the connection before. When I realized who she was, and found out her mother died, I rushed over to see if I could be of any help."

Aunt Sarah smiled, "Elly is lucky to have a good friend like you, Gabe."

Elly looked up, her crying over. "Yes, Gabe, thanks for coming over to check on me."

Gabe reddened, apparently embarrassed by the attention. He rose to leave and stated, "I'm glad your aunt is here with you. I won't be worried now that she is taking care of you."

Aunt Sarah didn't miss the tender connection exchanged between these two. She decided to take control, "Just where do you think you are going? Elly go upstairs and rest. You look like you haven't eaten in days. I hope Gabe can stay and help me make some dinner."

Elly, so used to taking orders complied immediately. Gabe, so unused to being ordered around didn't know how to react, so he just obeyed. Aunt Sarah so used to being in control, also felt comfortable. Elly was exhausted. Upstairs, she showered quickly and snuggled beneath the soft comforter on her bed. She fell into a dreamless sleep and slept the rest of the afternoon away. She felt like a new woman when she woke up. Aunt Sarah was right. I feel totally refreshed, thought Elly. She dressed in her favorite jeans and tee shirt, and started downstairs with a renewed sense of hope for the future.

Elly was totally unprepared for the spectacle in the kitchen. Aunt Sarah and Gabe were bustling around preparing dinner. Despite the occasion, the sight of Gabe in a ruffled apron, taking orders from an unmistakable taskmaster like Aunt Sarah, tickled Elly. She started to laugh. Both of the inhabitants of the kitchen seemed surprised, although pleased to hear it.

"I told Dr. Lopez here, that I want to prepare a small supper for you, before I return to my hotel, and he graciously offered to help," smiled Aunt Sarah. "However, from the looks of things, it wasn't much of an offer."

Gabe was trying to untangle long unused utensils and electrical cords that seemed to have a life of their own. It was a comical sight.

"Well it's good I'm not too hungry, because it looks like this could take a while," answered Elly.

Gabe, feigning hurt feelings, looked at Elly and mumbled something about her being a female chauvinist. This started the laughter again which became a release valve for all the pent up emotion Elly had bottled up for so long. Elly was delighted. Aunt Sarah and Gabe were having such a joyful time. The friendly banter and camaraderie was something new for this solemn house. Elly could only watch and enjoy. It was better than any comedy show she had ever seen.

"Here, try this, I hope you can carve a turkey as well as you carve up patients!" exclaimed Aunt Sarah as she handed Gabe a carving knife and a platter full of leftover turkey.

Elly remembered roasting the turkey three days ago while her mother took one of her infrequent naps. It seemed hard to believe, so much had changed in just three days.

"Well, now I can attest that carving a turkey from the freezer and one from the ER isn't much different, except in pay of course." His imitation of John Wayne brought more laughter.

Forty-five minutes later, three laughing friends sat around the dining room table enjoying a turkey casserole. Elly was so hungry she ate heartily. This was a better meal than she had enjoyed in a long time. The food was hot and delicious, and the conversation and company was just as warm.

Elly wanted to thank her Aunt for her kindness. She regretted the cruelty of her mother. Thinking of the way her mother cut her twin sister out of her will, Elly apologized, "I'm sorry you came all this way for nothing, Aunt Sarah."

Aunt Sarah reached across the table to hold Elly's hand, "What do you mean nothing? I came here to find my niece and I found one even nicer than the one I remembered."

Elly, so used to biting malice, did not know how to respond to a kind word.

Aunt Sarah, seeing her niece's embarrassment took the lead, "Let's clean up and then I have to head to the hotel, I'm afraid that I'm exhausted."

"Oh no," exclaimed Elly, "Don't leave. You can stay right here."

Aunt Sarah looked doubtful, "I don't want to impose."

"Oh, please," answered Elly, "I really don't want to be alone, you'd be doing me a favor."

Aunt Sarah looked to Gabe for a cue.

"I think it best Elly not be alone for now." Gabe's answer seemed to settle the question.

Aunt Sarah spent a week with Elly. It was a week of delight and discovery for Elly. Learning the truth of her extended family made Elly hungry for the sense of connectedness she never knew. She couldn't learn enough about her new relatives. Poor Aunt Sarah only got a break during Gabe's visits.

Thank goodness his visits were frequent and lively. He delighted in taking them out to the local theater and steak house. He was also just as comfortable sharing microwave popcorn, a video, and Aunt Sarah's simple cuisine. The house, so long filled with pain and darkness, was now full of light, laughter, and love. Elly felt as if a new life had begun for her. She looked forward to each day. Well rested, she enjoyed sharing her days with Aunt Sarah and Gabe. The pain of the past began to fade. The endless criticism of her mother was replaced by the love and laughter of these two wonderful people. The young girl never wanted the joy to end.

However, the week flew by, and a tearful parting from her new found aunt was only relieved by heartfelt promises that Elly would visit. They planned a visit in a few months. Elly could meet all her relatives.

The silence of the house gloomily descended on Elly even though Gabe continued his fun-filled visits. Gabe hated to tell Elly that his vacation was about to end. She seemed to look forward to his nightly visits. He knew she had to find a purpose for her life. She didn't want to be alone. Elly always wanted company. Elly complained to Gabe about the dreary days. She was depressed when he wasn't around.

"Look at this house," Gabe replied. "I'm not surprised! This house would depress anyone. What do you plan to do with it?"

Elly took a long look around her. The atmosphere of the dismally dank mansion was weary and depressing. After a few minutes of thought, Elly answered, "I hadn't really thought about it. Sell it, I suppose."

Gabe laughed, "Well, you'll never get a good price for it in this condition. Why don't you have some fun and clean, paint, and decorate the old girl? You may be able to triple the price if you make some repairs."

Elly looked around at the grime-covered windows and dusty drapes. It might even be fun to clean and decorate this house–at least it was something to keep her occupied. Her imagination started to re-do the place. Gabe laughed, by the look on her face he knew he'd won his point.

Gabe's visit with his family came to an end. He hated to leave. The overworked doctor had been very happy during this vacation. Not only had he rested and regained his strength, but he enjoyed his time with Elly. They spent almost every evening together and his feelings for the young girl were deepening.

His busy practice called him. There were patients he needed to check on, and Gabe couldn't put his return off any longer. He was worried about leaving Elly, afraid her deep depression might return when she was left all alone.

With the thought of keeping her mind busy, Gabe encouraged her. "I hope you're going to do something with that house while I'm away. I'll be looking forward to seeing what your decorating skills are like."

"I plan on making a lot of changes. I'll have to if this place is ever going to be sold." Elly was almost afraid to ask, but couldn't stop herself. "Just when will you be coming back to see it?"

So she will miss me, Gabe smiled to himself and said, "I'll be back to visit my family for a weekend in a month or so. Do you think you will miss me?"

Elly blushed, "I guess I might."

Gabe reached over and gave Elly a gentle kiss. "Well, I'll miss you Elly, and I'll be back as soon as I can. I'll call you every day. And I can't wait to see if you miss me."

Elly could feel the heat in her face as her blush deepened. Softly she whispered, as they said goodbye at the door, "I think I will miss you more than you know."

Another kiss ended their goodbye. Elly hated to see him leave. She was afraid of being alone. Elly decided that keeping busy was the best solution.

The very next morning Elly hired two cleaning girls. First the heavy drapes came down and the windows were washed to a sparkly shine. Light flooded the rooms, but only accented the worn carpets and heavy dark furniture. Elly cleaned the third floor with its six bedrooms and three baths. Then, she closed it off. Someday this floor might hold some use, but today it just held bad memories. Even her childhood room just reminded her of long days of loneliness.

Next, the painters and a local decorator came and worked their magic. New pastel carpets showed off the new, lighter and less formal furniture made of blonde wood and wicker. Light, lacy valances topped the windows and revealed spectacular ocean views. The fresh smell of paint mixed with the salty ocean breezes to lift Elly's spirit. Suddenly, her aversion to the ocean seemed to change and grow into a mysterious sense of love and wonder.

It took weeks of decorators and workmen stumbling over each other to finish the inside of the house. As the work was finished, and the house became quiet, Elly grew lonely. Until now the decorating had keep her busy. Now that the outside of the house was being scraped and painted, she was usually alone with no workmen inside.

Gabe called each night and she loved their long conversations, but she really want to see him. Elly couldn't wait for him to see the vast changes she accomplished. The house was so different. But his opinion of the house was not the real reason she longed for his visit. Elly really missed him. She felt so alone and insecure without him around. When he called and announced that he would be arriving on the morning train, she made arrangements to meet him on the ruse that she couldn't wait for him to see the house. The truth was, she couldn't wait to see him.

Gabe was stunned. The house was transformed from a horror into an exquisite ocean home. It looked like one of the homes often featured in a magazine. The plush carpets and cozy furniture changed the mansion from a forbidding abomination into a home. Each room revealed its own personality, each was light and inviting.

Gabe was more than impressed and exclaimed, "You've made it your own! It's spectacular!"

Elly looked around. She did feel at home now that her part of the work was done. She loved to cook in her sunny kitchen, and read in her plush easy chair.

With pride, Elly answered, "Yes, I do feel at home."

The formally dark and gloomy library was now joyful and full of light. Elly had deliberately set up decorations that were fun and carefree. Snow babies tumbled, porcelain angels smiled, precious moment statues shyly peeked out from the shelves. Next to these joyful scenes, were brown boxes. The boxes contained numerous heavy occult books, Ouija boards, and Egyptian icons which had belonged to her mother. Elly removed all of the dark reminders of the paranormal.

Gabe asked, "What are you going to do with these?"

"I don't know," Elly looked puzzled, "throw them out?"

"I've got a better idea!" Gabe carried the boxes out and placed them in a large metal barrel.

Elly felt a strong sense of peace as Gabe lit them on fire. It was as if all the evil of her mother was now removed from the house. The flaming barrel took on a solemn, almost spiritual quality.

Elly and Gabe spent the weekend together. They both felt the time passed too quickly. It wasn't enough time to be together, and Sunday afternoon arrived too soon. Elly knew Gabe had to leave in the morning and only one thought made it easier. Elly wasn't going to be alone, rambling around this big house. She had plans herself. She knew it would make missing Gabe easier.

Elly had promised her Aunt Sarah she would come for a visit, to meet the rest of the family. Dates had been confirmed and now that the house was done, she was looking forward to the visit. It was all arranged. Elly decided to take the train west to the small town that bordered Ohio, just outside of Pittsburgh.

"I'm sorry to shorten our last night together. I have to leave for Aunt Sarah's on the late afternoon train."

"I'll drive you to the train station." Gabe smiled. Tears sprang to Elly's eyes.

Gabe took her in his arms, and said, "I have a surprise for you this afternoon! My mother's making a huge feast, I want you to come and meet my family." Elly's immediate reaction was fear. Seeing the stress in her face, Gabe took Elly in his arms. Being held in Gabe's strong, protective arms calmed her.

Elly was nervous about meeting Gabe's family, but they soon put her at ease. Their joking and light hearted teasing astounded her. They were all such individuals, each with different interests and personalities. Yet, they seemed very interested in each other and able to disagree with love. And disagree they did, about everything from politics to how much salt to use. But, while there was a lot of jesting, there were no put-downs or insults.

For Elly, who lived for so long in fear of disagreement, it was amazing. Growing up, her slightest argument with her mother brought severe punishments. It was refreshing to see people argue with love.

Gabe's mother seemed so familiar. Elly knew she recognized her from somewhere. It wasn't until Gabe's mother touched Elly's hand that she recognized the dark, energetic woman as the cleaning lady she had met in the small church on the afternoon of her abortion. The memory of that painfully lonely day flooded Elly with a strong sense of shame. Elly realized Gabe's mother didn't know what Elly did that day, and tried to dismiss it all from her mind. If Mrs. Lopez placed her, she never said a word.

Elly didn't know which was better, the company, or the food. Whichever it was, it made for a joyous afternoon. She couldn't get over the good natured way Gabe's younger brothers and sisters teased him.

"We almost forgot what you looked like," badgered his sister. "When your picture fell out of my wallet last month, I had to think hard before I could remember who you were."

Gabe laughed, "I know I haven't visited in a long time, but I didn't realize it had been that long."

Gabe's sister giggled as she continued, "Well maybe we have good reason to hope we'll see more of you in the future." Elly blushed as she realized Gabe's sister was referring to her.

Gabe gently placed his arm around Elly's shoulders, "I realize it's hard, but you're just going to have to get used to them if you're going to be part of this family."

Elly was shaken. It was the first time Gabe mentioned any serious intention. She smiled, she already felt at home here. Elly so enjoyed the lunch that the hours just flew by. Gabe forced his family to let her leave, or she would have been late for her train.

After the excitement of the luncheon, the car seemed quiet. Elly tried to catch her breath and concentrate on the trip ahead. All her bags were packed and in Gabe's car trunk. Her tickets were in her handbag. After meeting Gabe's family, she was anxious to meet her own.

Looking across the seat, Elly couldn't help but notice how startlingly handsome Gabe was. She only wished she could take him with her. Her feelings for him were getting deeper. While she looked forward to this trip, she was going to miss him.

As if he sensed her thoughts, Gabe said, "I hope you won't be gone too long, I'm going to miss you."

Elly was pleased, "You're going back to the clinic, aren't you?"

Gabe grinned, "Yes, but if all goes as planned, I may have a surprise for you when you come back."

Gabe pulled into the parking lot, and after parking by the platform, he turned to Elly. "Finally, I may just get fifteen minutes alone with you before the train arrives."

Elly just smiled. She suddenly felt self-conscious, aware of her deeper feelings for him.

"Elly," Gabe softly spoke as he turned to her, "I hope you know how much I'm going to be lost without you." Reaching over, he gently stroked her hair.

"I'll miss you too," she whispered.

"We have a lot to talk about when you return." His dark eyes were piercing. Reaching over, Gabe softly kissed her cheek. As he gently cupped her face, the tracks rumbled with the clattering noise of the arriving train.

Elly whispered softly, softened by his kiss, "I should be back in two, three weeks at the most."

Gabe appeared lost in thought, as he carried her bags to the platform. "Don't worry, take your time. It's important for you to get to know who you are and where you came from. It doesn't matter if it takes time. I'll always be there for you."

A strange sense of peace fell over Elly. She wasn't afraid. She knew Gabe would be there for her. He meant what he said. She never felt such a sense of comfort. Gabe gave her bags to the porter and helped her to her train car. Bending down quickly, Elly softly kissed him. His eyes said all she needed to know.

With an overwhelming sensation of being loved, Elly started her trip. She brought a novel and a number of magazines for the nine hour train ride. As she entered the small empty compartment, however, she felt no desire to read. Closing her eyes and relaxing, she realized she hadn't had much time to reflect. The rhythmic clattering of the train wheels lulled her into a deep meditative state. Immediately her thoughts turned to Gabe. She needed to assess his role in her life, or her feelings about it.

From the first, he was good for her. When she was starving, he fed her. When she was depressed, he brought joy. When she was lonely, he filled her life with companionship. But there were some strange aspects of their relationship. Was he acting as her doctor or her friend? Were his feelings deeper? And how about her feelings? She heard of women falling in love with their doctors. Was that all it was, a misguided gratitude? No, she felt it was deeper on both sides. She, at least, knew she had strong feelings for him. What girl wouldn't? He was handsome and witty. He was intelligent and fun. But the reason she cared for him was much more profound. He was just so good. He was her savior.

"You already have a Savior!" Elly heard a strange voice, out of the blue. Thinking it was her imagination Elly ignored the voice and continued her thoughts.

There were problems though. They came from very different backgrounds. His family had love and such deep faith. Elly had never known love and had no faith. Money would probably not be a problem. Thinking of the little white church, Elly sighed. "If only I could believe."

"Faith is a gift!" This time Elly couldn't ignore the voice breaking into her thoughts.

Opening her eyes, she was startled to see a nun sitting across from her. She didn't hear anyone come in. Perhaps she dosed off. The nun's twinkling blue eyes set in an apple shaped face, attested to a habit of smiling more than frowning. The sweet, kind face appeared to find Elly's confusion amusing. Contrasted with the stark black and severely starched habit, blue veined hands fingered the large four-inch crucifix that lay across her chest.

"What did you say?" asked Elly.

"I said, faith is a gift, and if you want a gift you should ask for it."

Elly felt as if she was in a dream. "Will you give me the gift of faith, then?"

The nun let out a faint laugh. "Oh, I can't give it to you. You must ask God. Each day when you awake and each night before you sleep. Pray to God for the gift of faith."

"That's all?" Elly asked.

The elderly nun answered with assurance, "Oh, you can ask any time you want. Close your eyes and ask now."

Elly found herself obeying the strange woman sitting across from her, although she couldn't understand why.

The small shriveled nun instructed, "Repeat after me."

Bowing her head, the nun said, "Now pray. Dear Father in heaven, I believe, help my unbelief. Send me the gift of faith."

Elly started to repeat the prayer mentally.

"Out loud!" the nun demanded.

The nun repeated softly, "Dear Father in heaven, I believe, help my unbelief. Send me the gift of faith."

Suddenly, warmth flowed from the top of Elly's head to the tips of her toes. The warmth was followed by an overpowering sense of well being. Opening her eyes, Elly was shocked to find herself alone. Her eyes were closed for just a moment, and yet when she opened them the nun had disappeared. It wasn't until years later Elly would wonder how the nun knew her name and what she was thinking. It wasn't until seventy years later, at her death, that Elly would realize the nun was her guardian angel. Elly had never been taught the faith. She never realized each of us is given an angel to guide us. These guardian angels are our companions from the time of our conception and throughout our mortal life. They are our one constant friend, remaining with us for eternity. Elly's guardian angel had manifested herself in order to reach Elly. Angels often do, and are so seldom recognized, except as helpful strangers.

Pulling out her novel, Elly decided she would look for the nun when the train reached the station.

She did see Aunt Sarah on the Pittsburgh station platform, waving excitedly. Elly had packed two large suitcases, not knowing what events her aunt might have planned. Putting them down, she quickly hugged her beloved aunt.

"I'm so glad you're here, Elly. The whole family will be at the house to meet you in a week. The next five days are just for us."

She directed Elly to a small imported car. It was a forty minute drive to the town her mother had grown up in. On the edge of town, she pulled into the driveway of a 1920's Colonial and led Elly through the back door to the brightly lit kitchen.

"Want a cup of tea?" she asked, as she put on a kettle of water.

"Yes," replied Elly. She hadn't realized how tired the trip made her. "It'll help me relax. I'm excited about meeting the family, but I must say I'm glad to have time alone with you. I want to find out about my mother and I know practically nothing about my father."

"Slow down! I promise you, I'll tell you whatever you want to know tomorrow. Tonight let's just relax and get a good night's sleep." She poured the tea and sliced up some pound cake. "Tomorrow you can ask all the questions you want while you help me cook. It's a large hungry clan coming next weekend and they eat non stop!" With a knowing grin, Aunt Sarah introduced a topic dearer to her heart, "Tell me, how is Gabe?"

Elly laughed. Aunt Sarah's down to earth nature is what made Elly love her so much. Aunt Sarah didn't have any trouble saying exactly what she meant, what she needed, and what she would do for you.

I wish I could be more like her, she thought. Taking the last sip of her tea, Elly tried to stifle a yawn.

Looking sympathetically at her tired niece, Aunt Sarah announced, "Come on, your bed awaits you, madam."

Aunt Sarah led Elly upstairs to a small, neat bedroom overlooking the front of the house.

In her usual no nonsense manner, Aunt Sarah ordered, "Get a good night's sleep, we've got lots of work tomorrow."

Elly felt very relaxed after washing up and slipping on her nightgown. Snuggling between the clean crisp sheets, she felt her whole body relax. Elly was exhausted. She closed her eyes and couldn't understand why fifteen minutes later she was still awake. Then it hit her, climbing out of bed, she got on her knees and leaning on the side of the bed said, "Dear Father in heaven, I believe, help my unbelief. Please, give me the gift of faith." Climbing back into bed Elly felt nothing, but fell to sleep readily. It was a prayer she would repeat morning and night for the next month.

Fear Transformed

There is no fear in love, but perfect love drives out fear because fear has to do with punishment, and so one who fears is not yet perfect in love. We love because He first loved us. (1 John 4: 18-19)

She awoke confused. The rose papered room with lace curtains was flooded with the morning sun. It took her a moment to remember where she was. She decided to hurry and surprise Aunt Sarah with breakfast. Putting on her robe she rushed down the stairs, only to find Aunt Sarah already in the kitchen, with the coffee made and eggs frying in the pan.

"A late sleeper, huh," Aunt Sarah laughed.

"I thought I was pretty early, myself," answered Elly.

Aunt Sarah laughed, "I'm up with the sun. I'm what you call a daily communicant."

"What's that?" asked Elly as she munched on a crisply browned piece of rye toast.

Aunt Sarah answered casually, as she flipped the eggs, "It means I go to Mass everyday, not just on Sunday. I guess I should have asked you if you are, but I figured you needed the sleep. Do you go to daily Mass, or just on Sundays, Elly?"

Elly's face reddened. Aunt Sarah quickly picked up on her blunder.

Aunt Sarah quickly tried to make her niece more comfortable

and said, "I'm sorry Elly, I guess I just assumed. The whole family is Roman Catholic and the one promise your mother made to our parents, before she left, was she would raise you in the faith."

"I guess that's just one more promise she forgot," Elly sighed. Aunt Sarah's face filled with sorrow as she poured them coffee and placed the eggs before Elly.

"What other promises did she forget?" asked Aunt Sarah quietly. Suddenly, as if all the pain of a lifetime could no longer be held behind a facade of polite cordiality, Elly began to weep.

Elly cried, "She promised to always love me, but she forgot. She promised to always protect me, but she forgot that too!"

The eggs grew cold, as Sarah held her sobbing niece. She said nothing but allowed Elly to talk it out. And talk Elly did. She told her about the way she was raised, her mother's friends, and her mother's loss of interest in her. She told her aunt of her mother's involvement in the New Age movement, and the occult. She even told Aunt Sarah of the horrible way her mother chose to die and of the abortion Elly was forced to get, in order to care for her. Still, Aunt Sarah said nothing. A few times she sighed, but she allowed Elly to cry until the tears ran dry.

"I'm sorry!" Elly whispered, as she pulled away from her aunt's gentle arms. "I don't know what came over me. I didn't mean to burden you with all this. Now you can see why it's so important for me to find out about my family, especially my father."

Aunt Sarah scraped the cold breakfast into the trash can. She broke open new eggs and started new toast. Bringing fresh coffee to the table, she said, "I'm afraid you're in for quite a few shocks then. Are you sure you're ready for them?"

"Yes," Elly answered, with a renewed sense of strength.

Aunt Sarah watched Elly's face carefully as she said, "Well, we might as well start at the beginning, and to do that we might as well start with the biggest shock!"

"Go ahead," answered Elly, with great resolve. Little did she know what was coming.

Aunt Sarah sat at the table and began with the most startling news.

She asked with concern, "Elly, when you talk about your father, who do you mean?"

"Why, George Wilkin, my mother had his pictures all over the house. I know he was a banker, but she never seemed to want to talk about him. I guess it caused her too much pain. He died when I was just an infant. I don't know much about him. Did you know him?"

Elly's aunt took a moment to compose herself.

"Yes Elly, I knew George Wilkin, but I'm afraid you're on the wrong track here. You see, George Wilkin isn't really your father. In fact, your name is not Eleanor Wilkin. I have a copy of your birth certificate. Your real name is Eleanor Connor. Your father's name is David Connor."

Elly swallowed hard. Aunt Sarah looked with sympathy at the confused girl.

Aunt Sarah took a sip of her coffee, as if to strengthen herself for the revelations ahead, and said, "I know it's hard to understand, but let me explain the story."

Elly nodded. She needed to understand the truth, no matter what it led to.

"Your mother and I went to high school with David. I had a secret crush on him, but it ended when he started to date Louise in our junior year. They were inseparable. They went to every school dance. Both of them were very popular." Aunt Sarah laughed. "I know you would never believe it now, but I was the shy one. David and your mother were soon going steady. That means she wore his class ring and was considered his girl. Hands off to all the other fellows! I don't ever remember seeing Louise so happy. They were always together. They were even elected King and Queen of our prom. Everybody knew they were meant for each other. He was so handsome and she so beautiful, I thought they would forever be in love. They seemed to have it all. I, just like everyone else, assumed that they would marry after graduation and live happily ever after, but that's not the way it turned out."

"What did happen?" Elly was fascinated by the story of her parents.

"Vietnam, Vietnam is what happened. One week after graduation, David got his draft notice. I guess it's hard to explain to someone who wasn't there, but those years were very confusing years for our country. David was very patriotic, and although he didn't want to leave Louise, he was determined to serve his country. Louise was irate! She disagreed with the war. She wanted David to dodge the draft and flee to Canada, as many objectors did in those days. She thought they could marry and start a life of their own. David, of course, refused.

"Louise's reaction was totally out of proportion. She begged and argued. She pleaded and belittled him. And on the day he left, she was so angry she slapped him and told him he would never see her again. She even cursed him and told him she wished he would die over there. It was the first time I saw Louise behave in such a cruel and selfish way."

"Did he die in Vietnam?" Elly asked, astonished by the story.

"No, no he came home years later, after three tours of duty, but by then everything had changed. It was about a month after David left that Louise discovered she was pregnant. She was horrified. My parents tried to support her and wanted to help her until David came home, but the shame of being an unwed mother was too much for her. She had already started working at the bank, and her looks had already caught the eye of lecherous old man Wilkin. He was three times her age, but by then Louise had grown so cold. She even told me one night, 'If a man is as rich as George Wilkin, it's best that he already has one foot in the grave!' I felt like I didn't even know what happened to the loving sister I grew up with. She'd become so greedy.

"We were never well-to-do, just middle class people. But, we never suffered. Suddenly, none of this was good enough for Louise. I tried to think it was for you. That, perhaps, she wanted more for you.

She encouraged the advances the old man made, although I know she wasn't attracted to him."

Aunt Sarah continued, "Somewhere along the line, she must have convinced him the child she was carrying was his. One day, she never came home from work. They eloped. George Wilkin retired and left the bank. He certainly didn't need the money, as wealthy as he was. He set her up in the house you grew up in. She cut all ties with her family. She visited just once, and that's when she made the promise to have you baptized and to raise you as a Catholic. She never came home again, not even when our parents died. After that, I'm afraid I grew angry. I just gave up on her. I always prayed, however, both for you and for Louise. I just gave up trying to maintain a relationship. She didn't want it. Perhaps, for your sake, I should have tried harder."

"No, she wouldn't have changed," Elly answered. "There's nothing you could have done."

With a sudden longing to meet her real father, Elly asked, "Does my father still live in this town?"

Aunt Sarah looked visibly upset as she answered. "No Elly, I'm sorry, David Connor died. He is buried at the church here though."

Elly couldn't help but feel the disappointment. I'm just not meant to have a parent to love, she thought.

As Elly sat in her bed that night, she reviewed all her aunt told her. She had no doubts her aunt told her the truth, but it was so much to comprehend and changed everything. Even her name was not her own.

Throughout the next week, Elly and her aunt cleaned, chopped vegetables, and cooked in preparation for the large family gathering expected on Saturday. They also talked. Elly learned she had one uncle and one other aunt. Her other aunt was a nun. She had two cousins, and one of them was pregnant. Soon, they were expecting the arrival of the next generation.

Elly enjoyed preparing for the family she was learning about. It was hard cooking and cleaning for so many. Still, it was so different from the care she gave her mother. There was a sense of joy to the work. Elly was just starting to understand the difference between work done out of duty as opposed to work done with love.

Aunt Sarah complemented Elly on her cooking and Elly enjoyed the closeness and giddiness she never enjoyed with her mother. Often, throughout the sunny days, the silliness seemed to get out of hand as some things got burned in the rush of preparation. But it never seemed to matter to Aunt Sarah who could find nothing but joy in the entire process.

Amidst the laughter and work of their hands, the days just seemed to slip away. Elly, although exhausted, was surprised to see the sunset behind the billowing kitchen curtains. Looking around, she noticed they were almost done.

"Time to finish!" Aunt Sarah announced as if to confirm Elly's thoughts. "And don't think that I've forgotten our dinner!"

Elly laughed as the doorbell rang and her aunt returned with a large pizza.

With giggles, Elly asked, "After all that cooking we're having a pizza?"

"Of course, I have no intention of cooking any more or cleaning up either."

Elly watched with amusement as her aunt, with great gusto and exaggerated tribulation, set the table with paper plates and cups. Elly never knew a pizza dinner could be so much fun!

Looking around, her aunt appeared pleased. They'd accomplished a lot in four days. The refrigerator was filled with food, and the counter was lined with assorted cakes and pastries. The kitchen and the rest of the house sparkled

Aunt Sarah was full of pride as she said, "I'm proud of us, we work well as a team."

Elly, as tired as she felt, was pleased, and commented, "I really enjoyed this week. I never knew housework could be such fun."

Aunt Sarah laughed. "It is, if you're doing it for someone you love. The anticipation of their enjoyment makes all the difference. I'm afraid when I'm alone, I don't clean and cook as I should. Somehow everything in life is better if you share it."

Elly, who spent most of her life alone and unwanted, filled with tears. Tears of joy escaped down her cheeks. Never again would she feel completely alone. She was so grateful to at last have a family to share things with. Aunt Sarah appeared to understand.

"You'll love the others when you meet them, and I'm sure they'll love you." In such a warm atmosphere, the evening passed swiftly.

As the work was done, and dinner was being digested, the talk naturally returned to the family Elly was about to become a part of. The more Elly learned about them the nicer they seemed, and she went to bed looking forward to the next day. Still, it all seemed very strange to Elly. One day, she felt completely alone, now she found herself about to be surrounded by a large family. It was wonderful and yet she was afraid. What if she didn't fit in? What if she didn't know how to act with aunts and cousins? What if they just didn't like her?

She pulled the soft comforter up to her chin, and changing positions, tried to sleep. Her aunt promised to take her to visit her biological father's grave in the morning. Then she remembered the prayer, "Father, in heaven, I believe, help my unbelief. Give me the gift of faith." It was strange, but as Elly dosed off, she could swear she heard a response. The voice seemed to come from within her, yet it was from outside of her. What it said made no sense to her: "Perfect love casts out all fear."

She slept a deep and peaceful sleep, arising with a calm and joyful energy she hadn't felt in a long time. She started breakfast by the time her aunt arrived from Mass. She found herself looking forward to going out and seeing the town her whole family once lived in. Aunt Sarah advised Elly to dress comfortably in jeans and tennis shoes for the long walk.

The bright sunny day hid nothing and the town made no apologies for what it was. It was a working class town. Surrounded by steel factories, the middle class homes proudly displayed clothes lines and gardens, front porches, and children's bikes. Overgrown trees lined the worn cement sidewalks. Unlike the quiet places Elly always knew, this place was noisy. Summer breezes were gentle as voices trailed through the screens of each house they passed. It was the sound of fathers leaving for work, children fighting over breakfast, grandparents on the porches, sounds of teeming life which blended so beautifully, they became the symphonic background of the town. Factory whistles announced the changing of the shifts as armies of night workers shuffled wearily home. Other men, going in the opposite direction quickened their steps, as the whistle sang of their tardiness. Men with lunch pails greeted children at bus stops, as wives watched from front porches. To Elly it was a magical place.

Reaching the main street did not dampen Elly's spirit. It was not much of a street. A small market stood with a vegetable stand outside. A five and dime was just opening its doors. Two pharmacies stood on opposite corners. A two-pump gas station's warning bell rang as a car pulled up to the pump. The pizza parlor remained closed until noon. Two churches on either end of the small street stood proudly surrounded by the gravestones of their dead parishioners. The street delighted Elly. It was so simple, with no frills and no chain stores. How could mother have hated this place?

Aunt Sarah directed Elly to the right, toward the brown stone Catholic Church. She led the way through the gravestones to the back of the church. She searched the silent stones for Elly's father for a good ten minutes.

"Here it is!" Aunt Sarah exclaimed. Elly stood transfixed. A daughter standing frozen in front of the grave of the father she never knew. The flat grey stone read simply, "David Connor, beloved husband and father."

"He had another family?" Elly asked without emotion.

Aunt Sarah quickly answered Elly's question, afraid of the questions to come. "Yes, he married a nice local girl, a few years after his time in Vietnam. When he came back, he went to Louise, but she turned him away. He met you when you were a toddler, but she swore you were not his. I don't think he believed it. You look just like him, with that wispy soft, blonde hair and those almond-shaped blue eyes. You never looked like old man Wilkin, or Louise. In his heart he must have known, but I guess he decided not to tear you away from your mother."

Elly, transfixed, just sighed and shook her head. "I wish he had. I wish I could have at least met him." She felt as if she had been cheated. She had a father, a father who she could have loved. Louise blocked the love by denying the truth. Why had she cheated both Elly and her father of the chance to find love? The stone stood as if mocking her. It said nothing. It dared her to find something of the man who lay beneath it.

Looking at the headstone, Elly was stunned by the date on the stone. She suddenly felt faint, her head reeling.

Overcome with emotion, Elly whispered, "He died just this year! When did he die?"

This was the moment Sarah had been afraid of. The middle-aged woman answered softly, afraid of the response, "Four months ago, Elly. He was ill for a long time."

Aunt Sarah watched as Elly's face reddened with anger as it hit her.

Elly stared at the headstone as she responded, "She couldn't tell me about my father even though she was dying! I missed my only chance to meet him!"

Sarah put her arm around Elly and tried to comfort the visibly shaken girl. "It was her pride, Elly, she just couldn't tell you. You'll have to forgive her."

Elly's anger flared as she raised her voice. "Forgive her. I hate her! I'll never be able to forgive her. I feel nothing but hatred for her!"

Aunt Sarah reached out and grabbed both of Elly's hands. Speaking with firmness she said, "Forgiveness isn't a feeling, it's a decision. You trust what Jesus taught and decide to forgive. His Grace will bring the feelings. None of us are able to forgive on our own. Elly, you've been through a lot, but you haven't been nailed to a cross. He was. And yet, He said, 'Father forgive them, for they know not what they do.' Elly, make the decision to forgive your mother. Imitate Jesus, if you want peace in your heart. Your hatred won't hurt her, but it will destroy you. You don't need to feel that forgiveness, just decide it. Jesus will help you."

Aunt Sarah's eyes were feverish as they searched Elly's face. She was so full of confidence in Jesus. Elly needed to reach out to her Creator. Believe, Elly believe, Jesus will bring you the peace your heart desires. Reach out to Him, Aunt Sarah prayed in the silence of her heart.

Elly was confused. She trembled with fear of the unknown. Anger was all that kept her from slipping into the dark pit of depression. How could she give that anger up? Her face was pale. Who was this Jesus anyway? How could she trust someone she didn't even know? How could she ask help of someone she didn't even believe in?

Elly wanted to give her stock answer about not believing, but the words wouldn't come. Not just because she couldn't bring herself to repeat the words taught to her by the mother she now hated, but suddenly she was no longer sure she believed such words.

"Jesus," Elly stuttered. "Why would he help me now? He's never helped me before. I've been so alone, for so long. Why would I believe in Him?" Elly wept as she continued, "He's never helped me."

Aunt Sarah held the lost child and whispered, "All you need to know is that He loves you, Elly. You don't have to know a whole lot more than that Love right now. Pray with me, Elly. Let's talk to the Eternal One who loves you!"

And so Elly and her aunt prayed with their hands stretched over the grave of David Connor. And the Eternal One, who also loved David, allowed him to see the long-awaited answer to his prayers. Throughout his life, David had prayed for the daughter he was denied. In heaven, that prayer continued. Heaven and earth are separated by a thin veil. Those who have reached their eternal reward are not unaware of the struggles of those they love on earth. Love is eternal and continues. The love David Connor felt for his firstborn grew even greater. God too is a Father, a Father to both David and Elly. As a Loving Father, he rejoices in giving happiness to His children. He gave David sight and knowledge that would bring him the joy of answered prayer. It was one of the many joy-filled moments in eternity David would experience, as the Spirit of Love flowed through the communion of Saints.

Aunt Sarah said gently, "Just repeat after me."

Elly closed her eyes and they both bowed their heads. Elly repeated the words Aunt Sarah said. "Jesus, I love You. You are God and I am a sinner. Help me, Lord. My human heart cannot forgive, but I have made a decision to forgive. So, remove my stony human heart and replace it with Your Heart of Love. Give me your Heart, Jesus, for your Heart is Love and Forgiveness. With Your Heart, I could feel the forgiveness I have decided to give my mother. Replace my sinful heart with Your Sacred Heart, and I will be healed." Elly felt a warm glow as the Holy Spirit touched her. She felt as though she was being hugged.

She didn't feel the forgiveness Aunt Sarah prayed about, she simply knew it didn't matter. She sensed peace. The feeling would come when she was ready. Elly took a tiny step toward the God who never left her. It was a moment beyond words, as Elly would discover so many moments with God were. Elly didn't understand the feelings that flooded her. She felt a warmth flow though her. A profound sense of peace poured through her spirit. It was as if the Eternal God touched her. She had a strong sense of that Eternal Love, and it was an overwhelming feeling.

Suddenly, the loneliness disappeared. Elly felt a Presence. Strong and Powerful, she simply seemed to understand God's Presence had always been there. She had refused to see Him. Now, she sensed that God would always be there for her. The peace the knowledge gave Elly was beyond words.

The two women silently entered the small church. Aunt Sarah walked to the side after bowing before the altar and knelt before a statue of Mary, the mother of Jesus. Aunt Sarah lit a candle, and bowed her head in thanks to the Virgin Mary for her intercession. Mary, was given by Jesus at Calvary to be the mother of all the faithful. In that role, she acted like any earthly mother. She spoke up for her children. When her children prayed and asked for her help, she would fly to her Son. She would intercede for her children on earth. She had heard the prayer of Aunt Sarah. She had asked her Son, Jesus to help this devoted aunt reach her lost and confused niece. The Queen of Angels looked down and smiled at her devoted daughter.

Elly sat still on the long wooden pew. She truly felt she was in the presence of The Almighty. Looking at the large Crucifix which dominated the front of the ornate church interior, Elly stared. Was the man who hung on the cross two thousand years ago really God? If so, why had he died? What did He want with Elly? Looking at this suffering image of Jesus, Elly felt a strange sense of being watched. Not an unpleasant one, more of being watched over, with love. But, how could she believe in something she couldn't see? Yet she could feel Him. It occurred to Elly that she couldn't see the wind, but because she could see and feel the effects of the wind, she believed in it. Elly decided she would look for God in His works, and her own feelings. If this Jesus was the true God, she would know it.

A light tap on her shoulder aroused Elly from her pondering. Aunt Sarah was ready to go home. They still had a lot of preparation for the family's arrival tomorrow. There was a certain joy in preparing for the comfort of people you loved. Elly wanted to love these people. Most of all, she wanted them to love her. She was looking forward to meeting them.

While they worked Elly said, "Tell me more about my family."

Aunt Sarah was more than glad to talk about them. "Well there were four children, including your mother. Besides me, you have one more aunt and uncle. Your Uncle John is widowed and has two daughters, Sandy and Cynthia. Cynthia is about to have a baby. And the youngest is your Aunt Nora, who is a nun and now her name is Sister Immaculata."

Elly laughed, "It's hard to believe I have an aunt who's a nun!"

Aunt Sarah smiled. "I think you'll be surprised, she's a lot of fun."

"I'm glad to be meeting my family. It's funny but a few days ago, I really felt nervous about it. Now, I'm looking forward to it. Tell me about my father's family."

Aunt Sarah looked up. "There's not much to tell. Your father was an only child. Both his parents died around 10 years ago." Aunt Sarah paused to take the two apple pies out of the oven and set them on the counter to cool. The aroma of cinnamon filled the kitchen air. "You have a younger half sister named Joan. Both she and her mother went to Florida right after your father died. Your stepmother's family all live there now. Do you want to meet them? I could find them if I had to."

"I'd like to meet them, especially my sister. But, I don't think now is the right time. She's just lost her husband and Joan's lost a father she probably loved very much. I don't think it would be right to intrude on their grief. Maybe in a year or so, it wouldn't be right to hit them with an illegitimate daughter and sister."

Elly didn't appear upset. She said what she thought calmly and peacefully. Aunt Sarah was pleased. Elly was thoughtful and kind. She didn't just think of her own needs. She, unlike her mother, was sensitive to the needs of others.

A Blanket of Protection

And the Lord helps them and delivers them; He delivers them from the Wicked And saves them, because they take refuge in Him. And the Lord helps them and delivers them; He delivers them from the Wicked And saves them, because they take refuge in Him. (Psalm 37:40)

When Joseph awoke, he automatically reached for the warm bundle of humanity which was usually cuddled beside him. Slowly, as reality seeped in, the memory of the accident returned. Still, he arose with a sense of power. Everything was going to be all right. He was in control again.

Dressing quickly, and downing some orange juice and toast, Joseph felt great. The sun was bright as he drove to the clinic on the other side of the small, posh suburban town. Most of the people who stayed at the clinic were recuperating from cosmetic surgery or being monitored while on a starvation diet.

Joyce never needed the expensive indulgences most of the wives in this town needed. She was naturally beautiful and slim. Still, Joseph approved of the pains taken by his neighbors' wives to please their husbands. Money well spent, if you asked him.

Joseph decided to stop by the clinic on his way to the office. The elaborate gardens and fountains surrounding the clinic testified to the high cost of seeking eternal youth. Joseph chuckled, as he pulled into the clinic entrance. Dr. Simon had quite a set-up here. He must be rolling in dough, thought Joseph. A guard checked Joseph's identity and reason for visiting before he could enter the gate. With all the wealthy clients behind these stone walls, security was tight.

Joseph hoped a quick–yet concerned–fifteen minute visit would cover all his bases. As much of an inconvenience as it was, a short visit wouldn't interfere with all the work he had to do today. It was best to maintain a presence, and it was important to let all those involved know who was in control.

He was understandably upset when the front desk receptionist refused to direct him to his wife's private room. Despite his overbearing manner, the petite but stubborn woman stood her ground, and forcefully stated, "Dr. Simon left strict orders. You'll have to see him first. I'll buzz his office if you'll just have a seat."

The receptionist stood with her hand on her hip and stared at Joseph. He soon realized the receptionist wasn't going to buzz Dr. Simon's office until he took a seat. In a great display of anger he sat. Within a few minutes, he was led to the doctor's office by the receptionist. Joseph was irate. He didn't like being treated this way. The elaborately decorated clinic reminded Joseph he wasn't dealing with the tired, overworked physician, Dr. Andrews, whom he had overwhelmed last night. Dr. Simon had plenty of his own power. He carried influence in this town. Joseph would have to treat this man with more respect. His power and wealth was reflected in the rich décor of this clinic.

The plush, classic decor of Simon's office was enough to take your breath away. It was richly decorated with expensive, original art work. Classic antique furnishings were done in soothing earth tones with splashes of primary colors. Joseph was impressed. It was hard to be ostentatious with taste, but Simon accomplished it in this office. If Joseph wasn't so angry at the delay, he would have asked Simon for the name of his decorator.

Joseph's wait wasn't long as the crisply attired physician appeared promptly from a door behind his desk. Joseph immediately started an attack, "What is going on here? I insist you bring me to my wife immediately!"

Dr. Simon raised his manicured hands up to quiet Joseph's complaints, and answered, "I know you're in a rush to see Joyce. Believe me, I wouldn't disturb or delay you unless it was something extremely important."

Now, for the first time, Joseph's thoughts turned to his injured wife. Could something have happened? Did they find an injury they missed yesterday? If anything was missed, he'd sue them all. But Joseph knew how to play 'rope a dope,' as Mulhammed Ali once said–first, get all the information you needed by playing passive, allow your opponent to relax, and think he has won his point. When he least expects it, that's when you go in for the kill. With this in mind, he stilled his emotions and casually took a seat.

Sitting in the soft, leather chair in front of Dr. Simon's large mahogany desk, Joseph tried to remain calm. The doctor seemed relieved as he watched the patient's husband quiet down. Sitting behind his desk, Dr. Simon tried to defuse the emotional time bomb Joseph was. It seemed to work.

Keeping his face as empty of expression as possible, Joseph asked, "I hope there's nothing wrong. Nothing is wrong with Joyce, is there?"

Dr. Simon was glad to see Joseph speaking calmly. What he had to tell him was not going to be easy. Dr. Simon stated in a deliberately soothing voice, "Wrong is not exactly the word I would use, unexpected is more like it."

"What is it?" Joseph asked impatiently raising his voice. The doctor appeared uncomfortable.

Again in a voice serene and intentional, the well-tailored man said, "It will be a shock, but not anything we won't be able to handle. I'm more concerned about your reaction. I want you to promise to sit there and not say a word until I'm finished. If you'll do that, I'll answer any questions you may have."

Joseph was getting impatient and annoyed, and icily retorted, "Just tell me Simon, for God's sake!"

"Joyce is pregnant," Simons said.

"That's not possible," Joseph loudly interrupted.

Dr. Simon shook his head and raised his hands up to quiet Joseph. "Just hear me out. She most definitely is pregnant. And don't go jumping to conclusions. It is also highly possible that you are the father."

Anger was rising in Joseph as the thought of another man touching Joyce entered his mind. Joseph reddened with rage jumped up and shouted, "Don't be ridiculous. I've had a vasectomy done. You recommended the surgeon yourself. How could I be the father? There's only one explanation!"

"No!" The doctor's loud and commanding voice stunned and quieted Joseph. "This reaction is exactly what I was afraid of. Sit down!"

Joseph sat despite himself.

The physician, seeing Joseph sitting in stunned silence, lowered his voice and continued, "As I explained when I recommended the procedure, there is always a possibility of the vasectomy reversing itself spontaneously. There were never any guarantees. I don't want you going off half-cocked until we see if that is what happened. Let us test you. We'll have our answer by tonight. I want you to calm yourself, and say nothing to Joyce."

"You mean you haven't told her?" Joseph was incredulous.

With a commanding tone, Dr. Simon answered, "No, and neither will you. If Joyce is pregnant with your child there are still bigger problems to face. I don't want you to excite her about this pregnancy just yet."

Joseph sat in stony silence.

The doctor watched Joseph with disdain He had learned to despise the arrogance of the wealthy people he served. In this situation, he knew he had the power, and announced, "If you don't agree to keep quiet about this, I won't let you see her."

Joseph was too shocked to think. He allowed the doctor to take the lead.

Dr. Simon didn't lose the opportunity to control this volatile situation and stated, "Now go with my nurse for the test, and I'll go with you to see Joyce. Remember, you don't have any information yet. She knows nothing, so act as normal as possible." Joseph acted like a robot.

After giving his sample, he made a short visit to his wife. In a daze, he watched her as one might observe a stranger. He felt no connection to the woman before him. She seemed to sense something was wrong but mistakenly concluded it was his worry over her.

Joseph was glad to escape her presence, and leave for the city.

Driving the BMW well over the speed limit, he had some trouble seeing. The bright morning sunlight reflected off Joyce's rosary beads which were dangling off the rear view mirror. Stopping at a red light, the glare directly hit his troubled eyes. With overwhelming anger, he lowered the window. Joseph grabbed the beads and with rage threw them onto the asphalt. He watched with great satisfaction as the beads broke and the small crystals rolled like marbles all over the road. Enough is enough! Someone was going to pay. He didn't know whether it was Joyce, another man, or the doctor, but someone was going to pay for such a mistake.

Joseph found it almost impossible to concentrate on work. Every moment found him picturing Joyce with another man or worse yet, her body distorted with an advanced pregnancy. Whatever the answer was, Joseph knew one thing. This baby would never be born. Whether it was his or another man's he didn't want it. The more he thought, the angrier he became. Luckily, Joseph's large ego managed to keep his anger in check. Somehow, he couldn't imagine Joyce wanting another man. He decided this baby was more than likely his. He had Joyce under too much control for her to be having an affair.

Nothing seemed to be getting finished at the office, his mind was much too cluttered with personal problems. Joseph was glad when his secretary called and told him that Dr. Simon's office had called and wanted him to stop by the clinic for the results. Now he could get a handle on this situation. Once he had the right information, he could make the decisions necessary to return his life to normal. He could plan an effective strategy that would put him in control again.

It seemed a lifetime before he found himself in the doctor's office. Drumming his fingers on the arm of his chair, he longed to hear the right words. He wanted to know Joyce was faithful. He couldn't even think about what he would do if she had been unfaithful. He would probably have to leave her. The thought of living without Joyce sent chills down his spine. How could he live without her?

It would be hard, if not impossible. But what choice did he have? If she had been with another man, he couldn't stay with her, an unfaithful wife. The humiliation would destroy him.

"Joseph," Dr. Simon nodded as he closed his office door, "your sperm count showed just what I expected. The surgery must have reversed itself. You are most likely the father of Joyce's baby."

Joseph was relieved. The fear he was harboring over losing Joyce had overpowered his every thought. A sudden warm wave of love flowed through him. He pushed it away and quickly regained control. Looking up, he caught Simon quietly observing the conflicting emotions that played across his face.

Joseph mumbled to himself, "What will I do now? She'll want to keep the baby. She's prayed for a baby for so long."

For a minute, images of Joyce's novena and rosary flashed through Joseph's mind. Oh what nonsense, he thought, as he pushed the images from his mind.

Joseph pulled himself from his musings. He knew he had to take control before the situation was irreversible. Standing up to impose his will, he announced, "Well it doesn't matter whose it is, I don't want it. I want you to arrange an abortion as soon as possible."

Startled, Dr. Simon looked up from his desk and appeared thankful, "So, you already realize. I thought it was going to be hard to talk you into the abortion. Joyce had so many x-rays after the accident. I'm sure the baby must be affected at this developmental stage. There is no way I could guarantee a normal baby. Surely you wouldn't want to bring a baby with a birth defect into the world."

Joseph didn't know the x-rays could have caused a defect in the baby, but he caught on quickly and feigned understanding. Joyce would have an abortion and everything would fall into his lap.

Dr. Simon was relieved that Joseph seemed to understand and said, "It's going to be hard on Joyce. It'll be best if her doctor tells her. You be there for support. As a supportive husband, you'll have no trouble talking her into termination of the pregnancy. She won't agree at first, but I'm sure she'll see the logic of it in time. You can guide her toward the right decision."

Joseph was delighted. He would have no trouble controlling Joyce. He was confident he would have this fetus aborted within the next two days.

Two days later, Joseph sat in his BMW in the parking lot of the posh clinic and wondered what went wrong. When they told Joyce about the pregnancy, she was understandably excited and pleased. Joseph pretended the same. When Dr. Simon explained the horrible damage the x-rays could have done to the baby and his opinion that Joyce should have an abortion, Joseph pretended great grief. He knew how to convince Joyce, he would slowly lead her to the conclusion that it was selfish and cruel to bring a disfigured baby into the world. He pretended he was just as heart-broken as Joyce. He played on her kindness, sure he would convince her. But, it all went terribly wrong.

It wasn't difficult for Joyce to disappear. Once she realized the plans against her baby, she moved quickly. She enlisted the help of her parents and a Christian nurse. Joyce knew no believing Christian could condone abortion for any reason. Receiving help made her secret escape easy. She was gone without a trace.

She didn't have time to worry about Joseph. It was a matter of life and death for her unborn baby. She feared the abortion might be done against her will. Joseph wielded a lot of power. She wanted to get away quickly to a safe place where she would not be found. Joyce didn't even let her parents know where she was hiding. A secret is only a secret if no one knows. If known by even two people, it's no longer a secret. One person could always slip, even accidentally. This was too important a cause–her unborn baby's very life. She couldn't take any chance that Joseph would find her, and she had no illusions he would leave no stone unturned trying. Her parents were upset at first, but Joyce was firm in her resolve. It pained Joyce to see the hurt in her father's eyes.

When he held her close at their rushed meeting, he whispered, "Take care of yourself and my grandchild. And remember how much we love you."

She could feel the sobs that he tried to hold in. Her mother couldn't hide her feelings, she cried openly. Joyce knew it was going to be painful to be separated from them. She had never been apart from her parents for long. As an only daughter, she had always made sure to spend time with her parents. She shared the little things in her life, knowing how much they looked forward to her company. Now, because of Joseph's stubborn nature, she had to disappear. Joyce knew her husband. He would be relentless in his search for her. Her parents were hurt. They didn't understand why she couldn't trust them. Later, after being followed by Joseph's private detectives, they came to see the wisdom of Joyce's decision.

Despite the pain of hurting her parents, Joyce had no doubt about her decision. Surges of energy and optimism ran through her battered body. Snap decisions felt so right. She knew she was being guided by the Holy Spirit. At this most critical of times, each prayer seemed to be instantly answered. Guided by the small, still, voice she heard internally, Joyce made what appeared to be all the right moves. Angels surrounded her as she made her way to her new home. One angel cried rejoicing hymns of praise to God for protecting his beautiful charge. It was the baby's guardian angel. Every infant is assigned an angel to watch over them at the time of conception.

All of the angels present guided the young woman. Joyce felt drawn to the ocean. She always loved the Jersey shore. The steely gray power of the Atlantic filled her with a sense of the unending strength of Almighty God. Fortified with the loan her wealthy father was happy to give her, she purchased a small ranch home a few blocks from the ocean. Joseph would never look for her in such a simple, lower-middle class home. Here she could live peacefully.

She hated to leave the husband she loved so. He was so misguided. With his spirit broken by years of pain and poverty, he claimed to worship nothing. Joyce knew that to be a lie, he worshiped money, and the power money created. She forgave him his faults. Joyce understood them. But she had to protect her unborn baby. She had to trust Joseph to God. She would never divorce him. She would pray for his conversion.

A church was only a short block away. After her leg healed and the live-in nurse was no longer needed, she attended daily Mass. Each morning she took a walk on the deserted winter boardwalk. Bundled against the wind, she prayed and planned for the baby she already loved. She prayed for Joseph whom she loved. She prayed he would accept God and Truth and again become a part of her life. She loved him despite his misguided ways. He would always be her husband and the father of her child. She never doubted God would answer her prayers. But God's timing was better than man's timing. She would have to be patient. She planned a spring garden and a summer baby. Joyce found peace in trusting the Source of her strength.

Joseph found no peace. He lost control of the situation and the lack of control drove him mad. He hired the most expensive private detectives in the nation. He drove the local police up the wall with daily calls and accusations. He harassed Joyce's parents and friends relentlessly, all to no avail. Joyce had made a clean escape. He tried to sue the hospital and Dr. Simon for negligence but nothing came of it. Joyce was an adult and free to make her own choices. Joseph always knew Joyce was smart, but he never thought she would outsmart him.

On the day Joyce first felt the baby move, Joseph took his first snort of cocaine. Mixed with alcohol, it caused a blackout. He lost all memory of the time he spent in his drug-induced fog. He woke up next to a strange brunette who was destined to be the first in a string of nameless and forgotten women. The pain of losing Joyce was only dulled by drugs and drink. Under their numbing influence, Joseph began to mix with a criminal class of people.

His whole personality began to change. Joseph didn't notice the first time he decided a soiled and wrinkled jacket was fine to wear to work. He didn't notice it was three days since he shaved. Joseph's appearance and his business were ignored. Formerly terrified of not being in control, he became a true slave–to cocaine and alcohol. He lost control of his life. His friends shunned him. His business started operating in the red. The jobs his construction company contracted came in high above promised bids and behind projected deadlines. Joseph didn't notice. His only concern was where his next hit was coming from.

The sea air was good for Joyce. The pregnancy seemed to be going well. The morning sickness only lasted for a few weeks, and Joyce felt a spurt of energy that led her to long walks on the deserted winter boardwalk. There was something peaceful and calming about the closed amusement rides and stands. It was as if the world was taking a long winter nap, resting up for the laughter and excitement of summer children and suntanned beauties.

But, while the world of man slept, the world God created continued. Cold, fresh winds battered the shore, as the ocean roared approval. Nature screamed and testified that the amusements of man continued only at the whim of sky, sea, and wind. Man's buildings shook at a mild display of nature's power. Joyce found the power of nature reassuring because it reminded her of the power of God. The isolation of the boardwalk gave Joyce time to think and to pray. The walks strengthened both her body and her mind.

She prayed for Joseph and the baby. The doctor was not optimistic. She wasn't afraid. He suggested tests that would put the baby at risk. Joyce refused, after finding there wasn't anything to help the baby. The tests were just to convince her to terminate the pregnancy. She turned to Father John Burns, the local parish priest, who put her in touch with a devout Catholic doctor.

Joyce was pleased with his care and his attitude. Only Father Burns and the doctor knew the whole story of Joyce's marriage and pregnancy. Neither of them knew her real name. Joyce would not take the smallest chance with her baby's life. She knew her husband. If he found her, there was no telling what he would force her to do.

After a few months, Joyce's life settled into a peaceful routine. She volunteered to do office work a few afternoons each week in the rectory. She joined the charismatic prayer group which met each Tuesday evening and began to make some friends. The people seemed wonderful. Joyce assumed most of them thought she was a young, unwed mother. The wonder was, they never asked. They asked after her health, and they always lifted the baby and her up in prayer. They never intruded in her personal life and seemed to be almost protective about Joyce. Joyce suspected it was not the first time they met a young woman with an unexplained pregnancy. This was such a pro-life parish it probably was not unusual to have many young girls seek refuge here. No one asked Joyce about the father, and Joyce never volunteered any information.

In a pro-life parish, many of the people are committed to caring for women who reject the thought of an abortion. Some of the people donate money. Often, the people hold baby showers to insure that the young mothers have everything they need for the new baby. Some of the families are so committed to the concept of saving an unborn baby's life they take the pregnant girl into their home and even pay the medical expenses. The mother is given complete confidentiality, whether she keeps the baby or decides to give it up for adoption. Joyce didn't need any financial help, but the emotional support was gladly accepted.

She felt at home here, amongst God's people. She no longer worried about her baby not having a family. Her child would be a part of God's family. The baby would be loved and wanted among people who loved life. Joyce felt she was led to a place of hope, love, and life. This parish shone like a candle in the darkness against a world of despair, hatred, and death. Joyce was at peace.

She decorated the small, three bedroom ranch in a simple but comfortable style. Large overstuffed sofas and chairs filled the tiny rooms. Joyce liked to have her new friends over. She loved to cooked large, Italian meals for all who came. She made people feel welcome and comfortable, and t was unusual for Joyce to spend an evening alone. She spent much of her free time shopping and decorating the baby's nursery.

The nursery was lemon yellow and cool mint-green. Stuffed animals and music boxes lined the shelves of the frosted oak furnishings. Tiny pajamas and sweater sets hung in the closet. Joyce enjoyed buying for the baby because it was a testament to her faith. She only wished her parents could share the joy of preparing for their first grandchild. She missed her parents. New friends could not replace her family. At times, she was tempted to call her mother. The loneliness came in waves, washing over the isolated woman. On some nights her seclusion overwhelmed her, and Joyce cried herself to sleep. She longed to phone her parents, but resisted. She missed Joseph so much. She loved him, but knew she couldn't trust him. It was all so painful. The growing life inside her was her only comfort. She hated the solitude, but maintained it. Despite her loneliness, she knew she was doing the right thing.

The baby was going to live. She put all her trust in God. She felt His presence beside her in all she did.

Joyce worried about how Joseph was doing. She knew she had to accept that she had no control over Joseph's reaction to her disappearance. Joyce talked to the baby and prayed over the baby each day. She consecrated the baby to Jesus each morning at Mass. She felt no fear for the baby–she feared more for Joseph. Would he ever find his way? Would he ever find God and find his way home? Joyce knew God loved Joseph. But Joseph was given free will and God would never force anyone against his will. Joyce could only pray for him.

Joyce didn't have any way of knowing how much Joseph needed her prayers. His life had begun to unravel. His need for cocaine and alcohol grew daily. The cost of his drug habit was astronomical, and he started to borrow small amounts from the company. Small amounts he could pay back within a week, before anyone would notice. But the amount of money he needed grew as the amount of cocaine he used increased. Joseph started losing all of his money as his savings dwindled and his business declined. He spent most of his time high or looking for his next hit. Nothing else mattered to him as the strength of his addiction increased. He even sold the home that Joyce and he had taken such pride in. It didn't take long, just six months. A business like Joseph's was built on word of mouth. Within a few months, word of the shoddy and late work his company was turning out got around. Rumors of Joseph's drug addiction were whispered in union halls and board rooms. The company was all but lost. No one trusted Joseph.

When the dealers he used refused to extend him any more credit, he began to deal drugs. Joseph rationalized no one would ever find out. He told himself that once business picked up, he would stop dealing drugs. Joseph lied to himself, unable to face the addict he had become. All he really cared about was his next fix. He lost all pride in his himself, his business, and even in his reputation. Everyone knew the truth about Joseph. Only Joseph believed his own lies. Joseph didn't look at the truth. He blamed everything on Joyce. He told himself that when he found her everything would be all right.

As spring arrived, Joyce enjoyed starting her garden. She planted tomatoes, corn, pole beans, and zucchini. She loved the smell of earth and sun. She planted marigolds between the neatly planted rows. She surrounded her garden with fragrant flowers bursting with copper and red blossoms. Not only were they beautiful, but they kept the furry creatures away from the vegetables. Sweet corn and tomatoes grew best in Jersey's sandy soil, and Joyce loved them.

The tomato vines became weighed down with plump green tomatoes. It was while she watered the newly staked vines she felt her first labor pain. It was two weeks before her due date, so she waited. But when her water broke she knew it was time to go.

Her doctor wanted to deliver the baby in a hospital one hour north because it had a Stage Three neonatal nursery. Her baby might need special care. Joyce didn't waste time. She would do anything to help the little life inside her. Joyce's friends from the prayer group were quick to respond and Joyce was on her way with her packed suitcases within ten minutes.

The pain grew both in frequency and intensity as the car headed north. Joyce rested in the back seat while reclining on the fluffy pillows her girlfriend Pat supplied. Tom and Pat were an older couple, both retired from the telephone company. With white hair and kind faces they seemed to spend all their time helping others. Pat sat up front as her husband Tom drove. They tried to engage Joyce in conversation. It didn't help. Joyce was lonely and needed Joseph.

I miss him, she thought. *It's only natural for a father to be with his wife when his child is born.* The thought depressed her. If only it could be. Joyce felt a tear escape her eye and trickle down her cheek. *Stop it,* she thought. *Stop feeling sorry for yourself. God is with you and He gave you two good friends to comfort you.* Joyce resolved to stop thinking of things which could not be, and focus on the good things that were.

Pat held Joyce's hand in the labor room. But when the nurses wheeled Joyce to the delivery room, she was alone. Noticing all the women with their husbands, she felt herself filling up with tears again. She longed for Joseph. *Why couldn't he be like the other husbands she had watched? Why wasn't he there to hold her hand and wait anxiously for their first born? Why God, why?*

She felt terribly alone without her husband or her parents. The nurse thought she was crying because of the labor pains. The head nurse gave Joyce pain medication. It helped, making Joyce a little drowsy. She drifted off to sleep for a short time, until sharp labor ripped through her. Joyce was now in active labor and too busy giving birth to think of Joseph.

Joseph could not stop thinking of her. Numerous women fell short when compared to Joyce. Alcohol and increased amounts of cocaine could not dull the pain of his loss. Where was she? He couldn't find her no matter how he tried. The money was all but gone. Joseph moved to a tiny studio apartment in a questionable neighborhood. He ignored any friendly overtures from his new neighbors. He felt they were beneath him.

One morning he woke up with a long-haired blonde. With her back turned to him, he momentarily thought she was Joyce. His spirit crashed when he realized he didn't even know the woman's name. His life was spiraling out of control and he was losing all hope. He knew Joyce could help him. But all she cared about was that damn baby. He called the private detectives, but they refused to take his call. The bastards! Kick a man when he's down! He hadn't paid them in two months.

Joseph scraped the line of cocaine with a razor on the small mirror he kept on the chipped kitchen table. Taking a rolled-up dollar bill, he snorted what would turn out to be his last hit. As the drug flooded his spirit and mind, the pain lessened.

The sudden pounding on the apartment door startled him. The police yelled and asked him to open the door. He froze in fear, unable to move. When the front door was broken down, he just sat in shock with the evidence of his recent hit in plain sight.

A loud, tall cop pulled him from his seat. Spinning Joseph around and slamming him against the wall, he started to read Joseph his rights, "You have the right to remain silent, if you chose to speak, anything you say can be held against you…"

Joseph didn't listen. He didn't care. He was only concerned with his cocaine. Joseph was upset that the other cop was bagging up his cocaine. Where was he going to get his next hit? This high is sure to wear off soon, thought the lost man.

As the tall cop slapped the handcuffs on Joseph, he remained in a stupor. He was so coked-up he was unable to think clearly. Why is this happening to me? Where are they taking my coke? Joseph's head was spinning, full of senseless thoughts. He couldn't do anything to save himself. He had long ago stopped caring about himself. Someone still loved Joseph. God had intervened in his self-destructive life.

Joyce's worries about Joseph faded, as she concentrated on the birth of her child. The pain was overwhelming, and she felt as if she were drowning in it. Losing all track of time and day, she listened to the directions of her doctor.

Dr. Gadick commanded, "Push! Push!"

Joyce obeyed despite the pain.

The doctor was excited as he stated, "I see the head now, just one more push."

Joyce heard everything he said despite the delivery room noise. The machines whirled and the nurses moved instruments and equipment around the room. Another nurse arrived with an isolette for the newborn. The background noise was tremendous, yet Joyce remained focused on her physician.

His deep masculine voice announced, “Here’s the baby!” Suddenly the room fell silent. The newborn cried. But no one in the room made any comment. All eyes momentarily appeared mesmerized by the infant. Suddenly the special care nurse took the baby and, after a few measurements and assessments, wrapped her tightly in a bunting blanket.

No one said a word as the nurse handed the newborn girl to her mother.

Joyce immediately fell in love with the tiny, fine featured girl. Joyce, unlike the others in the room, looked at this gift from God, and saw only what the child had. The baby’s eyes strained to open with curiosity. The sweet disposition shone even at this early age. The thick dark hair shimmered in the delivery room light. Joyce, who exulted in all the baby had, wasn’t stupid. She realized right away what was missing. It just didn’t matter. She thanked God for what was given. The doctor and the nurses looked at the infant and saw she had no arms. Joyce looked at the infant and knew she was a gift, a sign of God’s pure love. Angels in the room knew that The Father gave special babies only to special mothers. Special Mothers who were capable of the unique love handicapped children required.

Washed in His Blood

Hic Calix Novum Testamentum Est In Meo Sanguine
[This Chalice is the New Testament In My Blood] (1 Cor:11-25)

The first joyful arrival was Sister Immaculata. Elly was shocked by how beautiful she was. Elly's first thought was why would such a beautiful woman give up her life and become a nun? It was a question she would later be ashamed of. It didn't take long for Elly to realize her young aunt had done anything but given up life, but instead had plunged into it. Sister Immaculata, or Nora as her family still called her, was so full of joy she infected all around her.

Even though she was just ten years older than Elly, she asked Elly to call her Aunt Nora. The cheerful nun gave her niece a hug and said, "After all, you're family!" A hug confirmed her acceptance of her grateful niece.

She was glad to appease Elly's curiosity and explained about her order and her devotion to it. It was a Franciscan community, devoted to following the teaching of St. Francis of Assisi. One of those teachings was a vow of personal poverty. Another was to care for any one who was in need. They were especially devoted to care of the poor. Their habits were simple Franciscan gray. Since Elly knew nothing about St. Francis her aunt offered to send her a book on his life. The community in which she lived was set up for the care of poor children–both foster and orphaned. Sister Immaculata kept both Elly and Aunt Sarah in stitches over the simple antics of the children.

It was in this state of laughter Uncle John and his two daughters found them. John, tall and bald, was the only brother of the family. He was a middle child, born between the twins, Louise and Sarah, and the youngest, Nora. He was a quiet man who had grown up in a house dominated by women. To his delight and exasperation, he continued his life with the female sex, by having two daughters. It was a point of constant teasing for the family.

"Oh no! It's started already!" he exclaimed as he entered through the kitchen door. His two blonde daughters, Sandy and Cynthia, followed him into the kitchen. Sandy was the single one, out-spoken, small and petite. Cynthia was married, tall, and very pregnant.

Sandy laughed, "It's always the same. Now he'll go hide behind his paper and pipe."

Uncle John walked over to Elly and gave her a bear hug. "Not until I meet my niece." Elly was fascinated. Uncle John put both his large hands on Elly's shoulders and took a step back. Taking a good look at her, he smiled and in a deep, masculine voice stated, "Welcome to the family! Don't let them give you the wrong idea. I love them, but it's not easy to grow up with three sisters, and then have two daughters. A man needs some peace and quiet!"

Everyone laughed as John hightailed it to the living room.

Cynthia spoke up, "Don't let him fool you, he'll hear every word we say."

She slumped awkwardly into a chair, and with weariness announced, "I think he's praying for a boy."

"When is your baby due?" asked Elly.

Cynthia smiled at her new-found cousin, "Another month, I can't wait."

The laughter and light-hearted batter continued throughout dinner and late into the evening. Elly was delighted with the food and the company. She was thrilled to find her family so interesting.

Early the next morning Sandy knocked on Elly's door and said through the door, "Wake up, sleepyhead, time for Mass."

Elly was startled. She had never been to a Mass. She decided to go, glad that her new family had included her. The ride in Uncle John's van was comfortable, and she recognized the brownstone church she had visited with her aunt.

Elly was fascinated by the Mass. Everyone stood up as the priest walked from the back of the church to the altar. Before him had come an altar boy, singing a song Elly never heard before. He was holding a staff topped by the crucifix high above his head. The priest followed lustfully singing with the congregation. Following the priest, a lay person carried a gold covered bible above his head, displaying respect for the scriptures. Two small altar boys struggled slightly as they carried heavy candles in large golden holders. It was a simple, yet profound procession.

After they reached the altar, the priest started with the sign of the cross and said, "In the name of the Father, and of the Son, and of The Holy Spirit."

The assembly responded, "Amen."

The priest blessed the people by saying, "The grace of Our Lord Jesus Christ and the love of God and the fellowship of The Holy Spirit be with you all."

The people answered, 'and also with you.' The priest then asked the people to bow their heads and be mindful of their sinfulness and the mercy of God.

After a few minutes of silence, all the people prayed, 'I confess to Almighty God and to you my brothers and sisters, that I have sinned through my own fault, in my thoughts and in my words, in what I have done, and in what I have failed to do. And I ask blessed Mary, ever virgin, all the angels and saints, and you, my brothers and sisters, to pray for me for the Lord Our God.'

The Lector announced, 'Lord have Mercy, Christ have mercy, Lord have mercy,' with the people repeating each phrase.

The priest prayed. 'May Almighty God have mercy on us, forgive us our sins and bring us to everlasting life.'

In loud and glorious voices, the choir sang, "Glory to God in the Highest and peace to his people on earth. Lord, God, Heavenly King, Almighty God and Father, we worship You, we give You thanks, we praise You for Your Glory."

Elly was overwhelmed. The movements, the words, and the atmosphere, all spoke of the unity of the people in their praise of Jesus Christ. The beauty of it left her speechless.

The congregation was not speechless. It turned its attention to the reading of the Bible. The lector stood up at the podium and read from the Bible out loud, "Thus says the Lord God: I myself will look after and tend my sheep. As a shepherd tends his flock when he finds himself among his scattered sheep, so will I tend my sheep. I will rescue them from every place where they were scattered when it was cloudy and dark. I will lead them out from among the peoples and gather them from the foreign lands; I will bring them back to their own country and pasture them upon the mountains of Israel (In the land's ravines and all its inhabited places). In good pastures I will pasture them; and on the mountain heights of Israel shall be their grazing ground. There they shall lie down on good grazing ground, and in rich pastures shall they be pastured on the mountains of Israel. I myself will pasture my sheep; I myself will give them rest, says the Lord God. The lost I will seek out, the strayed I will bring back, the injured I will bind up, the sick I will heal, but the sleek and strong I will destroy, shepherding them rightly."

Elly had never heard such beautiful words. She had never thought of Jesus as a shepherd. It made him seem so gentle and caring. *Was she one of his lost sheep?* she pondered. *Was Jesus looking for her, wanting to heal her of her pain and loneliness?* She had never thought of Jesus this way. Elly always thought of God as a Judge. Someone she should be fear. This reading presented God as a loving and caring Creator. For Elly, it was a new way of seeing God.

After more song and prayer, the lector rose to the podium again and read: "The love of God has been poured out in our hearts through The Holy Spirit who has been given to us. At the appointed time, when we were still powerless, Christ died for us godless men. It is rare that anyone should lay down his life for a just man, though it is barely possible that for a good man someone may have the courage to die; It is precisely in this that God proves his love for us; that while we were still sinners, Christ died for us. Now that we have been justified by his blood, it is all the more certain that we shall be saved by him from God's wrath. For if, when we were God's enemies, we were reconciled to him by the death of his Son, it is all the more certain that we who have been reconciled will be saved by his life. Not only that; we go so far as to make God our boost through our Lord Jesus Christ, through whom we have now received reconciliation.'

Elly pondered the meaning of these words, as the entire congregation stood. She rose too, realizing something important was taking place. As all people stand in respect for the national anthem, everyone stood for the reading of the gospel.

The priest rose to the pulpit and read, "Jesus addressed this parable to the Pharisees and the scribes. Who among you if he has a hundred sheep and loses one of them, does not leave the ninety-nine in the wasteland and follow the lost one until he finds it? And when he finds it, he puts it on his shoulders in jubilation. Once arrived home, he invites friends and neighbors in and says to them, Rejoice with me for I have found my lost sheep. I tell you, there will likewise be more joy in heaven over one repentant sinner than over ninety-nine righteous people who have no need to repent."

Elly was spellbound the words she had just heard. She sat with the rest of the congregation as the priest started to explain the gospel in his homily. Words of the tender compassion of Jesus flowed over her, overwhelming her senses – until she felt herself being lifted and loved by a God who was looking and calling for her. Elly never had the love of an earthly father. All her life she longed for paternal love. Ignored and neglected as a child, she felt she was unlovable. Now, feeling she was loved by her heavenly Father filled her with hope. She wanted to run to the arms of this Eternal Father who waited and longed for her. She finally felt the love of a Father. For Elly the emotion was so exhilarating tears began to form. She quickly dashed them away, not wanting to embarrass her family.

She steadied herself, realizing the Mass was not over. It simply moved from the proclamation of the gospel to the celebration of the Eucharist. The Eucharist is communion, the receiving of Christ's Body and Blood in the form of bread and wine. Elly listened as the priest repeated the words of Jesus at the Last Supper. It was so beautiful. The rituals were so unique, transporting Elly's mind and heart upward to thoughts of heaven. After the priest was done speaking, the people rose and repeated a prayer of faith.

Elly didn't know the words, but she listened carefully as the entire congregation prayed. "We believe in one God, the Father, the Almighty, maker of heaven and earth, of all that is seen and unseen. We believe in one Lord, Jesus Christ, the only son of God, eternally begotten of the Father. God from God, Light from Light, True God from True God. Begotten, not made, one in being with the Father. Through Him all thing were made. For us men, and for our salvation he came down from heaven."

Elly watched as the congregation bowed and continued praying out loud. "By the power of the Holy Spirit he was born of the Virgin Mary Catherine and became Man."

Standing straight again, the priest and the people continued. "For our sake he was crucified under Pontius Pilate, he suffered, died and was buried. On the third day he rose again in fulfillment of the Scriptures, he ascended into heaven and is seated at the right hand of the Father. He will come in glory to judge the living and the dead, and his kingdom will have no end. We believe in The Holy Spirit, the Lord, the giver of life, who proceeds from the Father and the Son. With the Father and the Son , he is worshiped and glorified. He has spoken through the prophets. We believe in one Holy, Catholic and apostolic church. We acknowledge one baptism for the forgiveness of sins. We look forward to the resurrection of the dead, and the life of the world to come. Amen."

Although Elly didn't understand the entire meaning of the

prayer, she was struck by the unifying affirmation of what these people believed.

Prayer continued as the lector rose and prayed for the bishop and the local parish. She prayed for the individual members of the parish, from infants to the elderly, the sick and the needy, and with each prayer the people responded. It gave Elly a powerful sense of the magnitude of the universal church, and the intimacy of the parish and its individual members.

Elly watched as bread and wine was brought up to the altar. Kneeling, the people bowed their heads and listened to the words of the priest. Elly knew she was in the actual presence of Jesus Christ. The priest blessed the people and asked them to lift their hearts to the Lord. The people proclaimed it right to give Him thanks and praise. Elly felt her heart lift as she heard the entire congregation sing, 'Holy, Holy, Holy Lord, God of Power and Light. Heaven and earth are full of your glory. Hosanna in the highest. Blest is he who comes in the name of the Lord. Hosanna in the Highest.'

Again Elly knelt with the people and bowed her head.

The priest said, "Let us proclaim the mystery of faith."

The congregation answered, "When we eat this bread and drink this cup, we proclaim your death, Lord Jesus, until you come in glory."

The priest concluded the Eucharistic prayer, 'through Him, with Him, in Him, in the unity of The Holy Spirit, all glory and honor is yours, almighty Father, forever, and ever Amen.'

Elly's heart beat quickly as the people all took each others hands and prayed the Lord's Prayer. The priest then broke the bread, preparing for communion as the congregation sang, 'Lamb of God, you take away the sin of the world grant us peace.'

Elly had heard Catholics believed the priest, through the Power of The Holy Spirit, actually turned the bread and wine into the body and blood of Christ. Awestruck and full of tears, she now knew it to be true. And why not, if the great God who created the universe humbled himself to become a baby and died to save mankind, thought

Elly, Why wouldn't he humble himself to feed the people he so loved? He promised to be with them. In the Eucharist, He sustained them by spiritually and physically becoming a part of them.

Elly knew, by the peace-filled faces of those returning from communion they had received the true Christ. She longed to receive him. She was so hungry for Him, now as she knelt in His presence, the longing was stronger and deeper than any physical hunger she ever felt. She envied those who could make Him part of themselves. She knew she had to do anything to be worthy.

How could I be worthy with all the sin in my life? Elly wondered. She would have to talk to her Aunt Nora about it. She doubted anyone who did so many bad things could ever be forgiven and accepted. But, she was afraid to tell her Aunt about herself. As the communion ended and the priest blessed the assembly, it was as if The Holy Spirit was answering Elly's question. The choir started singing the most beautiful song Elly had ever heard. The words of the song washed over Elly's heart and a sense of profound peace flowed over her as the choir sang.

'There is welcome for the sinner, and more graces for the good,
There is mercy with the Savior, There is healing in His Blood'.

Elly, who had so far managed to control her feelings, now broke down weeping. Aunt Nora held her and whispered comfort. As the tears subsided, Nora waved the rest of the family home, saying, "Elly and I will walk home. Maybe we'll stop for breakfast." And so the Lord started Elly's long journey home.

Elly and her new-found aunt walked arm in arm out of the church and toward the center of town. Aunt Nora led her to the town's only diner. It wasn't one of those diners which were redone with brick and chandeliers and linen tablecloths. It was a true diner, like the ones back home in New Jersey, without pretensions of being anything else. The walls were lined with stainless steel in a diamond pattern. Shaped like a railroad car, it looked like it could be pulled to any corner.

The only break in the stainless steel lining was the bright red stools and booths. The matching linoleum was worn from the shoes of many a scurrying waitress. Like the diner itself, the food was simple, plentiful, and just plain good. With coffee and a large breakfast before her, Elly felt comfortable enough to talk.

She would never forget the morning she spent with her Aunt Nora. She and the nun spent hours in the diner talking over coffee, long after the breakfast dishes had been taken away. Aunt Nora listened intently, as Elly poured out her heart. She didn't judge, she didn't advise, but with a well trained ear, she guided Elly to full recognition of her own feelings. She repeated back important points to Elly for focus and verification. She validated Elly's right to her own feelings. In the end, the energetic nun said very little, but Elly felt the burden of secrecy lift off her shoulders.

"Well Elly," said Aunt Nora as she sipped a coffee that had just been reheated for the second time. "You seem to know what you have to do and what you want to do."

Elly sat back and sighed. "Yes, it's really funny, but for the first time in my life, I really do. I want to get right with God. I want to be a member of the Church. I just don't know where to begin."

Aunt Nora smiled and said, "Well! I can help you there. It's really very simple. You go talk to a priest and join the parish RCIA program. RCIA is short for the Right of Christian Initiation for Adults. It is a teaching program, so you can learn the faith. It's easy if you want, I can call your pastor and make an appointment for you."

Elly reddened, and answered, "You make it sound so easy, but I've just told you what a life I've led and the things I've done. My pastor won't want me."

Aunt Nora reached across the booth tabletop and took Elly hand in her own. She softly said, "Your pastor represents Jesus. And Jesus wants you back. Who do you think has been calling you? He'll not only forgive you, He'll run to embrace you."

Elly smiled. She felt relaxed and sure of herself with her Aunt Nora. They walked home in high spirits.

The following week was one of great delight. With her burden lifted she enjoyed the simple joys of family life. Elly and Aunt Sarah prepared again for a weekend visit from her uncle and cousins. Aunt Nora took the entire week off and joined in the plans.

Amid all the laughter and fun the week seemed to fly by. Uncle John and his daughters arrived Friday night and only added to the fun. Saturday they took a ride to Pittsburgh.

Pittsburgh sits on the point where the Ohio, Allegheny, and Monongahela Rivers meet to form what is known as the three river area. Uncle John had made reservations for a river boat ride on the Gateway Clipper. They parked his van at the pier of Station Square. The lights of the city glowed brightly and reflected in the choppy river water. The riverboat was having a dinner dance known as the Big Band Cruise. Dinner was served on the boat as it churned up the Ohio River and the lights of the city glowed against the star-filled sky. It was delightful. A band played music as Aunt Sarah showed off her dancing skills. Elly danced with her Uncle. Everyone had a great time, and laughter filled the ride home. Elly went to bed happy and content.

When she heard the knock on her door, Elly, confused and groggy, assumed she was being woken up for Mass. Sandy's voice was urgent. Fumbling and reaching for her robe, Elly looked at her clock and realized it was three-thirty in the morning.

"What's wrong?" Elly asked.

Sandy gave a nervous laugh and said, "Nothing sleepyhead, it's just that my sister is about to give birth!" Elly sprang from her bed to the door.

The small blonde giggled, "You're more nervous than my father, the eternal worry wart! I'm getting everything packed and ready for Cynthia. If you what to come to the hospital you can, just get dressed."

"Oh, I want to come all right," responded Elly, as she sprinted to the closet for clothes. "I wouldn't miss this for anything."

Elly made a sour face at the pungent sip of her third cup of vending machine coffee and frowned. "This has to be the worse tasting swill, ever!" The whole family nodded in agreement.

They were waiting for what seemed like an eternity, but it had only been two hours. Cynthia's husband arrived. Despite his look of a calm, well dressed executive, the chief financial officer of a large company was clearly unnerved by the expected role of fatherhood. The couple had decided months ago that he was too squeamish to be in the delivery room. No one, however, appeared as jumpy as Uncle John, who wouldn't sit down and paced the floor in excited expectation. When the doctor came to announce the arrival of a healthy new baby boy into the world, no one could be more pleased.

The new grandfather started to weep and sighed, "If only your mother was alive to see him."

Sandy tried to comfort her widowed father and said, "She's here, I can feel her presence."

While Cynthia's husband went to join his wife, the rest of the family went to the nursery window.

"There he is!" gloated Uncle John. "I'd recognize him anywhere."

Sandy smiled at her father, "The fact that he's the only boy there wouldn't have anything to do with that, would it?"

Elly laughed along with Aunt Nora and Sarah when she looked at the nursery through the large single pane window. It contained only three babies, two in pink and one in blue. Besides, the obvious large card on the head of the glass bassinet announced the baby boy's last name.

"Oh, look at those eyes, Sandy!" Uncle John's own eyes moistened with emotion. "Those are your mother's eyes."

Tears rolled down his face as he fell in love with his new grandson. Sandy, who seemed to be enjoying every aspect of her nephew's advent, giggled and announced, "He also has his father's straight, dark hair."

Elly was amazed a child could display so much of the mixture of his parents, right from the beginning. Each baby was so unique. She felt a strange tug at her heart.

Aunt Sarah said, "Look at him, he's the first of a whole new generation in this family."

Instantly, Elly thought, 'No, he's not the first, there was another baby, a baby who never got the chance to be born.' Elly took a deep breath to steady her nerves. Aunt Nora picked up on Elly's feelings, and carefully watched her niece. She placed an arm of comfort and support around her. Elly witnessed her family welcome this small stranger into the world with great love. He already belonged. It would have been so different for her baby. No one would have wanted him. He was rejected and unwanted by his family from the beginning. And unloved and unwanted he remained as his small life was snuffed out.

Elly was just now beginning to realize the true scope of the tragedy. Her baby was unique, one of a kind. No baby would ever be the same. She felt a twinge of envy for this baby surrounded by so much love. She longed to hold her own baby. Elly walked away from the happy group. She didn't want to dampen their joy.

A Gift from the Cross

The Lord who gives sight to the blind
Who raises up those who are bowed down,
The Lord, who protects the stranger
And upholds the widow and orphan
(Psalm 146:8-9)

Sister Immaculata rubbed her forehead in exasperation. Only two weeks since her delightful vacation with her family and here she was back at work facing the most difficult part of her job. The most joyful part of her job at Blessed Trinity was finding a couple willing to adopt a child. It was not so joyful when the adoption split up siblings in a family. This was a unique adoption. The family's willingness to take both of the brothers was truly a blessing. It was challenging, if not impossible, to find a couple willing to adopt two children at once. It was a miracle to find a couple who would adopt two older children.

This couple was special. The boys would be loved and raised in a fine, middle class neighborhood. She didn't have a hard time talking the devout couple into adopting both of the boys. With three girls of their own, the couple seemed unable to decide between the two brothers.

Sister Immaculata was pleased that the two boys would always have each other. She knew she had made the right decision. The kind nun decided the O'Rourke brothers would be much better off adopted into the loving couple's home. A normal home, with loving parents was always the best way to raise children. The authorities had searched for the boy's father for six months without success. Without their father the children became wards of the state. This made all the O'Rourke children eligible for adoption.

If only the family had been willing to make room for the girl. 'Ah, well,' Sister Immaculata supposed, 'that would be too much to ask for.' It was going to be so hard to tell Mary Catherine. The O'Rourke children had adjusted to their life at Blessed Trinity. They were very close to each other. Mary Catherine even learned to love her baby brother, Thomas, and she spent all of her free time with her three younger brothers.

The nun picked up the phone on her desk and said, "Please, send Mary Catherine O'Rourke to the chapel. I'll meet her there."

Sister Immaculata knew there was no easy way to do this, but being in the chapel meant being closer to Jesus. Jesus was present in the tabernacle in the guise of bread. In this his consecrated Eucharistic form, Jesus would be bodily present and close. That closeness could only help.

When she received the summons, Mary Catherine was glad to get out of English class. She loved math, but the mystery of English grammar stymied her. Math was basic and clean. It had rules that were absolute. Once you knew the rules, they never changed. Mary Catherine wished all her other subjects were the same, if they were, she might even like school.

She wasn't afraid that she did something wrong. Mary Catherine felt like Blessed Trinity was home, and she was very comfortable here. She knew her brothers were being well treated, and she felt the pressure of their happiness was not on her shoulders alone.

Sister Immaculata, who awaited Mary Catherine's arrival at the small chapel, was on her knees silently praying, 'Oh Holy Spirit, give me the words to help Mary Catherine. Give me the wisdom to say the right thing. She's too small to have so much to deal with. Guide me.'

Sister Immaculata was so deep in prayer she didn't hear the small girl arrive.

Mary Catherine sat quietly by the nun as she prayed. She figured that it wasn't good to bother nuns when they were talking to their boss. Besides, it was peaceful here, with no sentences to diagram. The chapel was small, but ornately decorated with carved wooden panels lining both the walls and the ceiling. The plush red carpeting stood out. Numerous statues painted in colorful fashion glowed in the reflected light of the many votive candles. Sister was finally aroused by the stirring of the child next to her.

Looking down, she realized the child beside her was the subject of her prayers. Sister reached out to the girl and said, "Hello, Mary Catherine. I'm sorry, I didn't hear you arrive."

Mary Catherine smiled, and replied, "That's okay Sister, my teacher said you wanted to talk with me?"

Sister's heart broke as she looked at the small girl trying to act so mature. She had shouldered quite a lot of responsibility since her mother died. Sister Immaculata read all the reports from Sister Clements. She was impressed by the courage the young girl displayed. She hoped the courage she had clearly demonstrated then, would guide her now.

The nun moved closer and softly placed her arms around the child, drawing her near, and said, "Let me tell you a story. Once there was a family of orphans, they were very close because they had no one but themselves to care for each other. They had no mother or father, so the oldest girl kept them together and cared for the three younger brothers. She protected them and watched out for them. She did a very good job, but no matter how much she tried, she couldn't become her brothers' parent. Little boys need parents, don't you think?"

Mary Catherine didn't know what Sister was getting at, but she didn't like it. She was starting to get a nauseous feeling in the pit of her stomach. "Yes, I mean, I guess all children should have parents. But, some just don't, right Sister?"

The nun wished she could hold this young girl and protect her from the hurt and pain that was sure to tear her apart. 'Why does life have to be so hard? Some people just seem to suffer so much more then others,' the pretty nun's forehead wrinkled with the burden she was carrying. It was so painful to hurt a child. Yet there was nothing else she could do. She had to think of the two small O'Rourke brothers. They deserved a chance for a normal childhood. If only Mary Catherine could have a happy childhood. If only she could have parents to care for her. It seemed that no one wanted an older child.

Sister Immaculata looked at the girl who was starting to tremble. "Yes, some children lose their parents and become orphans. Sometimes they come to orphanages just like this one, and they stay here until they grow up. You like it here Mary Catherine, don't you?" Sister studied the girl for a clue to her feelings, and read the fear in her face.

Mary Catherine wouldn't look at the nun, "Yes, Sister, I like it here swell, and my brothers seem okay too. I guess we'll just stay here until we grow up."

The determination of Mary Catherine's resolve worried the nun. Sister could feel the thin shoulder of the child stiffen in stubbornness.

Sister Immaculata said with kindness, "It's all right to grow up here, but don't you think it would be best to grow up in a nice home with two parents who want and love you."

Mary Catherine didn't like the way this conversation was going. She had just gotten used to her new life at Blessed Trinity. She didn't want anything to change now. She couldn't understand what Sister Immaculata was getting at, but a deep fear was rising up, telling her she really didn't want to know.

Sister Immaculata felt like crying. This girl had been through so much. She had lost her mother and had been abandoned by her father. She hated to hurt her further. The longer I drag it out, the worse it will be, thought the nun. She decided to get to the point and asked, "Suppose I told you there was a nice family who want to adopt your two brothers Danny and Johnny. How would you feel about that?"

All the blood drained from Mary Catherine's face 'Was this nun kidding? No one was going to take her brothers from her,' Mary Catherine's mind screamed but her voice whispered, "What about Thomas and me? Will we be adopted by the same family?"

Sister watched as Mary Catherine's eyes widened in terror.

Talking as calmly as she could, the nun responded, "No, they just have room in their family for the two boys. It's wonderful that they want to adopt both of them. Most families only adopt one child. It's really lucky if we can keep the two boys together. They'll always have each other, and they won't be alone."

Mary Catherine was horrified! She couldn't comprehend what Sister was saying.

"No, no!" she pulled away from the nun, "You can't take my brothers away from me! I can't let them go, I promised my mother!"

The child was becoming overwhelmed. Sister pulled her closer.

Sister Immaculata was upset – she had never seen a child so distraught. "Mary Catherine, I know how you feel. You think being together is the best for your family. But, I want you to think and pray about it."

Mary Catherine burst into tears. "I don't have to think about it. I don't want to be alone. I have no mother. I only have my brothers! If you take them away I'll have nobody!"

The girl laid her head on the pew and sobbed loudly. Sister stroked Mary Catherine's hair, and knowing the basic goodness of the human heart, took a gamble.

Sister Immaculata looked with tenderness at the small girl. She knew she could trust in this girl's heart. In a trusting confident voice Sister said, "Mary Catherine, don't be afraid! I'm going to let you decide, I won't let your brothers be adopted unless you give me permission."

Mary Catherine was stunned. She never had control over her life. Now this nun was giving her total control over the situation. Shc couldn't believe it. She figured it had to be a trick.

Looking at the nun with a skeptical expression Mary Catherine asked, "Are you saying that if I say the boys can't go to this new home they'll have to stay here?"

The nun looked into the distrustful face and answered, "Yes, that's what I'm saying. If you tell me that you think it's best for the boys to stay here instead of having a real family, I will do what you say."

Mary Catherine figured this had to be some sort of trick. Grownups were really good at tricking children. She decided it was best not to give an answer right away.

Mary Catherine asked again. She didn't want the nun to be able to deny what she was saying, "Are you sure, Sister? I make the final decision about Johnny and Danny?"

The nun, reading the emotions that passed across Mary Catherine's face, repeated, "Yes Mary Catherine, all I ask is that you take the time to really think about it. I want you to pray and decide what is best for your brothers."

Mary Catherine already knew what her answer was, but she decided it wouldn't look too good to make up her mind so fast.

"So," asked the nun, "How will you make up your mind?"

'Oh no, here's the trick,' thought Mary Catherine as she asked, "I don't know, whenever I had a really big decision to make, I always asked my mother. But now, I don't have any mother. I have no one to ask for advice."

Sister Immaculata smiled as she answered, "You do have a mother to talk to, and she'll help you make up your mind."

Mary Catherine figured the nun was losing it.

She explained to the nun, "My mother's dead, Sister. I can't ask her what to do. I don't have anyone." The girl looked forlorn and was starting to cry again.

"Come with me." Sister Immaculata said as she took the girl's hand in hers, and led her to the front of the chapel. She took her by the shoulders and directed Mary Catherine to stand in front of the statue of Our Lady of Grace and stated, "This is your mother. You can ask her."

Mary Catherine was confused, what was the nun saying?

Looking at the statue, she said in exasperation, "This isn't my mother. This is a statue of Jesus' mother, Mary. She's God's mother, not mine."

The nun smiled at the young girl's impatience, and stated with confidence, "Oh, but that's where you're wrong. Jesus gave her to you. She's your mother and she wants you to come to her and tell her your problems, and she never, ever fails to help you. Just like a real mother Mary waits for us to ask for what we need and when we ask her, she hurries to her Son's side to present the prayers of her children to her Son. Jesus loves his mother so much that if what she asks for is within His Will, He won't turn her down."

Sister took the lonely child on her lap and explained to her that when Jesus was dying on the Cross, He gave his mother to the church and all the children of the world to be their mother. Mary Catherine was amazed by the thought that Jesus gave His mother to her. She needed a mother so bad.

Mary Catherine was intrigued, but didn't think the mother of Jesus would want to help her, "But, I don't know her. I don't know my prayers so good. I don't know what prayers to say."

Sister Immaculata smiled at Mary Catherine's humility and told her, "You don't need to know any special prayers. She likes it when you just talk to her. That way, she knows you trust her as your mother. Just talk to her like you would talk to your own mother. She always answers you."

The practical child looked puzzled and said, "But, if she is the mother of everybody, she won't have time for me."

The nun grinned, "Oh, she will always have time for you. She likes to help children who have no earthly mother the best. You know that the Pope was an orphan like you and she became his special mother."

Mary Catherine was astonished. "You mean the Pope talks to her and she answers him?"

"Yes," the nun responded, "she has since he was a little boy, after his mother died. She'll help you if you talk to her."

Ever practical, Mary Catherine asked, "But how will she answer me? This is just a statue of her, like a picture of my dead mother. It can't answer or move. How will I hear her?"

The nun put her arm around Mary Catherine and whispered, "She'll whisper the answer in your heart. Stay here as long as you need too. She'll let you know what is right."

Sister Immaculata left Mary Catherine in front of the statue of Mary. The nun had complete trust in the Mother of God.

Mary Catherine rubbed her eyes and took some deep gulps of air. She knew she had to steady herself. She felt so alone. Looking up, she watched the flickering lights of the candles dance with the shadows. The statue of Mary, the mother of Jesus, was about five foot tall and stood on a pedestal about two feet high. An iron rack that held rows of votive candle were placed before the statue. On the left side of the chapel, in the first wooden pew before the statue, Mary Catherine sat. So small, the girl was eye level with the feet of the statue. Two cherub-like angels peeked out from behind the Blessed Mother's robe. The Blessed mother had no shoes on. Barefooted, the statue of Mary Catherine stood on a globe of the world. Across that globe lay a long winding snake. The Blessed Mother was crushing the snake with her bare foot.

'Oh, God's mother must have been brave.' Mary Catherine hated snakes. She couldn't imagine stepping on one with her shoes on, never mind barefoot. Looking up, she caught her breath at the sight of the beautifully peaceful face on the statue. It smiled sadly at her. The arms of the Lady were held out, just like her real mother used to hold her arms out when she wanted a hug from her only daughter. The face of the Blessed mother was full of love. Mary Catherine started with a simple "hello." She began to talk, telling her heavenly mother about her problems. The Blessed Virgin didn't interrupt, she just listened. The desolate orphan poured her heart out to her newfound friend.

Mary Catherine was in the chapel for hours, sometimes in animated talk and sometimes in extended silence. The Sisters, who came and went, were worried about the child and immediately went to Sister Immaculata's office to report the scene. Sister Immaculata wasn't worried about Mary Catherine. It was what she hoped for. Mary Catherine had found her mother. She knew everything would be all right now.

Sister Immaculata wasn't surprised when she heard the gentle knock on her office door just a few hours later. The child seemed exhausted. She had been wrestling with angels. Sister immediately took the child on her lap. Mary Catherine sighed, and laid her head on the nun's shoulder.

"How are you?" the nun softly whispered.

"Okay, I guess." Mary Catherine remained silent for a few minutes and then said, "I guess I know what the right thing to do is. It isn't going to be easy."

The nun tightened her grip on the girl. "The right thing seldom is."

Mary Catherine looked up at the face of the nun said with resolve, "The boys should have a mother and a father. They should have a home and a family. I told God's mother that she didn't understand. I told her that what she was asking me to do was just too hard. She just kept smiling. I got so mad, I want to hit her. But, she was so nice. She listened to everything I said and then she showed me stuff."

Sister Immaculata tried to keep her emotions in check. She wanted to cry as she asked, "What did she show you?"

"Jesus' mother showed me how much she loved her Son. But she had to let him go, so He could be with His Father. It was so good, what she did, that now she gets to be with her Son forever. She really didn't understand why she had to give Him up when she did. She just knew it was right and best for Him. She missed Him for a little bit, but she is glad that she did what was best for Him. She told me I should do what was best for Johnny and Danny, and not to be afraid. She said that I would miss them, but I would be with them when I grew up."

The girl sighed, and continued, "I told her I couldn't do it. It was too much. I asked her why all these bad things kept happening to me. It wasn't fair! I told her that I just didn't care what was right. I was going to do what was best for me, the heck with everyone else. Do you know what she did?"

The nun was fascinated and asked, "What did she do?"

Mary Catherine continued, "She just smiled and said she knew I had a good heart and that she trusted me. It was so hard. I told her that I didn't care, it didn't matter what my heart said. I wasn't letting Johnny and Danny go. Then, she stopped talking. I cried and cried. I told her it wasn't fair. I cried until ran out of tears, but still she just smiled. Finally, I told her that maybe, just maybe, I would let Johnny and Danny be adopted. It was probably good for them. But what about me? I didn't want to be all alone. And guess what she said? The Blessed Mother said whenever I was lonely I could come to her. She said I could talk to her anytime I wanted to. She would be my mother, and I would never be alone."

Sister Immaculata resolved she would obtain the parent's permission to reunite the children when they reached adulthood. She would not allow this unselfish act to go unrewarded. Soft tears fell from the nun's large eyes as she listened to Mary Catherine.

"How did the Blessed Mother tell you this?" She caught her breath as the child answered.

"She whispered to my heart."

Two months later, six weeks after the O'Rourke brothers were adopted, Sister Josephine waddled down the long hallway to Sister Immaculata's office. She walked so quickly that she huffed and reddened with the strain of moving her large frame. Her body was unused to exercise, but her anger propelled her against her nature. She was sick of it! The thought of what that girl was allowed to get away with made her sick.

She was sick of all the special people. In her book, that was anyone who acted different, all those so called beautiful people who stood out from the rest. Oh, she was sick of it all right. God knows, she was a patient person. She had tolerated and put up with all the special people. But, this was the last straw. She would not have that girl thinking she was special. She was just an ordinary orphan. Not special in any way. The girl was not especially pretty, and from what Sister Josephine had seen of her work, she was not particularly bright either. She had better learn early on what was expected of her. She had better learn that people like her weren't anything. The little brat better learn to follow the rules!

What made her think that she could get away with acting like she did was beyond the heavy-set nun. It was probably her friendship with Mother Superior. *Ha! There's a laugh!* As far as the breathless nun was concerned there was nothing superior about her. She was too young to even know what she was doing. The fact she permitted the goings-on that she did only proved her incompetence.

Sister Josephine hated Sister Immaculata. Hate was not a word that was strong enough to describe the way she felt. Sister Immaculata, the new Mother Superior, was one of those people the world considered exceptional. She was beautiful and well educated. The young nun had all the advantages which were denied Sister Josephine. The rotund older nun had no doubts Sister Immaculata impressed everyone with her sickly sweetness and natural good looks. What chance was there against this interloper?

Sister Immaculata had grabbed the older nun's promotion right out from under her, and the older nun was out to prove it had been a mistake. The spiritual director of the order had given this young nobody what was clearly Sister Josephine's job.

Sister Josephine was sure she was to be made the new Mother Superior after the death of the last one. After all, no one deserved it more than her. She had been here for 30 years. She had been the first one here. When the building was built, it was Sister Josephine who fired up the coal furnace each morning and saw to it everything was ready before the other sisters arrived. For thirty years, she served the original Mother Superior with gusto. She enthusiastically advised her of her errors and kept unimportant issues from her attention. She didn't show it, but Sister Josephine was sure the original principal had appreciated all her help and guidance. She accepted the other nun as her boss, knowing her turn would come soon enough. But, it was a long time in coming. The former principal had hung onto her job for dear life! Sister Josephine figured she knew a good thing when she had it. It was an answer to the jealous nun's prayer when the original Mother Superior had been taken ill. *Oh, she cried and carried on like the rest of the sisters, but who's kidding who? It was about time.*

The older nun had prepared for this all of her life. She knew when she was in charge she would straighten them all out. Discipline was weak around here. Both the children and the other sisters tolerated too much fun. No one ever took their work seriously enough. Sister Josephine had plans though. She had a plan to adjust everyone's life in this place. She would bring about strict adherence to the letter of the law. She would teach them all what a good manager could do. Sister Josephine looked forward to the day she would be made Mother Superior.

During those years, she put up with them all. She had been forced to correct all their mistakes. She taught the only really strict class in the school. The fat nun spent the one year she had the students in her class beating the pride out of them. She was forced to undo all the harm the liberal nuns and their lenient ways had done. The children came to her prideful and disobedient. When they left her classroom, they were subdued and held the fear of adults all children needed. It wasn't easy! The children had complained. They didn't understand she was the only one who cared enough to correct their faults. She was made to look like the heavy, but she knew best what the children needed.

Sister Josephine formulated plans for all those nuns who reported her when the corrections she made required a heavy hand. She wouldn't fall for all their innocent routines when she was made principal. They would learn to run their classrooms correctly, under her directions. She waited for 30 years. For 30 years, she stood on her aching feet, trying to teach the ignorant refuse of humanity. Did anyone thank her? No, instead she suffered the veiled insults of the younger nuns, and the distance of the older nuns. She accepted the suffering because she believed that her day of revenge would come. Sister Josephine knew her day in the sun was coming! They couldn't deny her the place of respect she worked for all these years. She knew they had no choice. She assessed the competition and found them wanting. When Mother Superior fell ill, she couldn't kid herself, she was elated. At last, her day had come!

The bitterness she felt when an outsider was chosen as the new Mother Superior destroyed whatever goodness Sister Josephine had in her. Being passed over for the promotion confirmed her belief that she was unappreciated. It made her bitter. Sister Josephine felt the world treated her unfairly because of her looks and lack of education. She was furious! Spilling over with bile, she became even crueler, her remarks more callous. As the snake of jealousy wrapped itself around her hardened heart, her behavior became even more brutal. She felt safe because she only displayed it to the helpless children in her care. She ignored the nuns she lived with, she hated them all. But most of all she detested Sister Immaculata, who she saw as the source of the injustice in her life.

By the time the angry nun reached the office, she was out of breath and dizzy with anger. Her cheeks were deep red, almost purple. Sister Immaculata wasn't pleased to see her, but she tried to hide it. Whenever the younger nun faced Sister Josephine, her reaction was instant and guttural. She didn't like Sister Josephine but always tried to remember St. Therese of the Roses and her little way. When St. Therese was with a fellow Sister whom she by nature disliked, she took pains to make that sister feel that she was her favorite, her best friend. It was her way of suffering. St. Therese offered her suffering up to God. Like St. Paul in the gospel, she united her suffering to the suffering of Jesus for the redemption of mankind.

St. Therese was a popular saint because of her little way. St. Therese believed that we did not have to do great works to become holy. She taught we just needed to do the little, daily things to the glory of God. Sister Immaculata found St. Therese's teaching to be close to the truth. She sometimes felt it would be easier to face down the lions in the Roman Coliseum then to face this hateful nun. She smiled however, and offered it up to Jesus.

"You seem upset, Sister Josephine, slow down and tell me what's wrong?"

The short, stocky nun gasped for air, as she tried to spit out her concerns. "It's that girl," she had to stop to catch her breath.

"What girl?" Sister Immaculata was really concerned. Perhaps something was wrong with one of the children.

Sister Josephine, now able to talk, bitterly answered, "It's that girl you seem to like so much, Mary Catherine."

Sister Immaculata was annoyed with the sarcastic tone in the smug nun's voice, but tried to overlook it as she asked, "What about Mary Catherine?"

Sister Josephine raised her voice, "She's down in the chapel acting like an idiot! It's a sacrilege, what's she's doing. She's down there talking out loud to the statue of Mary! What's worse is that she is acting like she's listening while the statue is answering her. I think she needs a good smack, and you better do something about it."

The young Mother Superior was relieved that the young girl wasn't hurt, and she tried to turn away before the older nun could see the amused look on her face. Sister Josephine saw the smile, however, and her anger rose.

"You don't seem to understand, the girl is acting like the Blessed Mother is talking to her. She's talking to the Blessed Mother as if she were talking to a friend. She's just sitting there, having a conversation with the Mother of God." Sister Josephine was beside herself, her hands moving in excitement. Yelling, to emphasize her point, Sister Josephine continued, "She must think the mother of God has nothing to do but listen to the stupid needs of some child. She's actually telling the Blessed Mother that she needs new shoes that don't pinch her toes!"

At that point, Sister Immaculata couldn't hold her laughter in. Tears sprang to her eyes as Sister Josephine watched her laughter with pure hatred and disdain. The more anger Sister Josephine displayed, the less control Sister Immaculata had over her mirth. When Sister Josephine started to stamp her feet, the sight was just too funny. Sister Immaculata sunk into her desk chair.

Sister Immaculata's laughter made the older nun boil with anger, "So as usual, you're going to let that child get away with her horrible behavior. No wonder this place is going to hell in a hand basket. You're the most incompetent excuse of a nun we've ever had here. I think it's time I went to the Spiritual Director and let him know just how stupid you are."

The minute the Sister Josephine saw the change in Sister Immaculata's face, she knew she had gone too far. Sister Immaculata could feel the disgust she felt for this nun rise within her. She turned icy cold in order to control the rage she felt.

"I'm sorry you feel that way, Sister, perhaps you should take your concerns to Father. However, I order you to leave Mary Catherine alone. I only wish all of us had such a close and natural way of prayer. I'm sure it must delight the Blessed Mother to listen to Mary Catherine." Sister Immaculata realized that it was a waste of time to talk to this spiteful nun. "Leave Mary Catherine alone. If her behavior is causing a distraction in the chapel, I'll talk to her myself."

The angry nun slammed the door behind her as she left. She had no intention of listening to this nun who laughed at her and belittled her concerns. She knew, however, she had let too much out of the bag. She resolved to deal with Mary Catherine in her own way. She also knew she would have to be very careful when she did.

Sister Immaculata picked up the phone and said, "Please send Mary Catherine to my office." She resolved that she would talk to Mary Catherine before anyone else did. She didn't want anyone, even someone with good intentions, to change the close relationship this child felt toward Mary. Sister Immaculata directed the child when her brothers were both adopted to continue her talks with the Blessed Mother. The child truly perceived Mary as her mother. Sister was delighted the girl had developed such a close relationship with a mother who would always be there for her. Sister Immaculata didn't want anyone interfering with the child. She would talk to Mary Catherine and advise her that she didn't need to talk out loud. She would help the child to get even closer to the Blessed Mother.

When Mary Catherine received the message to go to the principal's office, she wasn't afraid. She loved Sister Immaculata. She had been so kind, and what's more she always treated Mary Catherine to some of the small cakes she kept in the top draw of her desk. Mary Catherine would have to hurry though. It was almost time for the hour Mary Catherine spent with her baby brother, Thomas.

Each day, Mary Catherine would play in the nursery with him. He was standing now, and ready to walk any day. Mary Catherine was sure he might walk today. She didn't want to miss it. She skipped down the hall with a light heart.

"Come in, Mary Catherine," Sister Immaculata said in answer to the knock on her door. The girl smiled as she took a chair in front of the large wooden desk. "Mary Catherine, how have you been? I haven't seen you in days."

Mary Catherine answered with a matter of fact attitude, "Oh, all right, Sister. I've been doing better with my English, even though I still hate it. I tried to think of it as a game like you said, but I still think it's a waste of time."

Sister suppressed a smile at her stark honesty. She was glad Mary Catherine wasn't afraid to say just what she thought. It was an endearing quality.

Sister Immaculata asked with amusement, "How's your brother, Thomas?"

She listened in delight as the girl, who once blamed the baby for all of her troubles, talked on and on with pride in everything the boy did. She bragged about each of the baby's traits. Sister was glad the girl had learned to love him. It wasn't healthy for her to resent her sibling. Sister didn't disappoint Mary Catherine. She pulled two small chocolate snack cakes out of her drawer and presented them to her. Mary Catherine greedily gulped one down and pocketed the other.

Mary Catherine said as she placed the small cake in her pocket, "I'll save this one for Thomas. It's almost time to see him."

The nun watched the anxious girl check the clock on the wall behind her desk, and decided to get to the point. "Mary Catherine, have you been praying with the Blessed Mother? I know I suggested that, after we talked about your brothers being adopted."

Mary Catherine was excited by thoughts of her relationship with the Blessed Mother, and sitting forward in her chair said, "Oh yes, Sister, I talk to the Blessed Mother every day. I tell her everything that happens and whatever I think. I know she tells Jesus all about me, 'cause whatever I ask her for, she helps me with."

The nun smiled with pleasure. "Do you pray with her in the chapel?"

"Yes, Sister. Oh, I know I can talk to her anywhere, but the statue of her in the chapel helps. I know it's just a statue, but it's like looking at a picture of someone. When I look at a picture of my mother, it seems easier to talk to her. It's the same with the statue of Mary. It just helps me to remember everything I want to say."

"Mary Catherine, I'm glad that you talk to the Blessed Mother in the chapel, or anywhere else you feel comfortable talking to her. You know, however, other people go to the chapel to pray."

Mary Catherine replied with exasperation, "I know Sister, sometimes the nuns are in the chapel saying the rosary out loud. When they are, I don't go in there to pray."

"Why is that?" the Sister Immaculata replied.

Mary Catherine shook her head in frustration, "Oh, I can't concentrate on what I want to say when they're talking out loud."

Sister Immaculata asked, with a smile, "Do you talk out loud when you pray?"

"Usually." Mary Catherine hesitated, as if something was just occurring to her.

Trying to make a point, Sister Immaculata asked, "Do you think that when you talk out loud, it might be hard for others to concentrate on their prayers?"

Mary Catherine looked up and smiled and answered with new understanding, "Oh, I got it, I should stop praying out loud in the chapel. It must be bothering the other people when they are trying to pray. I understand. The Blessed Mother can hear you when you just talk in your head anyway, can't she? I guess that I could just talk to her in my head."

"I knew you would understand, Mary Catherine. I don't want you to stop praying. Pray just the way you do, as much as you do. Just try not to pray out loud. The Blessed Mother must be very happy to hear from you. She loves you just as much as if you were her own child. In fact, you are her daughter, so don't be afraid to go to her with any of your problems. She loves you."

Mary Catherine's feet, which didn't reach the ground from the chair she was sitting in, swung nervously as she looked at the clock behind the nun's head. It was already five minutes past the time her recess started. Mary Catherine always tried to spend her recess time with Thomas. He couldn't tell time, Mary Catherine knew, but he always seemed to know when she was coming. He was probably waiting for her right now. Sister Immaculata understood body language. When a person couldn't keep their feet still it usually meant the person wanted to leave. From the way Mary Catherine's legs were swinging back and forth, she knew the child was dying to get to her baby brother.

"All right, Mary Catherine, I guess you can go now." The nun watched, and laughed at how fast the child exited her office.

Mary Catherine skipped down the hall to the nursery. As she had expected, the chubby blonde baby was watching the door for her arrival. He cooed and held out his arms for her to scoop him up as he saw her. Mary Catherine needed his love, as much as he needed hers.

She felt so alone now that Johnny and Danny were gone. Talking to God was all right and all, but sometimes you just needed a hug. Mary Catherine missed her mother. She used to sit on her mother's lap, and her mother used to put her arms around her and hold her close. She could still smell the sweet perfume her mother liked whenever she thought of her.

Everyone was nice around here, but they weren't family. Mary Catherine only had a sense of family when Thomas's warm chubby arms surrounded her. The smell of baby powder and lotion reminded Mary Catherine of home. Love was made up of warm hugs and remembered smells. Mary Catherine even missed the muddy, sweaty smell of her two brothers. 'I won't think of that now,' she decided. She would just enjoy Thomas. He was all she had of her family now.

Mary Catherine pushed open the heavy double doors that led into the nursery. She heard someone call her name. The loud call startled her. Mary Catherine looked up to see Sister Josephine calling her. She really didn't like this nun. It must be Sister Josephine's turn to be in charge of the nursery this afternoon. Mary Catherine decided she better see what the nun wanted.

Sister Immaculata was anxious to get started on her trip home. She was going to be away for four days. It seemed strange to be leaving the school after just being away for a week, but she was going to be a Godmother to her new nephew. She was overjoyed when the baby was born while she was on vacation at Sarah's house. It was such an eventful week. She had not only been there when the infant was born, she had also met Elly, a niece she never knew.

Meeting Elly had been the highlight of her trip. It was a pleasure to meet such a shy, yet friendly girl. Sister Immaculata was sorry she wouldn't get to see Elly at her nephew's christening. Besides, Sister Immaculata mused, Elly had enough to digest after meeting the family.

Sister Immaculata closed her office in a rush. If any more business crossed her desk today, she would be late getting to her sister's house. Besides, she hated to travel at night. She still needed to pack. The nun was glad she was around to resolve the problem between Sister Josephine and Mary Catherine. There's no telling what Sister Josephine would have said, or done to the girl if she had not been there to control the situation. As Sister Immaculata started on her journey, she had no way of knowing what she was leaving behind.

Sister Josephine eyed up the girl, who slowly answered her call. Mary Catherine grudgingly crossed the room, and lifted her eyes to look directly at the nun. Mary Catherine was surprised to see Sister Josephine in the nursery, and asked, "Where is Sister Nadine?"

The nun immediately took this as a sign of arrogance, and felt her temper rising. She would delight in teaching this brassy child her place.

"Sister Nadine is off on a vacation. I am taking her place in the nursery for the next week." Sister Josephine's nostrils flared with anger, "The question is not what I am doing here, the question is what are you doing here?"

Mary Catherine was shocked by the nun's anger.

"I'm visiting my brother, Thomas." Mary Catherine gulped, as she saw the vessels pop on the nun's reddened neck.

The red faced nun shouted, "And just who told you that you could come in here anytime you want to!"

Mary Catherine's face darkened. "No one Sister, but no one told me I couldn't!"

As far as Sister Josephine was concerned, the young girl's answer was arrogant and impertinent.

Sister Josephine bellowed, "I am in charge of the nursery today. I don't remember being asked if you could come for a visit. No one else is here today that you could have asked. And so, I imagine you just took it upon yourself. You just decided, without permission, that you could come here today and disrupt the nursery."

Mary Catherine was at a loss. She answered with what proved to be a bad defense, "I come here every day and play with Thomas, my baby brother. Sister Immaculata knows about my visits, and never said that I shouldn't. I come during recess each day. It makes Thomas feel good, he knows that I love him."

The bitter nun felt the bile of hatred rise at the mention of Sister Immaculata. It was just as she thought. This child thought she was special because of her relationship with the "special" nun. It made her sick!

"And just how do you think that makes the other babies feel? They must think that they aren't worthy of the special love Thomas gets. They must feel he is special, better than them?"

Mary Catherine was stumped. She had never thought about her visits that way. "Well, I guess you're right Sister. I should play with all the babies, so they don't feel bad." Mary Catherine smiled at the brilliant solution she had come up with.

Sister Josephine slapped the smile right off her face. She slapped her with all the anger that had built up over the years. She slapped the girl so hard she knocked her to the ground.

Mary Catherine lay stunned on the floor, covering her reddened face from further injury. For a moment the whole nursery seemed to freeze in confused silence, and then the wale of crying and frightened toddlers started. The sound seemed to bring the nun to her senses. What if another adult had seen? She would have to take control of this situation.

The nun reached down and yanked the small girl up by her arm. Mary Catherine could feel the pain in her shoulder as she was snatched up. Only her fear kept her from crying out. The nun's face was bright with rage as she carried the young girl to the next room.

"You need to find out who's the boss around here. You're not to come here without my permission, and you better not answer me back in the future!" The nun struggled with a heavy, wooden door that scraped along the floor as it resisted opening. "Perhaps some time alone will help you think!" The nun threw the child roughly against the back wall of the old supply closet.

Mary Catherine lay hurt and in shock as the nun locked the

door. She could hear the nun's footsteps as she walked away. The light disappeared as the door closed. Only dread of her abuser kept Mary Catherine from crying out in fear. She tried to catch her breath. The rapid-fire sequence of the last few minutes and the sting of the unexpected left Mary Catherine confused. What had she done to deserve this? Her face felt warm and sore. Mary Catherine could feel the trickle of blood coming from her lip.

The warm blood in her mouth had a metallic taste which nauseated her. Mary Catherine's stomach had sharp stabbing pains. The chocolate cake she had just eaten seemed to be attacking her.

Mary Catherine had never been afraid of the dark before, but it was so dark she couldn't even see her own hand in front of her. She was barely able to see the thin line of light at the bottom of the heavy closet door. Shelves full of office papers and supplies lined the closet. The smell of ink and dusty files was strong. The air was stale and dusky, and Mary Catherine felt as if she would suffocate in the small space. As the walls seemed to be closing in on her, the closet seemed to be getting smaller and smaller. She cried. She was terrified that the angry Sister Josephine would come back. She didn't want to be hit anymore, but she couldn't breathe.

Mary Catherine screamed. She yelled so long and so loud that she had to struggle for air. In between the screams, she panted as she tried to catch her breath for the next shout. No one heard. Mary Catherine knew that Sister Josephine was right in the next room with the babies. Either the nun didn't care, or the heavy, wooden closet door was muffling all the sounds of her sobbing. Mary Catherine ran out of tears. Sitting silently, she could barely hear the sounds of the nursery.

Time lost all meaning. By the silence, she realized the babies were no longer in the next room. They had been taken to another room far on the other side of the building for dinner. On the other side of the building the infants would be fed and put to sleep. It must be dinnertime, and if it was, she had been in the closet for about three hours. No one was in the room next door. No one would hear her if she called out. Sister Josephine was the only one who knew she was here. Surely, she wouldn't forget to get her out of the closet.

"Help me, help me. Please open the door!" Mary Catherine screamed and cried, as she beat the door with her fists. She called and screamed, "Let me out, I can't breath." Her throat was dry and sore. Her voice weakened. Unable to make her voice louder, the terrified girl banged and screamed, "I'm going to die. Please, don't let me die all alone in here!" No one could hear her. No one was coming.

Losing her voice, Mary Catherine continued to bang on the closet door. She beat the door with all the strength she had. Her fisted hands stung, and her knuckles began to bleed. The pain became too much. Mary Catherine, weakening, slapped the door until the pain in her hands overcame her.

Her eyes burned and stung from all the tears. She hurt all over. Holding her stomach, she laid down on the floor. She closed her eyes as she tried to listen for another human who could help her. The silence was deafening. No one was there. The weary girl realized that no one would come. Mary Catherine couldn't stand it anymore. She had to escape. The only way was to sleep. It wasn't until she started to fall asleep that Mary Catherine remembered her angel was with her. She dosed off with a silent prayer for help. Mary Catherine's angel covered and held the small child as she slept in the dark, forgotten closet.

Sister Josephine hadn't forgotten Mary Catherine was in the closet, but she considered herself lucky. Not only was she in charge when Mother Superior was away, but her night time assignment was to check the girl's ward. How lucky could she get? She wasn't worried anyway. All of the other sisters were too afraid of her. They wouldn't question anything she said. She decided she would leave the girl in the closet overnight. No harm could come to her there. And after all, she only had this weekend to straighten the girl out.

Sister Josephine opened the closet the next morning, letting the weak and subdued girl out. 'She'll listen to me from now on,' the nun thought.

A Friend Sent From God

Consider the work of God. Who can make straight what he has made crooked! On a good day enjoy good things, and on an evil day consider: Both the one and the other God has made, so that Man cannot find fault with Him in anything. (Ecclesiastes 7:13-14)

Joseph couldn't comprehend what was happening. It was all moving too fast. It was surreal. The cops, shouting to each other, tore his apartment to shreds. They tore out drawers and quickly found his stash of cocaine.

"Here it is!" the tall cop shouted as he bagged and labeled the cocaine. Joseph was numb. Suddenly, another cop reeled him around and walked him to the door. *What were they going to do to him?* He knew he should call someone. Someone would have to help him. He couldn't think. His mind was clouded from cocaine and shock.

Joseph was roughly walked down the stairs, and placed in the back of the police car. The cop slammed the car door shut, and he was left in the car alone. A group of cops stood outside the car and questioned the neighbors Joseph always snubbed. *What was he going to do?* Joseph's head began to pound. He needed to call someone. That much he knew. He should get a lawyer. He would call a lawyer and all of this would be straightened out. *They couldn't do this to him. Didn't they know who he was!*

His new-found sense of power quickly dissipated. Joseph

remembered that he fired the company lawyer. He was very nasty to the lawyer, accusing the older man of being at fault when the company contracts fell through. The truth was the contracts fell through because Joseph didn't meet the deadlines for construction. He screamed at the lawyer, throwing him out of the office. At the time, he needed a hit.

Looking out the window, Joseph could see all his neighbors watching the arrest. Why not? It made quite a show. He wanted the ground to swallow him. He wanted to wake up and find out this was a nightmare. He was actually glad when the car pulled out, taking him to the station. Anything would be better than giving this humiliating show for an eagerly entertained public. Anything had to be better than this. Joseph didn't realize how wrong he was.

When they reached the police station Joseph was taken into a room where he sat in a wooden chair and waited for twenty minutes. It was long enough for his temper to rise. When the door to the room opened, a dark-skinned man and a petite woman entered and introduced themselves, "Hello, Mr. McKenna, I'm Detective Lamia." Pointing to the middle-aged brunette who accompanied him, the tall detective continued, "And this is Detective DeMaio."

The two detectives sat across the table from the handcuffed man. The female detective started. "Do you know why you are under arrest?"

Joseph was annoyed. He didn't like her tone of voice. "No why don't you tell me. Could it be the cocaine?"

Detective Lamia stood up, as if to impose his height, and shouted, "I'd watch my mouth if I were you. You are under arrest for possession of nearly a kilo and for distributing cocaine in a drug-free zone. That alone will add time in prison to whatever sentence you receive."

Joseph didn't know what to say. He didn't remember selling drugs by a school. If someone was caught selling drugs within that area it required the Judge to give a stay in prison. Joseph couldn't remember doing it, but that meant nothing. Joseph's memory, mixed with cocaine, was poor. *I could use a snort right now*, Joseph thought.

"You've been read your rights," said Detective Lamia as he resumed his seat. "Do you want to call your lawyer?"

Joseph answered with arrogance, "I don't need any lawyer. You have no proof that I sold any drugs. When the cops came I was in my apartment. Maybe you got me for possession, but that's all."

Detective DeMaio, a tough masculine woman, answered, "I'm afraid you're in for a rude awakening. You tried to sell cocaine to one of our undercover detectives right outside a school. We have it all on tape. The only reason we didn't arrest you on the spot was because we followed you. We wanted to get your source. Once we got your supplier, we arrested you. I suggest you call your lawyer. That is, unless you've decided that you want to confess and save the state the cost of a trial."

Joseph didn't know what to say. He didn't have a lawyer to call. He didn't have any money. The company had gone belly-up months ago. He had nothing and no one. He couldn't let the cops see that. He had to let them think he was on top of his game. His head was buzzing, and the addict knew he wasn't thinking straight. *These cops have a lot of nerve. There was a time I could buy and sell them. Who do they think they are talking to?* Joseph thought as rage took over.

Joseph shouted, "Do whatever you want. I don't have to talk to you. My lawyer will destroy your case. And then I will deal with you."

The detective laughed. Opening the door, he called over a uniformed cop. "Book him, and then let him make his call."

Joseph was taken to another room and fingerprinted. He stood before a camera as his picture was taken. The policeman asked, "Do you want to make a call now?"

Joseph wanted to punch him. *Who did he think he was?* He screamed, "I make my call when I'm good and ready. You'll be sorry, believe me."

The cop just shook his head as he slapped the handcuffs back on the prisoner. Joseph expected them to ask questions, but they didn't. Instead they sat him down in a row with other handcuffed prisoners and forgot him. He didn't like the low life crowd around him. How could they do this to him? Sitting handcuffed with a lot of obvious criminal types was too degrading for him. Joseph started to shout. He wanted out of here. A passing policeman told him to be quiet.

"You'll pay for this!" he snarled. "I know a lot of important people. I could have your job!"

The laughter stunned him. The cops weren't the only one who laughed. All of the people who sat handcuffed with Joseph also laughed.

"Oh, so you'll have my job, will you," the red-headed cop retorted as he yanked Joseph to a standing position. "I can see you're the dangerous type. Perhaps, for my own protection, I better put you under lock and key."

The policeman continued amidst the encouraging regale of laughter, "However, Mr. Important, I wouldn't suggest you tell your new cell mates about your high position. They might not be as impressed as we were."

He was pulled and steered down the hall and around the corner to a large cell. Harshly shoved inside, he heard the lock click behind him. Now as his head cleared, rage flowed through him. The rage quickly turned to fear as he scanned the cell and the dangerous-looking characters he was locked up with. It was a large cell, with about six men in it. It smelled of urine and dust. Peeling paint chips cluttered the corners. The back wall was lined with cots that acted as seats to the waiting prisoners. One metal toilet without a seat and oozing a noxious smell stood on the side wall.

Withering under the probing stares of his fellow cellmates, he wisely decided to be quiet. Finding an empty corner, he slouched against the wall, and lowered his eyes. He didn't want to arouse the interest of any of these menacing looking men. He sat in silence, with no threatening movements. He made himself as small as possible. Fear kept him awake all night with his back against the wall.

In the morning, he decided he would find a way out of this. He would ask, politely, to have help in finding a lawyer. The snores of the men in his cell, normally sounds that would irritate him, was music to his ears. He dreaded the morning, when they would awaken.

When the morning did come, Joseph was surprised to find all the men were bailed out by wives or friends. He was alone in the horrid cell. The pealing paint and the stained mattresses sickened him. He longed to get out of there. But he had no one. There was no one for him to call. He had lost all of his friends. His spiral down was observed by all. They deserted him, all of them, as if he were a leper. He bothered with no one, except those who supplied his cocaine habit. All of his former cell mates had someone. As his throbbing head cleared of the drug-induced fog, the idea he had no one to call hit him hard. *How did he end up like this?*

Alone, without drugs to hide the truth, Joseph realized no one loved him, because he loved no one. He treated those who reached out in love as weaklings. Like a steamroller, he rolled his steel will over all the generous and gentle souls he ever knew. He rewarded only the most cruel and ruthless in his company and his life. He destroyed everybody else.

Wait, not quite everybody, there were two, the remorseful man thought. Two sweet and gentle souls he didn't destroy, despite himself. Two people in his past walked away whole, and even with dignity. He never understood them. Both John Meyer and Joyce left him confused and angry. Right now, he realized they were the only two he could ask for help.

Joyce would be his first choice, but he didn't know where she was. He paid the most expensive detectives and they searched everywhere and ran down every clue. Joseph ordered them to follow her entire family, but he never found her. Eventually, the drugs took over his life and all of his money was spent on cocaine as the company he spent years building failed. The detectives quit after not being paid. It didn't matter any more. Only the cocaine mattered. *I need a hit right now,* he thought as his hands trembled.

Joseph hadn't seen John Meyer since Joyce's accident. He hadn't been very kind to him. John rebuilt his business from the bottom up. Many of his friends helped him. Joseph was ashamed to admit it, but John's business had long ago outstripped Joseph's company. It was one of the largest construction companies in the area, and had a reputation for quality work and honest billing.

Joseph didn't know anyone else he could ask for help. John Meyer was the only man who had ever been kind to him. Joseph hadn't returned the kindness. When John's company was in trouble, he had reached out to Joseph he refused to help him. *Why had he turned his back on John in his moment of need?* Yet, John was the only person Joseph could think of. *How could Joseph ask John to help him now?* John was sure to laugh at him. Joseph knew he couldn't expect the man he had deserted to help him. John was kind, but was sure to gloat over Joseph's fall from grace. *After all,* Joseph thought, *a man has to have pride.*

The cell began filling up with assorted intimidating men again. When Joseph's fear surpassed his pride, he asked to make the call. He was relieved to reach John Meyer.

To Joseph's surprise, John didn't refuse his call, or take the opportunity to belittle him. He arrived in 30 minutes, and stood by him during the arraignment. He paid the bail. Joseph couldn't thank him. All Joseph could think about was cocaine.

John Meyer took Joseph to his brick ranch house in an upper-class neighborhood and gave him clean clothes and an opportunity to bathe and rest. Hours later, Joseph woke up in a comfortable bedroom and smelled dinner cooking on the stove. Joseph found John broiling steaks.

The older man looked up and smiled, "Oh, you're up! I was about to wake you. I'll bet you're hungry."

Joseph was shocked to see how healthy John looked, and answered, "Yes, I am, but you didn't have to go to all this trouble. I'll be out of your hair before you know it."

"Oh, it's no trouble, sit down, I love to cook. I don't often have the opportunity to cook for someone else."

John placed the sizzling steak and crisp baked potato in front of

Joseph who ate quickly. Looking up, Joseph saw John was watching him with a smile.

"Aren't you going to eat?" Joseph asked between hungry gulps.

"I will, but not steak, it hasn't been on my menu since my heart surgery. I'll have to settle for a salad and grilled salmon. I sure enjoy watching you eat the steak, however!" the gray-haired man laughed.

Joseph flinched at the thought of how sick John was the last time they met.

"You know, John," Joseph paused – admitting he owed another was very difficult for him, "I appreciate what you're doing for me. I had no one else to turn to, or I wouldn't have bothered you."

John was moved by Joseph's sincerity and answered, "You needed help, and I was there, that's all there is to it."

Joseph's face flushed red with shame. "If I were you, after the way I treated you, I would have laughed at you for asking me for help. You had every right to turn your back on me. After all, that's what I did to you when you needed me."

John looked Joseph in the eye, trying to discern his level of sincerity. "Yes, I suppose you could look at it that way, but that's something I hope I will never do to anyone. Revenge and anger is a losing game."

Joseph shook his head, "I don't understand why you did it. It took a lot of courage to do what you've done." Joseph was puzzled.

John smiled, and answered "It wasn't courage. It was grace, pure and simple."

With curiosity Joseph asked, "What do you mean?" Joseph swallowed his last piece of steak, "What's grace?"

John took his time as he put the dishes in the dishwasher. The spotless ranch was a testament to the older man's neatness. Turning, John reached for his jacket and said, "It's a long story, come on, I'll explain it to you as we drive over to the lawyer's office. I made an appointment with Eric Larson. He has a lot of experience in criminal law."

Joseph followed his old mentor without question out to the

driveway and into the Crown Victoria. He trusted John. He really had no choice but to trust him. John Meyer was the only one who came to his aid. Joseph shook with desire. The desire for cocaine was overwhelming. He felt as if he was going to lose his mind. *If only I could have one hit, my mind would clear*, Joseph thought as they pulled out of the driveway and headed to the lawyer.

John drove and his gentle conversation was refreshing after listening to the rough language of the men he shared his last accommodations with. The thought of how he spent last night began to depress him, so he pushed the thought away and tried to concentrate on John's conversation.

John talked as he drove through the beautiful neighborhood with the manicured lawns. "Grace is a word which like many English words has its root in Latin. It is derived from the Latin word "gratis" which means a gift freely given, without merit and undeserved."

Joseph's mind was quick, "So, by saying your help is given by the power of grace, you're saying it's a gift I haven't earned, but which you decided to give anyway. I agree, after the way I treated you when you needed my help, I certainly didn't deserve your help. What I don't understand is how you have the power to forgive me. I don't have the ability to forgive like you do. It's just not natural."

John smiled, as they turned another corner in the stylish neighborhood. "You're right, it's not natural, it's supernatural. On my own, by my own human inclinations, I wouldn't have the power to forgive you. It was only by grace that I could. That grace was first given to me by God and now I can share it with you."

Joseph was puzzled. He looked at the older man who drove well below the speed limit and asked, "What do you mean?"

John smiled again as he paused to greet some neighbors as they jogged by.

"I mean, Jesus died for me, and gave me the gift of everlasting life, even though I turned my back on Him. God the Father gave me the life of His only Son, even though I rejected Him and didn't deserve anything from Him. He should have turned His back on me, when I called on Him in my hour of need. He should have rejected me, but instead, He loved me." John was moved just thinking about it.

Joseph's whole body trembled as his need for cocaine grew stronger. He tried to focus on the conversation and asked, "Yes, I can understand your feelings, but what does that have to do with you helping me?" Joseph asked.

"When you love someone you want to be like them. It would be impossible for me, as a human, to forgive and help you. I'm no saint, and what you did to me really hurt me. But anger and hatred destroys the one who hates not the one who is hated. Bitterness in the heart is the main cause of mankind's trouble. I pray for the grace to overcome it, to treat you the way He treated me. A prayer for grace is always answered. I decided to forgive. He gave me the grace to actually do it."

The drive to the lawyer's office continued in silence. Joseph tried to grasp what John had just explained to him. Joseph always had trouble understanding other people's religious feelings. Joyce's thoughts and emotions always eluded him. Some people simply developed this sense of God he never developed. He always ridiculed the gift. Now, for the first time, he was beginning to see it as a potentially valuable gift. It seemed to help those who possessed it. Joseph thought of this faith as a mental gift, given to some like the gift of poetry or music. It was nice to have, even though it wasn't necessary. One thing was sure, he didn't have it, and what's more, he was pretty sure he didn't want it.

Eric Larson pulled no punches. Joseph was going away for his crime. The state had an airtight case. The pale blonde lawyer who always believed in telling the truth, told him, "You have two choices. You can plead not guilty and fight the charges. They have an abundance of evidence to prove you guilty. I don't think you can win, but I will do what you want. If you want to plead not guilty, I will still defend you. I think it is a risk. You have a better chance if you are honest, and ask for mercy. That's what I advise."

John and Joseph sat quietly before the lawyer's desk. Joseph trembled. His need for a fix grew with the fear of what his future held.

The office was as plain and direct as the lawyer. Heavy law books lined the shelves surrounding the simple room. Joseph panicked. *Something, somewhere, in one of these many law books had to save him.* He was getting antsy just sitting in this small office. *How was he going to stand sitting in a prison cell?*

In a whisper of dread, Joseph asked, "And what's the second option?"

Eric Larson took a good look at Joseph. *Good God, he's already in withdrawal,* the lawyer thought as he answered, "You can plead guilty and throw yourself on the mercy of the court. It is what I recommend. The court sometimes goes easy with someone who is honest and admits they are wrong. If you take that route, I would send you to a drug rehabilitation center right now. You would have to check in voluntarily. We could ask the judge for leniency. If we could convince the judge you have already tried to overcome your addiction, he may give you a break. If you tell the truth, and save the state the expense of a trial, he will probably take that into consideration in your sentencing. I would help you by pleading for mercy. If you did kick the addiction to cocaine, I could probably convince the court that you would become a valued citizen again. It's up to you."

Joseph wanted to run. He didn't want to check into rehab, he wanted to get some coke. Joseph was afraid but had to ask, "If I don't plead guilty and the court finds me guilty, what is the most I could get?"

Eric Larson looked across the desk and pronounced, "20 years."

The truth of his situation hit Joseph full force. For the first time since he was a child, Joseph started to cry. John sat still beside him. John Meyer knew that Joseph needed to understand fully to make the right decision.

The young lawyer knew he had won his point. Reaching into the top drawer of his desk, he retrieved a card and handed it to John. In a serious tone of voice he stated, "Better sign him in tonight. I don't think he will make it through the night."

John read the card, 'Coastal Substance Abuse Clinic.' It would take a half hour to get there. Collecting up the broken man, John drove Joseph to the clinic and had him admitted.

When Meyer returned home, he just caught the phone as it rang. It was Joyce. She had read about Joseph's arrest in the paper and prayed that he turned to his old friend. John filled her in on the situation. Joyce listened carefully as John explained the lawyer's strategy, "It's his best chance. I agree with the lawyer. He has to get over the addiction or nothing will help him."

Joyce wept as she blamed herself. John listened for a while, then intervened, "It is not your fault. You did what you had to do. Joseph has to find his own way. Don't worry Joyce, I will watch over him. You just pray for him. I will call you and keep you informed."

Four months later, John sat behind Joseph as the judge read the sentence. Joseph's legs shook as he heard the judge announce his sentence.

Looking down, the judge pronounced, "You shall be taken to a maximum security drug treatment center, where you will remain until the doctors are convinced that you are no longer addicted to drugs. Afterwards, you shall be transferred to the maximum security prison for a term of five years." Joseph collapsed from fright. The guard helped him up and led him out of the courtroom in handcuffs.

John Meyer was pleased. He had written to the judge with a plea for mercy, and the judge apparently gave it. Joseph could have received as much as 20 years for his crimes. The judge's decision to order drug treatment was the most important point, now Joseph had a real chance to straighten out his life. John prayed he would.

As soon as he got home, John made the phone call. It was the same call he placed each night since Joseph first called for help. He was happy with the news he reported. It would have done Joseph terrible harm to be found not liable for his sins. Yes, he was forgiven, but reparation and reformation still needed to be made.

"Hello, Joyce," John said. "I've got good news for you."

Joyce cried, as she thought of Joseph spending five years in prison. She knew the drug treatment was the best thing for him, however.

"I don't know how to thank you!" responded Joyce. They had grown close in the last four months as they tried to help the man they both loved.

"You can have me out once in a while to see that beautiful daughter of yours."

Joyce laughed, "I'll expect you this weekend, okay?"

John answered, "That sounds great. And feel free to cook. It's been a long time since I've had some of your good cooking. I really look forward to seeing you." The phone call ended, but the friendship which grew out of a mutual concern for a lost soul blossomed and solidified over the next few years.

Reaching Out

Lord, you are kind and forgiving, most loving to all who call on you.
(Psalm 86:5)

Even though the bandages were thick, touching his face sparked spasms of pain. It wasn't the first time Joseph had landed in the prison infirmary. The last time was during his seventh month in prison. When he was assigned to work in the laundry, he tried to quietly do his work and keep out of the other prisoner's way.

He initially spent six months in the prison drug rehabilitation. It was the hardest six months of his life. His addiction to cocaine was powerful. Withdrawal was excruciatingly painful. There were plenty of drugs in the prison, but so far Joseph was able to resist all the offers.

He heard the nurse rustling around in the ward, which contained ten Gurney-like beds. Four of the beds were occupied. The throbbing pain in his face, a result of a second prison beating, was getting worse.

"Nurse, please!" his voice was weak despite his effort, "Can I please have something for pain."

The heavy-set nurse answered in her usual dispassionate way. She was rough and direct. She had to be, working in this environment had seasoned her to the con artists and liars. Long ago, she learned to keep her emotions in check, keeping an air of professional distance from her patients.

Opening the chart, she scanned and quickly answered, "With your history, it won't be much. I guess the most I can offer you is Tylenol."

Joseph knew the drill. He'd gone through it after the first beating. This time, however, the pain was much worse. He was sure that his nose was broken, something he avoided during the first pummeling. When the nurse returned with a syringe full of liquid Tylenol, he started to realize just how badly he was beaten.

"I'll slowly drip this Tylenol in your mouth. Try to swallow gently." Joseph was amazed at how difficult it was for him to swallow the red syrup. The smallest movement hurt. When he had swallowed the last drop, the nurse continued, "The ambulance will be here soon. You'll have to go to the hospital."

The nurse's predictions proved right. The young intern at the emergency room ordered the x-rays that proved Joseph's nose, cheekbone, and jaw were fractured.

The doctor, looking at the x-rays, told Joseph, "I'm afraid that you'll need surgery."

Joseph tried to remember exactly what happened. His thoughts were fuzzy. He just knew that he opened his mouth when he should have kept it shut. Sometimes he just forgot where he was, and the old Joseph surfaced. The arrogant, cold, and sarcastic Joseph broke through his detached facade. When it did, he ended up in the infirmary. He had lived in the prison for just more than a year. Would he be able to survive another four?

Despite the pain the transfer caused, the feeling of exhilaration Joseph felt when

his ambulance left the prison was potent. He hated prison. He felt he was in Hell. The only bright spots in his life now were John's visits. Twice a month, he arrived full of joy and optimism. John managed in a one hour visit, to entrust some of his joy to Joseph.

When John visited, he brought the sense that there was life outside the cold prison walls. Hope awaited Joseph, and with John's visit, it became believable to him. Joseph never really understood why John took the time from his daily concerns to visit a so-called friend who had once betrayed him. Yet, John remained faithful. Joseph found himself looking forward to these visits as the only encouraging moments in his prison life. He found himself anxious for any news which made the outside world seem real.

The prison authorities informed John of Joseph's hospitalization. John was the only outside contact that Joseph had listed as next of kin. John arrived before the plastic surgeon did. He was dismayed at Joseph's fully bandaged face. Joseph could barely talk because of his injuries. But, if he was worried before, he was shocked when the doctor removed the bandages to examine Joseph. It was impossible to recognize the man he knew in the swollen and misaligned features. John was really worried. Although the plastic surgeon was reassuring, John could not imagine how he could repair the mangled features before him.

John kept his composure, however. He joked and laughed with Joseph as they prepared him for surgery. Secretly he prayed. He knew God had a purpose for everything Joseph was going through. He just hoped Joseph was responding to the grace God was trying to bestow. As two nurses wheeled Joseph down the hall to the surgery, John pulled out his cell phone. He just didn't know how he was going to tell Joyce without upsetting her.

Within 45 minutes, Joyce was in the waiting room, comforting John. He laughed to himself when he noticed the reversal of roles. That's the way it was with Joyce. Whenever someone set out to minister to her, she ended up ministering to them. She was so beautiful. Not only physically, but even more importantly she was beautiful spiritually. Joyce's calm, serene nature made the five hours of waiting seem like nothing. John enjoyed her company which included the latest pictures of baby Grace. If Joyce was disappointed in her armless daughter, it never showed. Her pride and elation at baby Grace's every accomplishment pulled one in. Within a few minutes, John found his pity replaced by laughter at the antics of the infant. He knew he would have to make an effort to get out and visit them more often.

Joyce stayed until the surgeon came and spoke to them. The surgeon assured John and Joyce the operation had gone well. The reality of Joseph's prison status startled her when a guard accompanied his stretcher to the recovery room.

"Are you all right, Joyce?" John placed his arm around her.

"Yes, yes," she sighed. "He just looks so helpless there." Her eyes filled with tears.

"I'll stay with him, and I'll let you know how things are going," John answered.

Looking into John's eyes, Joyce felt the closeness of their friendship. She wondered if Joseph would ever understand just how much this man did for both of them.

She hugged him goodbye and whispered, "I don't know how I'll ever be able to thank you for all you've done."

Joyce left for home with a clear mind. She knew Joseph was safe in John's care and knew her secret was safe with John.

Joseph slowly became aware of movement around him. The nurse took his blood pressure, but her light touch confused him.

"Joyce! Joyce, is that you?" He weakly called through taped lips.

"No, but dream on buddy," the nurse replied.

Joseph drifted back to his dreams. In his dreams, which he wouldn't remember, he was no longer a prisoner. Joyce was laughing and glad to be with him. If only his life was like his dreams. In his dreams, Joyce loved him.

Joseph was in and out of reality for the next 24 hours. The pain made it easier to sleep than to be awake. He was aware of John's presence at times, but still drifted off. It wasn't until the next morning he cut through the drug-induced fog. He became aware of his room and the guard standing by the door. He was back. And not all that sure he wanted to be. The pain was searing and burning. He knew he would have to live with it, and that it might even be worth it, just to get a break from the horror of his prison home. He just didn't fit in there. He told himself he didn't want to make friends with the other prisoners. Joseph told himself they were beneath him. The truth was they wanted nothing to do with him. Joseph was desperately lonely.

Maybe here, in the real world, someone would take the time to befriend him. He turned and saw the guard at the hospital door, and realized no one would trust him or befriend him. He was clearly marked as untouchable. No one wanted a con around.

Still, as painful as his isolation was, Joseph enjoyed seeing normal people. Patients walked the hall and joked with the nurses. The nurses gossiped, joked, and laughed with each other. Joseph wondered if they realized how precious their friendships were. No, probably not. People only missed what they didn't have. He doubted if any of them knew what true loneliness was. All of the patients seemed to be flooded with visitors. Joseph noticed the flowers and balloons, and the crowds of well-wishers spilling out of almost each room as the nurses, with the guard of course, walked him around the halls. He was really starting to pity himself when he noticed the room at the end of the hall. It was so isolated, no one ever seemed to be visiting.

"Who's in there?" he got up the courage to ask one of the nicer nurses.

"Oh, it's just an old woman. She's waiting for placement in a nursing home."

Joseph noticed the empty, pain filled eyes of the white-haired woman as he passed during one of his walks around the hall.

Joseph asked the nurse, "Doesn't anyone ever visit her?"

The nurse, wheeling her medication cart down the hall, shook her head, "She has no family. She's an old maid school teacher. Now that she's sick, there's no one to care for her. The state will place her in whatever nursing home has an opening."

Joseph felt pain. It wasn't a pain in his face. It was a pain in his heart. He could read the loneliness in the woman's face.

Joseph could not remember the last time he cared for anyone's feelings. Even in his family, he always put his own needs above others. Now he felt overwhelmed with empathy for this cloistered woman, a total stranger. He felt the urge to go and speak to her, but when he headed in her direction, the guard quickly ended his attempt.

The guard stopped him, "Where you think you're going, buddy?"

Joseph was startled as he was reminded of his felon status and replied, "I guess no where. I guess I'm not going anywhere."

The guard laughed, "You've got that right, buddy. If you want to make friends, you'll just have to stick with your own kind. You know, all the other losers and low-lives."

The guard seemed greatly amused by his own sense of humor. He laughed and looked at a young nurse for confirmation of his wit.

Joseph stood transfixed. The guard had meant to humiliate him. Instead, what the guard said enlightened him. *Yes, why wouldn't he talk to the other men he was imprisoned with? They were probably as lonely and frightened as he was. Was it because he was afraid? They were probably as distrustful as he was. And what was he afraid of? That they might reject him or ridicule him, or become violent?* Whatever it was, he wasn't doing too well with his current plan of ignoring his fellow prisoners.

Joseph was stunned by his thoughts. He would reach out to other convicts and make friends, and stop being afraid. He knew his life was about to change. He just hoped it would be for the better. He would look for the next opportunity to reach out to a fellow inmate.

Joseph spent two weeks in the hospital, and during that time even the guard noticed a change in him. Bill, the prison guard assigned to watching Joseph, noted a profound change in Joseph's attitude. Joseph was less surly and withdrawn. He appeared friendly and interested in the nurses and all who came in contact with him. He not only knew about the guard's young and pregnant wife, but he asked about her welfare each day, and really seemed to care. He knew about the head nurse's sick husband and asked each day about him. Joseph was starting to look at the people around him. He no longer viewed them as objects to be manipulated to meet his needs. And as he did reach out, he started to notice something. Each and every person, no matter what their status in life, had a story. And each story was pretty interesting. You couldn't just judge a person by what they did, or how they appeared. Often he found the person beneath the facade was nothing like you expected them to be.

Joseph also noticed that when you showed genuine care about another person's life, they seemed to open up. It was as if they were waiting for you to acknowledge them and recognize them as important. And when you did, they started to look at you differently. Joseph also found when you showed you cared about others they suddenly began to care about you. Of course there were people who didn't. They acted just as he did in the past, detached and unconcerned with others. They looked at Joseph as a nonentity, unimportant to them except as a chore. They apparently decided he was of no use to them. It was easy to spot them. They asked polite questions, but didn't care about the answer. These people never looked you in the eye. They related every conversation to themselves and what was best for them. Joseph wondered if he had been as cold and distant as these people. He thought he fooled others with manners and civility. He now realized there was no way to fake interest. You either cared or didn't. Your attitude showed, no matter how you thought you could hide it. Caring made eye contact, it reached out and asked questions, and it remembered. You can't fake it. Joseph found the more he reached out to others and showed he cared, the more they reached back to him. All the nurses found their way to his room on the morning of his discharge. The head nurse teased him, "How long do you think it will before we see you again?"

Joseph smiled and answered, "A long time, I hope! Although I admit there's no one there half as good looking, or as good natured as you."

The head nurse blushed and said, "I hope they treat you a little better this time. Maybe they will, I think you're much better looking than before."

Joseph really was going to miss the friends he made here. Even the gruff guard seemed concerned about Joseph's safety when he returned to the prison population. As they traveled back, Bill handed Joseph a Xerox of a prison program, and casually stated, "You know, you should sign up for this program."

Joseph read the paper that Bill had handed him, and answered, "This is no good. It's the same time I'm assigned to work in the laundry."

"That's the point, stupid," the guard laughed. "They'll have to give you another job so the times don't interfere."

Joseph was touched by the guard's manner. Although he acted casual about it, Joseph knew that he went through a lot of trouble to find out how he could keep the prisoner from returning to the site of his attack. Joseph looked at the paper. It was some kind of religious class led by some priest. It was just the kind of thing Joseph usually made fun of.

"Well, I guess I'll be signing up." He scanned the paper for the title, "For the Life in the Spirit Seminar."

Little did Joseph know how much that decision was about to change his life. Bill was just looking to remove the prisoner from a difficult situation which endangered his life. He didn't realize he was removing him from the danger of losing his soul. Joseph made sure he signed up as soon as he could.

He was surprised at the number and roughness of the inmates who signed up for the program. He found an empty desk in the middle of the class. The hoots and hollers of his fellow inmates alerted Joseph to the entrance of the small framed friar. Dressed in a brown habit tied by a rope at the waist, Father Dan laughed at the men's response to his appearance, and asked, "What's the matter fellows, not used to anyone in uniform?"

The men guffawed at the small priest and his lack of fear. No amount of intimidation, verbal or otherwise, seemed to faze the sandaled, bearded man. He quickly gained the respect of the hardened men in front of him. His courage was genuine, unlike so many others. The inmates could smell fear on a person, no matter how much bravado they might display. This diminutive priest didn't have any. The crowd of men seemed to simmer down in the face of pure spirit.

"Let us pray." As Father Dan bowed his head to lead the men in prayer, they imitated him. His voice was calming and sure.

Joseph prayed. He wasn't sure who he was praying to. But for the first time in his life, he did feel as if someone was listening. Father Dan asked The Holy Spirit to lead the session that was about to begin and to open the hearts and minds of all the men who were present. He then started his talk. Father Dan talked softly about God's love. All the men sat quietly listening to the priest. There was something about his face. It glowed with joy and peace.

All of the inmates seemed mesmerized by the concept that God loved them. Many of the hardened men didn't feel their families loved them. They had long ago learned not to trust any one's loyalty. Many of them were beaten and abused by the very people who were supposed to love them the most, their parents. The convicts felt betrayed by friends and family alike. They built walls around their hearts. Early, they learned not to be vulnerable to being hurt.

Now this priest was trying to tell them God, who they doubted existed at all, loved them. This God, all good and all perfect, loved them. Deep down, many of the men felt they were unlovable. The feeling of being unloved fueled anger, and the anger often led to crime. And yet here was this priest telling them God not only loved them, but He came and died for them. It was a concept that was hard for them to comprehend.

Father Dan ended with a reiteration of God's eternal love. He then introduced another inmate, to give something called a testimony. A grisly old man, bent and arthritic, shuffled up to the podium. Joseph recognized him. He often saw him sweeping the floors, and, in the past, ignored him as insignificant.

The scruffy-looking man began, "My name is Pete, and I'm here to tell you how God loves me. I'm a Lifer. I have been in this prison for the last twenty-five years of my life and I think that I will probably die here." Joseph couldn't believe his ears. How could this man think that God loved him? God let him live and die in this hell hole.

"I was born seventy eight years ago to an alcoholic prostitute who abandoned me on the steps of an orphanage and stopped coming to see me by the time I was five. I believe in my heart she died, but I'll never know."

Joseph was shocked by how much the man was revealing about himself. Pete continued with the story of such an unloved and abusive life that Joseph sat fascinated. Pete pulled no punches when he talked about his crime, and revealed, "I am guilty of the terrible murder of two young girls. I have no excuse. Life was cheap to me. It was as cheap as my own life was, until five years ago." Pete paused as he took deep breaths to control his emotions. "Five years ago, I met Father Dan and I went through a Life in the Spirit Seminar, like you are about to do. The hardest thing for me to comprehend was that God loved me. Me, Pete, who never did nothing good for nobody. My first question to any situation was always, what's in it for me?"

Pete, who had hung his head in shame, suddenly raised his eyes to look at the crowd of men and continued, "But when I was baptized in the Spirit, as you will be in six weeks, I felt God's warmth and love rushing though me. He touched my heart and mind, my very spirit." Pete paused as he choked with tears at this point. "I am no longer the person I was before. No, my circumstances have not changed. I will die in this prison. But I have changed, and now I know that God can even use me to do His work. I will be with Him and love Him for all eternity. And I am the happiest and luckiest man in the world because He loves me."

There was dead silence in the room, as Pete stepped down from the podium. Father Dan took over and led the men in a loud rendition of "Amazing Grace." Most of the hardened convicts were visibly moved by the blunt honesty they just witnessed.

They were directed into small groups of four men each and given a question to discuss with an assigned facilitator. The director of Joseph's group was another lifer convicted of kidnapping and attempted murder. All the men in his group had committed violent crimes of one kind or another. The burly man who led the group began with prayer, May the Holy Sprit be with us and direct all that we say or do tonight. May our minds and hearts be open to His prompting and may we all grow spiritually tonight. Amen.

"Well, our question tonight is, can we each tell of an incident in our life, when we felt the love of God?"

Two of the men told moving stories of life situations they claimed they never told anyone. One of the men refused to talk and was told that no one had to talk who didn't want to. Joseph was surprised to hear himself tell the story of his friendship with John. He told how he let John down and betrayed him. Yet, despite everything, John stood by him and was even with him during his recent hospitalization.

Joseph ended his story with, "I feel God has been good to me through John. I don't deserve such a loyal friend, especially when I was a selfish man all my life."

Joseph looked up expecting to see rejection and disgust on the faces of the men. He expected total rejection from men who now knew him for who he truly was. Instead he saw interest and sympathy.

The leader said, "Thank you for sharing, Joseph."

By the end of the night, Joseph felt he began new friendships. He looked forward to the meeting next week.

The Cleansing

Forgive us the wrong we have done, as we forgive those who wrong us. (Matt. 5:12)

Elly looked through her picture window, and gazed at the streaks of gold that lightened the morning sky. Sitting in the overstuffed chair, she couldn't help feeling a sense of satisfaction and pride in her home. The ocean rolled beneath the rising sun, and the morning light filled her with gratitude for the God who created such a world. The trip home was comfortable, but it hadn't been easy for her to leave her newfound family. Each one of them was special, each so loving and unique. But, it was the newborn who won her heart. He was so small, so dependent.

His world was full of love and interest. The people around him delighted in his smallest movement and action. His smallest coo brought a wave of delight from his doting relatives. Elly fell deeply in love with the little stranger while feeding him late one night. Each member of the family took turns giving the infant his bottle, so his exhausted mother could get a solid night's sleep. Aunt Sarah pointed out there would be plenty of sleepless nights in her future.

The infant opened his eyes and stared at her, as she gave him the warmed bottle. It was as if he was memorizing her face. His small hand held one of her fingers in acceptance of her friendship. It was impossible not to fall in love with this little life. It was very hard for

Elly to say goodbye to all of them. She resolved to buy the baby a present as soon as she got home. This was her plan for the day.

Arriving home, she found a letter from Gabe in the mailbox. He returned to his clinic, but he would be home soon. He had a surprise for her. Elly calculated he would be back, according to his plans, in three days. She really missed him. But she decided not to mope. Elly decided she would make the most her time by getting a christening present for Cynthia's baby. She also wanted to make an appointment with the pastor.

She hated to leave the sunrise scene she was enjoying, but decided she better shower and dress for the day. She did all of this and was about to head out the door, when the phone rang.

"Hello, is this Miss Wilkin?"

"Yes it is," Elly answered wondering who it could be.

"Oh, I'm so glad that I've reached you. I've been calling you for a week."

Elly answered quickly, wondering what could be so important, "I was away, how can I help you?"

The woman on the other end of the phone said, "Oh well, it's our policy to notify the next of kin when the gravestone is engraved and placed in the cemetery. It allows the family to check and see if the work is accurate and meets all their expectations. If anything is amiss, it's better to deal with it right away. Do you anticipate visiting your mother's grave site in the near future?"

Elly was silent for a moment. The call took her by surprise. The funeral of her mother seemed a lifetime ago. So much had happened since her death. The pain of her relationship came flooding back to her, and she wasn't prepared for it.

"Miss Wilkin, are you there?" the voice on the other end of the phone called.

"Yes, yes, of course, I'll be in town today. I'll visit the grave today. I'll let you know if anything is wrong." Elly shocked herself by what she said. She had no plans to visit the grave today, she didn't want to visit the grave at all.

"Thank you, Miss Wilkin, we're sure that you'll be pleased with our work. Please think of us in the future, if you need us."

The phone call took Elly's breath away. *Why did she say she would visit her mother's grave today?* She planned a day of joy-filled shopping and spiritual renewal. Dealing with her feelings about her mother was never part of her plans. She didn't want to think about her mother. Her life had been good over the last few months. She felt like a new person. She didn't want to think about her life before her mother died. She had blocked it from her mind. It was as if her life began after meeting Gabe, and her newly discovered family. This reminder of her past brought nothing but pain.

This is ridiculous. I should be able to handle such a simple task, Elly thought. She decided to be mature. There was no reason that she couldn't control her emotions. *Why did she let her mother bother her? She would look at the trip as anyone would, as a business transaction. She would evaluate the engraving on the stone, and not get emotional about it. She wasn't going to let anything spoil her day, or her new life.* Elly was determined not to let the past intrude on her current situation. With that resolve, she left the house and headed out on the long walk into town.

The air was cool and fresh. It invigorated Elly. The numerous small shops intrigued her. Finding the perfect baby present was not going to be hard. Choosing among all the exemplary selections was the difficult part.

Entering a small gift shop, Elly knew she found the perfect gift when she saw it. A complete crib ensemble, with the bumpers, pillow, sheets and comforter caught her eye. The beautiful colors would go with any decor. The comforter could be embroidered with the baby's name, birthday, and weight. Elly knew her cousin would love it. It would be ready in a week, and the clerk promised it would be shipped to the address that Elly gave her within three days of completion. Elly couldn't wait for them to receive it. It was such a delight to share things with loved ones. It was a new and pleasing experience for Elly.

Elly decided to lunch at the small coffee shop that caught her eye while she was shopping. The aroma of the fresh baked bread made her hungry. She was delighted with the creative menu the colorful cafe offered and settled on a sandwich and a flavor of coffee she never tried before. The shop was full. It was turning out to be a good day and she pushed the thought of going to the grave site out of her head. She would deal with that problem after lunch.

She was surprised she didn't feel awkward about eating alone. In the past, she would be too mortified. Worried about all the other diners looking at her, she would never sit at a table solo. It was funny how much a person could evolve in such a short time. She was actually enjoying being alone with her thoughts. She relished watching the strangers around her. The world was brighter. Flooded in a new light, Elly was seeing it for the first time with a sense of hope. She had a future filled with love. Elly smiled, thinking how much she was like her new nephew, seeing the world through new eyes.

After she delighted her taste buds with the freshly baked slice of carrot cake the waitress suggested for dessert, she felt full and sleepily satisfied. The bright September sun revived her as she leisurely walked the mile to the gated graveyard which stood just outside of town. Except for a few preoccupied visitors, the cemetery was empty. It was easy to find her mother's grave in the small yard. It wasn't like the search for her father's grave. She remembered the grave site. She tried to remain businesslike. Elly resolved not to let her mother ever hurt her again.

The stone was gray and glowed with the shine of newly polished granite, unlike the weather worn stones that surrounded it. The engraving was simple enough. Along with a few carved roses, it simply stated, "Louise Wilkin, beloved wife and mother." Elly tried to remain calm, but thoughts kept rushing through her. It was all a lie.

Louise wasn't any kind of wife. She married an old man for his money. She cheated a father of his daughter and a daughter of her father. She verbally beat down that daughter until it was possible to control and manipulate her. She hadn't loved and wasn't beloved at all. She was hated. Louise tried to destroy her daughter's spirit. She tried to kill Elly's soul. As Elly gulped back the tears of suppressed emotion, she gasped for the cool air. The rage she was suppressing broke to the surface. Elly couldn't understand her mother. She tried to kill everything unique about her daughter, including any God-given spirit in the gentle child. She tried, in every emotional and spiritual way, to kill a lonely little girl. Elly fell to her knees before her mother's gravestone and wept. How could Louise hate her so?

As she cried, Elly swore a voice which spoke only in her heart cried out, "She didn't kill you, I was always there."

Elly never heard such a soothing voice. She stopped crying and sat in stunned silence. She knew she heard the voice of her Creator. He was always with her. She was never really alone. He protected her, and while she was wounded her mother didn't kill her spirit. And then the truth hit her and took her breath away. *My mother didn't kill me and I hate her for what she did do, but I did kill my child. I've done worse than her. Who am I to judge her? Who am I to judge anyone? She tried to hurt me for her own reasons, but I killed my child for my own twisted reasons.*

A sense of guilt hit Elly full force. *What was worse than killing your own baby?* she thought as she stared at her mother's headstone.

Lately all her memories of her mother had been of a cruel and dominating manipulator. Now, Elly could remember Louise at moments of kindness. When Elly was very young her mother had shown her great love. *What had gone wrong? When had she changed?* It was such a gradual change it was difficult to pin-point the exact moment of her mother's downfall. It was after she got involved with all of her strange new age beliefs. At first, it seemed to be just a way for her mother to fill all the empty hours. A way to placate the curiosity she held about the unknown. But somehow Louise opened a door. It was a door to evil, and once it was opened, Louise lost herself to the spirits of the occult. She opened the door, and that's all evil needed to enter. She somehow lost the Louise God had made.

The occult, and those who practiced it, played to the very sin that caused the original fall of Eve. The occult played to Louise's pride. It played to the pride-filled need to know and control one's future. The pride was carefully fed and grown until it swallowed the person up. It drew Louise's soul away from the search for the True God, and turned her into a soul who worshiped her own false sense of power and knowledge. It caused a daughter to lose her mother.

But, I actually killed my child, thought Elly, I did worse than this lost woman. Elly stared at the stone. She started to talk to her mother. She now knew she had to forgive her mother. Elly fell under the spell of the Holy Spirit, and started to pray.

Elly felt a shiver arouse her. Looking at her watch, she realized it was already two in the afternoon. She shook herself. She needed to hurry if she was going to get to the rectory before closing time. She couldn't believe she had been sitting here so long. Elly didn't know this was often how the Holy Spirit ministered to a soul. She wiped the crisp brown leaves from her pants, and started on her way to town. Despite all of the heavy emotions she'd just gone through, she felt strangely at peace. Elly was unaware God had just given her the grace of forgiveness. It was starting to work on her. Elly was on her way to forgiving herself.

The small white church was on the other side of town. It took Elly about a half an hour to walk there. The autumn sun set early, and so she wanted to set up her appointment with the pastor, and be on her way home. It had been a full day and she felt a strange fatigue. The small brick rectory stood next to the white church. Elly stood on the sidewalk for a minute, hesitating. She was nervous about talking to the priest. *What if he rejected her?*

She rang the bell with some trepidation. A curly-haired receptionist answered the door and led Elly into a shabby office. After quickly and efficiently discovering Elly needed an appointment with the pastor, she dialed the inner office.

Hanging up the phone, she directed Elly to the door, "He'll see you now."

Elly panicked, "I just want to make an appointment to speak to him, I don't need to see him right away."

The receptionist seemed amused.

"Well, you're in luck. He's free to see you now. And what's more," the girl laughed as she gently pushed Elly through the door she opened, "he doesn't usually bite people on Monday!"

Elly looked around as the large wooden door closed behind her. The carpeting was worn, but clean. The walls were lined with bookshelves filled with large volumes that overflowed and spilled out to produce piles of books on the floor. A large metal desk stood in the middle of the room surrounded by strategically stacked papers. Behind the desk sat the pastor, a white-haired man with numerous wrinkles and twinkling brown eyes. He waved his hand and motioned for Elly to come in as he said, "Come in, come in, my child. Sit, and be patient as I finish this last paragraph."

Elly watched with amusement as the pastor struggled to type with his two pointer fingers amidst exclamations each time he hit the wrong key. He finally sat back and smiled with great relief, finishing whatever work he was grappling with.

He turned his attention to Elly, with an apology for her wait. "I'm sorry you had to wait, but if I stop while I'm writing, I always lose my train of thought. I'm Father John." He reached across the messy desk to shake her hand. "How can I help you, Elly?"

Elly was stunned. *How did he know her first name?* He did look familiar. He made Elly feel very comfortable. Still, she nervously shuffled her feet, as she struggled for the words she had planned to rehearse, after she made an appointment to see the priest.

In a whisper, Elly answered, "I guess, I've, well, I just want to find out about coming back."

Elly looked down at her feet. She half expected the priest to tell her to get out. She envisioned him asking her who she thought she was.

A sinner like Elly couldn't come to church. Only good people could come to church.

Instead she heard the soft-spoken priest say, "Welcome home prodigal daughter, Jesus has been waiting for you."

Elly looked into the priest's eyes and saw nothing but honest love and welcome. She had to ask, "How did you know my name, Father?"

The white-haired priest smiled and answered, "Oh, I'm sorry Elly, I guess you don't remember me, but I knew you as a child. You've grown into a beautiful woman, but you were a very pretty little girl, so I'm not surprised. I guess you were too young to remember me."

Elly really didn't remember the priest. But his eyes were so kind. Elly felt safe enough to talk and started, "I don't know how to go about it. My cousin, who I just met, is a nun, and she explained a little about the instruction for adults which I think she called RCIA. I guess I'm here to see how to sign up." Elly blurted out what she had to say, as if to say it all before she lost her courage.

The priest's smile was infectious, as he responded, "Well sure, as I recall, you hadn't made all of your sacraments and you will need instructions to make them. We usually have converts and returning Catholics who haven't made all of the sacraments study, so they can understand what the Catholic Church teaches. If they agree with those beliefs, they receive the sacraments they need to live a life of faith. They are usually received into the Church on Easter vigil. That's in the spring, the night before Easter morning, so you'll have plenty of time for your instructions. But tell me Elly, what made you decide to resume the faith-filled life?"

Elly hesitated. She didn't know where to begin. Then, the words just poured out. She gave the priest a short synopsis of her life and her desire to know God. The elderly priest came around the desk and sat in a chair facing Elly.

Taking both of her hands in his, he gently stated, "Elly, why don't we start by a good confession. I know you probably won't remember everything today, but the Holy Spirit will help you remember what you need to confess now."

Elly remained silent as the kind pastor prayed and asked The

Holy Spirit, with all His Power and Wisdom to touch Elly. Elly could feel warmth running through her which seemed to make the moment stand still. She felt the flowing peace of the Holy Spirit as the Priest continued in prayer. She felt the caress of God even as the words of the priest melted into a peaceful drone. At the end of his prayer, after a few minutes of silence, she heard him instruct her to begin her confession.

Elly answered his request, “I don’t know how to, I don’t remember!”

The priest gently instructed, “I’ll help you, repeat my words. Bless me Father, for I have sinned. It has been how many years since my last confession.”

Elly filled in the blank of 15 years. The compassionate guide before her led her through the Ten Commandments and Elly was incredulous. Memories flooded her. She covered all of the mortal sins of her past. Father explained the Spirit of God would reveal more to her. She could come back and confess what was revealed. The Church recommended monthly confession. Confession gave a sinner the grace to overcome tough sin patterns and grow in a deeper relationship with God. Elly was in shock. She told this priest the worst things she had ever done. She even told him about Michael, and the abortion. She told him of her hatred of her mother. He didn’t condemn her – he guided her with love at every turn.

The priest continued, “And now Elly, before I give you absolution for your sins, please say the act of contrition.”

She was embarrassed and stated, “I don’t remember it.”

Again the priest helped her, “I’ll help you, just repeat after me.” Elly repeated each line as Father John led, ‘O my God, I am heartily sorry for having offended Thee, and I detest all my sins because I dread the loss of Heaven and the pains of Hell; but most of all because they offend thee, my God, Who art all good and deserving of all my love. I firmly resolve, with the help of Thy grace, to confess my sins, to do penance, and to amend my life. Amen.’

Father John asked Elly to pray the fifty-first psalm each day as her penance.

Elly responded, "I have no Bible, Father."

Again the priest offered a solution and said, "I'll give you one before you leave. Now bow your head, and receive the Lord's forgiveness."

He gave Elly a blessing as he gave her absolution for her sins. Elly felt as if a large weight had been lifted off her shoulders. A flood of warming peace flowed through her.

Returning to his desk, the pastor opened up an appointment book and said, "Elly, I'm going to give you an appointment in a week, about this same time, if that's all right with you. RCIA doesn't start up for a month, but I want to see you at least once a week. If you have any questions, or if anything should come up, don't be afraid to call me."

Elly, filled with joy, just smiled. Father John reached out with a big hug, "Welcome back to the Kingdom of God, Elly."

She walked home as if on a cloud. She couldn't comprehend the feelings she was experiencing. For so long, she led a life of pain and sadness. The feeling of joy was a new thing for her. Oh sure, she was happy at times. When she met Michael and when she first wanted his baby. It was the way she felt when she saw Gabe approaching. She felt happy then. But this was different. She felt joy-filled. It was a deeper emotion. It was internal. It didn't seem to depend on outside events. It was a gift from God. Elly decided not to dissect it, just to enjoy it.

Arriving home, she felt great. She made a small dinner and watched the news. She felt distracted. It had been a busy day and much had happened. Her emotions were somewhat confused. She felt a deep sense of peace and joy that she couldn't explain. Nothing changed on the physical level. She was in the same house. She looked the same. She ate an ordinary dinner and watched her usual television programs. Nothing happened to change the very practical life she set for herself.

And yet, something was very different. Something was so

different she could only feel it. She could not explain it. It was as if she had been existing on only one level and now she was seeing many levels she didn't see before. It was as if she was partially blind or had dark glasses on. Now the bright light of the truth lifted her heart and showed her a new and better world. The better world was always there, but Elly couldn't see it. Each time it started to manifest itself in the past, she turned her eyes away. She was afraid of it, and refused to look at it. *Elly felt she was set free! Free to see the truth of the world around her.* Seeing through new eyes, she saw not only the temporal, but also the ethereal.

Elly didn't fully understand what was happening to her. She only knew that she was now a different person. She didn't understand that by turning to God, the God who called her, she started a new life. She was now part of the Kingdom of God. She was no longer living a natural life, but a supernatural life.

Elly felt too restless to watch television. She tried to read but couldn't seem to concentrate, so she decided to go to bed early, when the phone rang. She rejoiced to hear Gabe's voice.

"I just couldn't go to sleep without checking on you," Gabe laughed.

Elly smiled to herself and answered, "I'm glad you did, I've missed you." She was shocked at the freedom she felt about sharing her feelings with this man. In the past, she would have felt unsure about exposing her affections for fear of being rejected. Suddenly, it didn't seem to matter. She didn't feel any fear.

Gabe answered enthusiastically, "Well, I've missed you too. It seems that I've been gone forever. I can't wait to see you. I'm dying to tell you my surprise."

Elly teased and tempted him, but he would not give her even a clue about his secret. She lovingly decided that revenge was the best response.

Giggling, she announced, "Well, you're not the only one with a secret. I guess if you're not telling me yours, you'll just have to wait to hear mine."

"Oh, the revenge of a woman scorned," cried Gabe, after numerous attempts to make her tell her secret. "I guess both of us will have to wait until we see each other."

"And just when will that be?" queried a contented Elly.

Gabe smiled at her impatience, "I guess when I get there. It should be the day after tomorrow. That is, if you can take the time out of your busy day to see me."

Elly laughed, "Oh, I don't know, perhaps I'll be able to squeeze you in. What time do you want to come over?'

With all the pretense of not caring over, Gabe's voice became husky with emotion as he answered, "Elly, if I could fly through the phone just to see you and touch you and kiss you, I would. As it is the train will arrive in town about ten in the morning. Do you think that you could pick me up?"

Elly felt like crying when she heard the emotion in his voice. How could she be so lucky to meet someone as precious as this man? She knew she was falling in love with him. She wasn't afraid. It all seemed so right. Elly suddenly knew that she, like her small nephew, had a future filled with love and exciting new adventures.

She answered cheerfully, "I'll be waiting for you. I guess I could make you a nice brunch. You'll be hungry after the long train trip."

Gabe laughed, "Oh, I won't turn down food, but I'm really hungry for my girl!"

Elly smiled. It was the first time that Gabe had called her his girl. She hoped she would be his girl forever. She overflowed with thanksgiving at the gifts her new life was bringing.

She answered in a light-hearted manner, "Well, I'll make you some food anyway. I've seen you eat at your mother's house and I have no illusions about how long my looks will keep you satisfied."

Gabe pretended great offense as he answered, "Stung again with the cold practical truth. Have you no mercy in you, woman? It seems to me that you have no romance in your soul."

Elly laughed, "Oh, I have romance all right, but it's peppered generously with functional truth. A man may be glad to see his girl, but he'd be even happier to see his girl if she's holding a platter of his favorite food."

Gabe responded, "I guess I can't argue with you there. But it wouldn't hurt if you were just a little more romantic about our relationship."

Elly wished she could reach through the phone and kiss him. Instead she said, "I think that you've got all the romance we need for this relationship. Just keep it up. You swoon over me, while I make us food. It seems like a perfect plan to me."

Gabe's voice grew husky again, as he answered, "As long as I get to be with you, everything will be perfect. Still, it wouldn't hurt if you did a little swooning yourself."

"Well, I'll see if I can work up a swoon, when I see you. Until then, keep thinking of me," Elly retorted.

They said their goodbyes with regret. It was becoming harder and harder to remain separated. The newly discovered feelings they were developing longed for closeness. Elly was looking forward to telling Gabe about her new family and her return to the Church. Somehow, she knew that while he would be happy about the former, he would be thrilled about the latter.

The Dream

Such was his intention when, behold, the angel of the lord appeared to him in a dream and said, "Joseph, son of David, do not be afraid to take Mary your wife into your home. For it is through the Holy Spirit that this child has been conceived in her. (Matt 1:20)

Elly hated to end the phone conversation with Gabe, but she looked forward to seeing him soon. Elly snuggled under the soft goose down comforter that covered her queen-sized bed. The night had turned chilly. She prayed a Rosary. The prayer was so meditative on the life of Christ, that it relaxed her fervent mind. It brought her a comfortable peace, and she drifted off to sleep feeling she was in the hands of God. Elly fell into a deep sleep.

Elly found herself crawling. It was dark and she was surrounded by a bone-chilling cold.

Her knees were swollen and cut. The palms of her hands and all of her fingers were sore. The incline she was crawling up was rough and imbedded with sharp pebbles and rocks. The only warmth her cold, bleeding extremities could feel was the warmth of her own blood as it oozed from numerous cuts and abrasions.

She was exhausted. Cut and hurt, she didn't know how long she had been climbing in this dark place. She didn't know where she was.

She only knew she needed to keep climbing as she struggled against the cold and pain. She pushed on despite overwhelming fatigue. She somehow knew if she stopped, she would die.

Pulling herself one knee and one hand at a time, she knew she couldn't go on much longer. She reached her breaking point. One more reach and she would collapse. It didn't seem to matter anymore. She longed for the blessed sleep of death. As she reached up, she felt something sticking out of the ground. She grabbed it with one hand, and despite the pain from the deep lacerations on her knees, she reached up with the other hand and pulled herself up. She leaned her head against the object she gripped, and rested. It seemed a long time since she had rested. She felt warm. The cold disappeared. She now recognized that the object she grasped had the feel of a rough wooden plank. She felt safe now. She decided that she would rest for a while, until she could go on.

After she rested for what seemed like a long time, she became aware of a warm liquid she felt slowly dripping off her arms. At first she thought it was blood from the many gashes on both her hands. No, she realized, there was too much for it to be blood from her hands. And now she also felt it on her head. It seemed to be dripping down the wooden stake she was clinging to.

She was exhausted. She didn't want to open her eyes, but knew she had to see what was dripping on her. She struggled with the fatigue which seemed to seal her eyes shut. At first, her eyes flickered, unused to the light. She knew she was clinging to a wooden plank, but as she looked up, she could see it was not a wooden plank–it was a wooden cross. And on that cross was a man, who she instantly recognized as Jesus. The warm liquid that she had felt running over her was His blood dripping from his open wounds. It was His blood which warmed her.

She continued to cling to this rough cross as she looked up at the Jesus she had run from all of her life. She could do nothing else. The clouds swirled in the gray sky behind the cross, as harsh winds blew. The hill Elly found herself on was formed of rough stone and barren dirt with no vegetation. The winds blew the dry dust, stinging her eyes. Elly looked down at the tattered and dirty dress she wore. Variations of gray colored this desolate place. This dark hill, with a storm brewing in the distance, felt dark and forsaken.

Elly became frightened again. Looking up, she reached out to the only person there. She looked up to Jesus. Elly looked into His eyes, eyes of eternal wisdom and love. His eyes had indescribable depth. She was mesmerized. Elly couldn't look away. The dust and pebbles the harsh gales flung against Elly stung her exposed skin. The storm clouds gathered and darkened, covering the sun which became just a dull orb in the black sky.

Lightning crashed, flashing bright across the sky behind the cross. Elly felt so vulnerable and unprotected. She looked up to the man on the cross. Frightened and in pain, Elly called for help.

"Jesus, help me!"

Suddenly she was no longer in pain, she was no longer cold. The storm melted away. The sun brightened. The sense of love that radiated from Jesus warmed Elly. She wanted to touch this man on the cross and help him. The love she felt for him was overwhelming. She didn't want to look away. She looked at Him, and He looked at her for a long time.

Somehow, she just seemed to know that He wanted her to look away. It was an infused knowledge. They never actually spoke to each other. She knew He wanted to show her something. He wanted her to look to His right although it was desperately hard to tear her eyes away from His. She felt so much love she didn't want Him to leave. She tore her eyes away and looked to the right. She would never forget what she saw.

A beautiful woman stood glowing in an ethereal light. Her white and flowing gown and veils were luminescent, yet they didn't reflect as much radiance as her face. It was the most beautiful face Elly ever saw. Not because of its form or features, but because of its kindness. Elly basked in the glow of the kind face. She knew Mary the mother of Jesus, was standing before her. Again, Elly felt a sense of peacc and love overwhelming her. Elly noticed the compassionate figure before her was holding something in her arms. It was a baby, wrapped in a pink blanket. The face was so familiar.

Elly gasped as she realized the baby looking sweetly at her had Michael's face. *Yet she had her mother's eyes, eyes so like Aunt Sarah's. It was her baby. It was the baby she and Michael conceived. It was the daughter Elly aborted. The little girl she lost to fear, pain, and sin.* Looking at the sweet face of her daughter, Elly half expected the infant's look of love to turn to hate. Hate, because Elly's choice had denied a life to the infant.

Instead the babe stared at her with longing. She seemed to want Elly to hold her. Elly reached out, but quickly realized she couldn't hold her baby now. She realized her baby was in the arms of Mary. She suddenly understood that Mary would care for her daughter until she came to heaven to care for her.

Elly felt relieved. She never acknowledged the fear she had felt for her infant. She learned that the God, who created all life, never destroyed it. A soul once created had Eternal life. That is why God didn't destroy Satan. God would not destroy life.

The young woman had not acknowledged the tapestry of fears haunting her. She now knew that, deep down, she wondered what happened to her child. She was afraid to even think about this fear. Now she knew. She didn't need to be afraid anymore. Her daughter was still alive. Her child's spirit, like the spirit of all living things, was eternal. God created life. It was eternal, because life reflected Him, and He was eternal.

Elly wanted to hold her daughter. The pain of the separation grew. She longed for the baby. Her arms felt empty. She didn't want to wait. She wanted to be with her infant right now. The longing was intense, an instinct that only another mother could understand. She wanted to leave her life and enter the eternal realm. She wanted to be with her daughter and the Blessed Mother. She longed for this compassionate and loving God. Her longing grew, but the beautiful woman before her seemed to be showing her something. Again she knew that she would have to look away. She would have to tear her eyes away from a breathtaking vision to see something else she needed to understand. She looked to the right again as she felt the angelic vision indicated she should.

Elly saw a long road. It wound around from left to right. On each side of the road stood many people. She only knew a few of the people. She saw Gabe and some of her family, but most of these people were strangers. There were young women, children, and old men. There were people of all races and ages. At the end of the road, there was a bright glowing light. In that light, was the vision of Mary and Jesus, and a young woman whom she now recognized as her daughter.

She began to see what Mary was trying to show her. The knowledge overwhelmed her. Mary was showing her the road of her life. The people on the side of the road were all the people that Elly's life would touch. She needed to live the life this road represented. She needed to meet and touch all of the people on this road. At the end of this road of life stood eternity, and the God who loved her.

Elly suddenly knew what the Blessed Mother was telling her. There were no short cuts. Life was a gift that had to be used. She needed to fulfill her destiny before the reward of Eternal Life. There were others who would need her. She had other work to do. There would be an eternity to be with her daughter, right now she needed to live on earth. She needed to accomplish the will of God for her life.

Elly was given a most precious gift. She was given a glimpse into the everlasting love of God. She, in a dream, encountered the eternal meaning of life. In a moment, she was given a view of life. It was a view of life that all people were given a glimpse of. Life and the God of Life were reflected in the cycles of nature, in the words of the scripture, in the natural justice of the eternal meaning of love. In a vision, Elly was shown what we are all shown. Life has meaning and life is eternal.

Elly awoke from her dream, knowing instantly the vision was more than a dream. It was so real that she, now back in the earthly plain, felt disoriented. She awoke clinging to her pillow, as she had clung to the cross. She sensed the vision was the truth. And as it said in the Bible, the truth set her free. For the first time, Elly not only knew she was forgiven, but she realized she forgave herself. She had a life to live. She had immortality as a promise. She would never be afraid of death again. God had spoken to her in her dreams.

Elly wept tears of joy. She fell back to sleep in peace and wrapped in the knowledge of God's Love. She knew her life would never be the same. She understood life now. It was so emancipating to understand life. She had work to do, and she knew it was God's work. If she followed His Will, she would eventually reach Him. She felt a rush of contentment and serenity flow through her. Elly quietly enjoyed the most peaceful sleep she ever knew.

When she awoke to the late morning light, she was surprised she had slept so late. It wasn't like her. She was usually up with the sun and it was now ten in the morning. She never felt so rested. She vividly remembered the dream she experienced the night before. She didn't usually remember her dreams. It was too real, too detailed, and too intense to be just a dream. Somehow, Elly knew God had really reached out and touched her with a very personal message. She knew it was connected to the sacrament of reconciliation she experienced yesterday. The morning light didn't end her sense of well-being. Elly, through an ongoing faith, would maintain this sense of God for the rest of her natural life. Although her moods and feelings might change with the circumstances of her life, the very core of her spirit would always measure any incident in life against her sense of Eternal Truth.

Feeling wonderful, Elly showered and dressed for the day. She was so joyful she felt restless. After a light breakfast, she decided to take a walk. It was a bit chilly, but the sweater she wore was enough to keep her warm. She walked by the ocean. It was a rough day and the waves tossed the distant fishing ships around. It was a beautiful sight, in the bright sunlight. The beach was deserted on such a cold and windy day. Elly enjoyed the isolation. She was no longer afraid of the ocean, or of being alone.

Home was now this large house on the ocean. It no longer just held the memories of a painful childhood. New memories had been made here. Her aunt had met her at this house. So her new family was part of the new moments spent here. Even more important was the time Gabe had spent here with her. Elly had allowed love into this house. The house on the ocean was like her – newly renovated. The house was no longer empty and dark. It was full of love and light. Elly had a premonition that this new home would be a big part of her new life in Christ. She hoped that Gabe would be part of that new life.

In her heart Elly knew Gabe would be thrilled she had gone back to the church. She knew he was curious about what happened to the baby she was carrying when he last met her. He was man enough not to question her, or to force information from her before she was ready. She was ready now. She knew she could open up and tell him the truth now.

Elly sensed Gabe would be able to handle the truth. If he rejected her for it, she would understand. Still, it would hurt her deeply if that was his reaction. Elly suspected she was deeply in love with Dr. Gabriel Lopez. She was in love with the man she thought he was. If he turned out not to be the man she thought he was, she knew she would suffer. But, she also knew she would handle it. The point was to live in truth.

Elly spent most of her life in a house of lies. The truth was so painful Elly created illusions about the people in her life. She rationalized their behavior. She made excuses for everything they said or did, especially behavior which injured her. Elly had thought that denial was forgiveness. It wasn't. Forgiveness was facing the truth, accepting the truth, and then forgiving in truth.

Elly, with the grace of God, decided to always live in truth.

Sometimes that truth would hurt, she knew. But nothing could be worse than a life of lies. It was the lies of her former life that hurt her. She made excuses for her mother, herself, and everyone else she met. She lived a fantasy life. She projected feelings and thoughts into others she thought they should have. She vowed she would never do that again. *It's the lies we tell ourselves that do us in*, she thought as she walked along the beach.

Elly promised herself she would listen carefully and watch closely. She would take what people said and what they did at face value. She would believe them. If, for instance, someone said they didn't care about her, she would believe them. She would compare what they said to what they did, and if it fit, she would accept it as the truth. In the past, she would have made excuses for them, not being able to believe their coldness and disinterest. She would project her own feelings into them and find all kinds of excuses for their behavior.

She understood now that the truth stood alone. So often she ran around it. She refused to see it, because if she did, she would have to do something about the truth. When she did wrong, she found all kinds of excuses for herself. Elly pledged to herself she would always deal in truth. *If the truth was painful, so be it. It couldn't be worse than living a lie.*

Elly decided she would always look at the why of doing things. She was a generous soul, but she had a tendency to do good things so others would approve of her. She would wear herself out trying to win the love of those who didn't even have love to give. She did that with her mother and it become a pattern in her life. She now knew it was a sick pattern. *If someone has love, they have it as a gift from God. To try to win love from people by good works was just a waste of time.*

Elly knew that by being kind, she would demonstrate the kindness God gave her. *But to be kind and do works to win the love of others was wrong. Jesus said we should love others as ourselves. If we didn't love ourselves, then we couldn't love others. If others weren't acting out of love, they weren't acting in God. For God is love.*

It was a lot for Elly to comprehend. She knew her behavior

would take time to change. She would need to take each day and each situation as it came. She knew she couldn't do it alone. It would require God's grace and much prayer. She would fail at times, but she would learn. She had to act out of love for God, herself, and others, in that order.

Living in truth meant opening her eyes. She would have to see and hear the truth, accept it, and endure any hurt it caused. She would live in truth and live in the Spirit of God.

The cold wind was starting to bite. Elly started home with a sense of well-being. If she lived the new life, as revealed to her, she knew she would start to act as an adult in God. She hoped Gabe would accept her in truth, with all her failings. But if he didn't, she would accept it, and get over it.

She climbed the steep rocks up to the house. Elly loved Gabe, and she hoped that he loved her. She wanted to have a full life with him. Yes, she even admitted to herself that she hoped to marry him. The thought of marriage and children filled her with elation. She hoped for this with all of her heart, but if it wasn't meant to be, so be it.

Perhaps, because she knew God loved her, she was secure. She didn't just know it in her head. She knew it in her heart and in her spirit. The dream she experienced and the journey she was on convinced her that the Creator of the Universe loved her.

Elly knew and felt the love. She could handle anything, as long as she knew that love. If Gabe loved her, it would be a bonus. It would be a great gift from God. It would never be a necessity. The only necessity was God.

She made an early dinner. Not just a simple sandwich–she decided to treat herself to a full home cooked meal. She put a steak on the grill, tossed a salad, and cooked a potato in the microwave. The full meal was a blessing she gave herself, and she enjoyed it with relish. *I guess the fresh air made me hungry,* she thought.

She was washing up the dishes, when the phone rang.

Elly knew immediately that it was Gabe. She ran to the phone with glee. He confirmed that he would be back tomorrow. He sounded anxious to see her and she was glad he felt a little lonely. It proved she meant something to him. They talked on the phone for an hour, each of them unable to say goodbye. Elly longed to feel his arms around her. She wanted to share all of her new found knowledge with him. It only seemed right to share with him. She hoped he would make the early train. Tonight, she decided, she would go grocery shopping and buy something special for his lunch. She laughed as she recalled his hearty appetite. It was a pleasure to cook for someone who really appreciated it.

Joseph's Pentecost

Then there appeared to them tongues as of fire, Which parted and came to rest on each one of Them. And they were all filled with the Holy Spirit and began to speak in tongues, as the Spirit enabled them to proclaim. (Acts 1:4)

Joseph looked forward to the next meeting of the Life in the Spirit seminar. The talk he heard the first week really piqued his interest. The small group of men he was placed with were men he saw everyday. He just never noticed them. They blended into the crowd he once thought so beneath him. He found it pleasant to be recognized by a short nod, or smile. He felt human again. It amazed him that these men didn't reject him after what he revealed about himself.

It had occurred to him lately just what a horrific person he was. Joseph had turned his back on so many people who needed him.

It started with his mother. He turned his back on her when she most needed him. He was too afraid of being trapped in a world of poverty and Joseph associated the poverty with her. He hated her neediness. Now he remembered all the times she sacrificed so much for him.

She worked hard at menial jobs, especially before she became ill. The two of them shared meager and simple things, but there were many moments of joy. On her day off, Joseph's mother took him to all the free museums and shows throughout the city. Looking back, he now realized that she taught him, encouraged him to read, and placed within him the desire to be educated. She always told him that no one could take away your mind. Education was the way to rise up above the squalor they lived in. He learned a lot from her.

He remembered the joy she had for life. *How did he forget his real mother who was so good to him?* He'd forgotten when the illness wore her out. The cancer killed her long before she died. The pain caused her to lose all hope and her natural zest for life. He took care of her, and he resented it. How shallow he was, a teenager who only thought about himself. He let her know in every way he could that he begrudged the little things he did for her. And all she wanted was the same love in return that she had given him.

Joseph was ashamed of himself. *But what could he do? She was gone now and he couldn't make her understand how much he really loved and missed her. If there was a God and a heaven perhaps he could. Perhaps, she could hear him if he talked to her now.* And so Joseph spent the next hour alone in his cell praying. He prayed asking God to forgive him, and asking his mother to forgive him also. For the first time since she died, he cried. He had been so angry. Angry at her for getting sick and angry at her for leaving him alone in a world he couldn't handle.

He now realized he was angry because he needed her so much. It was always the two of them against the world. *Now how could he let her know how he really felt?* As he cried and wept, he suddenly noticed a strange odor. It was a familiar smell, an odd mixture of ivory soap and VO5 shampoo that he remembered from his childhood. It was his mother's fragrance. He couldn't believe it!

He hadn't remembered the distinctive smell until just now! The odor was so strong and so out of place. Joseph looked up, but he was still alone in his cell.

"No, I'm not alone, she can hear me. Thank you, God," Joseph said out loud.

A strange peace came over Joseph. His deep sobs stopped. He could feel his mother's presence. Joseph could sense her love. She had always loved him. *Why had he denied it?*

There was a God. And as Joseph washed his warm, tear stained face in the cold water from the stainless steel sink of his cell, he became determined to find out all about that God.

God, like John Meyer, loved him and was his friend, even when he didn't deserve it. He needed to get to know this God.

He was scheduled to see the assistant warden about appropriate work because his attendance at the seminar had conflicted with his work schedule. The assistant warden was a small, balding man who always seemed overwhelmed with his responsibilities. He looked at Joseph with a wariness that came from years of disappointment in the men he tried to help.

In a gruff voice the assistant warden asked, "So, you can't stop ticking people off, huh?"

Joseph smiled at the roughness that would have angered him just a few weeks ago. Brushing his hand through his thick dark hair, he looked into the eyes of the assistant warden, and answered, "No, I'd say that I had a way of talking that ticked people off. I probably deserved every beating I got."

The uninterested glazed look that dominated the warden's face changed slightly. "What do you mean by 'had'? Has something changed for you?"

Joseph paused to think about his response a moment, "I think everything has, although I don't expect you to believe me. I've started to attend the seminar that Father Dan gives each Tuesday, and it changed my outlook toward things."

Joseph saw nothing but disbelief and amusement on the assistant warden's face. The smug look would have infuriated Joseph in the past, but now he understood it. Looking around the shabby office, Joseph tried to put himself in the warden's place. Sitting at a desk, which had to be 50 years old, in an office with bars on the one small window that overlooked the lock-up, Joseph wondered at the lies this man heard over the years. Why would he believe anything Joseph told him? He'd probably heard it all before.

Leaning back in his squeaky swivel chair, the assistant warden's sarcastic face smirked with disbelief as he said, "So, you've found God, and seen the light, and you'll never be a bad boy again!"

Leaning forward and placing both of his muscular arms on his desk, the warden decided to push the prisoner even further. He was sure that Joseph's true colors would show as he continued. "I think you're a liar. You're trying to convince me that you've been transformed by a new found faith, huh? Well isn't that wonderful! I wonder if it would have been wonderful for all the kids who got hooked on the cocaine you pushed. You pushed drugs on kids, and all because you needed a few drugs to make your rich ass less depressed."

Joseph felt the blow as if it was a physical one. It was all the truth. *How could he deny the horrible things he did in his past?* He couldn't, and he answered the warden's accusations with contrition. "I know the things I did were atrocious. I can't go back and change them. I wish I could. I can only change what I do in the future."

The assistant warden was surprised. With Joseph's temper, he had expected him to lose it. Instead, Joseph handled the situation with calm truth and resolution.

The assistant warden decided to really test Joseph. "So, you want to do good in the future. Let's see then..." The warden paused as he looked over Joseph's file, and then continued, "You ran your own construction company, but your college degree is in finance and accounting, right?" He waited for Joseph's timid nod of acknowledgment. "So what work can you do? Oh, here's a job for you. The rest of the prisoners need financial help. Many of them don't know the first thing about budgeting. Many of them have families at home who live in poverty. Some can't even keep their kids and have to put them in foster care, just because they can't figure out how to support them."

The assistant warden looked up to watch Joseph's reaction as he continued, "Maybe you could work with the men who want help. Set yourself up in the library, and do financial counseling. Or is dealing with the poor too beneath you?"

Joseph was stunned. It had never occurred to him that he could use his skills to help the men around him. He gratefully responded, "Oh, I'd be glad too. I'll start tomorrow." The assistant warden was incredulous at the response that he got from Joseph.

Still wary, the warden announced, "I'll let the library guard know why you're there. He can let the other prisoners know about your service. And what's more, he can keep an eye on you. So you better show up and put in your time."

The possibilities were already filling Joseph's mind as he answered, "I'll be there, don't you worry. Oh, and thank you, Warden."

As Joseph left the office, the assistant warden shook his head. "I give him a week, at most," he muttered to himself.

Joseph, however, was totally enthralled by the new job. He was excited by the prospect and the privilege of being able to help others. It astounded him how God operated. And he had no doubt God's hand was in the new job offer. He prayed for a way to help the men around him. He also wanted to initiate restitution for the people he hurt and cheated in the past. The warden, while trying to rile him, gave him the perfect opportunity to start. It was surely the Holy Spirit who inspired the assistant warden.

Joseph was so enthusiastic about the new job that he ate his dinner without even noticing what it was. His head was so filled with ideas on books and budget planners. He could ask John Meyer to order the books for him. His mind worked at a fever pitch. The bland dessert did nothing to distract it. Only the need to prepare for Father Dan's seminar calmed him – he had been looking forward to it all week.

He grew very fond of Father Dan and the men in his small group. They were lucky to get Father Dan as their facilitator. Each of the men in the group had a unique history. There was a large man, a lifer, named Tyrone who committed murder. When Tyrone talked to the group, he began with great pride in his status as a tough guy on the prison block. In the past, Joseph was always afraid of him, but Joseph feelings toward the man changed.

Tyrone told his story of growing up in extreme poverty. His only joy in life was the girl he met and fell in love with in high school. He felt himself to be the luckiest man on earth when she married him. He found a job as a truck driver and worked hard, determined to get his wife and their small daughter out of the ghetto. Just when he thought he had enough money to buy a house in the suburbs, his wife became ill. As his eight-year-old daughter watched, his loving wife slowly wasted away with kidney disease. The medical treatments were expensive and his insurance coverage soon capped out. As his wife suffered, his savings dwindled. Finally, her frail body gave out. Right before she died, as if she needed to ask, she begged him to take good care of their daughter. She made him promise to raise their daughter Jasmine correctly.

His heart broke when she left him. Her funeral not only used the last of the savings, but left him in debt.

He spent the next five years working hard to save up the money needed to get Jasmine out of the ghetto. With his mother's help watching Jasmine, he spent long hours on the road. He reasoned he could slack off once he moved his Jasmine into a fine home. But as the months and years drifted on, he just became a stranger to the very daughter he was working so hard for.

It wasn't long before she was a teenager, and without a father around to guide her, she fell in with the wrong crowd. She experimented with drugs, and soon became addicted. Jasmine was just fifteen when he got the call that she had been found dead of an overdose. Tyrone lost it. He became filled with the raging anger he had suppressed since his wife's death. Blind with fury, his pain boiled over when he searched out and attacked the dealer who sold her the drugs.

His mother's face haunted him as she watched his trial. She

lost her granddaughter and now her son was being sentenced to life without parole. He bent his tear-streaked face, and held it in his hands as he begged God for forgiveness. He wished he turned to God instead. He learned too late that being with the ones you love was more important than where you were with them.

Joseph was touched by his story and he reached out to Tyrone without fear, and with a true human concern. They soon became close friends. It was that way with each of the men in the group. As they shared over the five weeks of the seminar, they grew to understand and care for each other. This meeting was the last before the Baptism in the Spirit, which was scheduled for the next week. Father Dan enthusiastically gave a talk on the gifts of the Holy Spirit, gifts which they could expect to be given during their baptism next week. Joseph was fascinated by the lesson.

The only gift that truly frightened him was the one called 'tongues'. Father Dan explained that it was a gift of special prayer. The Holy Spirit would pray through people in a language that they didn't understand.

Joseph heard others at the seminar pray in tongues, and while it had sounded beautiful when they all prayed together, he was sure that he didn't want that gift. He didn't mind getting any of the other gifts. Father Dan said that tongues were the least of the gifts anyway. He didn't like to admit it to himself, but he thought the gift would make him look ridiculous. He would just pray not to receive that gift. He was afraid of what others would think of him if he prayed in tongues.

He didn't like the idea at all. But he hoped the other men in his group, especially Tyrone, would all receive special gifts from the Holy Spirit. Joseph hoped the gifts would make their lives a little better. Joseph was glad when Father Dan asked them all to pray for the men in the group. He was a little nervous about the upcoming baptism, and he thought praying for his new found friends might help him forget how truly anxious he was.

Joseph didn't need to worry about it after all. The new job kept him too busy to worry. He went early to the library the next day and set up a long metal table in the back. He was able, with the help of the guard, to find the financial and tax books he needed and was given the use of a calculator and adding machine. The adding machine, like everything else in the prison was clearly old and dated. Still, it served its purpose.

The guards posted signs throughout the prison, but Joseph doubted anyone would come for help. He figured he would be lucky if one or two prisoners stopped by for advice. Joseph wasn't prepared for was the amount of men who came for help.

The line of inmates wrapped around the wall of the library. Joseph soon decided it would be best if he used today just to set up appointments. He still had men left over to see at the end of the week, and each day more came by to set up appointments. Joseph was unprepared for the great need the men had for financial help. Many of these men had families who suffered greatly by their imprisonment. Their wives often worked two jobs to keep up with the family needs, that meant the children were often neglected or being watched by aging grandparents. Like the warden had explained, many of the families could not even keep their own children.

Frequently, they were forced to put them in foster care with little prospect of ever bringing them home again. Thinking of Tyrone's daughter broke Joseph's heart. Often what the families needed was just a little more money or help to keep them together. Joseph, who always began with prayer seemed to find a simple solution by budgeting or finding some community help.

By the end of the week, he was exhausted and he was proud of the way he was able to help his fellow inmates. He couldn't help but get enthusiastic each time he saw a light of joy in the eyes of one of the men. Often that man was one who had just found control over a bad situation.

It was one of the most rewarding weeks that Joseph ever had. Joseph was too busy pouring over papers to notice the assistant warden look in on him. He was filled with the joy of good works.

The week passed quickly. Now, with permission to make phone calls, Joseph called his friend John with his needs. John seemed only too glad to help, and was very pleased with the work Joseph had undertaken. John even offered to donate some pricey budgeting books to help the men get started on the plans Joseph mapped out for them.

With all the work that consumed him, Tuesday evening came very quickly. Joseph had not worried about the baptism at all. It was just a quick prayer each night as he fell into his cot. He prayed for all the men in his small group and Father Dan. He also prayed he wouldn't get the gift of tongues. With a quick prayer for Joyce and John Meyer he fell quickly asleep each night with great peace. Still, he was very jubilant and curious about the baptism. Joseph was curious about what God would do for him. He was even more anxious to see what God would do for the other men in his group.

The baptism was held in the small chapel. Father Dan rose to the podium and read the book of Acts 1:1-4: 'When the time for Pentecost was fulfilled, they were all in one place together. And suddenly, there came from the sky a noise like a strong driving wind, and it filled the entire house in which they were. Then there appeared to them tongues of fire, which parted and came to rest on each one of them. And they were all filled with the Holy Spirit and began to speak in different tongues, as the Spirit enabled them to proclaim.'

Father Dan paused as he allowed the men, gathered in a circle of chairs before him, to ponder the word of God. Then the priest explained, "I want you to understand by this word, that the Holy Spirit will come to each of you today and bestow the gifts that will enable you to serve his kingdom. You need to be open to accepting the gifts that the Spirit wishes to bestow on you. You need to abandon the pride that led you to the life you lived before this baptism. You are now accepting a new life in Christ, Jesus. It is as serious as if you had died and were reborn. You will be called to live a life that is led by the Spirit, not the flesh, or the world. You must put away your old ways and turn to God for all your future guidance. You must now go wherever, and however, He wants you to go. Your journey through life is no longer your own, but His. But our God is good. He does not send us out into the world without the tools we need to live the life He wants of us. For alone, we, none of us, have the strength to live the life we are about to enter on. But, with Him we are given each gift that we need. He gives us spiritual gifts to strengthen us, as we need it. He gives us gifts today, not for ourselves, but gifts to strengthen the church. Let us read about the gifts we are about to receive."

Father Dan rose to the podium and opened his Bible. Looking up he said, "Let us read from the Word of God."

He turned the page and began reading. "There are different kinds of spiritual gifts but the same Spirit; there are different forms of service but the same Lord; there are different workings but the same God who produces all of them in everyone. To each individual the manifestation of the Spirit is given for some benefit. To one is given through the Spirit the expression of wisdom; to another faith by the same spirit; to another gifts of healing by the one Spirit; to another mighty deeds; to another prophecy; to another discernment of spirits; to another varieties of tongues; to another interpretation of tongues. But one and the same Spirit produces all of these, distributing them individually to each person as he wishes.

"Therefore," Father Dan continued, "it is not for us to decide what we want as a gift from the Holy Spirit. That pride of decision was part of our old life. We are to be open to whatever gift the Spirit wishes to give us. He alone knows what gift could best work through you for the building up of the church community. Put away any fear, for fear is never from God. Open your mind, heart, and soul to Him, and you will receive the gifts He wants you to have."

As Father Dan, and mature members of his prayer group prepared for the physical baptism, Joseph tried to prepare his heart. He was now ashamed of the way he had prayed all week, praying God would not give him the gift of tongues. It was because of personal pride. He didn't want to look like a fool, babbling in front of others. He was thinking all wrong. He should be proud to be a fool for God. He would open himself up to the Holy Spirit. If open, he would receive any gift God wanted him to have. If he was lucky, God would grace him with a gift that would help others.

The priest and three of his prayer team members started praying over each man by laying-on of hands. When they got to Joseph, he was open. Father Dan anointed his forehead in the sign of the cross with blessed olive oil mixed with frankincense and myrrh. It had a pleasant, spicy smell. Then Father Dan and three members of his prayer team laid their hands on Joseph, and began to pray.

Father Dan led the prayer, "Oh Father, we come before you with your beloved child, Joseph. Joseph offers his life, and soul, and body to you in faith, and hope. Baptize him with Your Holy Spirit. Come Eternal Light! Touch your servant Joseph and transform him in Your Light according to Your Will, Jesus."

The team began to pray in tongues. To Joseph it sounded like heavenly music, a chorus of angelic sounds that lifted and softened like waves upon his heart. As their hands grew warmer, and as their prayers mingled in harmony, Joseph felt warmth rush through his body. A profound sense of well-being overtook him. A warm peace seemed to permeate every cell of his body. A joy so profound it made his heart swell as if it was about to burst. In an instant, Joseph received an overwhelming sense of how much God loved him. It was so breathtaking, and so bright. He sensed the love God wanted to lavish upon him, and it was irresistible. The sense of utter, eternal intimacy flooded every fiber of his being. Tears flowed down his face as he felt the complete safety of being in the heart of the Ancient, Eternal Father. Never had he felt such security, such a flood of pure love. Joseph just wanted to rest in that love forever, to bask with the light of the Holy Spirit.

"Speak, as an infant cries for his father, so you cry out to your Father," the priest said softly. Joseph opened his mouth and tried to call to God. At first there was just a silent cry. But suddenly, as a babe might struggle to form words, a mumble came. The mumble became a song, and Joseph sang out in the gift of tongues. As he prayed in tongues, the feeling of God rushing though him brought fervent joy to his heart.

After a few minutes, he fell into silence, but the touch of God's hand continued as he rested in the Spirit. Completely at peace, Joseph was unaware as the Holy Spirit infused him with the gift of wisdom, faith and prophesy.

When he opened his eyes, and again became aware of his surroundings, the prayer team had finished prayers on the last supplicant. That supplicant was seven chairs down. He couldn't believe he had experienced God for so long, or for so little an amount of time. It seemed so short, and yet so eternal. He just knew that what Father Dan said was true. He would never be the same man! He had touched the face of God, only to find the Source of all Love!

The Sacrament of Marriage

My lover speaks; he says to me, "Arise, my beloved,
My beautiful one, and come! "For see, the winter is
Past, the rains are over and gone. The flowers appear
On the earth, the time of pruning the vines has come,
And the song of the dove is heard in our land. The fig
Tree puts forth its figs, and the vines, in bloom, give forth
Fragrance. Arise, my beloved, my beautiful one, and come!
(Songs of Solomon 2:10-13)

Beloved, if God so loved us, we also must love one another. No one has ever seen God. Yet, if we love one another, God remains in us, and his love is brought to perfection in us. (1 John: 4-1)

Elly couldn't seem to stop herself. She knew she looked undignified, but she couldn't help it. When she saw Gabe step down from the rumbling train, her heart leapt in her chest, and she just ran. Laughing with joy she ran into his waiting arms. He caught her up in pleased surprise.

"Well, what's happened to my shy, quiet girl!" he beamed, as she showered his face with kisses. Catching her face under her chin, he took the chance to give her a long, tender kiss. She responded by holding him in her arms.

Holding her back, at arms' length, his face glowed with passion, as he gazed into her mysteriously knowing eyes.

"What has gotten into you?" Gabe laughed.

"I'm just happy to see you," she replied with a smile.

Gabe teased, "Well, I hope all the good-looking girls in town are as glad to see me."

Elly softly slapped him on his arm in reply, as they headed to the parking lot, and said, "I hope you don't think I'm the jealous type, Dr. Lopez. Why just let me know your schedule with your many, many other women, so I can arrange my dates with the other guys accordingly." Elly secretly rejoiced at his loving response.

"Okay, Miss, just don't make any dates with other guys until I get back to you." Gabe stopped as they reached the car, and putting down his suitcase, he took Elly in his arms again. Nuzzling her neck, he thought about the thin woman who fit his arms so comfortably. She seemed so changed since he last saw her. Clearly something happened. She seemed confident and loving, no longer the frightened, wistful, and childlike girl he left. Maybe meeting her family gave her a renewed confidence. Perhaps in finding her family, she found herself. Gabe felt sure that this was part of it, but he sensed there was more to it. Gabe was curious, but patient. He knew he should never push Elly. She was pushed around enough in her life he suspected. He was confident she would explain everything when she was ready. Gabe loved her enough to wait.

Elly tried to get Gabe to tell her what his surprise was as they rode in the car to her awaiting dinner, but he was tightlipped. He seemed to enjoy her impatience, and teased her all the more. Elly had a few surprises of her own, as he was about to find out. Pulling into the driveway, Gabe stopped in awed silence. She loved watching his stunned surprise, when he examined the massive changes in the home on the cliff. He was truly impressed by her talent, and her beautiful taste in decorating. The dilapidated old mansion was now a beautiful ocean-side home. Elly was delighted with his response.

Gabe whistled, and asked, "You've worked magic! How did you

manage this in such a short time?"

Elly laughed. "Once I got started, I couldn't stop. I really enjoyed every minute of the renovations. It was worth it just to see your face."

Elly served the tired traveler a crisp salad and a warm casserole. She was proud of the bright, modern kitchen with the shining stainless steel counters and the large windows. She knew Gabe felt comfortable and at home.

Gabe was full, content, and drowsy. If he wanted to, he could easily stretch out in the large, overstuffed chair in the living room and fall asleep.

He laughed and said, "You better take me home to my mother's house, before I make myself too much at home."

Elly laughed, but she was secretly delighted to see him enjoying the new home. Now she knew why she had gone to such trouble. Gabe belonged here with her. She wondered if he felt the same. Only time would tell. And suddenly Elly knew she and Gabe would have a lifetime. She knew she loved him, and she felt he loved her. She wouldn't rush things. She drove him to his mother's home, and they made plans to meet the next day. Elly had so much to tell him.

She was a little afraid to tell him some things. Perhaps he wouldn't want her, once he knew what she did and how weak she was. If he was the man she thought he was, he would. She would talk to him tomorrow, she decided, as she drifted off to sleep. Tomorrow would be the beginning or the end.

The next day proved to be delightful in more ways than one. Gabe, rested and happy, came over in the morning. They walked hand in hand along the beach and as a cool salty breeze blew over the perfect cloudless day, Elly talked and Gabe listened. He was calm and nonjudgmental, as Elly softly told the story of her mother's rejection.

Gentle tears flowed down her cheeks as she told of her inability to fight her mother's determined will. In a muted voice full of pain and regret she told of the lonely day of her child's death. Gabe held her tightly as she sobbed in sorrow. The grief she felt was profound. She hoped he wouldn't leave her now.

Leaving Elly was the last thing on his mind. He was furious. He was angry at a mother who only thought of herself, not of her daughter, or her grandchild. But, he was most angry at himself. He had sent this child home to deal with a woman who intimidated her all her life. If only he investigated the situation more. He pressed her closer as she wept, and vowed he would never leave her alone again. The healing would take a long time, he knew, but Elly, who suffered alone, would not heal alone. And Gabe, as he wiped her tear-filled face, promised himself he would not push her. She needed time to grieve the child she lost. He would have to remain steadfast, ready to listen and guide her through the mourning process. A reliable friend is what she required. And he would fulfill that need.

The sun was high in the sky when they realized it was late and they hadn't eaten a thing. Elly, much calmer now, offered to make lunch.

Gabe wanted her to rest. "No way lady, you fed me last night, I can certainly treat you to a restaurant."

Elly smiled at his need to nurture her.

Soup and sandwiches were the specials of the day at the café. Elly always enjoyed Gabe's hearty appetite, it was a reflection of his appetite for life. She enjoyed spending time with him. He made her laugh with his zany and slightly corny humor, yet she never forgot the strength of character beneath that humor. She felt his strength as it enfolded her. He didn't reject her after she told him the truth and was kind and sympathetic. Elly realized now how much she worried about a possible rejection. She loved him. She felt a sigh of relief reverberate deep in her soul. Life with him was all she wanted. Elly wanted to have his strength around her forever. She silently prayed he felt the same about her. Only time would tell.

Each afternoon, Gabe would come and they would spend the rest of the day together. During these few weeks, Elly told Gabe about her religious experience and her return to the church. He seemed profoundly pleased. Elly felt free since her confession, and the dream that had followed. She felt God had truly forgiven her.

She felt drawn to attend daily Mass at the little church in town. She experienced comfort from the daily gospel readings and renewed strength from the Eucharist. Elly felt a sense of kinship with the group of people who attended Mass each morning. She grew to know the priests and was starting, for the first time in her life, to develop a sense of belonging to a community. She was beginning to feel she was part of the larger community of the worldwide church. Elly was embarking on a new identity as a Roman Catholic. It made her feel safe and whole. Just like being an American, being a Catholic was part of who she was.

She started to forget the sense of isolation she grew up with. Elly found most people were glad to be friendly especially if you showed a sincere concern for their welfare. But she loved the feeling of family most. Elly enjoyed joining in the banter of the table, teasing Gabe as they ate with his family. She loved the deep and profound friendship which blossomed between them. They spent all of their time talking and getting to know each other. And while they held hands and lovingly hugged and gazed into each other's eyes, there was no physical contact beyond that. Elly spent a lot of time talking about her abortion, and the painful emotional devastation it caused. Gabe just listened. He knew the best therapy was talking about her feelings. Bottling pain just made it explode later.

Dwelling on the abortion for the rest of her life was not the answer. She knew that she needed to work out her feelings. She did as Father John told her in the confessional to do. She named her baby. She lifted up her infant's soul each morning at mass. Nightly, she prayed with her child and asked the child for forgiveness. She felt as if she was forgiven by her child, and strangely she even felt as if she developed a relationship with her child. She knew she would have to stop dwelling on her pain and get on with her life. She would honor her child most by living a good and holy life. She would then get to spend eternity with that child.

Elly knew, as days passed, she was growing to love Gabe more. It would be hard to imagine life without him. After a few weeks, however, she found she was wearied of waiting for the surprise he promised he would reveal.

One morning, as she was leaving the morning mass, Gabe pulled up to the curb in his mother's car. Smiling, he waved and shouted, "Hop in. I'm finally going to satisfy that insatiable curiosity of yours."

Elly laughed as she opened the car door and jumped in. "Oh, funny. I'm curious! Maybe you shouldn't make someone wait for a surprise as long as you do!"

Gabe pretended to be hurt at her reprimand. "Just wait, when you see the surprise, I hope you'll forget the long wait."

Elly laughed at the excited sparkle in his dark eyes. He was like a kid on Christmas morning.

Gabe took her on a wild ride up and down all the side streets of the small town, only to stop suddenly on Main Street. Elly joyfully, caught her breath as Gabe raced to the red wooden door of a white office building. He stood dramatically pointing to the sign above the ornate door.

Elly eyes widened as she read the gold engraved letters. 'Dr. G. Lopez, M.D. Internist. Office Hours 9-5 Mon.-Fri.'

Elly's mouth dropped open. He was going to open a practice in their hometown! How he had managed to keep it a secret was beyond her. She spent many days with his family. How is it that no one slipped about the news? Gabe took Elly's hand and opened the red door, revealing the plush yet serene waiting room of his new office. She walked into the office unable to speak.

"I know you're in shock, but can you talk?" he laughed.

"I don't understand," she stuttered. "How did your family keep this all a secret?"

Gabe found her confusion endearing. "Nobody slipped, because no one in my family knew".

Elly just shook her head, "I don't get it."

Gabe took her softly in his arms and explained, "Nobody knew, just Dr. Crosby, who's retiring. He's the man who I rented this building from."

Elly answered with surprise in her voice, "Your mother, you mean, no one in your family knows."

Gabe answered, "No, why would I tell anyone else before I told you? You're the most important person in my life. You're the one I dreamed of sharing this with. I'll let the family know tomorrow. Now let me show you the rest of the office."

Elly blushed as she absorbed what Gabe had just said. Was it possible? *Was it really possible she could finally have the love she always dreamed of? Or would she wake up and find out this was just a dream?*

Elly had always been alone. The last few months she and Gabe spent together were the happiest of her life. But Elly learned a long time ago that happiness seldom lasted. Her mother had verbally beaten into her mind that she was unworthy of love, and she unconsciously accepted it as true. She was afraid of reaching out for love.

The one time she did reach out, it had terrible consequences. Her love for Michael turned into a tragedy. *Should she trust again? Would she be able to withstand more pain if love just wasn't meant to be part of her future?* As much as she felt she loved Gabe, she needed time to think. She needed to be sure this love was right for both of them.

Elly pushed all these thoughts aside in order to enjoy the moment. Gabe was proud of his new offices. He walked her through all of the examining rooms and the modern lab facilities. He glowed with anticipation of the many patients he would help. He felt his future was decided and enjoyed the thought of being a small town doctor. He didn't express what was also in his mind. He was sure his new future included the beautiful blonde who stood beside him. And with all the love he had to give her, he couldn't wait for that future to begin.

Elly laughed as Gabe picked her up and enthusiastically whirled her around in his arms. "And now I want you to go home and get ready! Put on your best clothes, tonight we're going to celebrate my new practice. I've got reservations for a hot Broadway show and reservations for the best restaurant in New York."

"Okay, okay. I'll put on my 'fancy going to meeting clothes,'" Elly answered in a feigned southern accent. She couldn't help but be caught up in his joy. It was infectious.

Elly had a hard time picking the right thing to wear. Despite her money, she hadn't indulged in an extensive wardrobe. She finally settled on a simple, yet elegant silk dress. She added gold jewelry and a Gucci bag and sling shoes for just the right touch. Sweeping her hair up and adding the make-up she seldom wore completed the look. Elly knew, by the look on Gabe's face, that she made the right decisions.

"You are the most beautiful woman I've ever seen!" was Gabe's instant response.

"You're not so bad yourself," Elly replied, as she took a long look at the exquisitely dressed man in front of her. He was dressed in an immaculate silk suit with a matching tie. Elly always knew Gabe was attractive, but she had only seen him in casual or work clothes. Tonight, he was positively suave. She was proud to be seen with him.

Elly enjoyed the excitement of the hour drive into Manhattan. She'd never seen a Broadway show. How Gabe obtained the tickets to a hot show like *The Producers*, she didn't know. And the view from the restaurant at the top of the World Trade Center afforded such a spectacular view that it took Elly's breath away. Gabe looked handsome in the flickering candlelight as the lights of the city glimmered below. His eyes glowed with warmth as the waiter cleared their table. Elly was so happy she wished this night could last forever.

"Elly, I have something to ask you," Gabe started. "I know it is kind of fast, and if you're not ready to answer, just tell me so."

For a minute, Elly was apprehensive. *What if his love depended on her answer? What if her answer was the wrong one? She shared all of her thoughts and feelings with him, what is it he now needed to know?* Anxiety made her heart flutter, but as she looked up into his warm face, all fear left her. Elly watched, in a daze, as Gabe got up and knelt before her. Reaching into his pocket, he removed a velvet jewelry box.

"Will you marry me, Elly?" Gabe whispered with an emotional catch in his voice. Elly's eyes filled with tears as she looked into the face of the man she so loved.

"Yes, Gabe, I would be proud to marry you."

The applause caught Elly by surprise. In the emotion of the moment, she hadn't noticed many of the restaurant patrons watching the proposal.

Elly blushed with the realization, as Gabe slipped the shimmering diamond ring on her finger. Elly's embarrassment could not take away from the overwhelming joy she felt as she absorbed the moment.

Staring into Gabe's eyes, Elly was overwhelmed by the happy future life now held. She loved this man more than anything on earth. He was intelligent and kind, gentle and strong. Her love for him was deep, reaching down to her soul. She thanked God for this wonderful gift, a gift of love from her Eternal Father. Elly vowed she would always be loyal and true to this man, her future husband. She would work at being the best wife she could.

A scattered ovation followed the two lovers as they walked hand in hand to the elevator. It was a night neither wanted to end. The ride home was full of excited plans for telling both families and of the wedding each dreamed of. Arriving home, it was hard for Elly and Gabe to part. They talked for hours of the future and their feelings for each other.

Laughing, Gabe tickled Elly with his statement, "I don't know what I would have done if you had said no. Imagine, with all those people watching."

"You were pretty sure of yourself, I might have said no."

Gabe acted shocked as he replied, "How could you? I got a real buy on the ring. I can't return it."

Elly was delighted with Gabe's rendition of a man worried about the expense of having a wife.

"I can always change my mind!" giggled Elly.

Gabe placed his arms around Elly and said, "No! You can't, I even have witnesses." He sighed, engulfed by powerful devotion to the delicate woman he was to marry.

Pulling away, with a face full of passion, Gabe grabbed his top coat. "I think I better leave. If I don't, I may have to elope tonight."

Elly smiled. They had already decided that a wedding in the small church in their hometown was what they both wanted.

Elly sighed, "Okay, but I hate to be separated even for a short time."

Gabe smiled. "Don't worry, soon we will be together always, a lifetime together. Besides, tomorrow we'll be busy sharing the good news with our family and friends."

Elly didn't miss the use of the word 'our.' She was so happy, she knew she would sleep peacefully tonight.

On the morning of her wedding, sunlight spilled across the floor of Elly's bedroom. A warm breeze, flowing from the open window, kissed her face and aroused her. All winter they planned and prepared for this day. And now that the roses bloomed and the air smelled of fresh mowed grass, the day had finally arrived. Elly thought she would be nervous. She wasn't. A strange, serene calm came over her. She experienced a sense of rightness, a feeling the marriage she was entering was her destiny. The house was full of family. She could hear the bustle starting in the kitchen. She longed for her first cup of coffee, but she knew once the day began she would be caught in a whirlwind. She took the time now to talk to God in prayer. She asked for her fathers' blessing. He couldn't be here. She had asked her uncle to give her away. Still, she liked to think her father would somehow be there, rejoicing in her happiness. Slipping out of bed and into her robe and slippers, Elly joined the boisterous crowd in the kitchen. Breakfast was a major affair in this family.

Elly enjoyed the banter, and feasted on blueberry pancakes, scrambled eggs, and hot coffee.

"You're not too nervous to eat?" laughed Aunt Sarah.

The bride-to-be laughed, "I'm not nervous, but I'm ravenous!"

There was a knock at the door. It was Gabe's sister, Maria, carrying her gown in a clothing bag. She arrived to prepare the bride. Elly had asked her two cousins and Gabe's sister to be in the wedding party. They enjoyed the shopping and get-togethers the wedding preparations afforded. The bridal shower brought them even closer, as everyone enjoyed filling Elly's new home with all the essentials. It cemented the connections of family by bringing the new relatives closer together. Elly really felt she was now part of an even larger family. She truly enjoyed it.

Elly ate her fill, and still there were copious amounts of muffins and eggs left. Aunt Sarah started to clean the breakfast dishes. When Elly tried to help, Aunt Sarah was outraged and said, "Oh no! Not on your wedding day. Soon you'll be a married lady and you'll spend the rest of your life in the kitchen. Enjoy today. Go get ready."

Thinking of Gabe's ferocious appetite made Elly laugh – there was more truth to her future in the kitchen than Aunt Sarah realized.

Pulling herself away from her musings, Elly answered, "Okay, if you don't need my domestic skills, I think that I'll relax and take a long bubble bath."

Elly and the wedding party had a one o'clock appointment to have their hair done. She had plenty of time to prepare for the four o'clock wedding. A bubble bath would relax and refresh her. Elly thought it would give her time to get away from the growing tumult of the house, and even better, it would give her time to dream about her favorite subject – Gabe. It was a beautiful and special day. Elly didn't want the importance of her marriage to get lost in the bustle of the wedding.

Before she knew it, it was time to get her hair done. The girls had great fun, getting their hair shampooed, styled, and curled. The hairdresser enjoyed all the lively laughter the women shared. The bride was so pretty, and it was a pleasure to work with her long, silky hair. And since the wedding was going to be in the small church in town, the hairdresser decided she would stop by and watch this gentle girl walk up the aisle. It was 21 years since she and her had Ralph tied the knot. She would enjoy watching the nuptials.

Maria, Gabe's sister, was dazzled by Elly's composed radiance dressed in her veil and gown. The chiffon dress was dazzling with a pearl-encrusted bodice and long tapered sleeves. An extended, layered train matched the flattering veil. The veil displayed her upswept hair and the shimmering curled tendrils framing the bride's face. There was something illuminating about this particular bride that made her more attractive. It was not an exterior quality. It was the brilliant joy in her eyes, and the radiant glow of her bright face that gave her the beauty no make-up could. Elly's euphoria was infectious. The entire wedding party was excited for her. Maria decided Gabe was a very lucky fellow to find a woman who loved him so much.

Elly held her uncle's arm, but her eyes were fixed on the handsome man who waited at the altar. Gabe was appealing in his crisp, stylish tuxedo. His eyes dark burned bright with passion and drew Elly in. She forgot all the other people. She was going to the man she loved. She would be with him forever and her fear of ever being alone and unloved was gone. He was waiting for her and that was all Elly could see.

Gabe was breathless as he watched his future wife walk toward him. The pipe organ followed the church choir in the sweeping refrains of "Ave Maria." She was more lovely than anyone he had ever seen. He knew how blessed he was as he was given her hand by her uncle. He hoped he would always make her happy. Gabe looked at the large crucifix behind the altar, and whispered a promise. He promised each day of his life he would remember to thank the Savior who gave him such a gift. Kneeling together, bride and groom, before the altar, they prepared for the nuptial Mass.

The first reading of the Mass was from the book of Genesis.

Gabe held tightly onto Elly's hand as they listened to Father John read the words from the first book of the Bible. "So the Lord God cast a deep sleep on the man, and while he was asleep, he took out one of his ribs and closed up its place with flesh. The Lord God then built up into a woman the rib that he had taken from the man. When he brought her to the man, the man said: 'This one, at last, is bone of my bones and flesh of my flesh; This one shall be called woman for out of her man this one has been taken.' That is why a man leaves his father and mother and clings to his wife and the two of them become one body. The man and his wife were both naked, yet they felt no shame."

Elly already felt as one with Gabe. She loved him deeply. He loved her despite the mistakes of her past. She vowed she would make no others. She would do all that she could to make the man next to her happy and successful. She prayed they would have many years together to share their love.

The Mass continued with the responsorial psalm and then the second reading. 'Rejoice in the lord always, I shall say it again: rejoice! Your kindness should be known to all. The Lord is near. Have no anxiety at all, but in everything, by prayer and petition, with thanksgiving, make your requests known to God. Then the peace of God that surpasses all understanding will guard your hearts and minds in Christ Jesus. Finally, brothers, whatever is true, whatever is pure, whatever is lovely, whatever is gracious, if there is any excellence and if there is anything worthy of praise, think about these things. Keep on doing what you have learned and received and heard and seen in me. Then the God of Peace will be with you.'

Amidst the songs of alleluia, the priest rose to the podium behind the altar to read the gospel. The entire church rose in respect for and in testimony to, the Risen Christ.

The priest announced the reading of the Gospel according to John. "On the third day there was a wedding in Cana in Galilee and the mother of Jesus was there. Jesus and his disciples were also invited to the wedding. When the wine ran short, the mother of Jesus said to him, 'They have no wine.' And Jesus said to her, 'Woman, how does your concern affect me? My hour has not yet come.' His mother said to the servers, 'Do whatever he tells you.' Now there were six stone water jars there for Jewish ceremonial washings, each holding twenty to thirty gallons. Jesus told them, 'Fill the jars with water.' So they filled them to the brim. Then he told them, 'Draw some out now and take it to the headwaiter.' So they took it. And when the headwaiter tasted the water that had become wine, without knowing where it came from (although the servers who had drawn the water knew), the headwaiter called the bridegroom and said to him, 'Everyone serves good wine first, and then when people have drunk freely, an inferior one; but you have kept the good wine until now.' Jesus did this as the beginning of signs in Cana in Galilee and so revealed his glory, and his disciples began to believe in him."

Gabe took Elly's hand and helped her to her seat as the priest began his homily.

Father John began by saying, "We all rejoice when we attend a wedding and rightly so, because it is the beginning of a new life. Two people begin a new life with each other, a wonderful journey. The readings we have selected point to just how important this step is. In the first reading, we are shown that God created marriage and that for any marriage to be truly successful, God must be an important partner. We are shown how close a man and his wife are. One does not dominate over the other. God took a rib from Adam's side, not from a man's head that a woman may rule over him. Nor did he take it from Adam's foot, that a man might crush his wife's spirit. He took it from his side, showing that each should be equal and close to each other's heart. In the second reading we have selected, God shows us how we are to live that marriage–by always looking for the good in each other. Oh, sure you will quickly find each other's faults. But our God tells us how to deal with these faults. We are not to dwell on them. Instead with perfect charity we are told to rejoice in what is good about our partner. We are to spend a lifetime finding and rejoicing in the goodness that Our Father, God has by grace, placed within us. And that is not all, we are to take the joy and the goodness and the charity that God has given us in the form of our partner and we are in turn told to give the same to others in the world.

"In Gratitude for the love God gives to each of you through your partner, you are then to share that love with all others God brings to you in need. If you follow this formula of giving love, God promises you peace. Not peace as the world knows it maybe, but a peace of heart that no one but God can give. Love is the one thing that grows only if it is given away. And as if that were not enough, the third reading gives us an additional aid to have a triumphant marriage. For in this reading He shows us how He listens to his mother. His mother is concerned with such a small thing in the eyes of the world. Mary did not want the bride and groom to be embarrassed by the shortage of wine for their guests.

"Mary, and always remember this, cares about the little day to day needs of her children. And what is more she turns to her son with complete trust to intercede for them. He always listens to her. And you should both remember to turn to Mary whenever life becomes overwhelming. She will talk to Jesus for you. But also remember to act like her. Always pray for your partner, always speak up for them on earth and in heaven. The bride and the groom may have never known what Mary did for them. You be like her. Quietly, and without any ulterior motive, be your partner's best friend. If you follow the formula God has so clearly laid out for a successful marriage, you will not only have a happy marriage, but a happy life. And now let us, before God and this assembly exchange our marriage vows."

As Elly and Gabe joyfully exchanged vows, the grace to live out those vows flooded them through the power of the Holy Spirit and through the privilege of the sacrament. They opened their hearts to that grace and became man and wife. The congregation applauded as they kissed and the Eucharistic celebration began. Jesus was invited body, soul, and divinity to the wedding. Introduced as Doctor and Mrs. Gabe Lopez for the first time, they proceeded down the aisle to start their new life.

That new life started with a small reception in the church hall. Gabe and Elly whirled in their first dance as a married couple. Looking into Gabe's eyes, Elly felt the warmth of his love. His strong arms surrounded her small waist, making her feel protected and safe. It was a new feeling for Elly. It seemed that everything she ever dreamed of had come true. She knew she could depend on Gabe's love. He was so reliable and steady. Life would be different for her now. God was now in charge of her life. It would be up to Him how things went. But Elly knew one thing, if she knew nothing else, Gabe loved her and her life would never be the same.

Elly kept the plans for the reception simple. She wanted everyone to feel comfortable and relaxed. She had always hated ostentatious weddings. She rented a simple hall and filled it with lots of plain, simple, and very good food from the local caterer. She bypassed the fancy cocktail hour, and instead offered a buffet with plenty of Hispanic and American foods. Like the menu, the music was also Spanish and American. It proved to be a winning formula. Everybody danced. Maria learned the twist. Aunt Sarah learned the meringue. There was plenty of food and drink, and everyone laughed, mingled, and had a good time. Even the priest danced a Scottish reel bringing tears of joy to all the guests.

After the wedding cake, as Gabe and Elly prepared to leave for a short honeymoon drive down to Cape May at the bottom of the Jersey peninsula, Sister Immaculata pulled Elly to the side. Elly was anxious to leave with her new husband but could never deny the aunt who had been so good to her. Sister Immaculata drew Elly to a private spot and said, "I hate to disturb your wedding like this but I just want to ask you to call me as soon as you get home. I have a special need, a young girl, I think that you both can help. She really needs someone, and I think that you are the very people who can help her."

Elly was intrigued. *What kind of help could the nun need from them? What kind of trouble was the girl in?* Only the thought of being alone with Gabe on a carefree trip stayed Elly's curiosity. Caught up in the joy of starting her new life with her handsome husband, Elly decided to postpone satisfying her inquisitiveness until she returned from her honeymoon. Elly didn't know how much the simple question Sister Immaculata asked would change her life.

The Birth of Friendship

A faithful friend is a sturdy shelter; he who finds one finds a treasure. A faithful friend is beyond price, no sum can balance his worth. A faithful friend is a life-saving remedy, such as he who fears God finds; For he who fears God behaves accordingly, and his friend will be like himself. (Sirach 6:14-17)

Joyce was thrilled that Grace fit right in at nursery school. Joyce had worried other children would reject Grace because of her metal arms. Grace adjusted very well to the use of her prosthetic arms, in fact, she was thrilled with them. She loved picking things up for Joyce, and worked many hours to learn to turn the pages of her favorite book. They were so happy, just the two of them. Joyce wished the heartwarming days of the two of them sharing their small world of play could go on forever.

Grace was so full of life. Her curiosity about everything kept Joyce on her toes. Grace was full of questions. She absorbed information like a sponge. It was gratifying to watch her blossom and grow. Her energy was without bounds, and Grace tended to enjoy each moment of her day. She fell exhausted into her crib at night. Joyce was often exhausted herself.

Their world was a small one. Their days consisted of playing, going to church, and marketing. There were no small children in the neighborhood, so Joyce and Grace spent most of their time alone together. They were both so happy that they saw no problem with the situation. But, as Grace became a toddler, Joyce began to think she needed to be around other children. She noticed children who didn't have playmates their own age while growing up always seemed to have trouble relating to other children.

The young mother admitted to herself she was being overprotective of Grace. Joyce was afraid the other children would belittle Grace because of her disability. She was sensitive to the stares of adults when they saw the small, dark girl without arms. *If that was how adults reacted, how would children behave? Children could be so cruel.* But, as time went on, she knew she needed to do what was best for Grace. Grace would have to live in the real world. If it turned out to be a cruel world, she would have to learn how to cope. It broke Joyce's heart to think about it, but she knew letting go was probably the hardest part of being a good mother.

Grace, on the other hand, had no fear. She was so excited about the prospect of going to nursery school and meeting other children, that she was ready for it two days ahead of time.

"Is school today?" she asked each morning.

Joyce would just smile and repeat, "Patience, Grace, just a few more days."

When the day finally arrived, Grace's worries about what toys she should bring made them run late. As they stood in line outside the large red metal doors, a small boy with a buzz cut pointed to Grace, and shouted, "Look Mommy, that girl has Transformer arms."

Joyce reddened, but not Grace. Grace answered the boy, "Hi, yeah, I have special arms. They're very strong, and I can pick up almost anything." Before the boy's embarrassed mother could stop him, the boy ran over to Grace.

The curious boy asked, "Can I touch them?"

Grace smiled, "Oh sure, let me shake your hand. My name is Grace. Do you like dogs?"

Soon all of the children gathered around Grace. Their questions about her arms didn't seem to bother her. She acted like her arms were quite special. Because she did, so did the other children. As Joyce watched, peace flooded her soul. It was at that moment she knew Grace's personality would carry her through any situation. Joyce would never fear again.

When the doors opened and swallowed up the animated crowd of children, one mother exclaimed, "Well, I like that, I was so worried and he didn't even say goodbye!"

The small group of women laughed as they headed home. The house seemed so empty to Joyce. She cleaned an already clean house. She baked cookies until the cookie jar was full. By the end of the week, she knew she needed to do something, and watching soap operas wasn't it. Grace was doing so well in school that she never wanted to miss. Joyce decided she needed to do some kind of work. But, she still wanted to be free, in case Grace needed her. Volunteer work was what she would look for. By the end of Grace's third week of school, Joyce was at the rectory talking to the priest, hoping to return to the post she had left when Grace was born.

Elly, on the other hand, was inundated with work. How it happened, even she would be hard put to explain. Gabe and she went on a wonderful and deliciously lazy honeymoon. They drove Gabe's mustang down to Cape May and stayed in a quaint Victorian Bed and Breakfast. For two weeks the loving couple swam and basked in the sun by day, and enjoyed the nearby restaurants by night. Just spending all their time together, planning their future and getting to know each other was like a dream.

Secure in Gabe's love, Elly blossomed into a woman with a calm, serene manner. And she surprised Gabe with a soft-spoken, dry sense of humor. They grew deeper in love, as they cultivated a deeper romance. The comfort of Gabe's love made Elly feel anchored. They explored the beaches and the beautiful shops of Cape May. Gabe's zest for life was infectious and Elly found herself looking forward to the adventure of each new day.

Elly didn't think about the comment that Nora made at the reception until they were almost home. They had lingered watching the ocean so long that it was night when they pulled into the driveway of their home. Elly's curiosity about Nora's need would have to wait till tomorrow.

As soon as Gabe left for the office the next morning Elly's curiosity got the better of her. The phone rang once before Nora picked up.

"Well, hello Sister Immaculata, it's your niece. I'm dying of curiosity about what it is you were talking about at the reception. You said that you needed some help?"

Nora laughed, "Oh, not so fast, first let me know what married life is like. And how was the honeymoon? It seems like ages that you've be incommunicado."

Elly was joyful as she answered, "Its great! We had a great time alone and I guess we'll have a lot more time alone. That is until the children start to come."

Elly noticed the pause. It was as if Nora was hesitating about telling Elly what she needed. She decided to encourage her aunt to speak up, "Come on, don't be afraid. Whatever it is, I'm sure that Gabe and I would both like to help."

Nora cleared her throat and said, "Okay, but you have to promise to tell me if it is too much for you. Or if you just don't want to do it, you'll just say no. It's a young girl. In fact, she is fifteen and well, she's gotten herself in the family way, if you know what I mean. The problem is she doesn't have a family. Or at least her family doesn't want her home. They demand she get an abortion. So does the boy who got her in this trouble. She's been staying with us, sharing a room with Mary Catherine, the young girl that I always talk about. It's not an ideal situation, but I wanted you to have a full honeymoon without burdening you with this until you came home."

Elly took all of the information in. She still didn't see how she and Gabe fit in to this situation, and asked, "Do you need some money for her?"

The nun hesitated for a moment, and then plunged forward, "It's more than that, she needs a home, with people who will care for her and help her do the right thing. I thought of you and Gabe, with that big home. Surely, you of all people understand what a difficult choice she has made. She has chosen to have her baby. Do you think you and Gabe could find a temporary place for her? She's due in four months, so it wouldn't be for long."

Elly was unprepared for the request. Of course, she would have to ask Gabe. The idea of taking in a girl who needed special care was so unexpected. She answered, "I'll have to talk to Gabe, and get back to you. I'll call you tomorrow, okay?" Elly could feel the joy coming from the other end of the phone line.

Nora smiled, "That's more than I hoped for! Please think about it, Elly. I think that you could be so good for her. She's so alone, and she needs someone who would understand her."

Elly's head was spinning as she hung up the phone. She could easily understand what the poor girl was going through. She remembered how alone and frightened she herself had been when she found herself pregnant and unmarried. Elly had been overwhelmed with fear. She, however, didn't have the courage to do what this girl had done. This girl left her family, and went out into the unknown, just to protect her unborn baby. Elly really admired her. So young too, Elly thought. *Where did she find so much courage? It must have been hard to go against her family and boyfriend. And what would she do once the baby was born? This girl must have great faith,* Elly decided. She also decided that, if it was all right with Gabe, she would have to help this girl. Perhaps, in helping this young girl, Elly could start to make some kind of restitution for the bad decision that she herself had made.

That is how Margie came to live with them. She turned out to be a delight. She was outgoing and fun. Gabe and Elly enjoyed her company. Elly enjoyed taking the girl shopping and the girl seemed to enjoy helping Elly around the house. She seldom talked about her family, and Elly didn't push her. Elly understood how painful the situation was. Gabe was able to give the girl free medical help and Elly's keen sense of what the girl was feeling gave her psychological support. Then, before they even had time to think about it, there were others – girls as desperate as Margie. Each had a heartbreaking story, and a courage that Elly admired.

Gabe and Elly looked around a few months later, and realized that their home was filled with love, laughter, and expectant life. They came to appreciate how full their life became. They decided this was why God so blessed them with wealth. The joy of helping these girls filled Elly's life with a purpose. As Gabe shared with her, so she shared with the girls. After eight months, they attended six births and reunited two families. One girl's boyfriend even realized his mistake and they funded a small wedding in the picture perfect church in town.

Lately, Elly had been tired. The fatigue seemed to increase each day. She sensed something must be physically wrong. Mentally, she was never better. She didn't want to worry Gabe, so she made an appointment with another doctor. Driving over to the neighboring town, she laughed at her own precautions. There was probably nothing wrong. She had been nauseous lately and thought she probably had a touch of the flu. She wasn't prepared for the diagnosis. The elderly doctor was happy to tell her that she had nothing to fear. She was pregnant! Elly was buoyant.

She felt like she was floating on air, as she drove home from her appointment. For the last eight months, she was surrounded by expectant mothers. Now, she was one of them. And the greatest joy was the prospect of telling Gabe. Elly knew he would be thrilled. She prayed the baby was a boy, and that he looked just like Gabe.

Elly was right. Gabe was beyond joyful, he was ecstatic. He was already making plans for the boy's major league baseball career.

As they celebrated, one of the girls shocked him, "What if it's a girl?"

Gabe looked stunned as he mumbled, "A girl, I never thought of that! She'll probably be beautiful, just like her mother."

All the girls laughed as Elly blushed.

Suddenly, Gabe looked worried, "Well, I won't be able to let her out of the house. All the boys will be chasing her!"

Elly laughed, "I don't believe I ever had trouble beating the men off."

Gabe looked tenderly at his blonde wife. That was one of the most precious things about her. She still didn't realize just how beautiful she was. Now with the expectant glow of pregnancy, she was gorgeous.

"I do know one thing," Gabe said firmly. "You're going to need some help around here. I won't have you running around all the time like you have been. You need to get some rest, and make sure you eat properly."

It had never occurred to Elly to ask for help. It's true, the things she needed to do each day had slowly grown to a full time occupation. She cooked and helped each of the girls with their needs. She did most of the shopping and cooking. The girls were really great about keeping everything clean. Elly helped the girls plan for their future and was involved in contacting many agencies and filling out lots of forms. It made for a full day. Who could she get to help with such an unstructured schedule? She would have to ask Father at the rectory. Perhaps he knew of someone.

Father John did know someone. He gave Joyce Elly's phone number and told Joyce of the home Elly was providing for unwed mothers. Joyce called Elly the next day and they set up a time to meet and interview. Joyce was impressed when she drove up to the beautiful ocean home. She was even more impressed by Elly herself.

Elly and Joyce hit it off soon as they met. Elly remembered seeing Joyce at the daily eight o'clock mass but she never talked to her. She was delighted with Joyce's attitude when she commented, "I'll be pleased to work for a few hours each day. My daughter, Grace, just started nursery school and I really need something to fill my time."

Elly liked her relaxed and sure manner, and explained, "I just found out that I'm pregnant. My husband would like me to take it a little easy. There's always something to do. Right now, we have 15 teenaged girls in various stages of pregnancy. We've had as many as eighteen stay with us at one time. They need to eat, and they usually eat a lot. There's shopping to do and they need rides to all sorts of appointments."

Joyce was impressed with the quiet woman before her, and replied, "I think I'm going to like this work. I'll be here tomorrow morning, right after I drop my daughter off at nursery school."

Joyce was dazzled by the beauty of Elly's mansion by the sea. It was impressive and decorated with wonderful taste. Elly provided a wonderful place for these troubled girls. Not only did they have a place to stay, they had a comfortable home to live in. Elly made the large house into their new home.

Each girl did chores, but didn't seem to mind doing them. Elly, like a mother hen, watched over each of them with affection. She seemed to know all the girls well and really cared for them. They felt free to tell Elly their dreams, and Elly listened. She never pushed them about what they should or should not do. She never belittled them. She wanted to encourage their dreams.

As she told Joyce later, "I believe that God places a dream in each person's heart, and if God has put it there, it must be a sin to kill it."

Joyce wondered where Elly learned such wisdom. Elly was so young, yet Joyce sensed that she was more mature then most girls her age. She had such a sweet demeanor, and yet carried herself with the confidence of a much older person. There seemed to be an inner joy in Elly that glowed warmly in her eyes. Joyce felt instantly comfortable talking to Elly. She found herself telling her more about her private life then she usually told others. Elly was so genuinely interested that Joyce found it easy to talk.

Within a few weeks, Elly and Joyce became best friends. Elly was impressed with the caring way Joyce shared with the girls. She also seemed like a devoted mother.

It was during a lunch of turkey sandwiches and tea that Joyce told her about Joseph. "He'll probably be in prison for at least three more years. We have a mutual friend who keeps me abreast of how he is doing." Elly was fascinated by the story of this woman's strength. It seemed to Elly that Joyce had displayed great courage in protecting both her handicapped child, and misguided husband.

Joyce continued, "He's just gone through baptism in the Holy Spirit, and I hope it changes his mind and his life. If time proves he's really found the truth of God, then perhaps, I can let him into Grace's life. I have to be sure though. I don't want a rejection by her father to hurt Grace. She has enough facing her in the future. I would like her to have her father. I think that it's important for a girl to have a man to love her, as she grows up."

Elly agreed, "I know that for a fact. My mother told me a lie about who my father was. I grew up not only without him, but under the illusion that someone else was my father. By the time I found out the truth, he had died and it was too late for us to have a relationship."

The sharing these two women experienced over the next few months sealed their bond of friendship. Three months after Joyce came to volunteer at the house, Elly took a call for Joyce while she was driving one of the girls to the dentist. It was a woman from the Little Giggles nursery school. The woman on the phone explained, "I'm afraid the teacher has come down ill. We are asking all the parents to pick up their children. We don't have the staff to watch the children."

When Elly told Joyce, she answered, "I guess that ends the day for me."

Elly realized Joyce was disappointed. The girls were cooking a special lunch. From the sound of the pots and pans rattling in the noisy kitchen, it promised to be a meal to be remembered.

Elly offered Joyce another option and said, "You know, you can bring Grace here for lunch, that is, if you don't mind her being around the girls."

Joyce smiled, "I think that's a great idea! I'll just pick her up, and be right back. It's about time you met the most important person in my life."

Grace walked in with an air of importance, taking in her surroundings. Looking Elly straight in the eye while shaking her brunette head back and forth, Grace pronounced, "Boy, you must be really rich, lady! I've never seen a place like this!"

Such a big statement from such a small girl tickled Elly. Joyce tried to stop her, but Grace walked around the large living room, swinging her metal arms up and down.

Grace sang, "It 's so big, I could take a walk around here." The child's antics had Elly in stitches.

Joyce looked at Elly with embarrassment, "I've tried to calm her down, but Grace has a way of saying whatever is on her mind."

Elly smiled at the tiny, honest child, and answered, "I think that's good, too many people are afraid. Grace has a way of telling the truth right away. I think that's a good thing."

Elly laughed, as Joyce exclaimed, "That's because you're not her mother!"

The pride in Joyce's eyes gave the lie to her statement. Elly could clearly see how proud she was of her daughter. Elly didn't blame her. The courage Grace displayed was something to be proud of.

Elly wondered if she would have a daughter. She started to imagine the love she would share with her unborn child. Looking down, Elly realized that Grace was staring at her. With a slight lisp, Grace asked, "Well, aren't you hungry? They just called us to lunch, don't you what to eat?"

Elly laughed, "Oh yes, I'm very hungry."

By the end of the lunch, not only Elly, but all of the girls fell in love with the three year old. It was a good thing too, because Grace became a regular visitor around the house. Grace loved her classes at nursery school and spent most her days there, but Joyce volunteered more and more as Elly's pregnancy progressed. It wasn't a problem having Grace around. Everyone loved her. But, while Grace might love all of the women, her main affection was for Gabe. Whenever he was home, she followed him around, asking questions, and tried to be his 'helper.'

They developed a special relationship. Elly thought it was good practice for when their child was born. With all the work and excitement in their life, the months flew by very quickly. Elly didn't have any problem practicing for the care of her new baby. Five newborns lived in the house, while Elly made arrangements for the mothers to start their new lives.

Some of the young girls decided to give their babies up for adoption, and Elly contacted all the proper agencies to insure that they would have a good upbringing. However, some of the girls, especially the older ones, decided to keep their babies. Elly knew that it wasn't going to be easy for them to be single mothers. She admired their courage and their love for their children. She helped them by giving them the best start that she could.

Once the baby was born, Elly would help arrange for a job or further schooling for the mother. She would help them find a good day care center and a good place to live. She would help them find all the programs that would make their life easier. Each girl was welcome to stay until she was ready to start her new life. In the meantime, the house was full of newborns and great commotion. Elly enjoyed every minute of it. With all the experience in the care and feeding of infants, she could hardly wait for her own.

Queen of Angels home grew crowded and busy as the number of girls who came for help grew. Some days were busier then others. This was one of those days and as usual Joyce volunteered to work late. One of the girls who had given birth a few weeks ago needed to be moved to her freshly painted apartment. That same afternoon, two new expectant mothers arrived. One of the new girls was in tears. Her family had totally rejected her because of her pregnancy. The young girl was overwhelmed with fear and sorrow. She had never even been away from home, now her father had banned her from the house. Elly spent all afternoon with the girl, comforting her and counseling her.

The accountant called about the quarterly taxes he was about to file, and complained about the lack of receipts he needed to make some deduction. Elly and Joyce spent all their spare time with the girls. Neither of them were great at keeping records of the purchases they made. They had lost many of the receipts, and would therefore not be able to take deductions they were entitled too. Elly promised the accountant that they would try to be more careful in the future, and added, "I don't know what to say. I know that I'm very bad at keeping accounts. Perhaps, I should get someone in to help with the books. I'll talk to Gabe about it."

The accountant seemed pleased with her solution and smiled, "I didn't mean to yell at you, Elly. It's just that whatever you pay someone will be worth it. It would save you a lot on your taxes. And the more money you save, the more people you can help."

Elly was touched. The gray haired accountant had a good heart. Still, the accountant's criticizing had topped off a busy day for a woman who was due herself in just two weeks. Joyce could read the exhaustion in Elly's face.

With empathy Joyce offered help, "Let me go pick up Grace and come back. Then you can take a long nap."

Elly was grateful, "Are you sure? Don't you want to spend some time alone with Grace?'

Joyce laughed, "When we're alone, Grace just wants to know about everyone here. If she's here for a few hours, her curiosity will be satisfied."

Elly was happy to sink into the featherbed she and Gabe usually shared. Her back was killing her. The first pain woke Elly out of a deep sleep. She rolled over and fell right back to sleep. The second pain was sharper and really roused her. It must be something I ate, she decided.

Looking at the bedside clock, she realized that she must have slept for two hours. Elly could hear the girls rattling around in the kitchen below her master bedroom. Well, maybe I'll just sleep for another fifteen minutes, she thought. But just as she was about to dose off, another pain hit. This one was harder than the first. Now, for the first time, Elly realized that it was a labor pain.

The thought woke her faster than a cold splash of ice water. She wasn't ready. She felt panic! Then she thought of Gabe, and how happy he would be. He was so impatient for his new child. Elly thought of her best friend, Joyce, who was just downstairs. Joyce would help her. Elly headed down the stairs before another pain could hit.

Elly was in the hospital and in the delivery room before she had time to worry. Apparently, her baby didn't intend to waste any time being born. Gabe arrived just in time, just as the pains became overwhelming. It was a relief to see him. Before she knew it, Elly could hear the lusty cries of her newborn son. Gabe was beaming as the nurse brought the boy and laid him in Elly's arms. The infant stopped crying the minute Elly's arms surrounded him. Gabe glowed with pride as he said, "See, he knows his mother."

'Mother,' thought Elly, 'I'm really a mother!' Gabe leaned over and kissed both of them.

"What's his name, Mom?" Elly's eyes smiled as Gabe offhandedly gave her the privilege of naming their new child.

Elly didn't hesitate, announcing, "His name is Gabriel David. He's named after you and my father."

Gabe's face displayed the pride he felt. It was a moment Elly would never forget.

Two days in the hospital proved enough for Elly. She couldn't wait to go home with her son. She missed her friends, family, and home Elly couldn't wait to introduce little Gabe to his newly decorated room. She prayed that she would be the mother he needed. He seemed to have his father's calm and contented disposition. He looked just like Gabe, except his hair was as blonde as Elly's.

The girls excitedly awaited her arrival with her new son. Gabe helped his tired wife into the house as Joyce carried the newborn into his new home. Amidst the adulation of all the girls, little Gabe slept in peace. The ride home was more strenuous than Elly expected. The birth took more out of her than she realized. She was gratified when Gabe helped her up the stairs to her bed.

Gabe pampered her and said, "You just rest. Our son seems intent on sleeping, so just rest."

Turning to Joyce, the proud father instructed, "Just lay the baby in the basinet at the end of the bed. If Elly or the baby need anything, I'll be in the next room."

There was no need to tiptoe out of the room, as the baby proved to be a sound sleeper. Elly was glad to close her eyes. She was just starting into her first dream, when the door to her bedroom opened. Looking at the door, the new mother didn't see anyone. Looking down, she saw the tiny figure of Grace. She tiptoed to the basinet and stood on her toes to see the new visitor. Elly laughed at the girl's curiosity. Elly was sure Joyce had told her to stay downstairs.

Grace was startled when Elly spoke, "Well Grace, what do you think?"

Grace, with a profoundly serious look on her face answered as only Grace would, "He's not very pretty, is he?"

Elly laughed as she realized what Gabe, both wrinkled and reddened, looked like to the small child.

"No, but we're hoping that his looks will improve!"

Elly rolled with laughter, as the look on Grace's face displayed her doubts.

A Sudden Detour

And Jabez called on the God of Israel saying, "Oh, that You would bless me, indeed, and enlarge my territory, that Your hand would be with me, and that You would keep me from evil, that I may not cause pain." So God granted him what he requested. (1 Chronicles 4:9-10)

Mary Catherine was disgusted. Nuns always took so long. *Didn't Sister Immaculata realize how important this was?* Nuns, especially this nun, always stopped to talk to everyone. Mary Catherine wanted to scream, as she saw the young nun stop to talk to another child. It had been this way since Sister had started teaching her how to drive. But today was even more important. Today was her seventeenth birthday, and she was all set to take the test for her driver's license. And driving meant only one thing to Mary Catherine – freedom! She had just graduated from high school, and Sister Immaculata enrolled her in the business school that Mary Catherine picked. Her future was looking bright. It all depended on one thing – getting her driving license.

Mary Catherine was confident she would pass the test. It hadn't always been that way. She was a terrible driver when she first began. Mary Catherine started learning to drive on the old beat-up car the nuns used. It had a manual transmission. Without an explanation of what gears were, she took the nuns on a ride that was worthy of any bronco-buster. It took her a few lessons to learn how to smoothly use the clutch. Sister was pleased when she finally got it.

The next problem was Mary Catharine's habit of turning without slowing. On one practice ride, Mary Catherine turned at 55 miles per hour into the unpaved parking lot of a local restaurant. As dirt flew, and restaurant patrons scattered, the nuns in the car all screamed. *Nuns sure are nervous*, she concluded. After that, the only nun who had the time to teach her was Sister Immaculata. The new driver was glad. Sister Immaculata and she had been close since she was a small, and Mary Catherine always thought of her as a mother. And besides that, she didn't scream as loud as the other nuns.

Still, she was always late. Mary Catherine, like most teenagers, didn't have much patience, and Sister was always telling her to try to develop some. It seemed to Mary Catherine that maybe the nuns could just speed it up. But especially now, her whole life depended on this test. Couldn't Sister see that? Sister Immaculata spotted her and waved. She hurried to the anxious teenager, and asked, "Are you ready to go, Mary Catherine?"

Mary Catherine answered with excitement, "Yes, Sister! I can't wait to get my driver's license!" Getting in the car, Sister had to laugh. Mary Catherine was never short of confidence.

The nun looked across the seat at the young girl, "You're not nervous then, are you?"

Mary Catherine was already pulling out of the drive as she answered, "Heck, no, Sister, I just want to get to the Motor Vehicle office before it's too late."

Sister tried not to laugh. All the other nuns refused to get in the car with Mary Catherine after the parking lot incident. She herself had prayed for the courage not to let the girl down. She had to admit, however, that she had become a pretty good driver. Sister prayed Mary Catherine would pass her test. It would be impossible to live with her if she didn't.

Sister need not have worried. Mary Catherine took the motor vehicle department by storm, and passed her driving test with flying colors. The nun took her out for a rare soda and pizza to celebrate. During the meal, she couldn't help but notice how much the Mary

Catherine had matured. It seemed like just yesterday that Mary Catherine arrived on the nun's doorstep with her brothers in tow. Mary Catherine was no longer a young frightened girl. She was an articulate, young woman.

Sister knew it hadn't been easy for the girl, growing up as she did. Mary Catherine watched all three of her brothers be adopted, as she was left behind. She made friends with other children who came to the orphanage, only to lose them when they were adopted. She was never picked for adoption. She learned not to get to close to the other children because it hurt too much when they left. Her only lasting relationships were with the nuns, and that wasn't always easy.

Sister Immaculata didn't suspect how hard it was for Mary Catherine. When Sister Immaculata was around, Mary Catherine was happy. She felt that someone cared for her. But Sister was required to travel a few times each year, and life was torture for Mary Catherine when she was gone. Sister Josephine never missed an opportunity to harass and belittle the girl. She confined her in the closet on more than one occasion. Mary Catherine could not explain and did not understand the hatred the red-faced nun had for her. She only knew that it grew over the years. If it was an all year thing, Mary Catherine wasn't sure she could have survived such bad treatment. She only knew that she developed a severe case of claustrophobia as a result of Sister Josephine's handling of her.

Now that Mary Catherine was older, the nun's cruelty was confined to verbal abuse. Even the verbal abuse eased since Mary Catherine lost her temper and confronted the nun. The memory of the incident still startled Mary Catherine. She didn't know where the courage came from. It just boiled over after years of battering. She told the nun that she wasn't even a Christian. That no one who believed in Jesus Christ could ever treat another human being as Sister Josephine had treated Mary Catherine. The nun was shocked. Until now, Mary Catherine just accepted her persecution. It wasn't reform that stopped the nun's abuse. It was fear. She realized Mary Catherine was now old enough to defend herself. Despite her feelings, Sister Josephine controlled her hatred. Still, she took every opportunity to harm the girl.

"I'm so proud of you, Mary Catherine," Sister Immaculata broke into the girl's thoughts.

"You are?" Mary Catherine looked at the nun with interest. "Why?"

The nun laughed at Mary Catherine's response and continued, "You've grown into quite a young lady. It hasn't been easy for you. I guess the hardest part was missing your brothers."

A look of pain overcame Mary Catherine. The nun longed to take the girl in her arms and comfort her, as she had done so many times over the years.

Reaching across the table to hold the young girl's hand, the nun said, "Mary Catherine, today seems like a good day to explain my plans to you. You seem old enough now to understand, and to be patient. I don't have, nor have I ever had, any intention of keeping you and your brothers separated. It was important to me they be adopted, so they could have a normal childhood. I wanted them to have parents, and friends. I know the loss of Johnny and Danny was very hard on you and Thomas' adoption was even harder. You were brave, even as a small child. It was so kind of you to put them first. I want you to know the truth now. The separation was never meant to be permanent. Before they were adopted, I made an agreement with their adoptive parents. When the boys are 18, you will be given their new names and addresses. That will be when you are 21."

Mary Catherine was shocked. She had dreamed for a long time of finding her brothers. She dreamed of miracle meetings. She prayed to the Blessed Mother, and her own mother for help. She assumed things would just work out and she would find them. Now the miracle was here. This nun, who was always so good to her, was her miracle. She would be 21 in just four years. It seemed like a long way off to a girl of seventeen, but it was an answer to prayer. She hated to wait, but she could understand the reason. They were both young now. When Johnny and Danny were old enough, she would be ready for them. She would work hard and make money and build a home for all of them. Sister Immaculata watched as the emotions played themselves over Mary Catherine's face.

The nun added, "Of course that offer extends to Thomas as well. It will be much longer, however, until he is old enough." Mary Catherine started to cry. This was the happiest day of her life. She knew now she wouldn't be alone. She would have her family.

Mary Catherine's head was spinning with plans as she said, "I'm going to spend the next few years getting ready for my brothers. I'm going to work really hard in school and become the best accountant in the world, Sister."

Sister was pleased as Mary Catherine hugged her and sobbed. It was good to give this girl hope. She was glad she decided to tell her. Mary Catherine now had a life and a family to look forward to. Mary Catherine was always a good student, and she never doubted that she would do well in business school. Sister kept her plan to herself for many years. She watched the lonely girl turn to the mother of Jesus with a special devotion. She was pleased with the way this child had grown. Mary Catherine professed a faith that could surpass many of the nuns'.

Sister Immaculata proudly told the girl, "Mary Catherine, you have been so brave over all these years. I never would have let the boys be adopted without these agreements. The records are all in my office. On the day you turn 21, I'll give them to you. Now let's go home. You can drive, I trust you completely."

Mary Catherine was so happy that she thought her heart would burst open. Arriving home, Mary Catherine rushed to tell her best friend the news. Kneeling before the statue of her mother in the chapel, Mary Catherine softly wept, "Oh, Blessed Mother, please thank your Son. I didn't understand how come I was all alone. I was afraid that I would be all alone forever. Thank Him for Sister Immaculata. I think that she must be a saint. I wish I could be good like her. Thank you for answering my prayers! I'll say my rosary now."

Mary Catherine pulled the beads out of her pocket. She said a rosary each day for her brothers. She loved the rosary. It was so peaceful to meditate on the important parts of Christ's life. Each decade brought her closer to an understanding of the wonderful plan of redemption that the life of Christ revealed.

She loved the joyful mysteries which concentrated on the birth and childhood of Jesus. She often cried during the sorrowful mysteries which concentrated on the suffering and passion of Jesus. Today she decided to say the glorious mysteries. Each mystery revealed the glory of God. From the resurrection, to the honoring of Mary, it seemed an appropriate time to reflect on the power of God.

So often through the years, God spoke to Mary Catherine though the rosary. On the days she missed her brothers, the suffering of Jesus had made her troubles seem little. When she was locked in the closet by Sister Josephine, she would pray the joyful mysteries. Meditating on the small stable surrounding the newborn Christ always made Mary Catherine feel better. Whenever she missed her mother, the mystery of little Jesus lost in the temple and Mary's search for Him made her feel secure. She knew, somehow, her mother would come for her when it was her time to go to heaven, just as Mary searched for Jesus. Lost in the joy of prayer, an hour passed with little notice from Mary Catherine.

Mary Catherine remained true to her word. She worked so hard in school that she managed to get her associate degree in just one and one half years instead of the expected two years. Sister Immaculata was proud of her. She watched her leave for the college each morning in the used Volkswagen bug the nuns managed to buy her. She was never late. After all this girl had survived, she proved to be an inspiration to the other children in the orphanage. When Mary Catherine received her diploma, the Sister Immaculata wanted to do something special for her.

All the younger children were excited about the surprise party which was planned for Mary Catherine. The hardest part was keeping it a secret. Sister managed, however.

The day of the party finally arrived, and she needed to get Mary Catherine out of the way. She assigned Mary Catherine to work in the garden. Mary Catherine wasn't too happy about it, but when Sister explained to her that she wanted to create a rose garden with a statue of the Blessed Mother, she became enthusiastic. The nun left Mary Catherine happily digging up weeds and turning over the ground with a shovel. The strength of the young never ceased to amaze her.

The rest of the children, most of them much younger than Mary Catherine, met Sister Immaculata in the large kitchen. They all loved Mary Catherine, and wanted to help make and decorate the large sheet cake that Sister planned.

She allowed them to help, each according to their abilities. They were making Mary Catherine's favorite – yellow cake with chocolate icing. They planned to decorate the sheet cake with yellow roses. Sister Victoria was a graduate of a course in cake decorating and promised to help. With all of the children helping, the batter was done quickly and the cake popped into the oven to bake. It was so much fun that all the children and the nuns were in a joyous mood.

When Sister Immaculata looked around the kitchen, however, she realized what a mess they created. If Mary Catherine came in and saw this, she would easily guess something was up. Following her eyes one of the girls, Rosie, realized the nuns' dilemma. It was time for noon prayers, and Sister was required to join the other sisters in the chapel. Yet, she couldn't leave this mess.

Rosie piped up, "Go ahead, Sister, we can clean this up! Don't worry about it. We'll have it cleaned up in a jiffy!"

Twelve-year-old Rosie, a chubby, confident brunette was always ready to help with a smile. Sister was pleased when all the children joined in the chorus of volunteers. Hurrying to the chapel, for the noon call to prayers, she left the clean-up to the children. The girls started by piling the dishes in the large double sink. Rosie took the sprayer and dosed the dishes in preparation for cleaning. She then took the sponge and started to wipe down the table and counters.

She assigned the sweeping of the floor to the crowd of boys. But the boys were fascinated by the sprayer.

Before Rosie knew what happened the largest of the boys, Billy, got to the sprayer and started to hit the younger girls with water. The younger girls screamed, and dispersed around the kitchen. The boys loved scaring the girls. The girls screamed as they ran and got saturated with water. The boys were hysterical. The girls and the kitchen were now wet and slippery. Rosie ran after Billy, and almost fell as she chased him away from the sink. The boys laughed as they ran out the kitchen door. Rosie looked around at the flooded kitchen and drenched children, and panicked.

Rosie realized she had just a half an hour before the nuns would be back and they would all get in trouble! Her first job, she decided was to dry and redress all of the cold, and soggy children. She took them upstairs and accomplished this in just a record twenty minutes.

But when Rosie returned to the large tiled kitchen, she the task before her overwhelmed her. It was only the thought of disappointing Sister Immaculata that started her cleaning. It was a great surprise to her when the younger girls started to mop and help. Rosie quickly washed all the dishes as the girls mopped and wiped up all to the water. Looking around, Rosie was pleased. The kitchen sparkled brighter then before they started to bake the cake.

Rosie was just finishing drying the last bowl, as she heard the sisters leaving the chapel. Looking around the kitchen, she was pleased with the great job the girls had done. As soon as this party was over, she would get those boys. She decided not to ruin Mary Catherine's party by ratting on them.

Sister Immaculata flashed one of her sweet smiles at the girls the minute she entered the gleaming kitchen. Rosie basked in the love this nun radiated. All of the hard work they did was worth that one smile. Sister removed the cake from the oven. The sweet smell filled the kitchen.

"It's perfect!" Sister Immaculata exclaimed as she set the cake on top of the stove to cool. "But I forgot to soften the butter for the icing. I'll soften it quick in the microwave."

Neither Rosie nor the nun noticed the puddle of water that had collected under the microwave. The girls missed it while doing their clean up. Placing the butter on the rotating plate in the fairly new appliance, Sister Immaculata reached for the switch.

Sister never felt any pain, as the jolt of electricity shot through her body. Her soul left her body before it hit the wall. Her physical form was killed instantly. The young nun watched as her remains slid down the wall opposite the microwave. She felt no fear, as she heard the screams of the watching children. Mary Catherine heard the children's screams and ran in from the garden. The other nuns came running, and everyone froze in fear.

Sister Immaculata's spirit calmly watched as Mary Catherine was the only one with the presence of mind to head for the phone and call 911. Sister Immaculata couldn't help but smile at the calmness Mary Catherine displayed while all the others were lost in panic. Then she turned to the awaiting angel and left the earth. Her Lord awaited her in the light, and the overwhelming peace and joy she felt as she traveled toward Him was indescribable. She had no fear that the CPR Mary Catherine started would not work. She knew her earthly life was over. She was joyous as she entered the Presence of Jesus.

Elly watched the young girl who sat so silently before the simple pine coffin which held the remains of her Aunt Nora. This must be Mary Catherine. Elly had heard many stories about her from Aunt Nora. The many antics of the beloved child brought laughter to all of their family gatherings. Aunt Nora so enjoyed the young, practical Mary Catherine. Elly felt as if she knew her. For so many years she enjoyed the stories about Mary Catherine and now she sat so still and silent before her. What could she say to her? Somehow she felt her Aunt Nora would want her to reach out and help the lost child. Sitting beside her, Elly watched as the girl just stared at the coffin.

"She isn't there, you know," started Elly. The young girl turned, and stared at Elly.

Looking back to the coffin, Mary Catherine answered, "I know, if anyone could make it to heaven, it would be Sister."

Elly smiled at the girl's devotion, "She must be so happy there, she was the only person I knew who really lived the Christian life."

Mary Catherine took a deep breath but couldn't stifle the sob that escaped her, "Yes, she's probably happy, but what about us? How are we supposed to live without her?"

Elly watched as Mary Catherine started to weep. Elly had some sense of how she was feeling. She knew what it was to feel all alone in the world. Her heart reached out to the young woman who was so sad. Placing her arm around her, Elly remained silent. She allowed Mary Catherine to sob on her shoulder.

Mary Catherine was distraught, "What am I supposed to do without her? Where will I go now? She always helped me to decide things. Now I'm all alone!"

Elly held Mary Catherine tight, as the younger girl released all her pent-up feelings of fear and grief. Looking at the serene face of Nora in her coffin, Elly decided she would take care of Mary Catherine. Aunt Nora helped her, and now it was her turn to help Aunt Nora's favorite child.

When the girl's weeping subsided, Elly pulled some tissues from her purse and wiped Mary Catherine's face. Elly tried to share some of the young girl's grief. "I loved her too. She was my aunt."

Mary Catherine searched Elly's profile, and answered in a matter of fact way, "Yeah, you do look like her."

Elly smiled at Mary Catherine's quick return to the pragmatic, and said, "My Aunt Nora often talked about you, Mary Catherine. She was so proud of how well you had done in school. She talked with as much pride as a mother would."

Mary Catherine stared at Sister Immaculata, as Elly talked. She answered quietly, "She was like a mother to me. I loved her."

Elly smiled at the girl's ability to clearly express her feelings.

There was nothing halfway about Mary Catherine.

Elly reached out to the young girl. "Aunt Nora told me that you got your degree in accounting. We discussed the kind of a job you would get."

"You did!" Mary Catherine seemed surprised that anyone found her life important enough to discuss.

Elly answered, "I begged her to let you come and work for me. I need someone to help me with the books. I am terrible at numbers, and my secretary Joyce is not much better. We run a nonprofit home for unmarried mothers."

Mary Catherine looked up at Elly with interest as Elly continued. "Do you think you would like to come and work for us? We could really use the help. The pay isn't much, but I can offer room and board."

Mary Catherine didn't have to think long. She was too old to stay at the orphanage. Now that Sister Immaculata was gone, her only reason for staying was also gone. The thought of living with Sister Josephine was not a pleasant one. If she took the job, she would have her own money to save. Mary Catherine wanted to save for a home–a home for her brothers.

She had been offered other accounting jobs since her graduation. All of them required a move to the city. She had looked around at apartments, but Mary Catherine didn't relish living alone. The thought of staying in one of the small, cramped studio apartments she had seen did not appeal to her. She did not relish living alone. Mary Catherine was too used to being around a lot of other people. She decided she would give Elly's offer serious consideration.

Within a few hours, Mary Catherine had made up her mind. Elly delighted in the very efficient girl before her. With the decision made, Mary Catherine returned to her grief, and the thoughts of the nun whom she loved. The wake was crowded with so many people that many were forced to stand in the hallway. Sister Immaculata touched many people with her kindness and her love.

So many attended the wake that no one noticed Sister Josephine was not there. She was very devious in letting each carload of nuns think that she was going in the other car. None of them cared for her, so each seemed relieved that she wasn't with them. She had big plans and attending the wake of someone who in her opinion, had stolen her job, was not among them.

She huffed and puffed her way to the office that should have been hers. With no one around to interfere, she knew she would be able to finally fix Mary Catherine. Her face reddened with anger as she remembered the day the runt dared to tell her off! Imagine the nerve of that brat, telling her that she wasn't a Christian! She decided on that very day she would fix her good. She had been patient. Like a spider, she waited for her opportunity. The death of Sister Immaculata gave her the chance.

Pulling the wheeled office chair over to the file cabinet, she lowered her girth with some effort onto the chair. Using the key she often observed Sister Immaculata hide under the statue of Our Lady, Sister Josephine opened the forbidden files. She grinned with evil satisfaction as she found just what she was looking for. Pulling the files from the cabinet, she took her time in looking through them. With great gratification, she found the files which contained all the information she was looking for. Sister didn't see the evil spirits directing her. She felt like jumping for glee as she headed for the shredder. In her pride, she just assumed the depraved sin she had just committed was her own idea.

She formulated the idea after she overheard Mary Catherine brag about her plans to find her brothers. She never expected to have so much luck. When the Mother Superior was electrocuted, it all came together. It just went to show you that with great patience, revenge was always possible. She was so joyful when she shredded the files that she laughed out loud.

The nun talked out loud to the empty room. "You'll never, ever find your brothers now! You little bitch!"

She laughed as the files were destroyed forever. No one will ever know what family adopted them. The records of the adoptions of Johnny, Danny, and Thomas were destroyed with relish. Sister Josephine delighted in causing pain to the girl she hated so much. She knew her act would break Mary Catherine's heart and she was delirious about it.

A Second Chance

But the hour is coming, and is now here, when true worshipers will worship the Father in Spirit and truth; and indeed the Father seeks such people to worship him. God is Spirit and those who worship him must worship in Spirit and truth. (John 3:23-24)

Joseph's lawyer had notified him of his parole board hearing two weeks ago. He hadn't been able to give it much thought. During the last three years, he became immersed in his advocacy work. Each day was a mission to help his fellow prisoners. With the many books John donated, and the new computer some of John's friends contributed, he tried to solve the financial burdens of the men and their families. The convicts' economic worries were sometimes harsher than their imprisonment. It was one thing to live within the physical walls of a prison. It was often more bitter to live imprisoned by poverty. Whenever Joseph could help he was happy. Often the solution was simple, and sometimes it was very complex.

Yet in all this time Joseph hadn't found a problem he wasn't able to solve. Often, he felt overwhelmed and tired. Discouraged, he often felt like giving up. It was during these times he would think of the testimony he heard at his first Life in the Spirit seminar. Tyrone's testimony was so powerful that even to this day it touched his heart. Tyrone's loss of family due to economics reinforced how important mismanagement of money could be. Joseph was determined not to let another family be lost because of bad budgeting or a lack of resources. He was tenacious in searching for the money each family needed. He would search until he found the means, or the resources they needed to keep the family together.

John Meyer worked with the assistant warden and Joseph, introducing Joseph and his program to outside social workers. With the warden's approval, they were glad to teach and help Joseph with his advocacy work. He often spent hours on the phones the warden set up for him, calling welfare departments, and food stamp programs. Joseph grew in knowledge and learned what charities he could depend on to help a family in need. He would work with the prisoner carefully, outlining a budget, getting more money in the home, getting in touch with all the needed agencies. Joseph would do anything to keep the family whole and together.

Sometimes he would even call an agency to find them a more affordable place to live. It was usually just a little amount of money–saved each month–which would make the difference.

Joseph would do anything to keep a family together. Sometimes, when it seemed he had hit a brick wall, he would remember how alone he felt as a teenager. He couldn't bear the thought of a lonely child being torn from his parents and placed in a foster home simply because of poverty. Thinking of how much these children needed their real parents kept Joseph going through many sleepless nights of research. Joseph was concerned for the fathers also. He didn't want any of these men to be forced to give a testimony like Tyrone's.

Through the years, Joseph had developed a profound life of prayer. No matter how busy, or overwhelmed his work made him, he always set aside at least an hour each morning for prayer. Today was no different. He spent an hour in the prison chapel, deeply immersed in listening to the Lord. Joseph learned it was much more important to listen than to talk. Jesus already knew what he needed. The answers he got in prayer confirmed that. It was often during prayer that the answers to one of the prisoner's problems were whispered to him.

Today, however, his calendar was clear. Today was Joseph's parole hearing. He didn't know how he felt about it. Joseph, if he was honest with himself, had avoided thinking about it. As he looked at the large crucifix on the wall of the chapel, Joseph admitted to both himself and Jesus that he was afraid.

He wasn't afraid of the hearing or of being denied parole. What frightened him most was the reality that he might be paroled. He was afraid to leave the prison. He was afraid of the world and what it might do to his faith. In prison, he knew his pride could not gain a foothold. He knew what his purpose was. *What would become of him out in the world? Would he lose his way again? Would he even lose Jesus?* Joseph closed his eyes and tried to clear his mind of his worries. He tried to listen to what God was saying.

"Joseph, my beloved son, walk by faith, not by sight. I have given you my Spirit. Do not be afraid, I am always with you." The familiar voice, heard in the whispers of his heart, brought Joseph peace. Suddenly, Joseph knew that wherever God placed him, He would be with him. It didn't matter where that was. It didn't matter what happened at the parole board hearing.

God, alone, knew where Joseph was needed most. The prisoner suddenly knew that if God removed him from the prison and his ministry, he would raise up another to take his place. To think otherwise would be the sin of pride. Joseph would go wherever Jesus led him. Suddenly, the image of Joyce came into his mind. He started to push the image away, as he had so many times in the past, until he realized the vision was from God.

"You have a wife and child also." Joseph was shocked. He had pushed thoughts of Joyce away for so long. Three years ago, during his baptism in the Spirit, he asked God to remove his obsessive thoughts of Joyce. Jesus was kind. Although his longing for Joyce didn't stop immediately, over next few months his obsession seemed to dwindle. He became absorbed in his work. He hadn't stopped loving Joyce. But the sick longing he carried for months seemed to disappear. Now it seemed that God was asking him to think of her again.

The image of his beautiful wife came easily. Joseph still loved her. He couldn't believe the way he treated her. Despite his behavior, she was always loyal. That is, until the day he threatened her child. Joseph crossed a line then. At the time he didn't see it. Now, he understood it. What he didn't understand is how he could have been so selfish. Joyce was strong, because she was strong in her faith. He understood that now, but he lost her. Joseph was sure of that. He didn't even know where she was. How could he ever hope to find her? And even if he did, he was sure she had gone on with her life. She wouldn't want anything to do with him. Why Father, are you bringing her to mind? Is it to remind me of my sins? I am well aware of them.

"Your wife and child need you too." The voice resounded through him. Why would anyone need me?, thought the broken man. If they need me, then I will trust in You. You will help me find them. You will bring Joyce and my child to me. Joseph was bewildered as he thought of the baby. The baby wouldn't be a baby anymore. The child would be about five years old. He didn't even know if it was a girl or a boy.

Whatever your Will, Lord. Just watch over both of them today and every day. And may your Will be done in the hearing today!

Joseph walked to the long narrow hallways on his way to the parole board hearing. Three lock-up doors had to be opened to let him through. As the guards let Joseph through, they all wished him luck at his hearing. Joseph was surprised and gratified. He was pleased that they cared enough to even know about his hearing. He took a deep breath as he was called into the main hearing room. Joseph was suddenly nervous. The next year of his life would be determined by the men and women in this room.

The parole board was made up of three people. In Joseph's case it was two men and one woman. Two middle-aged white men sat at the judicial bench, with a tiny elderly black woman. As Joseph stood with the public defender they introduced themselves to him.

One of the men said, "Mr. Joseph McKenna, this hearing has been called to decide if you are ready to re-enter society and become a productive citizen."

The white-haired board member continued, "My name is Mr. Johnson. And my colleagues are Mr. Hinko, and Mrs. Evans respectively."

Turning to address Joseph's lawyer, Mr. Johnson asked, "Mr. Williams are you and your client prepared to demonstrate his readiness to be paroled?"

Mr. Williams, the public defender, stood beside Joseph and answered, "Yes, we are."

Mr. Johnson sat back and stated, "Then proceed with any valid testimony."

Joseph sat while Mr. Williams called the first witness. Joseph was stunned when his lawyer called the assistant warden. The man Joseph grew to know well over the years didn't have to take the stand in such an informal hearing. He simply stood at a micro-phoned podium before the board, and gave his opinion. Joseph choked back the tears as he listened.

The assistant warden cleared his throat, and said, "Mr. Williams and board members, most of you have known me for many years and I would venture to say that this is one of the very few times that I have decided to testify at a parole board hearing. In the past, I have only testified against paroling what I felt was a dangerous criminal who I felt was trying to deceive the board members."

Joseph's heart broke as he thought that the man he had grown to respect was about to advise against his parole. It was not the loss of parole that upset him. It was the realization that the assistant warden thought he was a phony which bothered him.

The assistant warden continued his testimony. "When Joseph, the inmate and I first met I had little faith in the way he presented himself. I thought he was probably the best con-man I ever met. It seemed to me that, like so many others, he was going to use a so-called new found faith for his own benefit. I knew that as time went on, the truth would come out, and his true colors would show. I was not disappointed, they have."

Joseph couldn't believe the man he had grown to think of as a friend felt this way about him.

The assistant warden continued, "Joseph's true colors have shown, and to my surprise they have shown him to be a truly changed man." The assistant warden turned at smiled at Joseph.

"Mr. McKenna has, in my opinion, been one of the true success stories. He has gone through a profound religious transformation. As a result of that transformation, he has changed from an arrogant, pride-filled, and selfish human being into a truly caring individual. For the last three years he has spent each day helping other prisoners with their financial problems. He has put in long and unscheduled hours because he really cares about the other men. I have never seen such a change in any man. Over the years, I have seen him change the life and disposition of many other men. I have learned to respect him both as a human being and a friend. As many of you know, I am not a deep believer in the worthiness of my fellow human beings.

"When I first started my career I had a deep hope in rehabilitation, but during the years that followed I found myself conned by the best of them. My belief in the ability of the system to rehabilitate criminals was destroyed. If someone presented themselves to me a changed man, I just waited for the truth to be revealed. When Mr. McKenna came to my office, I was sure that his act of finding God was just that, a con job. But I must now say that he is truly a transformed individual. I believe that he is now a new person. I believe that he would not only not harm society, but actually benefit it. The only sad aspect is, that if you release him on parole, as he deserves we will lose him. He is a blessing around here and he will be sorely missed."

Joseph was stunned. He never expected such testimony. He never realized the assistant warden thought of him this way. Mrs. Evans, who did not seem as impressed as the other board members, asked the assistant warden some hard questions. He answered all of them well, but she seemed unconvinced.

"Do you have any other testimony?" she asked harshly as the warden was dismissed.

"I do," answered Mr. Williams. Joseph was overwhelmed, as his lawyer called many prisoners to testify. Man after man approached the podium to tell of the various ways in which Joseph helped to change their lives. Joseph was shocked by number of the men. The two men on the parole board, Mr. Johnson and Mr. Hinko seemed very impressed. During the testimonies, the board members asked questions of the witnesses until they were satisfied they were telling the truth. Mrs. Evan's face was skeptical.

The next witness called was Father Dan. He came to the podium with his usual radiant smile, and said, "Joseph came to our Life in the Spirit Seminar about three years ago. At first he seemed distant, but as the seminar progressed, he made some profound changes. He started to care about the men in his group. He started to care about them more than himself. He was flooded with the Holy Spirit at the baptism, and I believe from what I see that he was given many gifts."

Mrs. Evans, an evangelical, asked many questions of the priest. The priest answered all her questions. Father Dan ended his statement by saying, "Joseph gives his testimony each year, and is a group facilitator. I believe the Holy Spirit is able to help many lost men through him."

Joseph found himself getting choked up as he listened to the priest. He couldn't believe so many people came to help him. At this point, he didn't even care if he was granted parole. The love his friends had shown him was more than enough for any man.

Mrs. Evans, while obviously impressed by the priest, still appeared in doubt. She directed her next few questions directly to Joseph.

"It seems that you have made a good impression on many people in this prison. However the crimes you are guilty of are quite serious. Or do you claim that you are innocent of these crimes?"

Without looking at his lawyer for direction Joseph answered, "No m'am, I did all of the things I was convicted of. I even did worse things I didn't caught for. I can't deny who I was."

Mrs. Evans looked disturbed. "Oh, so your claim is that you did all these terrible things, but now you have changed."

Joseph answered, "Yes, with the help of God, and only by His Power, have I changed."

Mrs. Evans face softened as she saw the sincerity in Joseph's eyes, "I believe you, Mr. McKenna. I am concerned, however, how well all this will transfer to the outside world. Prison life is a controlled environment. Even if all we've been presented today is true, that doesn't mean you'll be able to make it in the outside world without back sliding into past behavior. What do you have in the outside world to ensure that your new way of life will continue?"

Joseph was stumped. It was the very question that he had struggled with in the chapel this morning. His silence seemed to speak volumes to the tough Mrs. Evans. Mr. Williams tried to quickly repair what he saw as real damage to Joseph's parole hopes.

Joseph's lawyer stated, "I believe the next witness that I call will be able to alleviate your worries on that account, Mrs. Evans."

Mrs. Evans face betrayed her doubt. "We'll see about that! However, we are going to break for lunch. You can present your final witness in an hour."

As the parole board left the room, Joseph and his attorney were left alone. The public defender seemed annoyed as he said, "Please, try to be more aggressive. It's bad enough that you got Mrs. Evans, she very rarely votes for parole. She has little trust in rehabilitation. You really have to convince her."

Joseph calmly listened to his frustrated lawyer, and responded, "I understand her concern, I'm not worried. If God wants me out of prison, I will get parole, if He wants me here, I won't. Worry is a sin. I'm happy to be wherever He wants me."

Mr. Williams, a nonbeliever, shook his head, and answered, "Well, it's not up to God. You might have a better chance with him! It's Mrs. Evan's you're dealing with. Let me explain something to you. You couldn't have gotten a worse deal. Twenty years ago, her only son was murdered by a man who was just paroled. That was when she first got involved in the parole board. Soon as I saw her, I knew your chances were slim. And if she decides against you, you've lost. All of the members have to vote for parole. If even one votes against it, parole is denied."

Joseph didn't respond. Mr. Williams wouldn't understand his trust in God and his docility to God's Will. He allowed the guard to walk him to the dining room for lunch. Joseph wasn't worried. He was, however, hungry.

The lunch hour went quickly. Joseph returned to the board room and awaited the introduction of the final witness on his behalf. Joseph was shocked when his lawyer called his last witness. It was John Meyer. He nodded at Joseph as he reached the podium and seemed pleased to be there. Joseph couldn't believe that he had left his busy business to come to Joseph's defense. The board also seemed impressed. John Meyer and his successful business projects were well known. He had even appeared on many cable business shows. It was not very often that an eminent businessman came to a parole hearing.

He talked about his long friendship with the prisoner and Joseph's spiral downward due to his drug addiction. He talked about the change he saw in Joseph after he turned to God. His support for Joseph's parole was very powerful.

Mrs. Evans was tenacious. "What makes you think that his so-called new ways will continue once he's out of prison?"

John smiled and answered, "You're right to worry. Normally, I myself would be afraid. Joseph could slip back into his old temptations if he didn't get any support."

Mrs. Evans frowned. "Oh, I'm sure even you, good man that you seem to be, would be supportive. But weren't you supportive the last time, as he got into all this trouble?"

John Meyer responded, "Yes, I was his friend. And yes, he did still go ahead and get into drugs and criminal behavior. This time, however, I can see two big differences that say to me that Joseph will make it."

Mrs. Evans looked doubtful, and asked, "Can you explain those differences?"

John paused for a minute to clarify his thoughts. "I would have to say that the defining change for Joseph is his faith, and his relationship with the Living Jesus. I believe Joseph has found the person that Christ meant him to be. When Joseph became lost, he didn't have any faith. This time I hope to direct him to a parish community where he will find the support to walk in faith. I want to set him up so that he can continue the good work that he began here. I believe with the fellowship of true believers and a Godly purpose to his life, Joseph will be able to walk in faith. I believe he will be able to transfer his faith into the outside world."

John finished speaking and hoped that he had made a strong case for Joseph's release.

Mrs. Evans spoke first, "I thank you Mr. Meyer for taking the time to speak for your friend. I wish that I had the same faith in him that you do. However, I do not see that he will have different support than he had the last time. I'm afraid I'm not sure what will make a difference. He may, in my opinion, get caught up in the world again. Can you tell me one real change in his life that may supply a profound change?"

John hesitated. He had not planned to broach the subject, but felt he had no other option. "Perhaps I can. Over the years Joseph has been in prison and without his knowledge, I have kept in close touch with his wife, Joyce."

Joseph felt his heart beat faster as his hands gripped the table before him. He felt the need to steady himself as John continued.

"His wife has been aware of all the events of Joseph's life. She did not want him to know that she was watching over him through me."

Joseph whitened as John's news stunned him.

"Joyce was not only aware of Joseph's drug problem and imprisonment, she was also aware of the hard time Joseph had during his first year in prison. She was with him when he had reconstructive facial surgery, after one of the many beatings he received during his first year here," Meyer continued.

Joseph couldn't believe his ears. Joyce was there, at the hospital, and he hadn't known it!

John's testimony continued. "She is aware of the changes Joseph has gone through. I'm afraid she, herself, was very skeptical of his reform. She had to be, she knew him better than anyone. She watched and waited, through me. Joyce wanted to see if Joseph had truly found the way of Jesus. I think that despite her prayers otherwise, she fully expected Joseph to fall into his old ways. For three years, since his conversion, I have been visiting and helping Joseph and keeping Joyce aware of his progress. He had no reason to lie to me. Joseph had no idea I even knew where Joyce was. Joyce is now convinced that Joseph is truly a changed man. The proof of that belief is that she wishes to extend to him an invitation. Joyce wishes, if Joseph is willing, to renew their relationship as husband and wife."

Joseph could no longer contain his feelings. He lowered his head into his hands and started to sob. Mrs. Evans noticed, but was too fascinated by what was happening to silence the witness.

"Joyce has always loved Joseph, but she knew he had to find God and change. She was afraid to allow him in her life without that change. And she had a very good reason to be afraid. She has a very special child. A little girl named Grace. Joyce told me she could never let Joseph in Grace's life if she thought Joseph would hurt or reject the girl because of her severe disabilities. She now feels that it would not only be safe, but beneficial to Grace to have Joseph as a father. I trust Joyce completely. If Joyce feels Joseph can make it in the real world then this court should have no worries. Joyce has more wisdom than any human I have ever known. If she is willing to let Joseph into her life, he must be profoundly changed. I hope that the board will let him out. He needs his daughter, and his daughter needs him."

Joseph couldn't believe it. Joyce was giving him a second chance. God! Oh, God! How good You are, he thought. Joseph was overwhelmed. He had a daughter. He had a little girl. Oh, how he wanted to see her. Mrs. Evans seemed astounded. She thanked John for his statement and turned her attention to a dazzled Joseph.

"Mr. McKenna, how do you feel about your wife?" she asked.

In a shaken voice, he answered, "I love Joyce, I have always loved her. But I did not always know what love was. Now, with God's help I hope that I can give her a happy life!"

Mrs. Evans appeared deep in thought as she looked at the prisoner. "Do you intend then, to take up your wife's invitation and start a new married life with her? Do you intend to live with her?"

Tears streamed down his cheeks as Joseph answered, "Yes, Yes! I want to spend the rest of my life with Joyce and my daughter!"

Mrs. Evans smiled. "This is exactly the profound life change I was looking for. I do believe now that you have a good chance to succeed in a new life. I myself cast a vote for your parole. It is up to my colleagues to finalize the decision."

The two men on the panel were stunned. *If Mrs. Evans thought the prisoner should be paroled, who were they to argue?* The decision was unanimous, Joseph was paroled.

Joseph stood outside on the sidewalk. He had stood under this tree for the last three afternoons. He gazed at the small ranch house before him. It was just like the woman who owned it, simple and straightforward. The rose bushes around the front porch were starting to bloom. The yard was small and neat. The tiny back yard had a small vegetable garden, and a swing set. A tiny table and chair was laden with a toy tea set. Two rag dolls sat at the table as if waiting for someone to pour them tea. Joseph wondered what his daughter looked like.

For three afternoons he stood here. His knees shook with fear. He simply could not get up the courage to walk up the porch and knock on the door. John encouraged him, but didn't force him.

John said each day, "This is something you are going to have to do on your own."

Joseph stood frozen. He deserved to be rejected. He had treated her so badly. How could he expect her to forgive him? He knew he could never face her. Joseph was about to walk away, as he had on the last two days, but when he started to turn he was stunned to hear the front door open. A tiny dark-haired girl opened the screen door and looked at him.

In a puzzled voice the tiny girl asked, "Dad, are you going to stand there all day! Why don't you knock, so I can let you in?"

Joseph couldn't believe the curious little face that looked at him. He found himself quickly up the walk, and on the porch.

The dark-haired girl introduced herself, "Hi! I'm Grace. You can come in. I know who you are."

Joseph noticed the metal arms for the first time, as the tiny girl opened the door wider. She led him into a small, beautifully decorated living room. Joseph couldn't take his eyes off of her as he sat on the sofa. She was like a small, precious jewel. Grace was so tiny and petite that she looked like a china doll. What stunned Joseph the most was that she looked just like him.

Trembling, Joseph asked, "How do you know that I'm your father?"

The dark girl laughed, "Don't be silly! Look around!"

Joseph looked around the room. He was shocked to see numerous pictures of himself framed on all the tables and walls. Many pictures were taken since his surgery. Joseph would find out later that John Meyer had sent Joyce many of the pictures he had taken of Joseph. That was how Grace knew who he was. Joyce told his daughter all about him. She wanted Grace to know him. Joseph was overwhelmed.

Grace came up to him and put her metal arms around him. Laying her head on his shoulder, she said, "Don't cry, Daddy. We've been waiting for you to get here. You don't have to be alone anymore."

Grace sat on his lap. The tiny girl comforted the large man who already loved her. This was how Joyce found them as she came out of the shower. With a large, white terry robe and a towel wrapped around her head, Joyce found the two people she loved the most together on her sofa. The man she loved softly wept as his daughter held his weeping frame in her metal arms. They had learned to love each other.

The Flight of Love

"Stop judging, that you may not be judged. For as you judge, so will you be judged, and the measure with which you measure. Will be measured out to you." (Matt. 7:1-2)

The crowd on the airplane was joyous. Most of them were headed for a long awaited vacation. There were a lot of children who were impatient to see the kingdom dedicated to the magic of childhood. There were some business men who worked on laptops and appeared annoyed by the ranting of the children.

Mary Catherine couldn't believe she was on this flight. What was she doing? She didn't want to go to Florida. It seemed to her almost every trip she ever took led to nothing but pain. First, she was removed from her home and left at an orphanage. At the orphanage, she lost everyone she loved. She lost her brothers. As a teenager, she lost the nun who was like her second mother. The trip she took to her job with Elly and Joyce proved to be better. In the ten years she spent at Queen of Angels, it became her home.

Mary Catherine didn't want to leave her home. He had a lot of nerve sending for her. What could he want now? Did he want to be forgiven? She had no intention of giving him any forgiveness. She couldn't stand thinking about it. She was blessed in many ways. During the last ten years, she formed friendships with two most wonderful women. Love seemed too small a word for what Mary Catherine felt toward Elly and Joyce. They became the family she lost. They gave her a home full of other young women. They were kind and gentle mothers toward her. At the age of eighteen, they transformed a young, grieving teenager to a competent, mature young woman.

She was full of pain when Elly first gave her the job as accountant. The death of Sister Immaculata rekindled the pain of her life, and brought it to the surface. She grieved not only for the loving nun, but for her mother, brothers, father, and the family she lost. She grieved for the life she would have had if her mother lived. She would never know that life. In the end, with Joyce's and Elly's help, she accepted life as it really was. That was no small task.

As Elly pointed out, "Mary Catherine, so many people spend their lives pining for the life they think they should have had. At the end of their life, they realize how they wasted the life that God really gave them. Always remember, it is not what happens to us that matters. It is what we do with what happens to us."

Mary Catherine never forgot those words. It wasn't always easy. It had been especially hard when they found that all of her brother's adoption records appeared lost. They searched the orphanage records and even traveled to search the diocesan records. Despite hours of hard work, they walked away empty-handed. It was so painful to Mary Catherine. She felt like she lost her brothers all over again. She spent many hours in prayer. It was during prayer she decided to save her money and hire a private detective to find them. The detective turned up some interesting clues but still they appeared lost.

During this time, Mary Catherine stayed in an upstairs room in Elly's house. It became her home. She worked hard each day, putting in long hours. Mary Catherine loved every minute of it. It made her laugh to think how their roles had reversed over the years. At first, she took the role of the child in their relationship. But as the years rolled on, the pragmatic and very practical Mary Catherine slowly became the adult. Elly was a dreamer–she wanted to heal the whole world. There was no one she seemed able to turn away. Joyce, while a little more practical, was hard put to tell Elly that they couldn't fit any more people at the home. Neither Elly nor Joyce ever seemed worried about the cost.

Mary Catherine, as the accountant, was the one who lovingly took care of the money. Mary Catherine with her short stylish hair, and no nonsense manner, was the one who managed the finances. She invested and tried to save. The home had long ago spent all of Elly's inheritance. Mary Catherine found discounts and had no shame about finding any government programs that might help. She was not past moving money around, or as they say 'robbing Peter to pay Paul.' She doubted whether either Elly or Joyce realized how often they came close to going broke. It didn't matter. It gave Mary Catherine a thrill to come through at the last minute. It often meant helping someone who would otherwise be turned away.

The home was still a home for unwed mothers, who were being forced by their families to have abortions. The families refused to help them unless they agreed to the abortion. Without help from their parents or boyfriend, or in some cases husbands, the women felt pressured into the abortions that they did not want. That was where the home came in. Elly's and Gabe's home, now called Queen of Angels, became their temporary home. She gave them food, shelter, and a safe haven until their baby was born. Through her husband Gabe, she also provided medical care for these girls who often had nothing. Without their help, many of these girls would have been forced to abort their babies.

Many of the parents and fathers changed their minds once the baby was born. They seemed willing to accept and love the child. In these cases' Joyce would, with her special touch, help the families to heal and learn to love again.

In the case where a girl was permanently estranged from her family, the team would meet and decide what the girl's and the infant's needs were. If the girl needed job training, the team would provide it. If she needed an affordable place, they would help her find it. The transition team was made up of five people, Elly, Joyce, Gabe, Father John Burns, and Mary Catherine. It was the part of the job Mary Catherine enjoyed most. Here Mary Catherine's special financial skills shone. She felt she was making a real difference in these girls' lives. It also gave her a real pleasure to keep a mother and her child together. She never wanted to see a family separated, like her own had been.

Pulled from her thoughts, Mary Catherine belted up for takeoff. So many children were on the flight to Florida. She watched as they sat beside their loving parents. Mary Catherine watched as one little girl who was afraid was comforted by her father. The father's strength calmed the girl immediately. Mary Catherine wondered if the young girl would ever realize how lucky she was. If only I had a father like that one, thought Mary Catherine. The sensation of the plane taking off drew Mary Catherine's attention to the clear blue sky outside the window, and back to her memories.

Despite her heavy work load at Queen of Angels, Mary Catherine continued to search for her brothers. She longed for her family. Mary Catherine watched as Elly's family grew. As the love between Gabe and Elly matured into a deep and profound contentment, their family also grew. Elly presented Gabe with five beautiful children. The boys reminded Mary Catherine of her brothers.

How lucky they are to have each other and grow up in a wonderful place like this, thought Mary Catherine, as she watched the boys play tag amongst the gardens. The flower gardens were planted and maintained by the garden club from town and were beautiful. Made up of mostly senior citizens, the garden club came each week to maintain and weed the gardens for half of what a professional landscaper would cost.

The freckled faces of little Gabe and his younger brother Jose reminded her of Johnny and Danny. Mary Catherine would often watch the two boys play through the window by her desk. She prayed she would find her brothers, but as the years passed it seemed as if they would always be lost.

Joyce had been reunited with her husband Joseph, who continued his advocacy work each day in his new position with Catholic

Charities. He worked in the worst ghettos of New York City and was gone for many hours each day. Still, Mary Catherine watched with joy as the little family grew in love. Grace was the glue that held that family together. Her loving ways with her parents gave them just the connection they needed to heal their marriage. Mary Catherine was happy for them. She just couldn't understand why she was always alone, searching for her family.

She loved Joyce and Elly. She had grown through her twenties with these wonderful women as her guide. She developed a loving relationship with both Joyce's daughter Grace, and Elly's five children. However, she spent much of her free time dreaming about finding her brothers. Danny and Johnny would be in their early twenties now. Thomas would be just eighteen. She wondered what they looked like. *What did they do? Did they ever think of her?* Sometimes these thoughts depressed her. Mary Catherine would be disappointed often, as lead after lead proved a dead end. Would she ever find her family? Sometimes, particularly after a deep disappointment, when a clue proved fruitless, she felt maybe it would be healthier to give up.

But she just couldn't. Someday she would find them. She would just have to keep praying. Some days were harder than others. The day that Johnny turned 21 hit her really hard. That was the day Sister Immaculata promised to tell Mary Catherine where the boys were. Mary Catherine tried to keep busy on what proved to be a very lonely day. Another day that hit her hard was the day that Thomas turned 18. She couldn't even imagine what Thomas looked like. Each time she thought of Thomas, she thought of her mother. She knew her mother wouldn't want her to give up the search, no matter what the cost. Her mother would want them together. At least I have a home now, a home with my friends and a beautiful house surrounded by beautiful gardens, thought Mary Catherine.

Everyone enjoyed the gardens. Each of the flower beds had their own theme, but the needs of the girls came first and soon enough even the small amount that the garden club charged became too much. Mary Catherine had to let the garden club go. She started the arduous task of finding a volunteer. Most of the landscapers she called laughed when she talked of the spiritual benefits of charity. Scottie didn't laugh. Mary Catherine was happy as could be, and arranged a meeting between Scottie and the board. Scottie was a young man who started his own landscaping business a year before. Blessed with a green thumb, his business took off. The morning of his meeting with the board of Queen of Angels Home was one he would never forget.

Joyce was stunned when she opened the door to admit Scottie. At six feet four inches, he was without a doubt one of the most handsome man she had ever met. Shining black hair and deep blue eyes were just part of his Celtic good looks. What made him even more attractive was his confidence and competence.

"I hope you'll allow me to keep the gardens for you." He smiled at Joyce. "I saw them on the way in, and they are magnificent. I would be privileged to maintain them."

Joyce was impressed and she could tell that the rest of the board was also. Scottie seemed as intelligent as he was good-looking. He smiled generously at them.

It wasn't until Mary Catherine arrived, unusually late, that he became awkward. Joyce and Elly exchanged glances. As soon as he looked at the petite and businesslike Mary Catherine, he became unglued. Suddenly the man started to stutter and shuffle his feet. Mary Catherine didn't seem to notice, but Joyce and Elly did. Scottie couldn't take his eyes off Mary Catherine. He stared at her as if he was seeing a vision from heaven. It was love at first sight. His moonstruck face reddened each time Mary Catherine looked at him. Mary Catherine, so immersed in business matters, never even noticed.

"Would you care for a drink, Miss?" the perky flight attendant asked.

Mary Catherine turned from the window. "Just a diet coke,

please."

She put on the headset to watch the movie the flight offered but couldn't concentrate. Her mind wandered to her favorite subject, Scottie.

After Scottie was approved as the landscaper to maintain the gardens, he was always around. Elly and Joyce had great fun watching Scottie hang around. He tried to find any opportunity to be with Mary Catherine, and then when he was with her, he became tongue-tied and unable to talk. Mary Catherine didn't seem to know what to do with him, and started just bossing him around and giving him extra work. Joyce could hardly contain her amusement as she watched this giant of a man bend to little Mary Catherine's every wish.

"Oh, this will never do," Joyce laughed to Elly. "If he's going to be with Mary Catherine, he's going to have to toughen up." Elly was amused.

"If he doesn't, Mary Catherine will be bossing him around for the rest of his life!" Gabe laughed.

It took Scottie three months to get up the courage to ask Mary Catherine out on a date. She seemed surprised by the request. Everyone else thought it was about time.

Scrubbed up, dressed up, and with flowers, he arrived to pick her up. Mary Catherine really looked at him for the first time that night. She looked at him as a man, instead of a worker. Mary Catherine found herself impressed by the man. He was caring and kind. She enjoyed being with him. She tried to make him relax. It took a few dates, however, for him to get over his awe of Mary Catherine. He thought she was the most beautiful girl he had ever seen.

Over the next six months their relationship grew. Mary Catherine remained the dominate one. It seemed that Scottie could never say no to anything Mary Catherine wanted. He seemed to hang on every word she said.

"He's smitten." Gabe laughed as he watched the large man follow the tiny woman around. Mary Catherine seemed to enjoy his company. She grew used to having Scottie around at her beck and call. Everything seemed fine until Scottie finally got up the courage to ask Mary Catherine to marry him.

No one was more shocked than Mary Catherine when Scottie pulled out the diamond ring. He had been saving for it for months. She never thought of getting married. Oh sure, she wanted to have her own family – she just never thought of getting married until she found her brothers.

"Scottie, I'm flattered. But I can't marry you now. We can just keep dating, can't we? I'm not ready to get married. You understand, don't you?" Mary Catherine watched in shock as Scottie's face reddened.

"No, Mary Catherine, we cannot just keep dating. Either you want to marry me, or you don't. I'm not going to wait around while you make up your mind! So make up your mind quickly. I want to get married and have a family. I hope that it will be with you. If not, then I don't see the point of wasting my time. Either you love me or you don't!" Scottie firmly announced.

Mary Catherine had never seen the gentle Scottie like this. They drove home in an uncomfortable silence. Finally, Mary Catherine turned to him and said, "Scottie, you don't mean it. I know you'll come to your senses! I really care for you, but I just can't get married yet. Why don't you stop being angry? Just think about it. You'll see that I'm right." Mary Catherine was sure he would give up this silly stubbornness.

Scottie took a deep breath and looked right into Mary Catherine's eyes. "I am not wrong, and I am not going to change my mind. Either you love me and you want to marry me, or I'll have to find someone who does. It's up to you. I don't intend to see you again, unless you change your mind."

Mary Catherine was ticked by his stubborn attitude and answered, "Well, we'll just see about that, Scottie. I give you two days and you'll come running to me and beg me to take you back. I don't think you'll be able to live without me."

To emphasize her point, Mary Catherine quickly got out of his car. She slammed the door, and walked away with an attitude. Two days, she thought. I'll give him one.

Those two days quickly turned into a week. Mary Catherine was miserable. She watched Scottie working in the gardens. He never even looked her way. *What was wrong with him?* She couldn't believe he really meant to give her up. She never realized how important he was to her. She really missed having the big guy around. She couldn't let him know that. *What was she going to do?* She had a pain in her stomach and it got worse each day. She couldn't concentrate on her work. Mary Catherine made more than one mistake during the week and everyone noticed. She just couldn't keep her mind on her work. *What was wrong with him anyway? How could he ignore her like this?*

He looked handsome out there in the sun. Mary Catherine never really appreciated how good looking Scottie was. She always noticed he was the kindest man she ever met. *Why was he being so mean to her now?* It really started to irritate her to see the way the young women looked at him.

"Mary Catherine! Didn't you hear me calling you?" Joyce stood watching the forlorn woman looking out the window. It was easy to see that she was staring at Scottie. She had called Mary Catherine at least five times. Mary Catherine was totally distracted. Everyone knew what was going on. Joyce and Elly encouraged the worried Scottie to stick to his guns. Mary Catherine, God love her, was too stubborn for her own good. Joyce wondered how many days of separation the girl could take. How many more days of the love-sick Mary Catherine could the rest of them take?

Mary Catherine reluctantly tore her eyes away from the man she now realized she loved. *What could she do?* He wouldn't bend. *How could anyone be that stubborn?*

"What is it Joyce?" A long sigh followed the question.

Joyce reddened with delight. "These tally sheets that you gave to Joseph to proof are all wrong. He says you better check them before he submits them to the IRS."

Mary Catherine looked at the stack of paper with disinterest, and sighed again. "Okay, I'll go over them."

Joyce felt sorry for the young woman and decided to speak frankly. "Why don't you just go out to him?"

Mary Catherine raised her head, "Go out to who?"

Joyce shook her head. "Mary Catherine, you are the most obstinate person I have ever known. Take my advice, love doesn't come along very often. Don't let it slip away, just because you don't have the courage to ask for it. Go to him. He loves you!"

Mary Catherine reddened. "But…"

Joyce interrupted her, "But, nothing. Go to him. Who told you that you're supposed to always get your way?"

Joyce was joined by Elly and they both watched with joy as Mary Catherine flew out the door and into the garden. Mary Catherine couldn't stand it anymore. She loved him. And she did want to marry him. Flying into his waiting arms, she found herself crying and babbling about her feelings. Scottie picked her up effortlessly and joyfully swung her around in his arms.

With great happiness Scottie said, "Mary Catherine, it sure took you long enough to realize that you should be my wife."

Mary Catherine laughed and cried at the same time. She never felt so happy. She never felt so safe. She knew Scottie would never leave her or hurt her. He was strong and dependable. He was the man she always dreamed of. She wanted this moment of joy to last forever. It was one of those defining moments in life that one never forgets. She could have stayed in the moment forever. Scottie lowered her to the ground and placed the diamond on her finger. The applause drew her attention. Mary Catherine hadn't realized that the whole place was watching.

She blushed as she clung to Scottie and admitted, "Okay, so I love him and we're going to get married. Are you all happy now?"

The cheers confirmed that everyone was.

Gabe was the first to interrupt the moment, saying, "Mary Catherine, I hate to bother you at a moment like this, but you have a long-distance call from Florida. I think that it may be important."

Mary Catherine smiled. Nothing could destroy her happiness. She tugged at Scottie's sleeve and ordered, "You come with me, Scottie. I'm not ready to let you out of my sight."

He went willingly. Mary Catherine figured that the phone call was probably business related, but nothing could have prepared her for what the call was actually about.

Mary Catherine started to tremble as she tightened her grip on the phone. Gabe watched her with concern. He knew what the call was about. Mary Catherine's face drained of color as she listened to the caller. Suddenly, she dropped the phone and ran out of the room. Gabe picked up the receiver and talked to the party on the other end as Elly followed Mary Catherine to the kitchen. Elly watched as Mary Catherine pounded her fists on the kitchen table. Elly never saw such anger.

"I won't go! I won't!" she cried as she talked to herself. "I hate him! I hope he dies!" Mary Catherine lowered her head on the table and wept. Elly hugged her. This was no time to ask questions. Gabe came into the kitchen with a pad.

Looking up in anger at the man who had given her the phone, Mary Catherine yelled, "How did he know where to find me? How did he know where I was?" Tears steamed down her face.

Gabe ignored her anger, and answered gently, "According to the nurse at the hospital, your father was brought in from a homeless shelter. The priest at the shelter found letters among your father's things from a nun named Sister Clements. It seems that your father wrote to her asking about you and she directed him to the orphanage. He also had some correspondence with Sister Immaculata before she died. When the nurse called Blessed Trinity, they directed her here."

Mary Catherine couldn't believe it. Everyone thought she should go see this man she hated. "Well I don't care how he found me. It was a waste of time, 'cause I'm not going!"

Gabe gave her a steady look and calmly said, "Mary Catherine, I have the address of the hospital. I'll call the airline and make you a reservation for a morning flight."

"I'm not going! You can't make me!" Mary Catherine shouted.

"No, I can't make you. But no matter what he is, he is your father and he's dying. I'll go and make the arrangements," Gabe answered gently.

Mary Catherine had fought the idea of coming to Florida for hours. Exhaustion and the gentle advice of Scottie had finally won out. Just a day after she became engaged, Mary Catherine was on a plane flying south to see the father who deserted her. She couldn't believe she was doing this. He was the man who was responsible for destroying her family and her life. She hated him.

A Father's Arms

Surely then you may lift up your face in innocence;
you may stand firm and unafraid
For then you shall forget your misery,
or recall it like waters that have ebbed away.
Then your life shall be brighter than the noonday;
its gloom shall become as the morning.
And you shall be secure, because there is hope;
you shall look around you and lie down in safety,
and you shall take your rest with none to disturb.
(Job 11:15-19)

The airport was a mess. It took Mary Catherine an hour longer than she expected. The lines were long and the people were short-tempered. There were just not enough employees to handle the summer crush. She impatiently waited forty-five minutes in a line to be assigned a taxi. The hassle added to her already bad mood.

It was one thing to suffer inconvenience for a good time, like a vacation. It wasn't even too bad to suffer for a necessary business trip. Mary Catherine was suffering in order to visit someone she did not want to see. It made all the headaches more of a torment. She was finally directed into a taxi. After giving the driver directions to her hotel, she took a deep breath and tried to relax.

Mary Catherine hated to admit it, but she was afraid. She was afraid to see the man that she hated for so many years. She didn't know what her reaction would be when she saw him. So far, she was able to keep her mind occupied with the details of this last minute trip. Now that she had arrived, there wasn't anything to occupy her mind. She had to face the fact that she was about to see her father. It was also true, at least according to the nurse who called, that her father was dying. Mary Catherine wasn't even sure how she really felt about his impending death. She had been in shock since she received the phone call. She never anticipated seeing her father again.

She thought about the day, many years ago, when he left her. She was only ten. Mary Catherine had just lost the mother she loved so much. How could he have left her?

She remembered the hospital. The scene the day her mother died was burned into her memory. The doctor said her mother's EEG was flat. She didn't know what "brain death" meant at the time. Mary Catherine did understand it now. It meant that her beloved mother was dead. Only the machines were keeping her body alive. Intellectually, Mary Catherine now understood that her father's decision had not killed her mother. Her mother was already dead. Mary Catherine knew he wasn't responsible for her mother's death, but emotionally it was impossible to forgive him.

Arriving at the hotel, Mary Catherine paid the taxi driver, and tipped the bellhop who took her two suitcases. She couldn't understand why she packed so much–she had no intention of staying long. It was ninety-two degrees and very sticky, even at 11AM. The air conditioning in the lobby hit her as a refreshing breeze.

It may be early, she thought, but I'm exhausted. The flight, although just two hours long, drained her. Mary Catherine hated to admit it, but the hard-hitting emotions of the last 24 hours had really pummeled her. She decided to shower and take a nap. She would visit the hospital in the evening.

Mary Catherine slept longer than she intended. It was the dinner hour by the time she awoke. She dressed and decided she was really hungry. She dined in the hotel restaurant. After a large dessert, she could find no further reason to delay her trip the hospital. I might as well get it over with, she thought. She hailed a taxi, and headed to Holy Cross hospital.

The hospital was large and modern. It served the large elderly community–retirees from the Northeast. She checked at the front visitor's desk, although she knew he was in the intensive care. Getting directions, she started down the long hall and up the elevator. The intensive care unit was on the fifth floor. The setting reminded her of the last time she was in a hospital.

Mary Catherine was only in a hospital twice. Once was when her mother died. The second time was when Sister Immaculata died. In that instance the patient never made it past the emergency room. They pronounced her dead on arrival. Both times were horrific! Mary Catherine hated hospitals. It always meant bad things, usually sickness and death. She hated being forced here. And she loathed the man who caused this trip.

The evening nurse showed Mary Catherine the way. She was glad it wasn't the same nurse she talked to on the phone. She wasn't proud of the way she had reacted on the phone. The nurse on the other end of the line had no way of understanding the relationship she had with her father. She must have thought Mary Catherine was a bitch. He was on the far side of the unit, in a cubby surrounded by curtains. Nothing prepared Mary Catherine for how he looked.

Patrick, if nothing else, had always been a handsome man. Mary Catherine looked a lot like him. At least, she looked a lot like he once looked. The fair skin she remembered was now ruddy. The thick hair he was so proud of was gray, matted, and very thin. His bloated face was full of stubbles, and unshaved. He looked nothing like the man she remembered.

He looked like a homeless alcoholic, the kind you see on TV. The cotton blanket rose and fell with each breath he took. It showed a grossly distended abdomen. Liver disease caused the swelling, and was also the cause of his impending death. As a coughing fit overtook him, a thick expectorant was produced.

The nursed wiped his mouth, and said, "He has pneumonia also, along with cirrhosis of the liver. Despite the swelling, it's easy to see that he is grossly malnourished. The homeless shelter couldn't wake him up the other morning. It seemed that they knew him well enough to know he was very ill. They brought him here, and he has been in and out of consciousness since."

Mary Catherine was shocked. She couldn't recognize her father in the man who lay before her.

"If you're lucky, he may come out of it. He does on occasion," the nurse said as she placed a chair beside the bed.

Mary Catherine took the seat quietly and sat beside the bed as the nurse left. She knew that he might wake up at any moment, but she prayed he wouldn't. She didn't want to talk to the man beside her. He was a stranger to her. Perhaps if she stayed quiet, he would just slip away. Mary Catherine couldn't deal with this.

Things were pretty quiet in the unit, except for the hum of machines and respirators. The nurses kept all the patients and visitors under strict control. The first hour that Mary Catherine spent sitting there seemed like an eternity. Mary Catherine never felt so uncomfortable. It was like being in Hell. She was glad that he didn't wake up. The few times that he stirred slightly had been enough to make her stomach knot. In a few minutes she would leave, she decided. She had put in enough time. Enough time to make it look respectable.

Just when she made up her mind to leave, it happened–her father moved! Mary Catherine's stomach was seized by a cramp. And then Mary Catherine who was known for always being cool, collected, and in control, did what she would have never predicted. When Patrick O'Rourke opened his bloodshot, yellow eyes, Mary Catherine bolted out of the unit and out of the hospital!

When Mary Catherine tossed herself on the large king-size bed in her hotel room she was trembling. The trembling started in the taxi and just got worse. The overwhelming hatred she felt made her heart beat faster. Waves of disgust nauseated her. Emotions of a lifetime were coursing through her body. She had no power to silence the memories. All the pain that she had suppressed was surfacing. It took just one look from Patrick O'Rourke to unsettle her. One look from the father who deserted her sent her running. Mary Catherine ran from the father she tried to forget. Fleeing from the father she longed to love her!

She laid in the dark of her room for what felt like ages. The conflicting emotions she felt left her motionless. She couldn't think. She couldn't even cry. She didn't notice the phone ringing until the third ring. Elly was on the other end, a person so familiar, from another life.

After saying hello, Elly asked, "Are you all right, Mary Catherine? Your voice sounds so funny."

Mary Catherine tried to clear her throat to no avail. She couldn't pretend with Elly, they were too close. Elly knew her too well.

"No, I'm not," Mary Catherine sat up and turned on the night stand light. "I'm in terrible shape and I'm coming home. I'm going to book the first flight tomorrow."

There was a moment of silence on the other end of the line, then Elly spoke. "Is he gone then? I'm so sorry Mary Catherine. I was hoping you and he would get a chance to work things out."

Mary Catherine couldn't believe her ears! What was Elly saying? "No, he's not gone. But don't you understand! He means nothing to me! I want nothing to do with him! Let him die alone! He left me alone, all alone! He never cared about me. Why should I care about him!" Mary Catherine tried to calm herself, but couldn't.

After a moment of silence Elly said, "Oh, I'm sorry I thought you were a Christian. You always go to church. I guess I was mistaken."

Mary Catherine still couldn't believe her ears. She was angry and she spat out, "You have a lot of nerve, Elly. Who are you to judge me! Do you know what that man did to me? He ruined my life! You think I should forgive him? God wouldn't expect that. That's too much to ask of anyone. How can I forgive him?"

Elly smiled to herself on the other end of the phone and answered, "Someone once told me that it is not humanly possible to forgive someone who has really hurt you. It is only by the Power of

Jesus Christ that we can fully forgive."

"I can't. I just can't!" sobbed the younger woman.

In a soft voice Elly instructed, "You just have to make the decision. You don't have to feel it. Just make the decision to forgive. Jesus will do the rest. Do you trust Him?"

Mary Catherine reddened with anger. "What do you know about it? Whoever treated you as badly as he treated me? You couldn't possibly know what I'm feeling."

Elly listened, but said nothing. Mary Catherine could not be helped with an explanation of her own past pains. Elly just let Mary Catherine vent. And vent she did, until she was tired and worn. Elly prayed silently while she did. She prayed to the Holy Spirit for the right words to help the young woman.

The words The Holy Spirit gave Elly were simple. "You know what's right. The right thing is written on your heart. Just pray about it. God will give you the answer you're looking for. I love you. All of us at home love you. We'll pray for you too. Now, pray and try to get some sleep."

The phone call ended on that calm note. Mary Catherine was exhausted. The strong emotions of the past day had worn her out.

Donning her pajamas, she said a quick prayer. "Mary, Mother of God, help me to know what to do, and give me the strength to do it. Pray for me."

Careworn, she fell asleep.

Her dreams came in waves as the Holy Spirit spoke to Mary Catherine. Dreams washed over Mary Catherine and answered her prayers in parables that only her spirit could understand. Mary Catherine had many dreams that night, but she would only remember the one that reached her heart. Mary Catherine dreamed she was at Calvary. She dreamed she stood beneath the cross as they crucified Jesus. It made her so angry. How could they do this?

Mary, the mother of Jesus, stood silently. She stood silently as Jesus asked His Father in Heaven to forgive them. How could He forgive them? Well, Mary Catherine decided, perhaps he could, he was God after all. But what about Mary? She was human. How could she forgive those who killed her son? How could she forgive all those friends of His who ran away just when He needed them most? But Mary not only forgave them, she helped them to start the church.

Mary was with them at Pentecost. She was with them in the Upper Room. She obviously forgave them for running away and deserting her Son in His hour of need. But then again Mary was a true Christian. She always allowed the Holy Spirit to operate through her. Could Mary Catherine do the same?

Mary Catherine awoke with a strange sense of peace. After two cups of strong coffee and a hot shower, she dressed in jeans, sneakers and a sweat shirt. It was going to be a long day at the hospital. Somehow she just sensed that she should dress comfortably. After a good night's sleep and in the morning light, the answer seemed clear. Her father was dying. And good or bad, he was her father. She would be with him. She wouldn't return evil for evil. She wouldn't desert him in his hour of need.

Taking a taxi, she made her way back to her father wondering if he would still be alive. Mary Catherine was a little shocked to see how much he had deteriorated during the night. His face was even more bloated, and his skin more jaundiced. He seemed to be going downhill fast. The nurses seemed busier on the morning shift, as tests were done and baths were given. Mary Catherine settled in the chair beside Patrick's bed. She planned to stay with Patrick until the end. Understanding it might be a long day, Elly brought a novel to help her pass the time.

For most of the day, she stayed beside him. He remained unresponsive. She ate lunch in the hospital cafeteria.

She was half-way finished with the novel when Patrick stirred. Instinctively, she panicked. Mary Catherine wasn't sure how long her resolve would last if her father actually talked to her. It was much easier to deal with a non-responsive abstraction.

Patrick did, however, open his eyes. At first, he seemed to have trouble focusing. Mary Catherine wasn't even sure he would recognize her. After all, he hadn't seen her since she was ten years old.

"Mary Catherine, is that you?" His voice was weak and feeble.

"Yes, Dad, it's me." Mary Catherine couldn't believe how calmly she answered him. "Do you need anything, Dad? She couldn't believe that she was calling him Dad.

Patrick's voice was weak as he answered, "Oh, Mary Catherine, I'm so glad you're here. I wanted to see you. I wanted to tell you how sorry I am. Can you forgive me, Mary Catherine?"

The chain of sentences seemed to weaken him. He slipped out of consciousness again. It was just as well. Mary Catherine didn't know what to say to his question. Could she forgive him?

Looking at him, she did feel some tenderness. It was hard to believe that Patrick was just fifty-eight. He was thirty when Mary Catherine was born. He looked as if he was seventy-eight. His arms were stick thin. It was true what the nurse said about his malnutrition. His skin was rough and weathered. He apparently spent many years homeless and exposed to the elements.

Why had he lived like this? Alcohol was the only answer. He was so addicted to alcohol that it destroyed his life. True, it started by destroying his wife and his children, but it didn't end there. It destroyed his hope, his home, and his body. He apparently lived a life of Hell. The scars on his body testified to the many fights he experienced. What had he fought for? Food? A drink? Or perhaps, just a cardboard box to sleep in. His addiction hurt Mary Catherine, but it destroyed him. It consumed his life. Alcohol devastated him.

Suddenly, Mary Catherine felt true compassion for him. He suffered more than any of them. He would never know his children, or for that matter any future grandchildren. He lived a life of pain and suffering all because of his need for the bottle. She could have compassion for him. He had hurt himself the most. And now the alcohol was taking his life. In a most painful way, it was killing him long before his time. He awoke a few hours later. Patrick seemed more focused this time.

Patrick called for his daughter, "Mary Catherine?"

She reached out and took his hand. "I'm going to your mother. She told me that I'm forgiven. But will you forgive me?"

She didn't know where the strength came from as she answered him, "Yes, Dad, I forgive you." Tears streamed down her face as she stroked his thin arm.

He responded, "I knew you would. You were always a good girl, Mary Catherine. I never deserved such a good daughter."

Mary Catherine was surprised. She had never known that her father felt that way about her. She asked gently, "Do you need something for pain, Dad?"

He seemed at peace as he answered, "No, I have no more pain. Your mother's coming for me. Can you see her?"

Mary Catherine didn't know what made her do it, but she pulled the brown Mt. Carmel scapular from around her neck. The Blessed Mother had appeared to St. Simon and gave the saint the brown cloth scapula. The story told and accepted by the church was that anyone who died wearing the scapula would be helped by the Blessed Mother to heaven. Tenderly she placed it around Patrick's neck.

With gentle tears she answered the man she had hated for so long. "Go to her Dad. She will show you the way home."

Patrick smiled tenderly. "Your mother always loved me, and I loved her. Now we can be together. Can you see her?"

Mary Catherine would have given anything to see her.

The tired man continued, "I've got to go now. But, here, I've been waiting to give this to you."

Gathering what little strength he could, Patrick reached to the bedside drawer next to his bed. It took great effort on his part to get what he wanted. He pressed a folded paper into Mary Catherine's hand. Falling back into his pillow, he took his last breath. The look of peace on his face brought peace to his daughter.

The machines shrieked and the staff ran. Mary Catherine was pushed out of the way as the intensive care staff tried to revive her father. Slipping the paper into her pocket, she watched from a distance as they coded her father. She knew they were wasting their time. He had gone home with her mother. The priest came and anointed the worn out body. Mary Catherine called the airline. She made arrangements for the body to be flown home. There would be no wake. There was only a daughter to bury him.

It was surreal to return to the small town where she spent the first ten years of her life. Mary Catherine had not seen this town since she left it on the train. She and her brothers were sent to the orphanage and as far as she knew, none of them ever returned. Everything seemed so much smaller than she remembered. But then again, she only had the memories of a child. It took all morning to make arrangements with the local funeral parlor. Mary Catherine was surprised to find that Father O'Brien was still alive. She thought of him as old eighteen years ago. He was pleased to do the funeral Mass and said he looked forward to seeing Mary Catherine.

She took a walk, curious to see the town she had once called home. Mary Catherine was surprised to see just how shabby the trailer park she lived in was–consisting of a few dilapidated and broken down trailers on the outskirts of town. They were poorer than she remembered. It was just a short walk to the school.

The red brick school looked just as she remembered it. She didn't have any hope of seeing anyone who remembered her. Sister Clements died many years ago. No one here remembered Mary Catherine or her brothers. The small church still seemed inviting. Mary Catherine was pleased to see that it had not been changed. After her eyes adjusted to the darkness, she walked up the left-hand aisle to the statue of the Blessed Mother. The sweet and loving face of the statue of Mary looked down at her. Mary Catherine said a short prayer. Tomorrow was going to be a sad as she buried her father. Mary Catherine was sure Mary, the Mother of God, prayed for her. She somehow knew the prayers of both of her mothers in heaven gave her the courage to deal with her fathers' death.

She returned to the hotel and placed a call to Queen of Angels home. She was glad when Elly answered.

"Hi, Elly, it's me. I'm calling to tell you how sorry I am about the way I spoke to you the other day. You were right. God helped me to forgive him."

Elly smiled, "I knew He would. I'm just so sorry that you lost your father, Mary Catherine."

Mary Catherine wished she could reach out and hug the woman who had become such a close friend. She answered, "No Elly, I didn't lose him. I found him. I wanted to thank you for that."

The phone conversation ended with Mary Catherine promising to be home soon.

After the funeral she would be glad to return home. She found some closure in Patrick's death. Mary Catherine wanted to begin her new life with Scottie. Scottie was right as usual. There was no sense living in the past. By living in the past, you could miss the present. Mary Catherine decided she would never make that mistake again.

The funeral took place with only Mary Catherine, Father O'Brien, and a few nuns present. The grieving daughter was sure Father O'Brien asked the nuns to attend. The nuns returned to their work after the Mass. Mary Catherine, the elderly priest, and the funeral director went to the cemetery.

Mary Catherine hadn't been to the cemetery since her mother's funeral. She was surprised to see the beautiful headstone Sister Clements had placed on her mother's grave. Mary Catherine would see to it that Patrick's name was added to the stone. He may have lived homeless, but she would not let him be buried in an unmarked grave. Mary Catherine was glad she decided to bury Patrick with her mother. As she watched her father's coffin being lowered into the ground, she was flooded with a great sense of peace. Patrick had said her mother came to bring him home when he died. She couldn't help but believe that they were together now. Not just physically in this grave, but spiritually in heaven. The whole experience of Patrick's death had been a renewal of faith. The sense of the eternal life of a person's soul gave Mary Catherine a feeling of tranquility. It meant that this was just a temporary separation. She knew her family would all find each other again–if not in this life, then surely in the next.

With that thought Mary Catherine returned to the hotel. She had to pack up and leave the past in the past. She couldn't wait to see Scottie.

Wanting to be comfortable on the drive home, Mary Catherine donned the jeans she wore to the hospital the day her father died. She checked out of the hotel with the intention of getting in her rental car and getting right on the highway. She found herself, however, headed toward the church. She wanted to say a quick prayer before she left. Maybe, she thought to herself, she wanted to drink in the atmosphere of her childhood church just one more time. Placing herself before the same lovely statue of the Blessed Mother, Mary Catherine thought she was alone.

She couldn't see her parents as they stood hand in hand. They watched her lovingly as she sat on the wooden pew. Reaching into her pocket for a tissue, Mary Catherine discovered the slip of paper in the pocket. It was the paper her father had given her before he died. With all the arrangements and the traveling, Mary Catherine forgot about it. As she opened it and read it, her face drained of color. She held the paper tightly, as she laid her head on the back of the pew. Her body was racked with sobs as she clung to the all-important paper. Mary Catherine couldn't believe it! The paper had the names and addresses of all three of her brothers!

Epilogue

Magnificat
My soul doth magnify the Lord
And my spirit hath rejoiced in God my Savior.
Because He hath regarded the humility of
His handmaid; For behold, from henceforth
All generations shall call me blessed.
Because He that is mighty hath done great things
To me; and holy is His name.
And His mercy is from generation to generation,
To them that fear Him.
He hath showed might in His arm; He hath
Scattered the proud in the conceit of their heart.
He hath put down the mighty from their seat;
And hath exalted the humble.
He hath filled the hungry with good things; and
The rich he hath sent empty away.
He hath received Israel His servant, being mindful
Of His Mercy.
As He spoke to our fathers, to Abraham, and to his
Seed forever. Amen.

Elly's arthritis ached as she climbed up to the boulder outside her home. It was the same boulder that she sat on as a child. However, she admitted the climb had been easier then. At seventy-two, her knees were not what they used to be. She took her time. It was not hard to find her way even in the dark. She could easily find her way around her lifelong home.

She had more time on her hands these days. The younger generation just seemed to take things over. It happened so gradually that she hardly noticed. Elly was glad. It was as it should be. The work would go on. There were always people in need. And as long as there was, someone would be there to help. That was what God intended. Elly watched as the workmen, by lamplight, set up the rows of folding chairs. It was a tradition for forty-five years. Every Easter, they had a sunrise Mass.

This was the first year Gabe, her Gabe, would not be here. He passed away eight months ago. Elly missed him so much. It seemed to her that she had lost so many people in her life. Life seemed to go by so fast. Elly couldn't believe how the children had grown. They all had families of their own now. I'm a grandmother. Inside I still feel like a young girl, the young girl who fell in love with Gabe, Elly sighed as she thought of Gabe.

Looking down she saw Grace, giving directions to a workman. Flood lights had been set up to guide the workmen. The altar had to be set up just right. This year was very special. The Bishop was coming to say the Mass. The Bishop was a frequent visitor here.

Grace had grown into a beautiful woman. She still glowed with that beauty even now that she was in her forties. Watching her as she directed the workmen to their tasks below, she though how proud Joyce would be if she could she her now. She was such a special woman.

Grace didn't look anything like Joyce. She was the spitting image of Joseph.

Elly sighed. She missed Joyce so much. It was over twenty years since she died from the complications of a stroke. Unlike Gabe, her death had been expected. The stroke left Joyce very debilitated. She never regained her ability to walk or talk and lived only two years after the stroke.

During those two years, Joseph cared for her. Elly had never seen such complete devotion. He bathed and dressed her each morning. He cooked and fed her and never complained. He was so in love with Joyce that he seemed honored to be able to wait on her. Joyce could never thank him. She seemed unaware of her surroundings. At least that was what they thought until the very end.

Elly visited Joyce each day and she did what she could to help. Grace helped her the most. It was really amazing–by the time Grace was a teenager, she had been given the computerized arms that she still used today. They looked like real arms. And what was really astounding was that they were stronger than real arms. Elly was always amazed by the numerous medical discoveries that came during her lifetime. With those arms, Grace was able to do whatever she wanted. If you didn't know Grace, you couldn't tell she had artificial arms. She was a big help to Joseph during Joyce's illness. Elly often thought that it was taking care of Joyce that inspired Grace to become a registered nurse.

Grace waved to Elly when she spotted her and yelled up, "You better rest, before the children get up."

Elly laughed. The children never did give her a moment of peace. Elly didn't mind.

"They keep me young!" she responded. They also keep me from missing Gabe too much, she thought.

Joyce died the night of Grace's wedding. Correction, Elly thought, she lived until Grace's wedding day. Despite the doctor's gloomy predictions, Joyce managed to stay alive until she saw her Grace get married. And she saw it, thanks to Joseph.

Joseph tenderly dressed Joyce in her finest clothes. She looked beautiful as he carried her gently up to the front pew of the church. The wedding was simple yet beautiful.

Gabe and Elly couldn't have been happier. Grace married their firstborn son. It made a permanent connection between the two mothers who had been best friends for years. It brought joy to both families. And even more important, the two children who grew up together seemed made for each other. Elly remembered it as one of the happiest, and yet one of the saddest days of her life.

Joyce sat quietly through the ceremony. No one thought she even knew where she was. Still, she seemed content. After the wedding, Joseph carried her carefully to the reception in the hall below the church. It was a great time. The caterers supplied great food and the band was so good that Joseph paid them to stay for an extra hour. Everyone and had a great time.

Even the bride and groom were reluctant to leave. The party could have gone on all night but the couple had a plane to catch. Elly was thrilled her son had found such a wonderful wife. After all the goodbyes, Elly went over to see if she could help Joseph with Joyce. It was the first time either of them realized just how much of the wedding Joyce had understood.

For the first time in two years, Joyce spoke. "Joseph, thank you. You've made me so happy. I've stayed as long as I could, but now that Grace is taken care of, I need to go. I'll wait for you. Please take care of him, Elly."

And then Joyce smiled. It was the most peaceful smile Elly had ever seen. She bowed her head and as quickly as that, she was gone.

Elly now understood that Joyce knew what was going on. She waited with the help of God until Grace's big day was over. Joyce wouldn't spoil Grace's happiness for anything. It didn't matter how much pain she may have suffered.

"Here's to you, Joyce!" Elly whispered, "You were a lady even at the end!"

Called from her musings by the greetings, Elly waved to the many young people who seemed to all arrive at once. Many of them were the babies she and Gabe had saved from abortions.

Elly couldn't miss Mary Catherine's entrance as she strutted in pushing the baby carriage. Mary Catherine was so proud of her first granddaughter. She always had her new granddaughter with her. Elly wondered if Mary Catherine's daughter-in-law ever got to see the baby. Elly laughed out loud at Mary Catherine's bragging. She could imagine it even from this distance.

Mary Catherine had grown into a wonderful woman. She returned home from her father's death full of profound faith. She married Scottie with much joy and she didn't waste any time in producing seven boys to carry on his name.

Best of all, she contacted her brothers. Surprisingly, Johnny and Danny lived close by. They were raised together by a wonderful couple and they never forgot their older sister who cared for them.

Mary Catherine was a little plumper and her hair was graying, but she still vibrated with overwhelming vitality. Her energy seemed boundless. It was a good thing too. Mary Catherine was never alone. She was always surrounded by children. Children seemed to gravitate to Mary Catherine, attracted by the childlike zest for life she had. It didn't seem to bother her. In fact, she seemed to thrive on their enthusiasm.

Elly laughed, as she watched the crowd of children surround Mary Catherine.

Scottie stood on the edge of the crowd of children clamoring for Mary Catherine's attention. He was trying to catch her eye. Scottie was fumbling with his tie and clearly needed some help. Elly watched as Mary Catherine found her way to him. Mary Catherine tied his tie, and kissed him on the cheek. Even after all these years, Scottie blushed. He was still madly in love with her.

Elly loved her too. She didn't know what she would have done without the practical Mary Catherine. They were closer than sisters. Mary Catherine, whose latest project was digging into her family's Irish roots, told Elly a story. Mary Catherine said that the ancient Celts believed that friends who shared a deep spirituality were called "Soul friends." They did share a special spirituality. They both came through neglect and abuse, and through the power of Jesus, learned to forgive. Forgiveness is the root of all healing. It is always the beginning of all healing. Forgiveness had brought both Elly and Mary Catherine tremendous blessings. One of those blessings was each other.

Elly waved to Joseph as he walked out of the house. Tall and lanky, dressed in a suit, his eyes scanned the lawn for Grace. She had become his life. His five grandchildren ran up to greet him. The joy in his eyes was profound. How strange life is, Elly pondered. The very child that he at one time wanted to abort was the focus of his life. Grace came up and hugged the man who worshiped her. Grace led him to a seat, with his family. How proud Joyce would be of this family, Elly thought.

The organist began to play as the congregation took their seats. All the metal chairs had been set up facing east toward the altar. The altar was raised up on a platform with the Atlantic as a backdrop. The floodlights were softened as the Mass began. The Bishop and several priests made their entrance amidst singing. Little Gabe, who was just five years old, slipped away from his mother Grace, as her attention was caught up with the Mass. He was Gabe and Grace's youngest child.

Little Gabe was so attached to his grandmother Elly, that he came to her at any opportunity. Grace looked around for him, and smiled as she saw him climb the hill to Elly. He had found his favorite spot, on Elly's lap.

Elly had stayed where she was on purpose. She wanted to watch from this vantage point. She loved all of the people below. Somehow though, being alone helped her feel Gabe's presence. She could feel his spirit with her, and it brought her comfort to pray for him. The Mass was beautiful. Little Gabe squirmed. He was too young to understand it. Elly's eyes moistened with emotion. How blessed she was. Jesus had given her so many gifts. Today was just one of them. Little Gabe reached up and wiped a tear of joy from her cheek.

"Look Nana! The sun is rising!" His brown eyes widened with delight as the golden rays lit the horizon. Elly looked deep into his eyes so full of wonder! Little Gabe was so like his grandfather. Each time Elly looked into little Gabe's eyes, she felt like she was looking into her husband's eyes. At that moment, as the sun rose in the background, the Bishop lifted the Eucharist above the chalice.

"Behold, The Lamb of God Who takes away the sin of the

world!" Bishop Thomas O'Rourke displayed the Body and Blood of Christ as his sister Mary Catherine wept with pride.

Little Gabe pulled on Elly's sleeve. As the globe of the sun followed its rays over the horizon he exclaimed, "Look, Nana, the sun is risen!"

Elly held the small boy close.

"Yes, Gabe, always remember. The Son is Risen!"

About Author
Karen Kelly Boyce

Karen Kelly Boyce was born in Jersey City, New Jersey. She learned her faith and love of reading at the hands of the Sisters of Mercy. Only a few blocks away from the Barron Library, she spent most of her summer days and weekends lost in the stories and biographies of famous people. The turbulent sixties led her away from her first loves of church, reading, and writing. The only part of her faith that remained was the belief that we were made to help others. That belief led her to graduate as an RN in 1974.

Karen married in 1975, and raised two children. After going through a Life in the Spirit Seminar, she found peace and eternal love in the faith that would sustain her. In 1990, she became very ill and was eventually diagnosed with end stage Lyme Disease and was unable to work as a nurse anymore. As a disabled person, Karen's love of reading was rekindled and her love of writing born again.

Karen is the author of two other books - *Into the Way of Peace* and a *Bend in the Road: A Year's Journey Through Breast Cancer.* The book you are holding and *Into the Way of Peace* have received the esteemed Catholic Writers Guild seal of approval.

All books can be purchased on line at :

www.queenofangelsfarm.com or
www.jacksonwritersgroup.com/boyce.html

www.ingramcontent.com/pod-product-compliance
Lightning Source LLC
LaVergne TN
LVHW020529100826
845148LV00010B/1401

* 9 7 8 0 6 9 2 0 0 9 2 0 8 *